THE SNAKE HARVEST

The Snake Harvest

Francis John Thornton

Coward, McCann & Geoghegan, Inc.
New York

To Mary Margaret, who inspires and bears with me, and Craig, who makes it all come true.

Library of Congress Cataloging in Publication Data
Thornton, Frank J
  The snake harvest.
  I. Title.
PZ4.T515Sn [PS3570.H667] 813'.5'4 77-20651

ISBN 0-698-10904-X

One

The body of Deanna Grayson was never recovered.

The few pieces of her life history were sewn together well after her death in a police report. It is only between the lines that are gathered up the random daubs filling in a profile.

Funny, how with a little distance and some notoriety. . . .

Having been born in the northeastern corner of the city, she made an almost preordained lateral move to northwest Philadelphia immediately after having completed the schooling required by law. There she found work in a sweatshop.

Justifiably she hated her work; for twelve hours a day six days a week, Deanna took a flat-based iron ring from an overhead railway, coiled a leather strap around it, fastened the strap tightly, and placed the gear on a treadmill. From the day that her left shoulder began to ache and her right hand started to swell from dogged repetition, the curse of imagination plagued her indentured mind. Above all, she sickened at the thought that at the end of the treadmill and the other steps in the monotonous process was a manure-coated boot ready for callous insertion.

She felt as soiled as if she herself were herding the riders onto the horses.

One winter afternoon, toward the close of the workday, a girl several yards down the assembly line, whom she did not know, caught a wisp of hair in a piece of machinery and was scalped before the wheels of the system could be stopped. While the plant manager carped about the carelessness of his personnel, listing a set of reasons why the company was not legally culpable for this "regrettable" matter, Deanna buried her face in her hands and tried to obliterate the echo of the girl's screams.

On the following Sunday afternoon, while a wet snow fell outside, she attended a meeting of the United Friends of Labor, Philadelphia chapter, and spoke her mind briefly but vehemently. By noon, Monday, Deanna had been fired.

As she considered such dire extremes as returning to northeast Philadelphia and her shabby, crowded home, her attention was drawn to the ragged photo of a young woman tacked onto a newsstand wall. The damp had rendered it dog-eared, but the girl had the exotic aura that always conjured images of the faraway. Responding to the chant of a newshawk, Deanna perused in passing a story relating to the limp photograph. She took no notice of the fact that the young woman in the picture was dead. The glitter quickly overshadowed the penalties.

She proceeded to a corner tavern. It wa a bit early for her, but no one reacted when she settled into her favorite corner at a respectable near distance from the bar. Women were admitted begrudgingly. The regulars recognized her and continued their discussions. The early-afternoon crowd preferred their drinking to the pursuit of a wandering female.

Tears of frustration blurred her eyes. She toyed with a small glass of cheap red wine, turning it one way, then the other.

She was now twenty-two, unmarried, unbetrothed, and unemployed. Deanna had but one working experience outside the sweatshop, a brief period as a chambermaid in a house on the Main Line after a fire had closed the factory two years ago. It ended abruptly when the mistress found her with the master in a suspicious arrangement late one evening.

She realized, of course, that she posed no threat to the Gibson Girl. But she could hold her own in her league, as her mother used to answer qualifiedly.

By five o'clock she had begun to talk to herself, and by seven the management had asked her to leave. Visions of comfort, thoughts of deep, warm carpets, delicate printed dresses, and food with more substance than chicken broth taunted her, and Deanna had to share the impressions with someone. And it was easier to elicit response from oneself.

She glanced at a man who was seated at a nearby table. He was sopping up ham fat with a crust of bread. The greasy stains on his vest could be overlooked. But he ignored her and ate a second helping that arrived automatically.

With only the cheap wine to sustain her, Deanna's unemployment somehow briefly changed form, summoning up reveries of freedom. Before long the wine helped her see through to the loneliness she had mistaken for liberty, and when she grew tearfully belligerent, the bartender had, in blunt terms, ordered her to leave.

When she awakened the next morning, her head throbbed, her stomach was entangled, and she felt lonelier than ever. Looking about the room, she saw the unmistakable evidence of her visitor. He had seemed rather solicitous, asking her if she'd needed support as she reeled across the avenue. On a whim she had mentioned a fee. Perhaps for amusement, he'd agreed. He was a college boy, she thought; they were supposed to be eager for anything that would stand still or lie down long enough. In any case, the episode had passed untraumatically. Deanna could remember little of it, save the ten-dollar bill she found on her cluttered dresser when she woke up to find him gone.

Standing under a gaslight, swathed in the foggy damp from the river, she might have thought of that evening. She yawned and tapped her fingers against the lamppost, awaiting the next one.

A year had passed: a busy springtime, a hot, difficult summer, an easy period in autumn, and now a gradually more lucrative winter. The Christmas season had been active; then a pious lull on the holiday; heated again at New Year's. Interspersed among the many sailors and businessmen, there had been doctors, lawyers, bums, and divinity students. Sometime during the easy period—around mid-October, when it had turned cool—Deanna realized that she'd become dependent on opiates. Within her new occupational sphere exotic drugs were not difficult to come by. She didn't really like her work; there were trolls all around her and demeaning tasks to perform. But the softening of the calluses on her hands and the aches and pains she no longer suffered since leaving the sweatshop outweighed all that. The food was more satisfying, too, although she learned to eat moderately since a fat trollop could find the going hard. When she thought about it, Deanna often wondered why she'd found comfort in drugs.

He waddled up to her from across the foggy street—a short, very round man, wheezing. Slightly hard of hearing after years in the din of the factory, she had not been aware of him until the heavy footsteps had become loud enough to cause her to look around.

He was well dressed, as was his companion lingering some distance away. While they politely enacted the business preliminaries, she puffed up her chest, placing her hand on her hip jauntily, striking an instinctive pose.

He tossed a cigarette into the street. His companion emerged from the fog, followed by a stranger little fellow whose giggling she had been prepared for by the first of the partners.

From a gramophone in a nearby house she could hear the faint, strident tones of a waltz. The party of four strolled up Market Street to Tenth and turned north, Deanna on the arm of the fat man and the others a few yards behind. As they spoke, their breaths could be seen in the damp, chilly air. She suspected that the strange little man was a half-wit, but since he was coming along only to watch, she paid no attention to him now, nor need his pleasure bear active consideration later.

Whatever scant recollections the police gathered dated her disappearance on the evening of February 14, 1898—St. Valentine's Day.

Had it been the type of issue to cause much concern it would have been swallowed up in any case by the events of the following day, for the *Maine* had gone down in Havana Harbor with two hundred and sixty more important lives aboard.

Amid various disappearances a set of killings had also been logged in police headquarters, but they too passed without fanfare. Philadelphia, along with the rest of the nation, turned its tunnel vision toward the Spanish menace.

First the body of Maura Ann Masterson, well-documented prostitute and drug addict, was happened upon by a group of children who were playing on the banks of the Schuylkill in March.

Then there was the badly decomposed corpse of Samantha Poole, also of indelicate reputation, which sanitation workers discovered under a rubbish heap in early April. Unpleasant outcomes were regarded as inevitable in careers of that sort, and the police, like many others, simply dismissed the deaths with a shrug of the shoulders.

When the remains of young Angela Whittingham were found, it became apparent that disappearances were suddenly rife, and that the victims were not limited to prostitutes. The press was at first suspicious, then excited, and at last determined to develop a scandal of major dimensions.

The newspaper fraternity had been greatly encouraged by its success in inspiring a war with Spain, but it needed an issue to fill in emotional gaps—something to tie public hysteria to the local level. A clerk employed in the coroner's office had, after her fourth glass of wine, giggled to a reporter the horrid details of mutilation that the police had hoped to keep classified for the time being. The clerk was summarily dismissed, but the newspapers, building on her shreds of information, had all they needed to fabricate a tale of deviate cults, foreign intrigue, police ineptitude, and assorted other monsters to pique the public imagination.

Lieutenant Hudson grunted and gestured toward the main desk, where a sergeant sat thumbing through papers. "So they poormouth you about promoting Curran, with fifteen years on the force, while the carpenters and decorators are so thick at the district attorney's office that you have to squeeze through them."

Captain Regis Tolan puffed on his pipe. "Politics, Charlie."

He picked up the Whittingham file and glanced at it, suggesting without words that the personnel issue was dead and whatever Hudson and he might think about it, further protest would only mean further frustration. . . . Miss Whittingham was neither a prostitute nor an addict. She was, in fact, the youngest daughter of a respected mathematics professor, and her only nocturnal activities had been restricted to volunteer church work.

"Who's on the Whittingham case?"

"McBride."

"Good choice. He needs the experience."

"Actually, Charlie, I had no choice, but I'm glad you approve. Now, may I get on with it?"

Lieutenant Hudson went his way, rubbing his neck with ice water. The April heat taxed much calmer nerves than his.

Nothing very bizarre could be said of the Whittingham disappearance. After a day's outing with her group of deprived youngsters, a day that had begun with breakfast at the church hall and featured an excursion to the university museum, she and her charges had returned to the church for lemonade and sandwiches in late afternoon. There were hints from here and there that Miss Whittingham was strangely infatuated with the zealous young Reverend Hopkins who headed her auxiliary's efforts. He described her as an exemplary Christian woman and identified her escort as a foreign archaeology student who was the last person to see her. Following dinner, Miss Whittingham and her escort had departed for the suburban trolley stop at Sixty-ninth Street about six o'clock.

The Whittingham disappearance had been duly logged in a missing persons report, as the unusual number of disappearances over the last winter had been, and Tolan's men resigned themselves to one more tedious marathon of legwork and interrogation.

Disappearances were laborious cases. They required as much patience and effort as stolen property. Often friends regarded the police as intruders, making the job singularly thankless. Half the time the subject turned up wearing an embarrassed grin after all the weeping and torment. But the newspapers loved such things; a good disappearance was news, sometimes a sensation, but solid human interest at least. And there had been eight of them since last autumn; mostly the lonely, the impure, and the dispossessed—and now Miss Whittingham. The condition of those two tarts, poor things, had sickened him.

Angela Christine Whittingham. Age eighteen. Light-blond hair, green eyes, small build. Plaid dress, black bonnet and shoes, plaid parasol, black purse. Her escort was a bit of a mystery: a German, not apparently well thought of by her church friends, especially the Reverend Hopkins.

Miss Whittingham belonged to something called the Fundamentalist Church of Christ the Proselyte, one of those rigid, thou shalt not smoke, drink, dance, or laugh bastard offspring of Methodism and Schwenkfelder. But it was established and, through fanatical tithing, affluent. Its prophet had schooled his disciples as thoroughly in economics as the virtues of spreading the Word.

* * *

Captain Tolan sent his most tactful, if least experienced, man, Nathan McBride, to the Whittingham home in the suburbs. Detective McBride had the rare ability of projecting a touch of sympathy without committing himself. It was an elusive quality, something of a remote vulnerability that put the concerned parties at ease, subtly coaxing them to divulge idiosyncrasies, however indiscreet.

Nathan didn't mind his resultant nickname. The Psychiatrist. It suggested more chilliness than he'd have wished for his caricature, but his nickname at least had dignity.

He found Angela Whittingham's mother in a bower that faced the back garden, shaded by a grapevine. The foliage and singing birds in the backyard were an agreeable change from the steaming rows of brick and mortar that marked his precinct.

"Mrs. Whittingham, I'm from the police department . . . Detective McBride." His voice was soft, almost a whisper. "Do you mind if I ask you some questions?"

She did not respond. He reintroduced himself as she continued to rock in her chair.

"I've been sitting here," she whispered after a time, "thinking of the mysterious goodness of Jesus."

"Oh. . . ." He was stopped for a moment. "I'm terribly sorry to have to disturb your meditation, Mrs. Whittingham."

No response.

"I'd like to ask you about your daughter's acquaintances if I may. Your cooperation may expedite our finding her."

Angela Whittingham's mother would not look up. As she rocked herself, she puckered her lips with determination. McBride found himself unconsciously imitating her.

"Have you ever met the Reverend Richard T. Hopkins?"

"Of course I have," she snapped. "He's my pastor's assistant."

"Do you know him well?"

"He's been here for dinner," she answered triumphantly, and Nathan felt momentarily encouraged.

"Often?"

"Often enough," she twittered.

He studied the white blossoms fallen from an overhanging apple tree. They had been borne down by a mild breeze, speckling the ground on which he stood. He felt increasingly intrusive, seeing the petals he bruised as he shifted his weight from foot to foot.

"Is he close to Angela?"

"Why don't you ask *him*?"

Nathan wanted to swear. The way his fortunes had been turning for the past few months, he really looked forward to making a breakthrough in a major case. He merely sighed patiently and looked up at the clouds.

Mrs. Whittingham's older daughter, meanwhile, had been standing in the doorway, blurred by an insect screen.

"He'd like to be, Officer," she said, causing him to turn abruptly.

Mrs. Whittingham stopped rocking. "Shoo, Betsy. You haven't been invited!"

Nathan had picked up a class picture from Angela's school on his way there. The features that had caused him to lose himself in Angela's picture while riding the suburban trolley had been refined from Betsy's profile. Betsy Whittingham was disappointing. Disheveled and washed out, she rubbed her hands vigorously with a dish towel.

"We're . . . rather unsettled these days, Officer," she added, casting a passing glance at her mother, and Nathan nodded that he understood. "Would you care for a glass of lemonade? Professor Whittingham doesn't permit our harboring anything stronger."

"Thank you, no."

"The professor would be here, but he probably feels there's little he can accomplish by it. Nothing must impede the Cartesian progress, as I'm sure you'll agree."

"That's very mindless of you, Betsy." Her mother sulked.

At the risk of offending Betsy, who seemed prepared to answer his questions, he hastened to add that his own grades in mathematics had been abominable; he realized the need for constant application to that particular discipline. Mrs. Whittingham, nevertheless, continued to sulk.

"Why do you ask about the Reverend Hopkins?" asked Betsy.

"No substantive reason, Miss Whittingham. We're just trying to get a clearer picture of your sister's customary movements and he's one of those who saw her before she disappeared."

"Have you spoken with him directly?"

"We can't find him."

"He's a fraud."

Mrs. Whittingham made no protest this time. She went on rocking and stared off at the apple trees, apparently feeling that such moments of trial were to be borne with self-possession.

McBride did his best to remain unaffected, although he had sensed in Betsy a seething willingness to implicate all about her.

"Why do you say that?"

She leaned against a fence post. "My sister was supposed to go to Bryn Mawr last September. They'd even offered her a scholarship. She wanted to be a Latin teacher, you see."

"That's interesting," he interjected. "I once thought of that, too. Quite a lot, in fact."

"Personally it always bored me." She shrugged. "Anyway, Angela seemed to like it until the Reverend Hopkins got her all excited about his religious crusading. She met him during a weak moment, I guess."

"Do the rest of you belong to his church?"

"Good Lord, no," she answered quickly. "Just Mother, only she's too old to go out and convert all God's riffraff. Father, of course, believes only in digits and fractions."

Mrs. Whittingham's rocking accelerated, her eyes seeming to bulge with pent-up anger.

Betsy warded off a yellow jacket. A pair of swallows squabbled over possession of a birdbath in the yard. "He has her trapped in her principles," said Betsy, "like Don Quixote. Every day she goes out to the slums to teach his doctrine for him. When she gets home, I make her bathe in the basement, and all her clothing is boiled in brown soap."

"Angela doesn't need you to tell her to bathe," countered her mother.

Betsy informed Nathan that her sister had been led to believe that her only purpose in the divine plan was the eventual conversion of Africa. Her mother avowed that it was somehow predicted in Deuteronomy that a young woman from Philadelphia would do that. He decided that he disliked the Reverend Hopkins.

"What do you know about this German student, Manfred Koch?"

"She doesn't talk much about him," answered Betsy indifferently. "I think he just hangs around her, hoping."

"Has he ever been here?" asked Nathan.

Betsy Whittingham looked uncertain. "Once," offered her mother. "Only once. He was very rude to Professor Whittingham. Thought he knew it all. He was never asked here again."

Nathan presumed that the German and Professor Whittingham had disagreed, probably on political or philosophical principles; hence the charge of rudeness.

After a few more questions whose answers reaffirmed Angela Whittingham's pristine life-style, Detective McBride returned to his precinct station with notes on sibling jealousy, religious dissembling, and an abrasive German, all jotted during the hot, rocky ride into the city. But in none of it could he discern anything of substance.

Two weeks passed before Miss Whittingham's remains were found in a steamer trunk in the basement of the condemned Peters Building. One of the two derelicts who stumbled upon her had fainted at the sight.

The report on Tolan's desk stated, in the most clinical wording possible, that internal organs had been removed from the body. Certain surgical skill was evident. Similar skill was apparent in the removal of large sections of skin from her inner thighs. On that evidence the police would have been tempted to believe that the butchery had taken place after death and sought a medical student perhaps, for what wouldn't those serious young gentlemen do to a cadaver? And there were those who wondered what some of them wouldn't do to procure the necessary subject.

The scorch marks on her breasts, however, had taken away their early optimism—such as it had been. There was no way of explaining that kind of mutilation without concluding that she had been tortured to death. A thong had been placed around the victim's neck so tightly that it had broken the skin. The police could hope only that death had come from strangulation.

Even the coroner's office sought to prove that the knife had been used after the fact in an attempt to soften the blow to the Whittingham family. But there was no way to determine just how long she had endured her torture. Nor could it be stated with certainty that Miss Whittingham had been sexually abused.

The two derelicts, James L. Thompson, better known around Fortieth and Darby as Whiskey Jim and a dwarf named Elmo

Zwink, remained sober and in shock for days. Tolan assigned Detective Lieutenant Hudson to their questioning. Detective Lou
James went out to investigate the families of the children who had
been in Miss Whittingham's care. Elmo Zwink recovered sufficient-
ly to chide his friend on his weak stomach.

"Believe me, Lieutenant, Jimmy ain't no feather, an' when he
keeled over, I had to pick him up."

It was Whiskey Jim who, waking up at midday, had noticed the
steamer trunk and, at Zwink's urging, had opened it in search of un-
told riches. They wondered if the lieutenant suspected them.

But Hudson knew society's dispossessed well; the Sink had been
his beat for years, and he knew its limits as well as he knew the lines
in his face. A drunken knifing, an inept attempted beating, sometimes a skull broken in pursuit of a bottle of muscatel—these were
the crimes of those indigenous to the Sink. If anything so involved
as the Whittingham murder had taken place there, it would have
been an affair between derelict and derelict. Outsiders were never
welcome within its purlieus, even as prey.

"No, Elmo, it's not your style," Hudson answered. "But we'll keep
in touch anyway."

He left them with two dollars, promising to have them released
from the drunk tank within twenty-four hours.

Hudson knew what most of the Philadelphia reading public was
gradually learning. Miss Masterson's body had been slashed vicious-
ly with a large blade—perhaps a butcher knife. Miss Poole had been
found with a large metal instrument protruding from her most private of parts. Both, like Miss Whittingham, were missing sections of
skin from sensitive areas. Both had been tortured by fire. It was also
believed that both had been sexually molested; such data were difficult to confirm in cases of women involved in their profession.
While the fact of intimacy could be established, it was not clear
whether it had taken place before or after death.

For the time being, however, the newspaper industry was happily
preoccupied. President McKinley had signed the war resolution, ordering Spain to surrender its sovereignty and resign from Cuba and
announcing that he was empowered to use the naval and military
establishments to carry out his demands. Having worked so feverishly for this resolution, which Congress was expected to ratify presently, the tabloids were congratulating themselves for bringing
about the independence of the Cuban people.

Two

Manfred Koch was close to hysteria. His usually precise English had failed him, and a German interpreter had to be employed. It was the introduction of Herr Koch, with his grimly romantic overtones, that truly piqued the imagination of the press.

He was young and very Teutonic, and his light-brown ringlets wilted in the heat as he alternately pleaded and protested, weeping and lashing out at those he called his persecutors.

Koch insisted that he had parted company with Angela Whittingham two blocks before the trolley stop because he was due at a lecture by six thirty. Witnesses would attest to his presence, if only because he had disrupted the lecturer's opening remarks as he maneuvered for an empty seat. Since the visiting lecturer was none other than Bernard St. John, the noted British Egyptologist, such matters did not go by unnoticed. Obviously he had not had time to do, well, all that had been done to Angela. Even if he had had the inclination, which he most assuredly did not.

"But you are a violent man, Mr. Koch, a guiding head of a dueling fraternity." The prominent scar on Koch's cheek seemed to pale as the color rose in his face.

"What would you know of a dueling fraternity, Sergeant James?" asked Koch scornfully. "Such phenomena are clearly beyond your intellectual restrictions."

Lieutenant Hudson sipped his sarsaparilla and observed, "It would hardly disturb you to take a sharp instrument and plunge it into another human being."

Captain Tolan, sitting still for the most part while Hudson and James grilled the suspect, tapped his pipe tobacco into an ashtray and reminded Koch of the Reverend Hopkins' allegation. Before deciding to turn silent, the minister had mentioned an instance when the deceased had rejected Koch's offer to take her back to Germany during the summer. The Reverend Hopkins attributed the rejection to Miss Whittingham's natural sense of decency, but Koch called it bourgeois timidity. Given Koch's arrogance and passionate reputation, it seemed a motive worth pursuing.

"Much of his opinion of me has been distorted ever since he discovered that Angela found me . . . attractive. He would have no false gods before him! You must ask him of *his* whereabouts on that evening if you really wish to be serious about finding poor Angela's murderer!"

Tolan glanced at Lieutenant Hudson. Both would have loved to have something with which to nail Hopkins but a flock of zealots had quickly come forward to offer proof of his alibi. By six thirty of the evening in question he had already begun his patented sermon against the Papist conspiracy to take over the South and Southwest.

"Just concentrate on your own problems for now, Mr. Koch," said Hudson. "You've never quite clarified your relationship with the deceased."

"*Sie sind ein Unmensch! Ich kann Sie verstehen nicht!*" he burst at Hudson.

Koch looked away haughtily. Tolan signaled the interpreter to repeat the question in German. The lazy whir from an overhead fan almost drowned out the interpreter's soft, hesitant voice. Judging by his obvious deference, the interpreter held Koch in almost feudalistic awe. Koch's tone as he responded was assuredly arrogant.

"Herr Koch," said the interpreter, turning back to Tolan, "feels that it would be improper and not in the best interests of Miss Whittingham to speak of their relationship without her written approval."

"You should know that's a pretty safe answer," said Hudson acidly.

In the stifling air of the back room, Tolan could sense the thresholds of patience lowering. All but Koch had removed their coats and rolled up their shirt sleeves. The suspect, in his usual Spartan manner, had merely opened his collar a bit and rejected the glasses of ice water offered him by McBride, whom he particularly despised.

It was Detective McBride who had uncovered the most damning evidence against Koch, but Hudson was the most likely to react to Koch's diabolically facetious answer. Tolan motioned to Hudson that it was time for some fresh air, and the two left McBride and James to question the suspect.

It was a sultry night for this time of year. Thunder rolled lightly in the distance while fireflies blinked in the park across the street. Tolan refilled his pipe and, with Hudson following, strolled across the cobbled roadway to a park bench. Koch was not a good suspect really. Even his motive was essentially flimsy, and Lou James had admitted only a moment ago that he and Hudson both felt they were begging the question each time they resumed their interrogation. Much of their efforts resembled burlesque, despite their best attempts at affecting sincerity.

A block away a newsboy hawked headlines of the war with Spain, now entering its third week. Tolan was ambivalent about that entire affair: On the one hand, he was grateful to have the press kept busy with the new sensations; on the other, he fully realized that the recent wave of national pride could make Manfred Koch a perfect monster. Koch's arrogance seemed to grow as his fears mounted. The suspect could give the press enough rope to hang him many times over.

Hudson propped himself against a tree, listening to the crickets and observing the maniacal dance of the moths that clustered around the white globe outside the station. Young couples strolled by, the men overdressed and probably uncomfortable in their Saturday night finery, the women fresh and breezy in their printed dresses, seemingly laundered in heaven.

"Do you have the photograph, Charlie?"

"The Masterson dame? Yeah." Hudson removed a picture from a folder that was crammed with material relating to Manfred Koch's life and habits. "A good likeness, I'd say. Every bit as good as the one in our files."

"It should be. It was taken by the same photographer."

"Andrew Sutton?"

"Our own Andrew Sutton," said Tolan. "No one else could ever get such clarity. That's why we hired him in the first place."

"I never thought the sanctimonious Mr. Sutton would permit a lady of the evening to get so close."

Andrew Sutton was as unlikable as he was talented. Sutton's album of mug shots was a priceless asset to the precincts, but his aloofness rivaled that of Manfred Koch.

"For the right price"—Tolan grinned—"he might even photograph Satan himself."

The photograph had been found in Koch's possession shortly after his arrest. Even in the dim light of the streetlamp, the freckles on her nose and cheekbones were discernible. Her mug shot contained, of course, many more freckles. This photograph had been retouched to advantage for advertising purposes. The hair was like the wing of a raven and the eyes a vivid blue. So blue, in fact, that one felt it in black and white. Both these features were true to the original; only the slightly prominent mouth and rather full cheeks had been modified. But for these minor defects, Maura Ann Masterson had been as pretty as anyone on the Broadway stage.

"Koch must be quite the sport," said Hudson, "paying an Andrew Sutton fee just for a strumpet he'd found enjoyable."

"I suppose it explains his antiseptic relationship with the Whittingham girl," mused Tolan. "This one took care of his more primitive needs."

Hudson perked up. "That was nice work on the McBride kid's part, wasn't it, Regis?"

"He's coming along, Charlie."

Frustrated by his visit to the Whittinghams, Nathan McBride had vowed to accept no more embarrassments. Within seventy-six hours he insinuated himself into the university community and gathered a fund of information on Manfred Koch and his comrades. He learned that their moments of relaxation invariably involved the services of prostitutes, that among those prostitutes were Samantha Poole and, in particular, Miss Masterson. He also happened upon some members of the community who complained of the ungentlemanly behavior of Koch and his crowd, especially as it applied to those they considered their inferiors.

When the body of Angela Whittingham turned up, McBride had already amassed a thorough profile of the suspect. Beginning on the night when Miss Whittingham had rejected him, Koch had engaged the Masterson girl's services on a regular basis. She was a knowledgeable professional, having worked at her trade for eight years. She had been addicted to opium since the age of eighteen.

"I guess she was pretty flattered by Koch's attention, Charlie. Customers had been getting harder to come by. The word had gotten out, you see, that she'd contracted the occupational disease."

"Hmm. . . ." Hudson smiled. "No doubt he's been on arsenic treatments then. How long do you think he can go on denying he'd ever met her?"

"Unless I'm totally naive, he must think his chair is on fire by now."

"I'd say that's motive enough right there," Hudson speculated. "He could still have done in the Masterson tart when he discovered she'd handed him a nail."

"No." Tolan shook his head. "I wouldn't say that at all, Charlie."

"Okay. Why not?"

"I feel reasonably certain that it's *a* case and not a series of cases. Whoever killed Angela Whittingham is also responsible for the Masterson and Poole deaths and probably most of our disappearances, such as the Grayson lady in February. Some person or persons—and I'm pretty sure it involves more than one —must fit the *total* pattern. We could hang them on one count if that's all we can prove. But I don't think we can justify ourselves by building what looks like a good case against Koch or anyone else without satisfying ourselves that he did it all. Do you see what I mean?"

"What if he confesses?"

"Oh, he won't. Our man, if it's one man, is cold-blooded, vicious, and criminally insane, but I'll bet my last penny that if he were here right now talking to us, you'd think him the most respectable, most civilized person in the Western world. Koch is almost everything you'd ever want to send to the hangman. If he confessed, I'd be suspicious of it. He may be blaming himself to some degree for what happened to Miss Whittingham."

Hudson scratched his head. "I don't know, sometimes I don't follow you, Regis. According to what McBride discovered, Koch is practically an encyclopedia of torture, for Christ's sake, and you think we've got the wrong man."

"You can't fault a man for having a scholarly curiosity, no matter the subject."

"He's violent. If McBride hadn't boxed in his college days, Koch would have turned him into hamburger. As it is, Nate's sporting a lot of bruises."

Tolan's pipe had gone out. He emptied the ashes into his palm and deposited them in a clump of grass. The street was beginning to fill up with Saturday-night strollers, although the thunder had got louder and more frequent, threatening to disrupt the band concert in the park later on.

"That's another feeling I have, Charlie. When we find our man, he'll probably come along meekly. Koch lets it out. He fights, and he fornicates."

"That fraternity of his doesn't just collect weaponry. They have a whole trainload of instruments of pain in their cellar," Hudson countered. "Now you can't tell me that's a purely academic interest."

"He's written a paper on the subject, you know. It was published last winter in a very reputable history periodical. I'd say that sounds rather academic."

Hudson sighed and remained silent for the moment. "I was hoping to get you on that last one, Regis, but I didn't know about his magazine article."

"You don't really think he's our man either, Charlie. He's just the one that all the evidence points to. There's a difference."

"There *is* a difference," Hudson acknowledged, "but we'll have to book him anyway. That's an inescapable fact, my friend."

"I know. Letting Koch go would be hard to explain."

"As the fellow says, he's the only game in town."

Hudson returned to the office. He was rather anxious about McBride's apparent concern for the suspect's rights; his charity toward the accused might someday cause him to overlook something pertinent to the case for the state. He had total faith in Lou James, however. No superfluous milk of human kindness there.

Tolan watched Hudson cross the street, smiling warmly. The complete cop, Tolan thought, the indispensable cog in his machine. How many ball games would have been over in the first inning without Charlie Hudson?

He wondered just how the Reverend Hopkins should be handled, just who should question him and how. Hudson probably, since Charlie was a Protestant, though certainly not devout. But then, Charlie and a man of the cloth—that could become an even more sensitive issue. He wondered whether Lou James had a religion and, if so, whether he'd know how to handle a minister. Cases like this often made Tolan think of retirement.

Christ, what if Koch were really guilty? The newspapers would parlay that kind of thing into an international incident in a matter of days. And then the German government would have to claim that Koch was only the victim of Yankee corruption or inefficiency or—

"Working long hours, I see, and on a Saturday night. Must be something good."

A short, round man had approached unseen, out of the crowd of passersby, and seated himself on the unoccupied portion of park bench. Tolan would not have made a welcoming gesture had he been aware of him. Haloed by the lamplight, Stanley Butterfield's mean pig eyes were hidden behind thick spectacles.

"On the contrary, Stanley, I was just about to doze off. Boredom."

"Entertaining erotic dreams, no doubt."

Stanley was forever trying to be disarmingly friendly, but his hungry transparency made those who knew him at all wish he'd started his career in San Francisco. That morning a by-lined article had accused the department of dragging its feet in the Whittingham case, dwelling on the seizure Professor Whittingham had taken when his daughter's remains had been found. There were thinly veiled hints of incompetence in Tolan's ranks, and Tolan had been called down to sit through a lengthy harangue in City Hall.

"What's on your mind, Stan?" he asked, his voice an uninviting monotone.

"I think the heat must be getting to you, Captain Tolan. Where's all that Irish charm I keep hearing about?"

Tolan got up and stretched. "I'd better be getting home. I'm taking the boys to the ball game tomorrow. They've never seen the New Yorks."

"You should have let me know sooner." Stanley Butterfield's smile never slackened. With his slicked-back hair, he reminded Tolan of a beaver. "I could have gotten you some press passes. Great seats for the boys. I can even get them Napoleon Lajoie's autograph."

Captain Tolan had received such offers from the press before. Frankly, he'd never liked any of them enough ever to have accepted a favor. It definitely bothered them.

"I'll remember that next time, Stanley. Now, if you'll excuse me. . . ." He started to cross the street to the station house. "Good night, Stanley."

Butterfield got to his feet.

"Stanley, I heard something about Admiral Dewey and the Spaniards in Cuba or the Philippines or somewhere today. Why don't you find out where it is and go cover it?"

"They say the German really hacked her up. She was a real mess, like she'd been attacked by some wild animal."

"You'd better watch what you eat before bed, Stanley. Your nightmares are getting worse."

"I have that on good authority, Captain Tolan. You can't hide the facts forever, you know. What about the German?"

Despite the threat of a storm, the band in the park was warming up. There was something surreal about Butterfield's silhouette, the streetlight reflecting from his eyeglasses, and a background of undirected music.

"Tell me, do they give you a gold star or a column or something if you can inspire a lynch mob? I have nothing for you, Stanley. Good night."

Tolan proceeded up the steps of the precinct station. He thought he heard Butterfield mumbling something under his breath and stopped. He was silent for a moment. Yes, that was the word. . . . He realized he'd heard the word "clown."

"I think you'd better run along, Stanley, before I have to turn myself in for cruelty to animals."

Butterfield froze, wondering whether to dart down the roadway. Tolan clenched his fists and fought the impulse to rattle Stanley. He suddenly envisioned Stanley scurrying fitfully along on those fat little legs and, turning, made a laughing exit through the main door of the station house. Stanley pounded his fist in impotent anger; the crickets and marching band grew louder behind him, as if mocking his efforts to be effectual.

Inside, Tolan almost knocked over the interpreter. The German excused himself brusquely and hastened through the doorway. Tolan looked at Hudson. Hudson just threw up his hands in innocence. Tolan then turned to Sergeant James for an explanation.

"He got irked at Charlie's language, Captain. Nothing serious."

"Look, sometimes we have to get graphic, right?" said Hudson. "Did he think I like to say those things in English?"

"That's too bad. I might have needed him. Did you find out anything?"

Lou James said, "Koch met the Whittingham girl at a sociology lecture. Aparently their relationship was quite prim."

"Well" Tolan yawned—"how good is your German, Nate?"

"Nothing very poetic, Captain," said McBride, "but I can hold my own in a low-class restaurant."

Tolan put his hand on McBride's shoulder. "I think this should be stated in the subject's own language lest the gravity of his situation be misinterpreted."

Koch fixed his gaze on Tolan as he went on. "Please inform Herr Koch that although we have by no means exhausted all avenues of investigation in this case, he is at present our principal suspect and the only one with a plausible motive. The German consul will be advised of Herr Koch's status, and all measures will be taken to assure a thoroughly fair treatment in this unfortunate matter."

McBride nodded and began rather haltingly. "*Herr Koch, obgleich der Untersuchung ist bestimmt nicht beendet.* . . .

Koch waved him aside in midsentence. McBride emitted a sigh of gratitude. The best he could boast of was fair reading knowledge of German.

"It must be quite a relief, Captain Tolan," Koch said bitterly, "to know you have your most appropriate scapegoat. Your superiors will love you for this. You will never have to punish the real murderer, and the journalists will stop hounding you."

"We haven't convicted you yet," said Tolan calmly.

"It is ignominious, believe me, to know that I've been brought down by such liars and cowards."

"We'll have to lock you up now, Mr. Koch," said Hudson, taking the young German by the arm.

"I could not," Koch asserted as he was being led away to his cell, "I could never have done those ugly things. I loved her. Angela was beautiful . . . like a flower. I simply wanted to marry her. I tried very hard to make her think better of me."

"And with that," Sergeant James announced, "I'm going for a beer. It's been a long, hot day. McBride can book him. It's his case anyway."

Lou James threw his jacket over his shoulder, bounded out the door and down the steps, heading up the street toward the nearest beer parlor. In the distance, under a street lamp, he could make out the silhouette of the lanky German interpreter, followed closely by that of portly Stanley Butterfield. Lou smiled to himself.

"I think we're going to lose Lou pretty soon, Regis," Hudson observed as he returned from the lockup. "The romantic call of the Army recruiter has touched his adventurous soul."

Tolan continued to thumb through Koch's file absentmindedly. "Ah, to be so young again, to be able to get excited over the insanity of the times. . . . I remember the day I got off the cattle boat from Cork. There he was, majestic, like a soldier in an opera, promising us food, money, above all, citizenship, if we'd rally 'round the Union. I was only fifteen, and the sight of Boston was more frightening to me than whatever the American Civil War was about."

"I didn't need a recruiter," said Hudson. "I was just glad to get out of Camden."

"Anyway, I got a good look at my new homeland, from Tennessee to Gettysburg at least." Tolan straightened the papers in the folder. "Had I landed in Charleston instead of Boston I'd have become a Confederate for all it mattered to me at the time."

"Shame on you, Regis. Are we still going to look into the Reverend Hopkins?"

"Not we, Charlie. You check him out. You're the Protestant. Only, please try to remember he's a righteous bastard, so I expect you to be a perfect gentleman. On second thought, you'd better take McBride with you."

On May 1, just before daybreak, Admiral George Dewey slipped into Manila Bay and leisurely and methodically destroyed the Spanish squadron under Admiral Montojo.

Spanish dead numbered three hundred and eighty-one with many more wounded; of the American personnel not one was killed and fewer than ten were wounded. Statistically, at least, it assumed major proportions. That the Spanish squadron was generally unseaworthy and, in this instance, badly outnumbered, seemed of little importance in the warmer months of 1898. For the first time in more than thirty years the nation was at war; more than ninety years had passed since it had last humbled a major power.

A decade or so later Theodore Roosevelt was to observe that "it wasn't much of a war, but it was the best war we had." At the time, however, the man in the street was much less inclined to dismiss the war's importance. A strong wave of nationalism produced songs and limericks applauding our new heroes and scoffing at all things European. The yellow press was beside itself with self-importance.

Shortly after Dewey dropped anchor in the bay, a German squadron appeared on the horizon and, with incredible insouciance, settled within firing distance of the American ships. Dewey and the German commander, Vice Admiral Otto von Diedrichs, exchanged heated words. Only the good offices of the British commander, Captain Sir Edward Chichester, whose squadron also lay in the bay, circumvented the serious threat of hostilities.

The crisis had been inflamed by the press, which was firmly convinced that Germany wanted the Philippines for itself. Cartoonists competed to see who could contrive the most grotesque depiction of Kaiser Wilhelm II—the Spanish King Alfonso XIII had been rendered so effectively.

Three

May 5 dawned overcast, but the dark hints of showers faded into a milky blue sky by early afternoon. The air in the city was nauseatingly close. While Hudson was questioning the petulant and uncooperative Reverend Hopkins, Captain Tolan was entertaining one Mme. Natalia Cheever, an obscure mystic who claimed to have helped the police in Buffalo and New Haven with her clairvoyant powers. Her elegant demeanor and supremely tasteful appearance had gained her quick access to Tolan's desk in the inner office.

Despite the intermittent touches of Brooklyn which crept into her lightly alien accent, it was some time before Tolan concluded that she was mad as a March hare and escorted her politely to the door. He threatened Lou James with a sudden reassignment to the waterfront if he ever failed to screen out the lunatics again.

Sergeant James bristled. "And just how long did it take you to find out for yourself? I watched you in there pouring tea as if you were visiting Sarah Bernhardt in her parlor. I'm no Sigmund Freud, you know."

Through the open window Tolan watched Mme. Cheever—whatever her real name—raise her parasol and float up the street. With her flowing leg-o'-mutton sleeves and long, trailing skirt, she reminded him of a sailboat on calm waters. "I have to admire one thing about her. She certainly looks unaffected by the heat."

"I really have more pressing matters to attend to, Captain." Sergeant James went back to his typewriter and continued to peck away at his report.

"So have I, Lou. I can't waste my hours talking to people who belong in a sandbox."

Yesterday a lanky, sallow, young man from the Pittsburgh area, who identified himself as John Stanklow, had claimed to have been sent by heaven with his gifted dog, Joseph. Joseph, half beagle and half Staffordshire, was supposed to be able to sense not only the guilty, but also those who harbored evil intentions.

Joseph licked the hand of a well-known felon. Joseph tore the cuff off Captain Tolan's trousers. As Stanklow nervously recited lines from Samuel, Corinthians, and Ezekiel, the dog left its personal mark under the captain's desk.

The German consulate had been surprisingly cooperative. A

thorough life history of Manfred Koch arrived less than a week after Tolan's formal request. It included Koch's grades at the University of Leipzig and a letter of high praise from a local commandant of militia. Added to McBride's efforts, this brought the Koch dossier to more than two hundred pages.

Koch, meanwhile, sublimated his tensions by working on his master's thesis: a study of Scythian artifacts recently unearthed in the eastern Ukraine near the Sea of Azov. His faculty adviser, Professor Theophilus Flood of the University of Pennsylvania, having received Tolan's permission to visit Koch daily, brought books in Latin, Greek, French, Russian, and Hebrew. Professor Flood, thoroughly unconcerned about anything unrelated to archaeology, claimed it would be "a definitive study on a profoundly enigmatic people." Sergeant James nodded his tacit approval.

One item in Koch's background was disturbing. A letter from a Professor Ehrlich in Leipzig, attached to a copy of a distinguished service award, noted that Koch had volunteered to take part in a bufotenine experiment—under strictly guarded conditions, of course.

Bufotenine. Something once spoken of at a criminologists' convention. It had stuck in Tolan's mind. The "berserk" drug. Could the suspect have taken it at the time? That would have to be looked into very soon. Very soon.

Zoltan Mroszek tiptoed past his landlady's door. Then he stumbled up the dimly lighted stairs, over a sleeping tomcat on the first flight, through a group of children playing tag at the stairwell turning on the fourth. He passed an argument between two round Italian housewives on the sixth and crept into his room on the seventh. He was careful to avoid disturbing Mrs. Leibowitz next door since it was commonly known that she was the landlady's principal spy.

He groped under the bed and found, amid the clutter of bottles, one three-quarters full of muscatel and gulped two quick mouthfuls before collapsing on the bed.

He sat up and drowsily removed his scarf, a tattered garment that he wore always. He took another deep drink of muscatel in a vain effort to clear his head and picked a book off one of the stacks. When his eyes focused for a moment, he stared at the fair-haired girl in the photograph that marked the page in his collection of Swinburne.

Let us go hence, my songs; she will not hear.
Let us go hence, together without fear;
Keep silence now, for singing-time is over,
And over all old things and all things dear.
She loves not you nor me as all we love her.
Yea, though we sang as angels in her ear,
    She would not hear.

The smile was sensuous, rather feigned, carefully practiced—like
the roguish tilt of her shoulder. Her eyes did not really smile, and
her thick, luxurious hair seemed to be only crudely assembled atop
her head.

But to Zoltan Mroszek, Samantha Poole, with her nasty temper
and roughneck vocabulary, her cold indifference and constant un-
faithfulness, had been the most beautiful, the most exciting woman
alive.

In the beginning Zoltan had spent his energy on painting. But the
galleries were repulsed by the untrammeled and undisciplined anger
of his works. Then he had turned to acting. But the producers, believing him irresponsible, had soon refused to cast him. Now his
rare sober moments were devoted to his writing; in the hot, tiny
room the unpublished plays mildewed; the unfinished novel about
bohemian life had not been touched since autumn; imitations of
Baudelaire, Rossetti, Symons, and, lately, Dowson were scattered
about incomplete. He had lost his Cynara, his remote ideal, and
when the one proper word was needed, his English usually failed
him.

It did now. He tore up the poem he had begun and slammed his
pen into the picture of Samantha Poole. In his muddled frustration,
he imagined her scornful laugh coming out of that shallow smile.
He hissed the word "slut" under his breath.

After draining the last of the muscatel, he crossed to the bureau.
He opened the top drawer to select a handful of press clippings and
tumbled back on his bed to read them. Within a few minutes he had
fallen into a deep, all-day sleep.

Troubled and weary after days of attempting to fathom the Whittingham case in the midst of bureaucratic hysteria, Tolan called on
Dr. Ian Blakeley. An Englishman, Blakeley was a forensic patholo-

gist who worked as a consultant to police departments of the East Coast when not involved in his own private investigations. Together he and Tolan had unraveled many mysteries over the past five years, and in the process a solid friendship had evolved, once Tolan's inherited antagonism to Englishmen was overcome.

Sipping cognac in Blakeley's study that evening, Regis Tolan once again marveled at Blakeley's prodigious sense of recall.

"Bufotenine . . . yes, it was perhaps the single most important factor behind the military effectiveness of the Vikings," said Blakeley. "In fact, we've gotten the word 'berserk' from a particularly fierce cult of Viking warriors who used it before going into battle. They cultivated a mushroom of the *Amanita muscaria* variety, indigenous to Scandinavia and northern Europe, for that purpose."

"Could it be cultivated in the climate and soil conditions of eastern Pennsylvania?"

"With a little care and scientific understanding, definitely," Blakeley answered.

"Do we know of any recent use of the drug in this area?"

"Until you mentioned those people in Leipzig, I'd no idea that anyone had used it since the eighth century," Blakeley admitted.

"Ian"—Tolan leaned forward, his eyes strained and his voice subdued—"you must know why I'm asking about this. You've read the papers. Stanley Butterfield collared an interpreter the other night and, after a few drinks, got some information that I was hoping to tone down for a while. It's that case—the ugly one."

Blakeley nodded. Tolan's words had come as no surprise. Tolan got up and paced around with his cognac before stopping before a portrait of Blakeley's delicately beautiful wife, Sophia.

Blakeley mused, "I take it you have serious doubts about this young German suspect of yours."

"It's all circumstantial, you know, every bit of it." Tolan sat on the ledge within the large Tudor window. A breeze ruffled his curly white hair, causing some of it to fall forward to his bushy eyebrows. "When you pare it down, all we've really got is his ambiguous relationship with the victim. The rest you could put into a glass no bigger than the one I'm holding. Those disconnected minds in City Hall are pressing us to make him look like Jack the Ripper."

"Does the fact that he's a German national enter into it at all?"

Tolan chortled ironically and got up to pace about. "Actually, that part of it is helping us because Washington seems to want to play down the German element. I had a visitor from the State Department today, and his sole concern was for the suspect's welfare. No, the jingoists I've got are in the press, but that's enough in an election year. You can pick up a lot of votes these days if you can just follow the tides of hatred."

Blakeley poured more cognac into his glass and loosened his ascot. The heat was impossible to ignore despite his wishing to remain proper. Philadelphia vexed him.

"Is there anything else that you may have missed? Something more in his past perhaps?" asked Blakeley. "I'm thinking now of what could happen were the press to come up with something useful before you do."

Tolan put his cognac down and folded his arms. "Butterfield claims to have interviewed some grocery clerk. Madigan. Patricia Madigan. She's supposed to have said she once refused Koch's attentions and received a clout or two for it. We have our informants, too, even in the press. You'll read about it in the papers tomorrow morning, I'm sure."

"No truth in it?"

"Well, that I really don't know yet."

"You've said he's capable of violence."

"But Butterfield is capable of worse. You can be certain that by the time we've proved that he's bribed the girl to tell her lie, the papers will have raised a howl to wake the dead. And the politicians will take it from there. I have my share of enemies in City Hall, and I'll be in the frying pan for days. Ian, I'd retire right now if I didn't find the whole thing so offensive to me personally. Between the reporters and the politicians a soul can't find an ounce of justice." Tolan picked up his cognac and stood silent.

"Which reminds me, I have two theater tickets for Friday and Sophia can't tolerate the playwright, a Norwegian named Henrik Ibsen. His plays haven't been done in Philadelphia up to now. Sophia claims he's also a boor because he's obsessed with the ugly truth. I think you'll appreciate him, Regis."

Tolan raised his cognac in agreement. "By the same token, Ian, I've got tickets, three of them, for a boxing match next Sunday, and Maggie hates the idea. I thought we might take Ralphie along. He'll probably want to climb into the ring and take them both on."

"Oh, yes, Ralphie. . . ." Blakeley was transparent in his desire to change the subject.

Tolan took a token sip of cognac and obliged. "How likely is a man to commit a truly odious act while under the influence of the bufotenine drug?" he asked.

Blakely thought for a moment. "It juggles the irascible appetite, as rational psychologists might put it. In Freudian wording, it blots out the superego. One acts entirely without fear or conscience."

"Could someone act coolly, if brutally? That is, take one's time to make sure there was a maximum of pain to the victim?"

"Oh, yes. One need not salivate, or even perspire, to inflict pain," Blakeley pointed out. "The Viking berserks could fight like madmen while adhering to a carefully thought-out plan of attack. It's conceivable that our own murderer could go about his terrible work with scientific detachment."

"Leave his own body, so to speak?"

"Yes, he could. It's a common schizophrenic trait as a matter of fact. Of course, a true schizophrene would require no narcotic inducements to do so."

"Hmm. . . ." Tolan placed his snifter of cognac, mostly untouched, on a table and started to leave. At least he'd determined that the proper focus of his investigation should be the university district. "Vicious, isn't it, my friend?"

Blakeley joked with Tolan as he accompanied him to the door. "On the other hand, if Beowulf really existed, he must have used quite a lot of it. Finn MacCool no doubt used it as well."

Tolan adjusted his derby and bade his friend good-night. "Finn MacCool no doubt used it better."

After lunch Manfred Koch's attorney interrupted Koch's research. The consulate had made an excellent choice of defense attorney: the much respected Geoffrey L. Van Zandt of Harrisburg, who delighted in upsetting the smugness of the Philadelphia county bar. Fluent in German and bearing a proud record of scholarship, Van Zandt was one of the few men capable of commanding Koch's cooperation, and the consulate had no apparent qualms about his lofty fees. With the preponderance of circumstantial evidence, it was expected he would have Koch out on bail within a fortnight.

In the back of Tolan's mind, too, as the pressure from City Hall for a conviction at all costs grew in intensity, was the memory of the celebrated Molly Maguires case in the coal fields. The press, the politicians, and a great deal of circumstantial evidence had hanged eighteen of Tolan's friends and relatives upstate during those shameful days after the Civil War. The bitter memories had never left him. He had left the coal region an angry, disillusioned young man. It was not at all hard for him to sympathize with the German now that he was on the other end of the issue.

The Reverend Hopkins, though treated with a deference bordering on obsequiousness, was almost infantile in his resentment of the police for having involved him in this unseemly affair.

In addition to Detective McBride, Tolan had assigned a young woman stenographer to the interrogation of the Reverend Hopkins, just in case Charlie Hudson should revert to form. Not that the captain was without his own impatience. In Tolan's estimation, the Reverend Hopkins would have been much happier faith healing down South. Had the Reverend Hopkins not found religion so lucrative and so satisfying to his ego, he would undoubtedly have made an indelible mark on the belligerent fringe of politics.

"We know more than you'd ever imagine, Reverend Hopkins," snapped Hudson. "You'd be *appalled* at how much we know."

Hudson eventually left the questioning to Nathan McBride, whose well-practiced, soft-spoken technique was more in keeping with the tone Tolan wished to maintain.

Virtually every answer given by the Reverend Hopkins was so obviously aimed at incriminating Manfred Koch that his entire testimony had to be viewed with skepticism. Although he seemed more willing to cooperate with Detective McBride, whom he considered sensitive for a Roman Catholic, his responses were no more useful than they had been all afternoon.

Angie Sutton, née Angélique-Marie Cordier to sharecropper parents in Lac Petit, Louisiana, a little more than twenty-five years before, was all aquiver. She had awakened an hour earlier than usual with every intention of being fresh as a daisy by noon, but she could recall, rather vaguely, having mumbled a good-bye to Andrew around seven thirty and then drifting off until nine.

Going to the kitchen cabinet which housed the bourbon, she took no notice of Andrew's neatly washed and dried breakfast dishes. Andrew's shadowy presence had become part of the mornings, though Angie found him easier to overlook than her morning nausea and jitters.

Seated before the dresser, she took special care with the dark areas under her eyes, more than ever a problem. The eyes were particularly important today. When she'd first met David, during the intermission of that dull concert Andrew had dragged her to, David had gone on and on about how much he admired them. He said she looked like a little China doll. In fact, as she recollected proudly, all her visitors had liked her eyes. But David was kind of special because he never failed to say something really nice about the way she looked and smelled.

Between delicate touches of rouge and rice powder, she sipped the second of the three glasses of bourbon that she would allow herself this morning, just in order to clear her head before her visitor arrived at noon.

When she had satisfied herself that the lines and circles were subtly camouflaged, she got up, removed her robe, and powdered her body with lilac sachet, paying particular attention to surround her breasts.

The grandfather clock that Andrew was so proud of, the one he'd toted all the way up from New Orleans along with all his other precious knickknacks, sounded eleven times in the hallway. Angie posed before the full-length mirror, inspecting and admiring her very pleasing body; seeing what she saw was still the most gratifying moment of her day.

David was, of course, too much the gentleman ever to say so, but she knew for sure he admired much more than her eyes. Other, less genteel men had been much bolder. One of her visitors had even admitted once that he'd be just as happy if all he got to do was look at her in the altogether. She had blushed and notified the gentleman that he would not be welcome until he'd learned the rules of decorum.

Pouring her third glass, she noted that her hands shook not half so much as an hour ago. She now felt confident enough to rouge her lips, always the most painstaking operation of the morning. As she decorated her brilliant red hair with emerald-green ribbons, she once again concluded that she looked like a real gracious plantation lady. She would hide just how much the heat and humidity bothered her.

Four

Regis Tolan picked up the evening newspaper with weary resignation. Stanley Butterfield had found a way into his home and could
taunt him even there.

That morning's account of Koch's alleged assault on Miss What's-
her-name?, Madigan, was a rare masterpiece of pathos and moral
indignation. It had been printed—not so coincidentally—opposite a
tale about a supposed insult to our ambassador to the German
court. Scanning it over his fried eggs and rye toast, he put it aside in
favor of a second cup of tea and a rare chat with Maggie.

The pressures of the day had made the story fade into relative
unimportance until midafternoon. The priggish senior secretary
had answered the telephone and hastily informed him that the district attorney's office wished to see him immediately. As many times
as he had warned her that he was to be out of the office to certain
people, her queer sense of public duty had combined with her natural fear of the higher-ups to cause her to inform on him. Why had
he not fired her? But a senior secretary with arthritis was certain to
play more upon his heart than his mind. Cursing the invention of
the telephone, he had appropriated a horse and buggy better used
on other errands and reported to the district attorney's office.

Though they cherished the same ideals—they were sure he was
well aware of that—they were feeling the pressure now and let him
know where the damage would most occur should a political embarrassment come of his obstinance and ingratitude. Tolan pictured his
pension turning into air. The district attorney was looking ahead to
the mayoral election and the mayor to the governor's mansion.

His wife reminded him that he'd been staring into space like a
holy man for the last ten minutes.

He unfolded the paper and thumbed through it in search of the
editorial page. There, in the left corner of page nine, was a column
assailing the district attorney's office for withholding information
that the public had every right to know, for caving in to pressure
from Washington because a German national was involved, for
indifference to the rights of Miss Whittingham's survivors, for grasping at legalistic straws when they had in custody a man of desperate
capabilities.

"Why, that dirty little hypocrite. . . ."

Stanley Butterfield had gotten an interview with the Reverend Hopkins.

Maggie, sensing an outburst at any moment, called Tolan's youngest daughter out of the living room and into the kitchen. In all, there were seven children, counting Kathleen in the convent and Kevin in the priesthood. None had ever heard their father utter anything beyond a mild oath; nevertheless, Maggie took no chances.

Essentially the same statement given to Hudson and McBride—supposedly confidential material in the first place—the article contained additional evidence designed to tighten the rope around Koch's neck.

The reverend had intimated to Butterfield that the late Miss Whittingham had expressed fear for her safety on several occasions. The reverend himself had warned Koch to stay away from Miss Whittingham. The warning had, of course, been ignored because "Mr. Koch, in his consummate weakness, had been under the influence of an intoxicant at the time." Tolan wasn't sure whether he loathed Stanley or the Reverend Hopkins more at that instant. "The Reverend Hopkins admitted that he too had been threatened with serious consequences to himself and to his congregation by Koch and several of Koch's arrogant associates."

Tolan put the newspaper aside, feeling suffocated.

The next morning, despite Van Zandt's arguments about the absence of any substantial evidence, Manfred Koch's bail was refused. Tolan sent Lou James for the Madigan girl and made his way through the detention corridor to Koch's cell. Antiquated, foul-smelling, and unhealthy, it was pleasantly cool inside. The dampness which seeped through the basement walls at all times and the relative lack of sunlight always made summers better than winters there.

To get there, one descended a series of steps made of stone and heavy wood and followed winding paths lined with cells now used for storage. Tolan's precinct possessed one of the last of these lockups, throwbacks to a bygone era of civil unrest and moral severity. The others had been replaced by the most part by the new county prison.

He did his best to sound cheerful. Koch chose to ignore his tone. Ever the disciplined gentleman of the Old World, he had rolled down his shirt sleeves and put on his coat when Tolan entered.

"Surely you must have other cases to occupy your time, Captain Tolan."

"Well, you're a celebrity, Mr. Koch." Tolan lifted the glass from the coal-oil lamp and lit his cigar from the flame.

"Ah, yes," said Koch sarcastically. "Do sit down, please, Herr Tolan."

Koch waited until the captain had settled atop a wooden stool below the grimy window before seating himself on the side of the bed. Tolan's pause must have lasted an awkward thirty seconds. "I came down here because I don't expect I'll have an opportunity to speak with you after today. You're being transferred to the city jail across town."

"Good. One might anticipate better conditions in a larger facility. Will I be able to consult with my attorney there?"

"Of course."

Koch paused this time. His resentment seemed to abate somewhat. "Would you happen to have another cigar? I'm told that fleas cannot stand the smell of smoke."

Tolan drew two panatelas from his vest pocket, adding that it would be wise to save them for after meals, in which case they might last a whole week. He added that personally he preferred a pipe but had left it in the office.

"Actually, considering that I am essentially a political prisoner, I have not been treated badly here at all. I expect I have you to thank for that, Captain."

"Our system is much different from yours, Mr. Koch. We usually treat our political prisoners with kid gloves. Do you know that expression?"

"It means you keep them in isolation while your press excites the public to unprecedented heights of moral indignation."

Tolan looked at him quizzically, as if he did not understand Koch's real meaning. He cleared his throat.

"What I mean is that we're taking special pains to see to it that some self-righteous rabble in the cells around you don't take it upon themselves to hang you. People accused of the type of crime that has you here seem to inspire that sort of thing. Besides, you're still a suspect. That's why we still have these cells in precinct stations. When you're arraigned, it will be another matter."

"Arraignments, indictments." Koch laughed contemptuously.

"Legalistic mumbo jumbo. Your newspapers have already convicted me!"

Tolan got up and looked out the window, wondering how much protection the bars would afford if someone should decide to get at Koch while he was detained there. The window was only about six inches above street level.

"It's probably a good thing your bail was refused. You're better off until this matter is settled anyway." Tolan's tone was matter-of-fact. "Hysteria is just below the surface of everything. Cultural anxiety is probably the term you'd choose to define it. Your people beat the French twenty years ago. You're much too young to remember. Anyway, it's the same thing. People don't know if they want to explode in anger or joy, but an explosion is imminent nonetheless."

"Very astute, Captain." The sunlight squeezed through the small, bespattered window and illuminated the suspect's angry countenance.

"We're awaiting word from Leipzig about something on your record. Mr. Koch, did you ever take the berserk drug?"

"Berserk drug . . . ?"

"Bufotenine. You experimented with it once."

"Bufotenine? Oh, good Lord!" Koch laughed nervously. "Don't tell me those swine you work for dredged that up!"

"Did you use it?" Tolan persisted.

Somewhere in the corridor a drunk was being escorted to his cell amid shouted obscenities from the resident prisoners.

"What would you or any of those other fools know of bufotenine, what it is, what it does? To you it is only an exotic new term to be used in connection with the Case of the Hateful Prussian." These last words were a reference to a nickname recently coined by the yellow press. He gestured toward his breast modestly.

"You love your new title, don't you, Mr. Koch?" Tolan inquired with a strange smile.

Koch looked at him as if he had just declared that the earth was flat. "Love it? Of course." Koch laughed. "It is precisely what I came here for!"

"In a way, I'm beginning to think so," said Tolan evenly.

"My brother Sean used to say," Tolan proceeded, "call me a son of a bitch often enough, and that's just what I'll be, a son of a bitch."

"So am I also, Captain," Koch agreed monotonously.

"You've trapped yourself in your own rhetoric, Koch. Ever since this case began, you've been strutting about like a Prussian caricature, vilifying all the sacred cows, actually *defying* us to hang you. No wonder the newspapers are having such a grand time with you. For a man of your supposed intelligence, you seem to know nothing about the prevailing emotional winds of the time and place. I don't believe you'd recognize yourself beneath that outmoded façade of yours."

"I take it someone gave you a book on behavioral science, Herr Tolan," Koch answered cynically.

"Son, I could write a book on behavioral science. I've seen much wiser lads than you hang themselves in the same way. Every time a turnkey overhears you calling your attorney a Yankee moron or my staff a pack of barbarians you pull the knot a little tighter. Frankly, you aren't making my task any easier."

"It is not for me to make your task easier, Herr Tolan."

"It is, you know. I don't want to have these bodies turning up weeks after they've hanged you. I don't want them saying the *police* got the wrong man. Is that clear, Koch?"

"You don't think I'm guilty?" Koch seemed puzzled.

It would be highly irregular to admit to an incarcerated suspect that he considered him innocent. Koch apparently understood.

"The next time I send one of my men to ask you something," said Tolan, his determination unabated, "I want you to give him answers instead of lessons in sophistry. And if you ever give the press another hint of your playacting arrogance, you'll very suddenly think you're in one of your own German prisons. Is that clear, Koch?"

"Very clear, Captain," said Koch awkwardly.

"Now," Tolan resumed, glancing at his pocket watch and pacing across the cell, "did you ever take bufotenine?"

"No, Captain. I took part in the experiment, but as an observer. I was never so zealous a student that I would consider ingesting it personally. I counted pulse rates and took notes."

Someone in a distant cell commanded the drunk to quiet down, and a brief lull followed.

"What were the circumstances?"

"Very respectable circumstances. Professor Ehrlich had, I believe, intended it for eventual use on patients who have withdrawn into themselves. He needed more data regarding levels of safe dosage." Koch's voice trailed off, as if something painfully relevant had just occurred to him.

"Go on," said Tolan quietly.

"It . . . it was administered to inmates of a prison not far from the university. I can tell you it was very fascinating to watch, but certainly not so much that one would ever wish to use it on himself."

"And that's all there was to it?"

"The whole truth, Captain."

"Well," Tolan quipped, "when you get back to Leipzig, you must remind Professor Ehrlich to be more thorough the next time he commends you. It was very unscientific of him."

"You don't do that sort of thing here, I presume? Experiments and the like?"

"No, we just feed you badly."

While they were awaiting the jailor, whose keys could be heard jangling as he strode up the corridor, Koch touched him on the arm.

"How can you think I'm innocent when the herd around you say otherwise?"

"I'd never swear to your innocence on a Bible, Mr. Koch. Not yet anyway." He wished that Koch would drop the issue immediately. He'd already intimated more than he should have.

"I'm obliged to you, Herr Tolan."

He left the cell feeling somewhat better, if unsure that it was not already too late for Manfred Koch. He knew he could not let the German go to trial within the next few months. It would take time and a few more suspects to allow the defense a chance at impaneling an objective jury, if, indeed, that would ever be possible.

Strolling up the corridor toward the stairway, he dwelt upon the panoply of horrors that would no doubt in time come of putting pressure on the simpering Reverend Hopkins. How he and Hudson—all of them, in fact—wanted to get the reverend into this. But the evidence just wasn't there, and before you could say benediction, the city would have his whole precinct shut down.

He finally admitted that he had no more reason to believe the Reverend Hopkins guilty than Manfred Koch innocent. He simply disliked the man.

In truth, he knew he had nothing of value to go on.

* * *

Jennifer Figge stood poker-faced while a veterinarian and a groom tended to Hubris III. Scarlet lash marks ran diagonally over the stallion's sleek chestnut body, converging on his forelegs where the flesh had been stripped.

Sighing, she crossed her arms and leaned against a stall. "Do you expect to stop the bleeding this month or next?"

"We've just about controlled it." The veterinarian never looked up. He had been at it since midmorning.

"You're very efficient," she said icily.

"But . . . I'm afraid he'll be badly scarred."

The groom stroked the white diamond patch that decorated the stallion's forehead. Jennifer remained motionless but for the slight nervous twitch of her left eye.

"What I'm waiting for you to tell me, Dr. Simms, is what the scars will look like. Are they—"

He looked up sharply. "Miss Figge, there is no way in the world that anyone with eyes could think that this horse had run off and got caught in a thicket. Your father knows this animal well."

"But there are briars all around here," she insisted, "especially along the creek where he could have gone for water. It's very warm, you know."

"Look." He removed his glasses and wiped his brow with the back of his wrist. "I'm not going to lie to your father. He can certainly tell the difference between briar scratches and whip marks."

"You've lied to him before."

"Oh?"

"When you said you were a veterinarian. Father should have hired you as a court fool!"

He resumed his swabbing. The stallion's deltoid muscle was still bleeding profusely. At such times it was all he could do to keep himself from taking the whip and returning the beating in kind.

"I won't argue with you, Miss Figge. As you see, I have work to do." It had happened on several previous occasions.

"You don't seem to comprehend, Dr. Simms, that Hubris Three is Father's favorite horse. I'm not even supposed to go near him."

"You should have thought of that before you picked up the whip."

"I have every right to get on and ride him if I want," she objected. "He threw me."

"If I were you, miss, I'd be somewhere else when your parents get home tomorrow night."

She pulled a saddle from its rack, sent it crashing to the ground, and began to kick it. When the men failed to respond, she left the stable. She wept and cursed as she headed toward the house. Along the bridle path she scuffed her heels and kicked up dust in a fit of temper.

Leaving the bridle path, she turned toward the gravel road which led downhill through rows of apple trees to the creek. The road was covered with layers of white blossoms, heightening the brilliant green of the estate's sprawling manicured lawns. It was a pretty time of year in Devon, a world of ivy and blooming rosebushes.

She knew she had to get away for a few days. But if she went back to school early, Father would surely come down there in a rage. She needed time, enough for Father's anger to cool. There was the party for that insipid Olivia Ragsdale, the one whose face had always reminded her of a foot; she hadn't planned to accept the invitation. If she could only disappear until the spring vacation was over and then slip into her room at school, Father would never think of raising a ruckus there. Probably he'd be so relieved by the time she'd telephoned him from school that he'd forget all about Hubris III and his cuts and bruises anyway. She tossed a stone into the creek.

Or better yet, what if she let it be thought she'd gone to Olivia Ragsdale's home in Chestnut Hill but went to see Max Toberman instead? After all, what with everything she knew about him and his strange friends, the least he could do was to hide her out for a few days. He'd been helpful before.

A tiny water dragon, disturbed by the splashing of the rock, fluttered busily along the bank of the creek. She leaned forward to wash her hands, drying them on her dark-brown riding pants. Plucking a handful of huckleberries from a low-hanging bush, she lay back in the sunshine and nibbled confidently.

Patricia Madigan reminded Captain Tolan of a glass of milk with blemishes. Her dull eyes and sullen mouth rarely changed expression. From the outset, her mother, a lantern-jawed frump with a whiskey nose, did most of the talking. She had accompanied her

daughter because, as Lou James put it so aptly, the police are only
human, and what man could resist the temptation to ravage the sensuous young thing?

Hudson had commented off the record that Miss Madigan would
probably be safe aboard a Turkish pirate ship.

After the initial questions had been asked, Miss Madigan's attorney, a prissy fellow obviously in the employ of Stanley Butterfield,
arrived in a great huff and demanded to know why his client had
been brought here in the first place. In the second place, he was appalled by Captain Tolan's disregard for her right to have counsel
present at all times. Moreover, presenting his credentials, he intended to see to it that the police would not be permitted to exploit
his client's confused state of mind.

"She agreed to come down here, Mr. . . . Cooper, is it? No one
forced her," said Sergeant James, turning to Miss Madigan. "Did
we, miss?"

Miss Madigan's mouth opened as if to speak but instead it merely
remained agape. She looked at her mother.

"Captain Tolan," said Cooper, posing as if he were Socrates confronting the village bully, "my client will answer only those questions which counsel deems fitting."

Sergeant James rolled his eyes. "Very shrewd, Counselor."

"You know very well what I mean, Sergeant . . . James, is it?
Only those questions which I consider proper for Miss Madigan to
answer prior to the trial and nothing more!" Cooper shouted indignantly.

Lou James shrugged and walked away. He made a surreptitious
obscene gesture toward Hudson as he poured himself a cup of
coffee.

"Mr. Cooper, we've brought your client down here as a possible
witness for the *prosecution*," said Tolan calmly but with a hint of
amusement. "You appear to have the roles a trifle confused. Am I to
presume you've been engaged by the defense?"

"Miss Madigan is *my client*, Captain Tolan." Cooper closed his
eyes as Hudson shook his head in disgust.

"Miss Madigan," recited Cooper, his fists clenched, "has a complaint of her own against the defendant."

"The suspect, Mr. Cooper," Tolan amended. "Or doesn't counsel
know the difference?"

"The arraignment is taking place at this very moment, and you know that," Cooper shot back. "Don't play semantics with me."

"Objection sustained . . . asshole," said Lou James from the far corner of the room.

Cooper turned white. "I must protest this, Captain Tolan! My client and her mother are not accustomed to such vile allusions, nor is it considered appropriate to sanction such commentaries during a formal interrogation session involving parties of both genders!"

"Yiz ain't very funny," carped Miss Madigan's mother. "This here's a bona fide member of the jurisprudent that yiz'r abusin', an' he don't have to take nothin' off yiz."

"Good Lord," Cooper muttered.

"Well now, Counselor," Tolan proceeded, "you were saying something about a complaint against Mr. Koch. I presume that's the central issue here, or do you think we've contacted Miss Madigan simply because we wished to meet *you?*"

Cooper gathered himself. "I am here, Captain Tolan, simply because I do not wish to have the cases overlap. My client intends to press charges against Mr. Koch apart from the state's case against him. Assault and battery with intent to ravage. Whatever you ask her is, naturally, of material interest to me."

There was a brief exchange of glances between Tolan and his men. "Do you have anything else to add, Mr. Cooper?"

"Yes. I wish that you would . . . I'd like you to. . . . "

"Counselor?" asked Tolan impatiently.

"Would you please"—Cooper blanched—"ask Sergeant James to apologize?"

Tolan stared back for a moment and, when he was satisfied that Cooper was suitably uncomfortable, said, "Now, if you have no further objections, I'd like to speak with your client. You may hold her hand if you wish."

"No need to be flippant, Captain."

A secretary was summoned to record the conversation.

"Miss Madigan," Tolan began, stifling his cigar in an overcrowded ashtray, "you are willing to attest to the fact that no force was involved in soliciting your cooperation here, are you not?"

Miss Madigan nodded uncertainly. Her mother looked at Cooper. "She's willin' to do her part," said her mother sternly.

"About the question of force, Miss Madigan?" Tolan looked at Cooper, who was jotting notes on a pad.

"No force, sir."

"Are you fully cognizant of why we wish to question you?"

Miss Madigan looked confused again.

Cooper jumped in. "We are not exactly clear on that score, Captain Tolan. Would you care to enlighten us?"

"Certainly, Mr. Cooper. It's a simple matter of wishing to protect the state's interests in this case. You see, the defense counsel, Mr. Geoffrey Van Zandt, has a reputation for turning witnesses into dog meat, and we'd like to get an impression beforehand just what his chances are of doing that."

"Van Zandt." Cooper winced. Evidently no one, not even Stanley Butterfield, had told him that. Tolan wondered how he could have missed it. The look Cooper gave the Madigans was poisonous.

"Yes, Van Zandt, Mr. Cooper. I believe you people call him the Shark. We don't want him turning our case into a slapstick farce."

"Is that the only reason, Captain?" hissed Cooper.

"Is there a better reason, Mr. Cooper?" growled Hudson.

"Yes," answered Cooper, leaping out of his chair, "your attitude toward the Whittingham case has been ambivalent from the onset. One might justifiably inquire into your own sentiments when interpreting whatever answers my client may proffer. We are not easily deceived."

"Right, Counselor," said Miss Madigan's mother, "we sure ain't."

Cooper sat down and played with his earlobe. Tolan repeated his original question, and Miss Madigan stated that she understood.

"Hasn't anyone ever told you, Miss Madigan," Tolan followed, "that it's not exactly responsible to bring charges against someone by reporting him to a newspaper? That is, there are other, more customary, measures."

She glanced with obvious pain toward Richard Cooper, who reacted hesitantly. "It isn't a matter of bringing charges, actually. She, my client, has merely cooperated with an investigative reporter."

"Why didn't you come to us, the police, when it happened to you, Miss Madigan? That is the usual procedure."

Miss Madigan looked away. "I . . . was scared."

"Of what, Miss Madigan?"

"Of what he might do to her next time," interrupted her mother. "The bastard's evil!"

"Mr. Cooper, will you please take us home?" Patricia Madigan was close to tears.

Tolan picked up a copy of that morning's newspaper, opened it to the article, and cited a reference to Manfred Koch's having torn away the front of her dress. "That must have been a terribly frightening experience for you, Miss Madigan."

"Yes, it was."

"I suppose you still have the dress, just in case it's needed as evidence?"

She looked at her mother, who nodded assent. Cooper was now tapping his pen unrhythmically against his note pad.

"Yeah," she answered barely audibly. "I got it at home."

"It was her best one, too," added her mother. "The one she got fer her last birthday."

Tolan glanced at Hudson, who winked. "Your best dress, Miss Madigan"—he smiled—"and you were wearing it to work?"

"That's possible, Captain," Cooper snapped. He then turned to Mrs. Madigan to ask her please to refrain from answering for his client. She refused to look at him.

"I didn't do nothin' to get it dirty. He tore it off me." Miss Madigan gulped.

"Well," said Tolan, "as your attorney says, that's possible. Now, did he do this before witnesses?"

Patricia Madigan's eyes streamed with tears and her lower lip was quivering. "Mr. Cooper," she repeated, "I, I'd like to go home."

Cooper started to get up, but Tolan waved him back into his chair. He scented an answer to the Stanley Butterfield problem in the stuffy air and cigar smoke of the office.

"You shoulda seen what he done to her," shouted Miss Madigan's mother. "Busted her nose an' kicked her in her privates. An' her goin' into the convent to become a holy sister! A ghoul he is!"

"Did he break your nose, Miss Madigan?" Tolan pressed.

Cooper crossed his legs huffily. "She said so, didn't she?"

"Did he *break* your nose?"

"No," she murmured, "it was just . . . busted."

Hudson accepted a cup of coffee from Lou James and grinned at Cooper. "I'll bet you're glad you don't have to prove *that* one, Counselor."

Cooper jumped up. "Why are you humiliating my client in this manner? Captain Tolan, instead of cooperating with the commonwealth, as you're expected to, you and your men act as if you're trying her."

"Counselor, these are all questions that *you* should have asked your client before accepting the case. You should be grateful. If my men and I didn't care at all, we'd just let you go into court and then enjoy the sight of Mr. Van Zandt making a monkey of you. Don't you understand that your meddling could destroy the prosecution's entire case?"

"Cup of coffee, Counselor?" Lou James asked consolingly. Cooper turned his back and paced a few steps.

Tolan asked the secretary if she'd got everything so far. She replied that she had. Broken pieces of dialogue could be heard amid the tapping of typewriters in the outer office. Cooper unbuttoned his wilting collar as Tolan thumbed through a large photo album.

"Miss Madigan," Tolan said finally, "I wonder if you'd identify his photograph for us."

"Who?"

"Your assailant, Mr. Koch. As I recall the newspaper article, you offered something of a description to the press."

"Yeah . . . I said he had weird eyes," she mumbled.

"Then it should be no problem at all. They say the eyes are our most memorable feature."

Patricia Madigan struggled visibly to recall the description of Manfred Koch given her by her mother. Eventually she looked directly at her mother.

"She'll pick him out. She'll pick him out. Who the hell do yiz t'ink yer dealin' wit'? We're no liars!" She sat up straight.

Cooper grimaced. Patricia Madigan looked at him in her usual vacant manner, but he refused to return her gaze.

Tolan placed a set of photographs before her. Since Manfred Koch's photo was not included, he sat back in his chair and folded his arms, awaiting the inevitable. She squinted at the pictures, looking at several of them for what must have seemed to her attorney an interminable period.

"This is an outrage," grumbled Cooper.

At length Miss Madigan, satisfied that she had at least convinced the police that she was serious, picked up one of the photographs and held it out as if it were on fire.

"That's him. That's the one."

"But"—laughed Tolan—"I thought you said he had weird eyes."

"Nate McBride wouldn't like that very much," mused Hudson. "It's his college graduation picture."

Tolan propped himself against the desk and looked into Patricia Madigan's eyes. "Do you know what God meant, Miss Madigan, when He said, 'Thou shalt not bear false witness against thy neighbor'?" He was starting to feel very sorry for her. "It's a terrible thing to do."

"That's him!" screamed her mother. "She said that's him! What the hell more do yiz want?"

Cooper shielded his eyes. Why had Butterfield got him into this?

Patricia Madigan seemed frozen for a moment. Starting to weep, she pointed a finger at her mother. "If you have any more questions, you can ask her! She's the one who knows it all. I don't even know what I'm doin' here."

In the girl's sobs Tolan read a vivid tale of pipe dreams, ignorance, and a mother's tyranny.

"Well, say somethin', Counselor," she commanded Cooper. "Don't just sit there wit' yer glasses foggin' an' let him do this to me daughter!"

Cooper rose feebly to the occasion. "Don't badger my client, Captain Tolan. We'll sue."

Nathan McBride came in. He had been looking into some of the families of the children involved with Angela Whittingham. Not noticing the women and having nothing really to report, he made a perfunctory comment about the heat. He observed Patricia Madigan, whose puzzled eyes were fixed upon him, and he drifted off to his desk, shaking his head, followed by Hudson and James' raucous laughter.

"How much did he pay you, Miss Madigan?" Tolan asked softly.

"He didn't pay me nothin'," she sobbed. "He paid Ma fifty bucks."

"Lovely," quipped Hudson.

Cooper preferred to stare through the window at the steaming sidewalk. Although the sun was hidden from view by the heavy overcast, its oppressive presence could be felt everywhere. Cooper removed his glasses and, with shaky hands, cleaned them with a very wrinkled handkerchief.

Miss Madigan's mother's face was starting to resemble the absent sun. "Where the hell did yiz get yer diploma, Cooper, Alaska?"

Tolan handed Patricia Madigan a handkerchief to dry her tears. "I'd be kinder to Mr. Cooper if I were you, Mrs. Madigan. You're going to have need of a lawyer very soon." He was enjoying this.

"Not that shite-house. A soul could wind up on Divil's Island wit' him representin' ya." When she sulked, the resemblance to her daughter was more evident.

Cooper searched for something to say. "Clearly, Captain, my client is not herself. She's under duress and has been in a singularly difficult state ever since the incident."

"What incident, Mr. Cooper? I think it would be an understatement to say we don't consider your client a very good witness for the prosecution." He lit up his cigar again and puffed smoke toward the ceiling. "On the other hand, I'd say she'll make a spectacular witness against your employer. Who was it, Stanley Butterfield or his newspaper?"

"It must have been Stanley himself, Captain," suggested Hudson. "The publisher would be too smart to hire a ham-and-egger like this."

Miss Madigan was petrified and looked as if she would be sick at any moment. Her mother, however, made one more noisy effort.

"A fine one you are, Captain Tolan, protectin' that dirty Prussian after he beat up on me little girl. Bejaysus—you'd t'ink we was the criminals here, an' all we done was try to help yiz out!"

Cooper threw up his hands in total defeat.

"It serves you right, Counselor"—Tolan was pointing his cigar at the nervous Cooper—"for dealing with the likes of Stanley Butterfield."

"That was his name. . . ." Patricia Madigan's voice was only slightly above a whisper. Tolan asked her to repeat herself.

"That was his name. Butterfield. A little fat fella. He runs around with Ma now an' then, only Daddy don't know nothin' about it or he'd kick the shite outa him. I think I'm gonna tell. . . ."

Lou James, who had drifted away some time ago after Tolan had taken over, said, "Tell your dad I'll point Butterfield out to him."

McBride, who had chosen to listen in instead of writing his report, could not contain his laughter. Tolan did his best to be very controlled; this was, after all, his precinct.

"That will be all for now, ladies. We'll be getting back to you."

All three started to leave, but Tolan stopped the lawyer in the doorway. "As for you, Mr. Cooper, I rather doubt that we'll be seeing much of each other. At the rate you're going, the Pennsylvania bar will probably see to that sooner or later."

Ah, darlin', he thought as he studied Maggie's picture, *you may be seeing a lot more of me soon.* It hadn't taken long to settle that one.

Five

Ian Blakeley got up early, made himself a pot of strong tea, and luxuriated in a steaming hot bath for more than a half hour. Peacefully humming to himself a number of familiar Gilbert and Sullivan tunes, he leafed through Isaac Ray's *Contributions to Mental Pathology* and savored the gentle scent of wild strawberries from the hillside.

He had drawn the bath himself because the servants balked so of late about their working hours that he knew the tea would be too weak and the bath water too chilly. More than most other comforts, Dr. Blakeley enjoyed his sunrise solitude.

He trimmed his salt-and-pepper beard to an even quarter of an inch all around and combed his full mustache so that it overlapped the beard just below the corners of his mouth. Another cup of tea, and he slipped into a tan linen suit with brown vest and dark amber silk tie.

Carrying his tea with him, he went down the broad, winding stairway, crossed the marble foyer, and surveyed the waning shadows from the porch. Since coming to Philadelphia where, as his old friends had warned him, the summer heat could resemble the sub-Sahara, he had eschewed his customary practice of rising at ten. Now he looked forward to the work he could accomplish in the soft, quiet morning hours, before the heat and his family—the latter in their delightfully nonchalant way—could conspire against him.

The orioles and wild canaries chattered on while a delicate breeze from the Schuylkill blew through the cherry trees and across the sloping dew-saturated lawn. Blakeley watched a young cardinal alternately preen and chirp at a distant comrade. The willow trees seemed to be kneeling in graceful supplication over the water.

Blakeley loved this home, with its lofty gables, turrets, and chimneys, its white and umber façade, at once so rustic and refined, and its acres of pasture rolling down to the river. At times he could envision shepherds and flocks, but that tended to make him homesick; the April rains brought the clematis and convolvulus to bloom early, conjuring poignant memories of the Kentish countryside. In the early mornings and late evenings the air was heavy with woodbine and sweet william.

When, after long, agonizing months of deliberation and compromise, the Blakeleys had finally reached the decision to move to America, he was pleased that Sophia had agreed upon Philadelphia. When Scotland Yard had sent him here years ago, his extensive travels had convinced him that this was the only happy medium. It did not deserve all its excoriating comments, whatever its obvious faults.

On his third trip he had brought Sophia with him. New York was too brash and tinsely. They were in immediate accord on that. She had rather enjoyed San Francisco, but however hard it tried, it was still much too far from civilization. Sophia had remarked that they might as well move on to Australia as remain there. Denver, still very young, simply tried too hard, and the mountains, though magnificent, made her nose bleed. There had been some pleasant moments in Chicago and Pittsburgh, tempting them to stay in the honest, hardworking center of the country. Ian could never quite articulate his negative feelings, but nevertheless felt them strongly. Too much like Newcastle and Manchester perhaps—no need to explain. Boston, now that had been a poser. They'd liked it very much, both of them, for its obvious advantages. But they'd finally agreed that it was England all over again, and that was, after all, hardly what this emigration was intended to simulate.

Philadelphia, forever troubled old lady, with its lush gardens and damp air, its bustling foundries and cobbled streets, its old edifices so jealously maintained, and its hugger-mugger population, just seemed to survive with unpompous dignity. It was London, in a way, and they'd both felt it, felt it different enough, too, from London.

They had built this house as if it were on the Afton. Polished oak railings adorned the stairways and vestibule. Pillars of the same timber supported the diagonal beams which flew overhead, evoking reminders of a medieval cathedral. Cedar ran along the walls, below Grecian designs by William Morris that looked like large cameos when seen from afar. Silver-plated ornaments appeared to grow out of the ebony furniture, toward the medieval tapestries and tall paintings, some of them by Sophia's own inspired hand. Bathed in light in the late evening, it must have seemed, through its stained glass windows, like an Elsinore without sin. Blakeley was satisfied that they had taken with them all the best of what they had known in Victoria's England.

He adjusted his monocle and went to his desk in the study to work on his favorite project, a book he had been researching for the past year. Sophia claimed that the mere presence of the manuscript in the house could cause nightmares. Blakeley was oddly pleased by the significance of her words; he'd had no idea that his work was so powerfully stated. To Sophia Blakeley, as far as the uninitiated listener was concerned, there had never been a Sodom and Gomorrah. The loathsome, the impure, the deviant—these were all phenomena born of vicious imaginations, matters unworthy of record or discussion. There had never walked this earth the likes of Herod or Nero or Lucrezia Borgia. Privately, however, Ian knew she often sacrificed decorum in the interests of curiosity. When he had offered to lock his notes in the safe, just to assure her peace of mind, Sophia had protested vigorously. Since then, although he'd never brought it to her attention, her vocabulary had become gradually and undeniably laced with the language of forensic medicine.

Still, it had become his practice to work at this project in the early hours and to put it by when she awoke. He finished his pot of tea and worked through the morning on the chapter dealing with Gilles de Rais, the fifteenth-century homosexual who had tortured to death more than two hundred young boys with the sanction and to the evident applause of his leisured friends. Curiously, Seigneur de Rais had been a comrade of Joan of Arc. An amiable and witty gentleman, he had been respected by most of his peers and welcome in the highest circles as a competent soldier and administrator. The court had agreed to his guilt begrudgingly and executed him apologetically, despite a wealth of horrible evidence.

To Ian Blakeley the arcane peregrinations of the homicidal mind were the most fascinating studies on earth. For years with Scotland Yard he had been involved in cool, isolated probings into causes of death. He had conducted countless mathematical analyses of the depths and angles of wounds, the severity of powder burns, the relative effectiveness of hundreds of poisons, even the time and energy it would require to strangle a certain victim. Dubious honor that Sophia suggested it was, Blakeley had become perhaps London's leading authority on murder.

But Scotland Yard had wanted to leave it at that: the how, when, and where of the matter. When the question of why had arisen, the

Yard had invariably deferred to the judgment of one Dr. Chidsey, whom Blakeley had come to regard as an egomaniacal simpleton. It was the Jack the Ripper debacle which had convinced Blakeley that his truest attachment was to forensic psychology. The Yard had never spent sufficient time on constructing personality profiles, he thought, and he'd told them so. Dr. Chidsey, however, had wisely reaffirmed their overworked methods, and Ian had realized that it was only a matter of time before he'd have to persuade Sophia to re-settle the family. His fervent wish was to design a valid method of pinpointing those mental quirks that one tosses off as afterthoughts but that might indicate probable homicidal tendencies. Then, per-haps, one need not be mired in the shortsighted implications of the how, when, and where. It was all still elusive, he admitted, but he needed time and freedom to pursue it.

The most interesting why of all was that of the multicides, the thoroughly ruthless, thoroughly amoral ones, whose victims usually numbered in scores—men like Gilles de Rais and Jack the Ripper. He was convinced they were not just sex criminals; that was a con-venient label. The motives of the multicide ran beyond sex, money, or jealousy—beyond all empirical data. They were hidden under layer after tortured layer of personal, perhaps even ancestral, an-guish. The subject challenged Blakeley as none other ever had.

When one disregarded all the newspaper gibberish, the Whitting-ham case was rather fascinating in its own right. He had not men-tioned to Tolan the fact that he'd been following it closely, even considering the possibility of involving himself; Tolan, under his own inexorable pressures, had not been of a mind to listen. With its odd pattern of brutality and surgical skill, it reminded Blakeley of the Count Orsino affair in the Calabrian mountains a half century ago.

With the exception of Miss Whittingham herself, the victims had all been prostitutes. Now, that could mean simply that these ladies were the most readily accessible to the perpetrator. They were, after all, in a business where availability meant prosperity, and their ir-regular life habits made their sudden disappearances less conspicu-ous. Thus, the automatic impulse was to look for a religious fanatic; it had always seemed to Blakeley, to some few of his colleagues, too, that whores and zealots were birds of a feather, each inspiring in the other a terrible indignation spawned by real or imagined guilt.

Miss Whittingham, however, blurred that theory. It was shameful, perhaps, to speculate about the possible turns of mind a spotless girl like Angela Whittingham might have had had she enjoyed a to-morrow, but there were examples in the Spanish convent tradition of many who had left their pristine backgrounds to wallow in sin. Had Miss Whittingham ever met the questionable ladies, if only in the course of her religious duties? Was there another side to her life that the authorities had missed?

Of course, the idea of a sadistic fiend with no interests other than the sexually perverse could not be ruled out entirely. Blakeley de-spised such creatures. Their purposes went nowhere beyond the bounds of a dog in heat. It was this randomly brutal sort whose acts blunted the edge of all his theories. How little we'd climbed on the evolutionary ladder!

There remained the matter of surgical skill to temper the image of mere savagery. Our man took his time, perhaps even mapped out his methods of inflicting pain. That is, if we were actually concerned with a man. There is the theory, well recognized by now, that wom-en are even crueler than men when it comes to dealing with other women. Unhappy competitors, sexual deviants, frustrated mother superiors, the plain and inadequate—there were many varieties of women capable of enjoying the death pangs of prostitutes or of poor Angela Whittingham.

Blakeley was not indifferent to the possibility of a cult. Anxious times produce such phenomena, and more often than not they grow like microbes in university districts where the disciples await a saviour, reading Rabelais and Proudhon while sipping cheap wine in bohemian haunts. There seemed to be a ritual involved; the missing organs suggested that. They might have been removed after the death. A number of works had been published of late on the Aztec and Mayan cultures, and the subject of human sacrifices had no doubt been tossed about. It was, as he recognized, grasping at a straw to pursue that theory.

At eight thirty, as he composed the final sentences in the De Rais chapter, there began the usual rumbling and shaking from Ralphie's room. Ralphie's morning exercises involved the use of weight-lifting contrivances strongly resembling in size and weight the axle and wheels of a locomotive. Tapping his fingers on the desk, Blakeley counted to ten and once again reminded himself that Ralphie, the herculean Ralphie, was sprung from his own being. Very small at birth, given to mysterious fevers, Ralphie had caused his parents to fear for his survival. Accordingly, at age three Ian had devised a special diet and exercises for him. Ralphie, like a plant under the influence of an exotic new fertilizer, had sprouted into a sinewy mountain. Blakeley wondered if the beams would hold should Ralphie ever lose his grip on the hundreds of pounds of steel he held overhead.

At nine another commotion, this from the direction of the kitchen, threatened to awaken Sophia. When he heard the clatter of pots and pans on the kitchen floor, he knew Sophia was awake.

He closed his books and placed his notes in the top drawer. Confrontations of this sort between Victor, the butler, and Snopkowski, the cook, were not uncommon. He usually chose to ignore them until they'd burned themselves out. Domestic laissez-faire, he liked to call it. But the truth was he would do anything to keep Snopkowski, whose cooking was unequaled, and the stuffy Victor was like a page out of an eighteenth-century conduct book.

"Ian, you must do something." Sophia flew into the study, her lavender robe trailing regally behind her. Blakeley got up and kissed her on the cheek.

"She—she's just impossible, Ian." Angrily she seated herself in the chair next to his desk. "She wants to serve the coquilles Saint-Jacques this evening with something called progies."

He thought for a moment. "Pirogis?"

"Whatever." Sophia tossed the term aside. "And when Victor objected, she flew into a rage. Just listen to her. She sounds like Ivan the Terrible."

"And what has Victor to do with the menu, my dear?" There was the matter of proper channels to be considered, he reminded her gently.

"Nothing really, except he felt it quite inappropriate and merely proposed alternatives." Sophia crossed her arms and legs simultaneously, an unmistakable signal that she was truly agitated. "You must speak with her, Ian."

"They're quite good, you know. We've had them before, my love."

He chafed a bit; Snopkowski, like Ralphie, was the product of his overindulgence. Awed by her skills and given to savoring them as delicious relics of a bygone era of unimpeded excellence, often he'd felt more like her patron than employer. In another time and place she would most likely have been the king's personal chef and would have received similar preferential treatment. He couldn't blame Snopkowski for sensing all that.

"What *are* they?"

"Little fried things with a cheese and potato filling."

Sophia looked up suddenly. "That must have been what I saw then."

"Yes," he continued with a smile, "crunchy little dumplings, so to speak, with a smashing good potato and cheese filling."

"Hmm . . . then that's what it must have been," she said. "All over poor Victor," she went on sharply. "She threw it at him!"

"Oh?" He slapped at a mosquito which had somehow found its way from the river, into his study, and onto his arm. Damned early in the day for them, he thought.

"Yes, and you'd better see to it posthaste or Victor will surely pout all day and night, and we shall need him this evening. We have guests for dinner."

He chuckled at the thought of the imperious Victor soiled with peasant fare. The second half of her statement then sank in, and he asked in a low voice, "Guests?"

"Yes"—she winced—"the Peacocks, Murvin and Petula."

"Good Lord, the cosmetics salesman?" He frowned and drifted toward the large Tudor window.

"He has influence, Ian."

"What kind of influence?" he asked impatiently.

"Well"—she sighed—"he may be able to get Ralphie into a school next September."

"Oh, really?" he grunted. This subject, above all, provoked him. At that moment the upstairs shook as Ralphie lowered his barbells to the floor. "Where?"

"Somewhere out west. North Dakota, I believe."

"That won't work." Ian shook his head. "Ralphie will get lost trying to find it."

She smiled demurely, but with obvious amusement. "Be serious, Ian."

"Yes, well"—he became serious again—"must I listen to one of Peacock's confounded travelogues?"

Sophia hesitated, then continued resignedly. "Entirely possible, my love. They've just come back from the Low Countries."

He had been to the Low Countries, too. . . . "Well, I suppose I must speak to the cook. Meanwhile, you should see to it that Rosalie comes down to breakfast at ten sharp, before she starts nibbling on those damned chocolates."

He went to the kitchen, where he found Snopkowski thoroughly absorbed in cutting meat. Blakeley guessed that with each angry thud of the cleaver was severed one more of Victor's joints. He cleared his throat and advanced cautiously.

"You really mustn't use such language before Madame, Snopkowski," he began. "Madame has a profound reaction to such terminology, even if she doesn't know what it means."

Snopkowski went on chopping, oblivious to his presence. She had an uncanny way of making one feel totally inane and useless.

"You really must learn to control your temper," he kept on. "We've had to discuss this matter before, you will recall." She glanced up nonchalantly, a wisp of gray hair dangling over her left eye.

"But pirogis and coquilles Saint-Jacques would be much too heavy. One should be concerned about such things in this warm weather."

"You too goddamn skinny anyhow," she scoffed. In such moods, Snopkowski always lost herself by cutting meat.

"I say," he answered disconcertedly.

"So is Madame," she grunted, "too goddamn skinny."

He felt about his waistline. "I say, thank you." He blushed. "As for Madame, she enjoys being, well, thin."

There was no response from Snopkowski. Blakeley decided to go on in any case; the die had been cast. He readjusted his monocle and drew in a deep breath.

"I mean, can't you think of something besides pirogis?"

She placed her hands on her hips, and the meat cleaver hung suspended like a dormant predator. "Like what?"

"Well"—he proceeded warily—"Madame was thinking of something like scampi."

"Dot's cat food!"

"Cat food?" He'd never thought of it that way. "Nevertheless, it goes with coquilles Saint-Jacques much more suitably. Madame and I concur on that."

She resumed her chopping. "It's no Friday," she mumbled. "Why you want fish?"

"*Sea* food, Mrs. Snopkowski," he insisted, his tone now betraying exasperation. "Madame and I agree with Victor that—"

"Veektorr!" She brought the cleaver down with such force that it sank deeply into the cutting board. A slice of meat slithered across the floor, coming to rest against a garbage can. Snopkowski's face was livid.

"Bottler—ptui! He should empty spittoon an' wash dish! You keep him outa keetchum! You tal him Snopkowski say she trow cheeckum guts next time! You tal him. Goddamn chewtabacca goddamn!"

By the time she'd finished her opening remarks she was rattling pots and pans and shaking her fist. Blakeley realized why he preferred writing about the theory of violence to encountering it. Domestic affairs, he also remembered, had always tended to leave him unhinged.

She waved her finger in his face, delivering her ultimatum as if she possessed the secret of Armageddon. "You keep dot yonko out keetchum an' maybe I no make pirogi. You lat him in, dan maybe I tree, maybe *four* time a day makink dem, by Jesu!"

He sensed his collar chafing and his shirt going limp. Snopkowski had gained the upper hand, no doubt of that, but he knew he could not leave the kitchen without having imposed at least a semblance of control. Well, he calculated, compromise must begin somewhere.

"Actually," he replied calmly, "I like pirogis personally."

"So do I," she said, still unpacified. She was struggling to remove the cleaver from the chopping block. "Dot's how come I make dem."

"But," he ventured, "wouldn't it be better to serve them with some of your exquisite boeuf bourguignon? I've just been picturing them on the side, garnished perhaps with sprigs of parsley and accompanied by chilled Beaujolais. We might even call them by another name. How does pirogis Snopkousse sound to you? The Peacocks would never know. They might take them for a variety of crepes Suzettes."

"You call dem pirogis. Nottink else. Who ever hord of dot stuff you say?" Her tone was still belligerent, but she'd eased her grip on the cleaver. He was encouraged.

"As you wish, Mrs. Snopkowski."

"No parsley." She glowered. "Dot would make dem look like rocks an' weeds. I put in bowl jost like last time."

"Very well," he granted, wondering when he would start to win some concessions of his own.

"Ralphie like dem," she pointed out.

"Oh, most assuredly."

"Good boy dot," she muttered. "I fix him dozen jost for him."

She cooked in massive quantities, and Ralph went into ecstasy. "Don't lat Snopkowski hear nobody say nottink about Ralphie goddamn!" She flashed a menacing glance at no one in particular.

She was cooling off. "You agree then on boeuf bourguignon?" he pressed.

She nodded. "Bot no Beaujolais. You give dot stuff to gasts. You drink some o' Snopkowski homemade."

His eyes lit up. Now *that* was a genuine concession. Snopkowski regarded the best vintage wines of France as feeble imitations of her own and protected her private stock as if it were the Ark of the Covenant.

"That, that does sound delightful," he said, his voice clearly showing his astonishment. "Outstanding, in fact."

"You betchum good," she answered triumphantly. "Bot . . . you keep dot yonko Veektorr outa poor Snopkowski keetchum or I cookink him insteada pirogi."

She bent over the waste can to retrieve the cut of meat. A shocking thought occurred to him as he noticed the devilish look on her face.

"Now don't give that cut of meat to Victor," he said. "Give it to the dog."

Snopkowski grumbled something in Polish. Blakeley left the kitchen, feeling something like a successful arbitrator. Victor could be placated later.

Victor Primrose, born Stashu Popnofnik, had had dreams of becoming a matinee idol, but for years he had played butlers in a long line of drawing-room comedies while James O'Neill took all the plums. Finally, when O'Neill had monopolized the Edmond Dantes role in *The Count of Monte Cristo* and a director refused to cast Victor as a butterfly in an operetta, Victor had given it up and retired into what he knew best. In reality, Victor was a terrible butler, but Sophia was convinced that he added something to the decor.

By ten o'clock Sophia was dressed in a crisp high-necked blouse and pale-blue skirt, impatiently awaiting the rest of the family at the breakfast table. In the spring and summer the Blakeleys breakfasted on the patio, surrounded by the Scotch heather that Sophia had planted shortly after they'd moved into the house. Ian, as usual, had decided not to wait for the others. Having had nothing since his pot of tea at dawn, his appetite was prodigious. Snopkowski, in a further gesture of appeasement, had prepared some excellent eggs benedict and baked fish.

Ralphie's heavy footsteps came down the stairs, through the ground floor, across the patio, and to a sudden stop at the table. In his shirt sleeves, he looked rather like a laborer. Sophia remarked that at least he could have taken the time to comb his hair.

"Jeez crumps, Ma," Ralphie retorted woundedly, "I thought I did."

Feeling chipper after his little victory in the kitchen, Blakeley had to remind himself that Sophia had got off to a bad start. The servants one found in this country were much different from those she had known in England.

"Listen, Mr. Blakeley," she chided Ralphie, "this household is not prepared to accept your customary pleas of ignorance today. Because of you, we have to put up with the wearisome Peacocks this evening."

Ralphie looked with confusion at his father.

"What your mother means, Ralphie," said Ian as he moved his chair slightly to make room for Ralphie's Brobdingnagian presence, "is that Mr. Peacock has intimated that he can get you enrolled in another university. So we want you to be all sharpened up by suppertime. It's quite important to your mother and me."

Ralphie nodded as if he understood while the stone-faced Victor served him his usual dozen eggs and pound of bacon. Victor made it perfectly clear that he was not speaking to Blakeley, to Blakeley's immense gratitude.

"What's for supper tonight?" asked Ralphie as he scooped up a mouthful of scrambled eggs.

"Ralphie, you must promise you'll take this one seriously," she said. "We're running out of schools. This will be four of them in less than two years."

Ian sighed and picked at his dish of prunes. First, it had been Princeton. Ralphie left there one hour after the end of the final game of the football season. The following term he had entered the state university, where there was no football. But when spring came, Ralphie had counted the number of available young ladies in the town and, finding them sorely scarce, had come home. This last year had been an improvement, they thought. They had sent him off to a little state normal college tucked away in the Pocono Mountains, and he had even succeeded in completing the fall term. One week ago, however, he had appeared just in time for lunch. After finishing his sixth plate of stew he confessed that there was no use in trying to finish another semester. His grades were so low that the final examinations would have been mere formalities. Sophia had refused to consider it, but Ian was slowly becoming convinced that it was hopeless to try to mix Ralphie and higher education.

"Have you seen your sister?" he asked.

Ralphie's mouth was too full of toast and jam to answer. He gulped and mumbled something that sounded like "messed up in Boston."

"Try once again, Ralphie," said Sophia.

"She's gettin' dressed up in her suffragette costume."

Ian sighed again and looked over at Sophia, who smiled sheepishly.

"What's the name of the school, Dad?" Ralphie was now prepared to show some interest.

His father confessed that he did not know.

"It's . . . something like the North Dakota College of Agriculture and Mining."

Ralphie dropped his fork. "North Dakota?"

Sophia hastened to explain, lest Ralphie misconstrue this as attempted banishment. "Yes, Ralph, you see, Mr. Peacock's sister, Clotilde, is married to the cousin of the vice-president of—"

"Wow!" He let out a whoop and waved an imaginary Stetson. "Out West—golly!"

"Ralphie, stop that," Sophia demanded. "The neighbors will think we're running a home for the terminally bewildered."

"You mean I can go out there an' punch cows?"

"We had hoped," answered his father, "that you'd go out there and study."

Ralphie leaped out of his chair, swinging an imaginary lariat. Sophia looked on appalled. Blakeley looked up and observed two young chambermaids giggling in a third-floor window. He demanded that Ralphie cease and desist his whooping and hollering. Ralphie had a faraway look and couldn't hear him.

Then, as suddenly as he had begun, Ralphie stopped and looked somewhat dumbfounded.

"Only I can't go," he said.

"What do you mean you can't go?" Sophia flushed and stood up. At the moment the thought of keeping Ralphie out in North Dakota never seemed more appealing.

"I, gee, Ma, I don't think you're gonna like it." He went over to his father and whispered something in his ear.

Sophia wondered if, God forbid, Ralphie had been seeing the wrong kind of woman up there in the mountains. Something about Ralphie's abrupt departures from three colleges had made such thoughts difficult to avoid.

Blakeley's monocle dropped into his dish of prunes. "You've what?"

Ralphie nodded that it was true no matter how they might feel about it.

"Sophia," said Ian, "Ralphie's joined the Army."

For an instant she looked as if she were about to swoon, but at length she arched her brows and spoke in a husky voice.

"It can't be true. This is preposterous."

"It's true, Ma," Ralphie repeated. His head hung slightly for a time; then he shrugged and returned to his scrambled eggs.

"Well"—Ian smiled, wiping prune juice from his monocle—"there shall be no need to entertain the Peacocks this evening at least. You may instruct Victor to call them with our regrets. It will do him some good. He does enjoy using that telephone."

"But what reason should we offer?"

"Why don't you tell them that we've discovered smallpox in the house and that we shall all be quarantined indefinitely? And," he said, turning to Ralphie, "you can eat pirogis to your heart's content this evening. You'll get none of them in the Army, I should imagine."

"Wow—pirogis!" Ralphie was about to let out another yell.

Sophia cut in quickly. "However, you must bathe before dinner, Ralph."

Ralphie went on with his breakfast, never looking up at either of them. Sophia sipped her tea resignedly. Blakeley grumbled that his baked fish was cold. Victor continued to pout at a respectful distance.

Rosie entered in her suffragette costume, the most prominent feature of which was the severe collar with black tie. She sat next to her mother, not wishing to fraternize with the Men.

Her father bade her a good morning. Rosie answered coolly.

*   *   *

The three o'clock sun was demonic. The horse drawing Jennifer Figge's carriage stepped lazily over the steaming cobblestones. The sweltering coachman hummed softly to himself, daydreaming of shady groves and waterfalls.

The leisurely ride from Devon had taken two hours, but except for the heat in the darkened cab, it had not been too irritating. They had crossed the city line between the hours of heaviest traffic, and the coachman had taken a meandering route to remain on the tree-shaded avenues. Jennifer had sharply reminded the coachman that she was due at the Ragsdales' by four.

She counted the blocks along Fifty-fourth Street and gathered her skirt, awaiting the most propitious moment for her departure. The little shops and neatly trimmed trees reminded her vaguely of Paris or Bayreuth.

Silently, slowly, she turned the bronze handle on the carriage door and, amid the monotonous din of the traffic, stole out of the coach and trotted around a corner. She was smiling to herself at the thought of the old coachman's chagrin when he had to explain his empty cab to the crowd at the Ragsdales'.

When the coach finished its turn and disappeared behind a corner hedgerow at Armitage Street, she brushed her clothing and strolled past a realtor's office, a barber shop, and a bakery, then climbed a flight of whitewashed steps. She went into the office of Max Toberman.

At the other end of the city at that moment a seedy man scratched under his soiled white shirt and fixed his gaze upon a building across the street. The voices that only he heard were urging him to go in, to go in and do it.

The evening papers again featured news of the conflict with Spain. The War Department, now anticipating the need for an invasion of Cuba, was calling for a large number of volunteers to supplement the Regular Army. The response on the nation's campuses, in the sweatshops, and on the farms was immediate and overwhelming. Although the government reports stated that the Spanish garrison on the island amounted to no more than eighty thousand men, the press insisted that the number was two hundred thousand, exhorting the flower of American manhood to aid in the destruction of tyranny and oppression in our hemisphere. A massive force was to be concentrated in Tampa under the command of General William R. Shafter.

Stanley Butterfield's article on the recent "unimpeachable" evidence against Manfred Koch and the emergence of "damning testimony" against him appeared in bold type farther down on the front page. The type having been set, the exigencies of the newspaper medium kept Stanley in print for one more issue, despite his feverish efforts to stop the presses at the last minute.

Tolan let out a roar of laughter. The proof of bribery would soon reduce poor Stanley to composing advertisements for bladder and kidney remedies. Thanks to Stanley's bungling, Tolan now had the newspaper, as Hudson had put it, by the scrotum. It was a very satisfying turn of the wheel.

Kathleen Whalen really liked those uniforms. The soldiers wore dark-blue tunics, light-blue trousers, and jaunty slouch hats of a khaki color to match their leggings. She had never imagined men so beautiful.

From the backyard she heard her mother, Ellie, gossiping with Mrs. Foy about Father McDonnough from Saint Francis Xavier's and that Eyetalian lady. Kathleen fanned herself and wondered just what kind of woman would ever consort with the likes of that fat, phony crayture. Ye'd have to be daft or desperate or both, she thought.

The soldiers fascinated her. Young men she used to see in their greasy work clothes, dragging their lunch pails to and from the pits, as they called the railroad yard, had now taken on totally different dimensions. It was said they were going off to some place called Porta Rica, where all they'd see would be "nigger" women and wild Indians. Somewhere down in South America or Mexico.

Tinker Whalen still hoped to make an advantageous marriage for Katie. He almost despaired that she would tempt the right boy into a serious commitment. Always trying to frustrate her—so far as he knew—unsuccessful attempts to get rid of her virginity was a constant drain on the strength he marshaled for the days he worked.

But unbeknownst to him, Katie was sneaking off at odd moments, after midnight or just before dawn, crossing the bridge over the creek, running through the churchyard, and meeting her soldiers in

the long grass that bordered the cemetery. She had to remind herself that they might never return from that godless and faraway
place before she ran breathlessly to meet the soldier boys.

First there was Leo Dougherty; he told his brother Kenny, even
though he'd sworn he never would. After Kenny Dougherty there
was Seamus O'Hanlon; he told—despite her complete faith in him
not to—Kevin McLaughlin, Peter Gannon, Jimmy O'Riley, Moose
McGee, and little Eddie Conroy.

Then, on Good Friday, she told Ellie that the curse had so destroyed her that she'd never make it through the Three Hours' Agony; she met that drippy Harry Nolan since he'd always said he loved
her. And what did he do but bring along his cousin Dickie! That episode, of them all, plagued her conscience during contemplative moments; sometimes at mass on Sundays she had imagined, to her horror, old Father O'Rourke interrupting his sermon to call for hot
coals where she'd sinned on Good Friday. But she steeled herself
with the resolution that if ever such an accusation should arise,
she'd simply fire back a comment about his pompous curate, Father
McDonnough, and that Eyetalian lady. And wouldn't *that* be a
puck in the puss?

In any event, Kathleen knew her time was running out. She knew
that no one would ever tell her brothers, especially big Michael, unless he wanted to wind up maimed and crippled. The day could not
be far off when Tinker would so aggravate one of the neighbors—
probably Bird Martin, whose personality closely resembled Tinker's
own—that the tale of her adventures would be told. And then she'd
find herself in a fine kettle of fish.

Lately, however, Kathleen had been seeing just one soldier. At
first he'd been simply one among the gathering legion. Then he'd
turned up more frequently, rewarding her favors with little gifts of
flowers and candy. Now she was seeing him exclusively.

He wasn't really much to look at, a bit of a runt if the truth be
told. But she thought he loved her. At times she even thought she
felt a little twinge of that for him, too. He was kind at least—and he
did tell her he thought she was beautiful. None of the others ever
said that; they either joked or said nothing.

Last night he'd brought her a bunch of peonies. She was sure he'd
plucked them out of old lady McNiff's garden on his way to their
meeting place, the clearing by the brook. She had curtsied as he
held them out to her and wondered if he saw the tears in her eyes.

Six

"I wish you wouldn't call me Toby in front of my patients and other casual observers, Jennifer," said Max Toberman as he tapped a perfumed cigarette against his desktop. "It's very poor form."

She opened the cigarette box and removed one of the thin black cylinders. "A bit stuffy, ahn't we?"

"Do you understand me, Jennifer?" he asked. *"Miss Figge."*

She looked up indifferently, struck a blue-tip match, and applied it to her cigarette. "Careful now, Max. Or I might just pass your name on to Daddy. And you know what that could mean."

She could see by the flush of his cheek that she had made her point.

"I do understand, Max, your need for surface respectability. Really I do. Incidentally I wish you'd dismiss your receptionist. Her breath is quite foul."

He lit his cigarette and answered in a monotone. "I shall order her to chew licorice and cardamom on the occasion of your next visit."

She exhaled a puff of pungent blue smoke. "That's so good of you."

It was so easy to hate Jennifer Figge, he thought. She worked too hard to affect consummate boredom. "And so"—he got up and stood looking into a tall medicine cabinet—"since you are obviously not suffering an ailment, what exactly has brought you here?"

She paused. "You might say I've come to have my psyche massaged."

"Oh?"

"Oh, yes. It's a very delicate matter requiring your special skills."

He laughed nervously. "You are doing a good job of obfuscation."

"You're not listening, Max. You're more concerned with how long it will take me to leave." She affected a sulky look. "You're very cold, Dr. Toberman."

He glanced at his pocket watch and nodded agreement. "Five minutes already. I still do not know why you are here."

She rose and stepped forward. "Tell me that you do not find me attractive, Max. Go ahead. Look me in the eyes and tell me that."

"Very well then, I—" She stopped his mouth and placed her arms around his neck. He studied her closely for a moment and then flicked his cigarette through the open window. Both hands were free now. She was uncommonly self-assured for her age.

"And charming? Tell me I'm charming and delightful."

"Jennifer." He took her hands gently and removed them from about his neck. "I have no times for games now. You are beautiful, of course, and, in your own Byzantine way, amusing. But we who must work for a living are the unfortunate slaves of clocks and calendars. Your time is up. You may pay the receptionist or ask her to bill you."

"But, Max. . . ."

He broke away and crossed to the door, wishing she had never slithered into his world. In the waiting room a child sobbed and a man was having a terrible coughing spell. Jennifer refused to move. Her cuteness was maddening.

"Look, Jennifer. Day and night are different settings for different scenes. You were simply *one* of my patients, just like those others out there. Did you even see the really sick people who must wait to see me? Now, why don't you return to Miss Fudderman's Latin School before they miss you?"

"I can't go back to school." She snuffed out her cigarette. "I can't go home either, Max. You've got to hide me for a few days."

"Hide you?"

She leaned against the arm of a swivel chair and swayed very slightly. "It was worth your while last time, wasn't it?"

"I had no idea that I was *hiding* you last time. As far as I knew, I was simply practicing medicine for a fee."

"A substantial fee," she added pointedly. "Only the best and most discreet for a Figge. Daddy taught me that, and I'd never disobey Daddy. All I want you to do now is hide me out for a few days. I'll pay you well for it. You know that." Her tone was showing more impatience. Max Toberman was a small man, delicate in fact, and she thought that she could bully him.

"I could lose my license, you know."

"To be sure. But you could lose it even faster if you don't take me seriously, Max." He was silent for a moment. She folded her arms, and her smile took on an almost Circean cast. "Do you still think I'm playing a game? We do have our little secrets, you and I. I've often wondered just how Daddy would react to your tampering with his dynasty."

"You'd never do that, Jennifer," he said, his mouth turning dusty. "You're spoiled, and you're vindictive, but you're not stupid enough to incriminate yourself."

"Daddy," she said with a dulcet ring, "can forgive little Jennifer anything given time. On the other hand, he'd no doubt insist that *someone* be punished. . . . Guess who?"

For a moment neither spoke. The noises of the traffic along the street drifted through the open window. He glared at her with a burning hatred to which her frozen sensibilities remained impervious. She took another cigarette from the box and looked about for a match.

"Now don't look so indignant, Max." She chuckled. "You may be tempted to cross me. But I know too much about you and your peculiar associates. You know who I mean—the fat man and that giggling little moron who hangs onto the thin, effeminate one with the pox. I even know their names, Dr. Toberman, but I won't tell a soul . . I think."

When Captain Tolan transferred the assignment from Detective McBride to Sergeant James, the latter tried his best to connect a drunken father, or even an addled mother, to the Angela Whittingham case. The facts could not be made free with, but such an angle made for a more interesting report. But it was all to no avail. He was bored.

And in a weak moment between his last interview and the precinct station, Lou James enlisted in the Marine Corps.

"Wonderful," Tolan growled, totally unimpressed by Sergeant James' patriotic pretenstions. "I suppose McBride will be the next one to quit us." McBride, so serious a young man that he sometimes made Tolan feel his junior, gave one of his aloof glances and peered again into a file cabinet.

Lou James was blushing and sheepish. Tolan growled, but his actual feelings shortly surfaced. Soon he was joking with Lou about native girls and traveling salesmen. He really liked Lou. It would not be easy to replace him. Good detectives were always difficult to replace. They were a unique breed, actually—part soldier, part scholar, an odd blend of the realist and the romantic. Lou James embodied that concept; he had moved up from the patrolman's beat before he was much beyond twenty-five.

Lou wanted to say something about respect and gratitude and the past three years, but he let the sentiments pass. Someday, he thought, he'd write a letter. No need to get serious when Tolan was in such an effervescent mood.

From a nearby church the Angelus tolled softly as they made their way down the street to Nellie's.

The coroner's report had suggested the use of a paring knife in the murders. Though they'd both agreed that the conclusion was infantile, they had their orders to come up with a paring knife bearing Koch's fingerprints. That, of course, produced more laughter as they followed the street up the rise and around the corner. The absurdity of their superiors' decisions was more often frustrating than humorous.

They discussed that and the absence of scratch marks on Koch's face—one more piece of material evidence the city would not believe was not there—after finding a place at the bar. There was also the matter of Koch's having no plausible motive to speak of. They concluded that the entire case against Manfred Koch was simply an expensive waste of time and that the investigation was bound to continue.

Nellie's Tavern was hot and smoky, and the sawdust on the floor dulled the shine on Lou James' shoes. The bartender, an ex-footballer named Casimir Zbigniewski, but known generally as Toes, made a practice of treating the captain to a free one. Toes seldom said much, rarely smiled, or showed any particular emotion for that matter, but he had a sense of people. Tolan and James ate ham sandwiches and boiled eggs and drank cold mugs of porter while the conversation drifted deliberately away from business.

In a far corner of the tavern, at a table out of their vision, Zoltan Mroszek sat over a bottle of cheap wine. It would have to do for now; later on he would try to treat himself to absinthe dreams. He was composing a sonnet. The Muse, apparently, had stopped frowning upon him for the time being.

From his station along the rear wall Zoltan could hear the faint rocking of thunder outside. A busy barmaid eyed him warily whenever by coincidence his eyes caught hers. She, from experience, was content to leave him unattended in the corner where the management habitually isolated him.

Closer to the university there were European cafés where one might enjoy fine wines and *haute cuisine*, even an occasional orchestra. But Nellie's was the most congenial establishment. Nellie, of course, was long gone, as was the "beershop" label; Tolan, though, could remember both from his days as a patrolman. The management had retained the good old atmosphere that appealed as much to families as to thirsty gentlemen. The patrons were thus, on the whole, respectable, and Tolan need not be concerned about some City Hall informant's spotting him at the bar.

No one really paid much heed to Zoltan Mroszek after his first few quiet visits there. With the university district nearby, an occasional oddball was expected. Only Irwin Heester, nicknamed the Gouger for the sweaty manner in which he conducted his loan company business, ever complained about Zoltan's presence. But then, no one ever voluntarily paid much attention to Irwin Heester either.

The tales of Heester's merciless handling of tardy debtors were sometimes exaggerated; he had, nevertheless, been personally responsible for thirty-two evictions in the last five years. Irwin, by judicious lending, had accumulated blocks of real estate and control of two local factories. If one were not in debt to him, it seemed one was working for him—and, in the case of the very unfortunate, paying rent to Irwin Heester. What always bothered Tolan most was the fact that the Gouger stayed within the law. Tolan and his men hated to be part of Irwin Heester's evictions.

Irwin customarily seated himself at a fair distance from, but directly in view of, Zoltan and issued loud expressions of disgust. If ever Zoltan had heard him, which was doubtful in light of his constant stupor, he had never acknowledged Irwin. This only served, naturally, to aggravate the Gouger even further. As he observed Zoltan writing, or staring vacantly ahead, or picking his nose, Irwin would emit horrible retching sounds. Usually customers simply moved away from Irwin.

The conversation turned abruptly away from Manfred Koch as soon as the eggs had been peeled and salted and the mugs of porter set before them. After commiserating over the Philadelphia club's inability to hit left-handers and the defensive weaknesses of the infield, they piled ham slices atop pieces of rye bread and discussed the progress of the war effort. Soon a patrolman entered and wended through the tables in search of the captain.

"McBride sent me, sir. We've got a new suspect in the Whittingham case."

Tolan blinked, removed his pipe, and looked anxiously at Lou James. "You don't say."

"Not really a suspect, Captain," the patrolman said with a grin.

"He already confessed it. And he's not really ours, I guess. They got him up at Broad and Erie. A real loony."

The piano player was warming up, and at a nearby table someone had just told a joke to huge applause and laughter. Tolan smiled back at the officer.

"Thank you very much, Riordan. Take a sandwich with you."

What the hell was he doing all the way up there? Tolan wondered. Broad and Erie was at the far northern end of the city. Leave it to the boys in the Twenty-third Precinct to catch the bouquet again. He doubted that there was anything more than hot air in this one, but at least it was a break from the frustration and tedium.

He bade Sergeant James a good-night and left a dollar on the bar to abet his celebration. The sky was darkening, and a faint rumble of thunder came from the distance. The band concert across the street was under way.

Walking across the cobbled roadway, Tolan tipped his hat to a couple of elderly ladies out for a stroll and nodded respectfully to a priest standing among several well-dressed gentlemen on the corner. The gaslights were on, and the evening crowds gave the neighborhood a rather festive air for midweek. Usually the concerts were given only on Saturdays. One of the nicer by-products of the war was the solidarity that seemed to be everywhere lately. Fervently he hoped that the spirit would not pass with the first intrusion of casualty lists.

What had been a lazy breeze earlier in the evening had grown into a series of strong gusts, raising havoc with ladies' skirts and causing the linden trees that lined the sidewalk to shiver. He held the brim of his well-worn derby and lowered his head to shield his eyes from the dust kicked up in a vacant lot nearby.

Well, a break's a break, he mused. *At least it upsets the case against Manfred Koch. That ought to upset a few stomachs in City Hall.*

The wind was now muffling the strains of a Sousa march. The tuba in the band sounded like a solo instrument.

"Well, is that it?"

"What?"

"Are you gonna sit there typin' a dumb report an' wearin' a silly grin on yer mug, or are you gonna do sumpin' about it?"

"Such as?" Nathan McBride asked with a distracted look. Her story, to say the least, was bizarre. Not that that alone diverted him from seriousness. He had missed supper, thanks to her; his lunch had consisted of a bowl of bean soup taken with black coffee. Hence, he was principally concerned that Mrs. Wolfe would hear the embarrassing rumbles emanating from his stomach. Then, too, his little scuffle with Manfred Koch had left him with a black eye and other bruises which, at times, made him wonder what it might be like to enter the ring with Bob Fitzsimmons.

"Get out there an' arrest them, fer Chrissake! Whattaya think?"

He mused at the appropriateness of her name. The angrier Mrs. Wolfe became, the more canine she looked. Heavily slung jowls waved like empty sacks under her prominent teeth and small, beady eyes.

"I don't know, Mrs. Wolfe. It may even be a matter for the men in Washington."

"Huh?"

"You see, had they been anything other than Spaniards that you say you found tunneling under your house, it would probably fall within our jurisdiction. But, well, Spaniards. . . ."

"Hmph!" She got up and waved a finger at him. "An old lady could get buggered to death before God an' everybody, and you guys would pass the buck somewheres else. I want them Spaniards outa my basement by tomorrow mornin' or I'm callin' the mayor!"

McBride was beginning to enjoy this. He looked at her earnestly and asked, "These Spaniards, do they have whiskers, prominent front teeth, and long, thin tails? Do they make squealy little noises?"

"Hey! Listen here, Clancy. I pay yer salary!"

"Aha!" he said. "*You're* the one. Funny thing, that we should meet like this. . . . About my salary. I find it frankly inadequate when you consider the present rise in the cost of living and the projected inflation of the wartime economy. And not only that—"

"Get offa me! I got my own troubles. I don't hear of no Spaniards tunnelin' under *your* place. Hey! I think you're missin' a few marbles!"

Captain Tolan started up the steps, singing in a furtive tenor as the wind began to howl with a frenzy. "'I wandered to-day to the hill, Maggie, to watch the scene below. . . .'" He was taken unaware and almost knocked over by the force of Mrs. Wolfe's body as she flew through the doorway.

"A pack o' fools," she snarled. "Every last one o' yiz!" She hurried off into the storm. He tipped his hat in her direction, covering her disappearing figure, and mumbled an "excuse me." The rain began with a thunderclap. Tolan wondered what had gone on but decided not to ask. McBride was shaking his head and laughing to himself as Tolan entered.

"Nate, see if you can get me Doyle from the Twenty-third on the telephone. I want to find out if someone's pulling my precinct's leg."

McBride obeyed, and Tolan went off to his crowded little working space to await a reply. By this time the rain was pelting the building and the wind blew through the open window, scattering papers around the room. The station house was almost deserted. Tolan puffed thoughtfully on his pipe and paid no attention to the storm.

The wind was buffeting the shrubbery and elm trees, causing little dusty whirlwinds to form along the still-unpaved street where Andrew Sutton lived. As Sutton unhitched his buggy and led his horse into the stable in back of the house, he worried about his newly planted rosebushes.

The stable door flew open, propelled by a sudden gust, and slammed against the entrance side of the stable, frightening the horse. The wind blew Sutton's striped silk tie over his shoulder. After a brief struggle he managed to lock both the horse and buggy in the stable, collecting in the process several mud and grease stains on his neat gray linen suit.

Sutton's home, with its tidy interior, well-kept study, well-equipped darkroom, well-kept lawn and hedges, reflected his orderly mind. To him the house symbolized his rediscovered stability. It afforded a controlled form of anonymity as well, for he'd made certain when he chose it that there was ample distance between him and his neighbors.

He walked to the front of the house and paused to survey the ambitious flower garden. When he removed his straw hat to prevent its being blown away, his thinning sandy hair was disarranged by the wind. Satisfied that his shrubs would weather the storm, he entered the house, hung his damp coat on a clothes tree in the vestibule, and called out for his wife.

The heavy maroon drapes in the parlor windows were billowing madly in the draft. Sutton rushed to fasten the windows before the pewter and chinaware above the fireplace and the glass figurines on the coffee table were damaged. He called again, this time for aid.

At length he succeeded in locking the windows and shutters. Kneeling to retrieve some sheet music which had been blown from atop the paino, he muttered to himself about Angie's incorrigible thoughtlessness.

In the closed room, gradually, Sutton noticed an acrid odor. Looking about, he noticed a circle of smoke forming near the ceiling.

He got up, sniffing as he walked through the dining room toward the downstairs sitting room; sometimes he found Angie there, taking a nap in the early evening. He turned on a lamp, but the sitting room was empty. The odor grew stronger.

Through the hallway, carefully arranged with some of his prize photographs, he could see the smoke now. It billowed in from the rear of the house in the direction of the kitchen.

Thick and black. He waved his hands before his face to keep the stinking smoke out of his eyes as he entered the kitchen.

"God, Angie—Oh, my God. . . ."

"He confessed it, Regis. He confessed it, and we didn't even ask him."

Tolan had asked Nipper Doyle to repeat some parts of his story. Nipper was notorious among his fellow detectives for a really droll sense of humor. More than once he had involved Tolan in practical jokes and on one occasion even duped his old friend into taking the long ride out to the Twenty-third Precinct.

"You're not up to your old tricks this time, are you?"

"Regis," squawked the voice on the other end, "even *I* don't make jokes out of matters as gruesome as this."

"What's that name again?"

"Piggy Spaganoli."

"How do you know he isn't just imagining things? We've had a few confessions, too. And they've all turned out to be publicity loonies."

"Not this time, Regis. This one is too good. He has a reputation out here as a first-class creep. He likes to beat up women. When he drinks, he blacks out and God help the woman who crosses him. He looks like he's been on the drunk of the entire century this time."

"Piggy Spaganoli," Tolan mused. "Even the name sounds like one of your jokes."

"Yeah, I know"—Nipper laughed—"but I'm serious this time, Regis. Honest."

He thanked Nipper Doyle and hung up. The storm had caused a great deal of static on the telephone; now and then he thought his eardrum would be affected by the noise, so much louder than the voice on the other end. But the rain had let up considerably, so he opened one window to permit the air to circulate. McBride had come by earlier and closed them all. McBride got up and opened another as Tolan started to sing low to himself again. He was beginning to sense relief from the unremitting pressure of the past few weeks.

"Does it sound good, Captain?" McBride asked.

"It's not the man, Nate. But it's good enough for now."

"You mean, good enough to let the German suspect go?"

"Indeed it is, Nathan." He beamed. "Indeed."

As Tolan tapped his pipe against an ashtray and fumbled in his vest pocket for his watch, Charlie Hudson entered, cursing the assignment that had got him trapped in the storm. Soaking wet, he looked like an aging terrier.

"You'll never guess who I just ran into, Regis," he said, draping his damp coat over the back of a chair. "I just saw our old friend Stanley Butterfield."

McBride, who had been about to return to his typewriter, looked up. "I hope you didn't invite him over for a drink, Lieutenant."

"Not exactly, Nate," said Hudson impishly. "I think you're gonna appreciate this, too."

Hudson sat down near a window and let the cool air envelop him as he rubbed his head with a towel.

"You know that place where the newspapermen hang out at Fiftieth and Lancaster, Patsy Dowd's? I ducked in there when the rain started, and I see Stanley with one mean load on. By that time I'm pretty fed up with everything anyway. Pounding the sidewalks in the heat all day, talking to road apples like the Reverend Hopkins and getting nowhere, so I don't need much of Stanley. He didn't see me at first, so I went over to a corner of the bar to avoid him. It just crawls with his associates. You know. Anyway, I only wanted to go over my notes. But I guess his eyesight improves with drink. Pretty soon he spotted me. I guess he'd been chewing the rag all day about how we, in his words, set out to ruin him because he was on to our game, whatever the hell that is. I told him to stay over at his end. But the little twerp actually had the nuts to come over and call me a name."

"What did he call you?" asked McBride.

"A clown," muttered Hudson.

Tolan sat up. "I think I'm going to like what's coming next."

"So," said Hudson, "I gently removed his glasses. Then I broke his nose."

After a round of laughter and congratulations, Tolan bade all a good-night. He was near to exhaustion. The thought of a long sleep and breakfast with Maggie was even more satisfying than his relish as he vicariously broke Stanley Butterfield's nose over and over. How he wished he'd been there, though, when Stanley hit the floor!

Flooded gutters spilled onto the sidewalk. He stepped gingerly over a puddle and turned toward Market Street. Thunder still rumbled far to the north, and sporadic heat lightning broke the gathering darkness.

So, he thought, *Manfred Leopold Koch III is free at last.* Tolan gladly accepted the smoke screen that Piggy Spaganoli's arrest would provide him. Now, with a little luck, they could concentrate their efforts on finding the real killer. No need to feel much compassion for Spaganoli—not if Nipper Doyle's description fitted. The man sounded like one worth locking up for a good long time. Anyway, he'd have to be let go sooner or later, that is, after they fell all over themselves at City Hall in exploiting the arrest of Spaganoli. The press, he concluded, should have another field day with this one.

Hands in his pockets and whistling a tune, Tolan strolled through a narrow street and passed an abandoned gymnasium. Torn and faded notices of many bygone boxing matches remained affixed to the walls. He always glanced at the bill featuring Killer Albertson and Lemonade Larry Higgins. He'd seen that one. It must have been ten years ago, but he remembered losing a couple of dollars on Albertson. Served him right for betting against an Irishman. Higgins was a Dublin boy, he recalled, out of the bay district, tough as they come.

A little stray dog, black with a bushy tail, tagged along until Tolan reached the corner of Hilton's Alley and Sixtieth Street, then deserted him to join a group of urchins splashing each other in a swollen creek on the outskirts of the park.

The air was thick with the smell of honeysuckle and lilac.

Seven

Since Grundy's Patch was on the periphery of Tolan's precinct, Tinker Whalen had to walk two miles to the nearest trolley stop and stand in the rain for at least a quarter hour while awaiting the trolley car. When it finally arrived, the car was crowded, so Tinker had to stand in the sweltering aisle for the three-and-one-half-mile ride down Lancaster Avenue.

Because of Ellie's damned silliness about the police, Tinker had to do it himself. Instead of taking his customary nap after dinner, he had been forced to put on his good clothes and rush to catch the trolley because there would be no other till nine o'clock.

It was Nathan McBride's long shift, and now that Curran, the desk sergeant, had finished with his preliminary paperwork, McBride was preparing to sneak out for a ham sandwich. Hudson left shortly after Captain Tolan, giving McBride a chance to get his records up to date.

He made another mental note to continue the profile, which he'd been constructing on his own time, of Angela Whittingham's sister. It was an admittedly farfetched hypothesis, but one that McBride wished to have in escrow in the event Manfred Koch was released, and that was, of course, imminent now. McBride's theory had Betsy Whittingham conspiring to have her sister only kidnapped, not murdered, in order to frighten her away from the riffraff. The murder, he thought, had been merely an unfortunate turn of events. Now there was no looking back for Betsy.

In his research he had discovered all the probable motives. She was older and much less attractive than Angela. Bryn Mawr had offered Angela a scholarship; Betsy had simply eked out a diploma from an uninspiring private school in Ardmore. Angela mastered Mozart in her teens; Betsy's larger, clumsy hands were judged more appropriate for housework. Angela wrote religious poetry which she had read during Sunday services; Betsy had had to be forced even to read her Bible assignments. Certainly Betsy Whittingham had good reason to wish to check Angela's next giant step in her father's eyes.

Her mother's assessment was immaterial, but Betsy's feelings for Professor Whittingham were clearly strong.

Had he been reading too many psychology texts? The odds against his theory were discouraging indeed.

The desk sergeant was lecturing Patrolmen Riordan and Shipley about the illegibility of their scrawl; he had not been able to record their daily reports for weeks.

A third patrolman, Wilmer "Bones" Fatzinger, who had come down from the Reading area with one of those giddy Pennsylvania Dutch accents, stood some distance from the others, looking characteristically absentminded. Fatzinger was so obtuse that it was a mystery he'd ever passed the minimal requirements. Sergeant Curran aimed his comments at Riordan and Shipley, having long ago given up any dreams of making Fatzinger do anything in a logical manner.

Bones was an inevitable by-product of the city bureaucracy. The commissioner had a niece who, in spite of her light-headedness, was the apple of his eye. She had been put on the payroll, and the commissioner, wishing to run the smallest risk of disrupting his operations, had finally decided to make her a clerk in personnel. After about six weeks the niece had beguiled her supervisor into letting her take part in an actual employment. As the supervisor—whose demotion followed—perspired over her shoulder, the commissioner's niece had interviewed long, gaunt Fatzinger.

First, she had mistaken Fatzinger's vacancy for nervousness; every time his mouth dropped open soundlessly in confusion at her questions, it had counted for him. Secondly, mistaking the Pennsylvania Dutch dialect for German, she had explained to her horrified uncle that it was an asset if you worked in Germantown. Finally, discovering that Fatzinger had come down from the upstate farmlands, she had recommended him for the mounted patrol (you have to know how to ride a horse if you live on a farm like that).

The niece had been quietly transferred to the supplies department. She had soon fallen in love with a clerk—whose demotion had followed—but the force had inherited Bones Fatzinger for the duration.

When the mounted patrol found Bones unable to fathom the complexities of a saddle, he had been promptly reassigned to a foot patrol in Germantown. When he had slept through his third armed robbery there, the commissioner, actually meeting the man and smelling his lunch pail, remembered an obscure incident: Tolan, on being passed over for promotion, had delivered a ton of manure to his doorstep. The commissioner sent Fatzinger to Tolan's precinct. Captain Tolan was too kindhearted ever to fire Fatzinger, whom he found oddly refreshing, so Bones had been allowed to stay long enough to establish seniority.

Watching Fatzinger chewing on a pickled egg made McBride even hungrier. He sorted his papers and placed them in the top drawer of his desk. As he started down the outside steps, filled with visions of his long-overdue supper, he was accosted by a knobby little man in a wrinkled suit.

"There's a sergeant at the desk. You can talk to him about it."

"Hey!" shouted Tinker as he grabbed McBride's arm. "Where da hell do you t'ink yer goin'? I ain't finished yet."

"I'm off duty, mister," said McBride, who forced a smile as he deftly plucked Tinker's hand from his forearm. "Just tell the nice desk sergeant your troubles, and he may even give you a free drink and a room for the night."

"I don't need no free drink. Me daughter's missin', an I wanna find her! What the hell's the matter with ye? Are ye deef an' dumb?"

"Okay, okay," he said resignedly, "let's go inside."

If this guy turned out to be a bum out of Charlie Hudson's Sink, and the daughter only a wino's hallucination, McBride vowed to lock the little man up until he imagined his cell being overrun by snakes and pink elephants.

"Name?"

"Dennis Whalen."

"Address?"

"Grundy's Gardens Number Five."

McBride wrote "Grundy's Patch" on the form, but Tinker quickly detected that and corrected him indignantly. "I said Grundy's *Gardens.*"

"Grundy's Gardens, right." McBride scratched in his correction. "Now, name of missing person?"

"Kathleen." Tinker sniffled. "An' I bet she was took off be one o' them goddamn bums in the Patch! A lovely girl, a saintly girl. . . ."

"Be careful, Vincent," snapped Dr. Toberman at the fat man struggling to place a large, heavily wrapped bundle neatly on the floor of the wagon. "Give him some help, Fred."

Fred Bowman looked up from his parcel. He had been staring in dull fascination at its contents for the past five minutes. When he smiled, the few rotten teeth seemed very long, like a rodent's, because his gums had shrunk back almost to the roots.

"And close that valise," hissed Toberman. He exchanged a weary glance with the tall, ashen fellow who stood near him and apart from the activity.

Fred Bowman giggled and did as he was ordered, placing the valise on the seat of the carriage and scurrying around to the other side to assist the fat man. Together they arranged the package against the base of the seat on the passenger's side of the buggy and set the valise down where it would not be jostled by the ride. Now and then the buggy would shiver a bit when the thunder stirred the horse.

The fat man closed the door and reported to Toberman, who added some last-minute instructions.

"What do you want me to do with Fred?" the fat man inquired. "He wants to go along."

"What do you think, Arthur?" Toberman turned to his ashen-faced companion.

"Why don't you just give him a piece of raw meat to play with?" snorted Arthur. The fat man reacted with amusement. Fred looked on stupidly.

"You'd better take him with you until you've taken care of the larger parcel," said Toberman thoughtfully. "Then you can drop him off. Don't let him tamper with the valise, however. Do you hear?"

The fat man nodded, then signaled Fred to get into the buggy. They drove off in the gathering storm.

The fog was warm, and it seemed to be growing denser by the minute. Tolan trudged on along a row of padlocked offices and noticed that someone had once again scratched the word "Gouger" on the wooden step in front of Irwin Heester's door. The big white lettering on the window read LOANS AT COMPETITIVE RATES, and he could recall the many times he had listened to Heester's outrage when some poor dupe had thrown a brick through it. He thought of the motley assortment of characters he'd collected over the years, the good, the bad, and the bruised, pathetic in betweens, like Felix Wellington, the aging pickpocket he had passed a way back—he no longer could clip the predatory rich and lived nearby. Most were not the kind you'd want next door, a lot of sick and weary old drunks and losers now, but it had been a colorful tapestry at least.

He plodded past a vegetable shop which featured a sale on artichokes and red peppers and a haberdashery with striped blazers in the window. *Faith,* he thought, *wouldn't I be a proper sight in one of them?* He paused to survey the corner lot, where an unsightly old firetrap had just been torn down to make way for the new grammar school.

At Easterley's meat store, where he usually tarried to study the next morning's offerings, he crossed the street, and when he neared Castleman's livery stable, he stopped.

Market Street was empty, and but for the muffled clopping of a distant horse, the constant cry of the katydids, and the gentle rustling of willow trees, the neighborhood was silent.

After dousing the pot of burning yams in the sink and opening the kitchen door and windows to clear the air of the heavy, acrid smoke, Andrew Sutton tried to rouse Angie from her stupor. The empty bottle lay near her feet. His initial fears had quickly subsided, and with each effort to awaken her his rage had grown more difficult to contain.

Her head rested as dead weight upon the table, a pose of total insensibility. It was not an uncommon sight by now. He considered leaving her there.

God forgive him, he even played with the idea of her drowning in her own vomit. Angie always got sick a few hours later. It would be poetic justice; God must have special ways of dealing with gluttons and sensualists just as He punishes the bully by the sword.

Finally, under wobbly legs, he carried her limp body upstairs and left her fully clothed on the bed. He had not dared leave her downstairs for fear that she would awaken in one of her vile tempers and alert the neighbors to his carefully guarded shame. His was a lonely burden; Jehovah had sent him Angélique-Marie Cordier as his very special cross. And so he chastised himself for his thoughts of a moment ago, for he well knew that it was not everyone whom Yahweh would give a means of atonement before the day when He would judge us all.

He returned to the kitchen, closed the door and windows because the storm had now worked itself up into a frenzy, and started to make himself a cup of tea. He prayed that the thunder would not awaken her.

It had been a busy day for Sutton, and his work load had mounted during the past month to such an extent that he wondered if he'd ever fulfill all his obligations on time. Beyond his regular work for the police, increasingly loathsome of recent weeks, there had been a number of private sessions. Somehow his prestige had grown, and with it the chance to do more suitable things. No longer was he trapped in a world of police records, identification numbers, the cheap, defiant faces of the riffraff, the maimed and decomposed bodies.

That morning he had photographed Lieutenant John C. Groome, the commandant of the First Troop, Philadelphia City Cavalry, due to embark for Florida within a fortnight. That afternoon it had been four university gentlemen who were leaving for Texas in a week to join Colonel Theodore Roosevelt's elite guard. Sutton's fees for the day had amounted to more than sixty dollars. Late that afternoon, through an introduction by Dr. Blakeley, he had made arrangements with a theatrical producer to photograph Lillian Russell when she arrived in Philadelphia later in the summer.

Still awaiting his attention in the darkroom were the greatest prizes of all. It had taken a year of bargaining, after the passing of Herbert Wilson, to secure the commission. The pictures he had taken of this season's debutantes would require his total concentration. They must be flawless.

He took his cup of tea into the living room and buried himself in the Scriptures in an effort to calm his nerves. The storm buffeted the house for a time, then ebbed into a steady, less determined downpour. He concentrated on the condemnation of Ashtoreth, in whose worship such lasciviousness was committed that she became a symbol of all things carnal and odious. Sins of the flesh most displeased Jehovah, and the torments of hell were especially bitter for those who followed Ashtoreth.

Sutton closed his eyes and once again offered a prayer for heavenly intervention on Angie's behalf—his most despairing measures had been of no avail. He was constantly considering taking matters into his own hands and putting the fear of God into her himself.

He rose from his easy chair to refill his cup of tea, taking the Bible

with him. She had been leaning against the archway that divided
the living and dining rooms, staring at him for the last few minutes.
In the noise of the wind and rain she had found her way down the
stairs without breaking his concentration.

"Why ain't yew in the dahkroom earnin' some money?" she mumbled. "I guess yew don't care that the roof's leakin' an' there's water
all over yer goddamn floor up there, do yuh?"

As her body swayed drunkenly, her hands left misty marks on the
polished wood. He watched as her body seemed to undulate beneath the distorted smile and heavy-lidded eyes. It brought to mind
today's caller, whoever that one happened to be, and he wanted to
call her a trollop but did not dare.

"Y'all mad at me again, preacher man?" She stared back with a
taunting gaze.

"Just disappointed again, Angie."

"That's fine. Jist so's yew ain't mad at me."

He excused himself to go refill his teacup. She stopped him, placing her body in front of him. If, after all, he were not angry. . . . She took his hand and rubbed it against her breast.

"Then," she purred, inserting his hand beneath her bodice, "how
come yew left me up there all alone? Don't y'know the devil coulda
crawled in bed with me an' pulled down my breeches? Then how
would I explain it if'n yew come in an' found him ridin' me?"

"You're disgusting," he snapped, jerking his hand away. "Why
couldn't you have stayed in bed and left me alone for the night?"

Carefully she released her grip, turned around and watched him
disappear. She took a hesitant step toward the kitchen whence she
could hear him preparing the kettle. "I wouldn't want yew to touch
me anyhow, yew half a man," she mumbled to herself, floundering
through the hallway. He was seated at the kitchen table with his
eyes fixed upon his Bible.

"I said"—she threw her head back in a queenly pose—"I don't
need yew to help me find it."

He sighed wearily and continued to ignore her. She demanded to
know where something was. He did not answer.

"Where is it?" she repeated, fumbling around the kitchen until at
length she'd begun to root through the cupboard. Then in frustration she pulled some pots and pans from their niche and let them
clank to the floor.

"My bourbon."

"You drank it."

She leaned forward, and he thought for a moment she would spit at him as had happened at times in the past. "What gives yew the right t' take my licker, yew bastard? Tell me where it is!"

He realized his eyes were focused over her shoulder on the rack of knives above the sink.

"If you crawl around the house and sniff long enough, you're bound to come up with it eventually."

She stood up and paused to make certain her feet were planted firmly. "Yew prob'ly got it locked in that blessed dahkroom that yew keep sealed up all the time. What yew doin' down there that y'all don't want me to know? Huh? Are yew abusin' yerself?"

"I keep the darkroom locked," he said, getting up to pour his tea, "because I don't want you down there knocking my equipment over in one of your monolithic stupors. I keep it locked because I don't want you down there drinking my chemicals. They're much too expensive. And I keep it locked because it's one small circle of dignity that I wish to keep unsullied by you and your"—he sought the correct word—"your companions."

"Companions," she sneered. "I *do* like yer choice o' words, Andrew. Allus so delicate, aren't yuh?"

He put his teacup down on the table and started out of the room. Angie followed him closely, badgering him in slurred, sometimes incomprehensible terms, and he felt his mouth go dry as he held back his anger and hurt.

"Yew goin' out to take some more dirty pitchers now, preacher man?" she asked. He put on his jacket and, with trembling hands, slicked his hair into place.

"Like the ones yew took o' me in New Orleans back before yew found more fun in Jesus, remember? The ones without a stitch o' clothes on," she jeered. "Yew wasn't hidin' my bourbon in them days, was yew?"

"Good night, Angie. Please don't wet the bed tonight."

"Who'd yew sell them pitchers to anyway, Andrew? I bet they paid yuh good fer them, didn't they?"

He opened the door, and a draft ruffled her hair. Tears ran down her cheeks, forming dark rivulets of makeup along the creases of her mouth. Her tone changed abruptly.

"Ah, c'mon, Andy," she whined, "now don't y'all be difficult. I need a drink bad." Her eyes flashed with inspiration. She fussed with the stays of her dress, making a cumbersome effort to remove it in a hurry. "What if. . . . "

How very much like a foul and filthy prostitute his Angélique truly was. He felt his hands rising from his sides and shoved her to the floor.

He went out the door, choking with pent-up rage as she screamed after him.

"Sonbitch! I hope y'all *drown* in that storm!"

He walked through the pelting rain, unaware that it was drenching his clothing, unaware of the thunder and distant lightning, unaware of everything but his desperate attempt to impose serenity on his thoughts.

Dawn broke with a soft drizzle which would continue well into the day. The streets took on a renewed life in the cooler air, and by seven thirty they were teeming with parasols and black umbrellas. By eight the sound of trolleys along main routes was joined by those of hucksters who barked from their stalls and wagons the prices of onions, tomatoes, freshly caught seafood, and the first blackberries of the season. Newsboys, too, cried out: headlines of the war and of Piggy Spaganoli's arrest. At nine a messenger from the German consulate arrived with a report for the captain. Charlie Hudson looked up from his desk, clearly stunned.

"Don't you know? Haven't you heard? Captain Tolan . . . passed away last evening?"

The messenger, who knew nothing of the personalities whose correspondences he carried, looked blank at first, then tried his best to appear appropriately saddened.

"That is truly awful. Herr Captain Tolan vass always a very agreeable gentleman."

"Yeah. . . . " Hudson looked toward Tolan's desk. "They found him outside Castleman's Livery Stable up Market Street. Took a stroke I guess. . . . " He observed the awkwardness of the young German. "Oh, yeah, the report. Why don't you just leave it on his desk? I'll get to it later."

The messenger placed the folder, which was marked "Confidential," reverently on Tolan's desk between an ashtray, in which rested a spare pipe, and a stack of papers and lawbooks.

"And," continued Hudson, "you can tell your superior that Herr

Koch was released from prison during the night. He's probably at home now."

The messenger, whose English was still elementary, looked confused again.

"Released," repeated Hudson, "let out. We found our man."

"*Ja.* The consul will be most . . . encouraged to be of this intelligence." He smiled.

Hudson added tersely, "Tell your people they'll receive an official apology from the city, as well as from the federal government."

Jesus, thought Hudson as the messenger clicked his heels and went out the door, what a mess poor Regis had left him with. With Lou James, green as he was, going off to fight the Spaniards and no one around but that even greener McBride kid. It was a damn good thing Spaganoli had popped up when he did.

A Tolan family portrait faced the report confirming Koch's assertion that he had never personally taken the bufotenine drug during the experiment at Leipzig.

Koch heeded the advice of his consulate, abandoning his graduate studies in Philadelphia and taking the first available berth on a tanker bound for Hamburg. But uncertain of his government's foreign policy, he disembarked at Liverpool, sailed instead to Cádiz, and promptly enlisted in the Spanish Army with the understanding that he would be assigned immediately to Cuba.

At nine thirty another messenger arrived—a detective out of the district attorney's office. He was directed to Hudson back where the files of long-standing cases were kept. After expressing his sadness over Regis Tolan's passing, he told him of Piggy Spaganoli's suicide.

Hudson gawked in disbelief at the story of the jailor's incredible incompetence. Spaganoli had draped a strip of bed sheet over a steam conduit in his cell and hanged himself during the night.

"What can you do about it, Charlie? When a guy wants to get rid of himself, that's all there is to it."

"Yeah, I know, I know, but it's a pretty shabby bit of police work when he succeeds."

Hudson poured another cup of coffee and announced resignedly, when he was alone, that whatever remained of the ugly affair was no longer in his province. It was time to move on to other matters, such as the missing persons report McBride had made out the previous evening. Fervently hoping that it was in no manner connected with the earlier disappearances, he sent the weary Detective McBride out to Grundy's Patch. Then he stole off to Tolan's home to offer whatever consolation he could.

"Well, it's your goddamn case, isn't it? You took the damn report, didn't you? Whattaya want me to do—send Fatzinger?"

McBride clenched his teeth and picked up a handful of trolley tokens. Muttering sotto voce about the inherent unfairness of the shift schedules, he was embarrassed to realize that it had been of Captain Tolan's making. He gulped down his cup of coffee, scalding his throat and making the tears rise. He picked his umbrella from the stand and entered the drizzly street to retrace Tinker Whalen's steps of the night before.

In the gloom of the morning crowd he thought of the day just two weeks ago when the captain had observed that the day had been mercifully uneventful and that he had two tickets for that afternoon's game with the Pittsburghs. They had taken the city's most uncomfortable trolley all the way to North Philadelphia to sit eating peanuts and saw Ed Delahanty hit a grand slam. It was especially important to McBride that the captain had chosen that day to be understanding since McBride had pulled a classic blunder on a burglary stakeout the day before. It was one of many hunches which had gone sour on him at the time.

Unlike Lou James, who had progressed rapidly from a patrolman's beat along the Delaware without benefit of an education, Nathan McBride had made detective through examinations. James smiled with benign condescension whenever McBride expressed what he thought were sophisticated motivational theories.

But Tolan had been different, asking him now and then what he was reading these days, how he felt about a suspect, what he thought of something in the newspapers that morning, encouraging and approving. One day, however, in an odd moment, he'd asked Hudson why Tolan had chosen this unlikely life. "What the hell was a big mick to do in them days? Become a soldier, a priest, a drunk, or a cop." McBride guessed that Hudson had often had to answer the same question.

He remembered stopping in Nellie's on the way home after the ball game and Tolan's insisting on buying the chicken sandwiches and beer before the staff meeting at six because he could recall what niggardly salaries they paid rookie detectives. McBride had not protested.

* * *

Zoltan Mroszek tossed and turned, muttering fitful comments in his half sleep. For the past hour or so he had tried in vain to shake off the haunting, disconnected horrors of his dreams. Somewhere on the stairwell he could hear the clucking of Mrs. Leibowitz and the landlady. He buried his head under the covers and drifted briefly back into sleep.

Fragments of his nightmares returned and tormented him: a fat man who wheezed as he struggled with a lock, a smaller man who fretted and urged the fat man on, Glorianna Bowman's heavy steps on the level above him, the fat man's angry voice demanding something, old Glorianna spitting on the floor, the bludgeon. . . .

Zoltan had left Nellie's in high spirits, tipping his hat to a plump barmaid and wandering off to his other havens. As he made the rounds of the university district dens, reading his poetry to anyone who would listen, he had partaken of more wine at the bequest of some bored acquaintances until he had eventually encountered a man with some absinthe. In a shadowy corner of an apartment near his home Zoltan and his friends had lounged about the floor while a newcomer with an exotic accent read from the works of Baha Ullah. At one point in the evening, as the absinthe took effect and Zoltan, engrossed in the Eastern prophet's words, had shushed his hostess, he had been dismissed curtly from the gathering.

He had stumbled over an abandoned rag doll and struggled up the front steps, his brain afire. He had slipped through the front door and tiptoed as if on eggs up the first three flights. Even in his stupor something reminded him that his rent was three weeks overdue. He vowed that as soon as he could borrow enough to pay her off, he would demand a room nearer the ground. One of these nights, he knew, he would tilt backward and roll seven flights to the lobby. But he also knew that the management tolerated his decadent presence only as long as he remained tucked away in a far corner of the building.

Somewhere near the fifth floor he had seemed to hear their voices. He'd peered upward from the shadows at the turning of the stair, thinking he saw the fat man bring the bludgeon down on old Glorianna's head, thinking he heard a terrified wail from poor bewildered Fred before the door had shut. Zoltan had shaken his head.

He could not be sure of anything. Ever since Samantha had gone, his visions, his absinthe haunts, had been filled with violence, with death and dying, with wretched little figures like Fred and monstrosities like the fat man. Often in his dreams he'd seen worse.

He had stepped out of the shadows, rubbed his eyes, and crept up the remaining flights to his room. He had not even paused as he reeled past old Glorianna's door, but he seemed to recall a series of sickening thuds. . . .

The voices outside rose to an excited crescendo, then fell into a sudden hush. Zoltan sat up, his body soaking wet and trembling in fear.

The voices resumed severally: now a man, then an old woman, the sounds of children gasping in wonderment. He got out of bed and opened his door slightly to peer through the crack. Tenants were gathered one flight below. Amid the gabbling of the landlady he heard the name Bowman, and he hastened to don his trousers.

A uniformed policeman stood outside the Bowmans' door. The landlady carped about the risks involved in taking in riffraff like Fred Bowman and his gypsy mother, whose rent was one month in arrears. On the floor near the landlady's foot Zoltan saw a large bloodstain. A second policeman called to the other to enter the apartment. In a moment both reappeared, bearing a stretcher. From under a canvas sheet a dirty little hand protruded. The policemen started to negotiate the narrow stairway.

Zoltan darted back into his room and locked the door, groping under the bed for whatever wine remained from nights before.

McBride boarded the trolley and studied a copy of the missing person's report on Kathleen Whalen as the car rolled roughly over the cobbled avenue. At Rupert Place a young lady boarded and, glancing around the car, McBride observed that all the seats were occupied, so he quickly offered her his own. She had a nice smile.

Two miles of dirt road concluded the journey from the trolley stop to Grundy's Patch. Walking on the trampled grass beside the deep yellow quagmire, over ruts and ducking beneath low-hanging bushes, McBride felt a pang of conscience. No wonder the little guy had looked like a bum. It was the hard lot of the poor to be forever misunderstood and suspect. He must remember his own people had come out of one of these patches, too.

At the end of the road, after stepping into several unavoidable mudholes, cursing the birth of Lieutenant Hudson, he entered a clearing and followed a narrow path into the little community, knowing precisely what to look for first.

In the rows of houses that looked as if they had been erected on toothpicks, open sewers that spilled over the walkways, roofs of tin and tar paper, the modest rectory of Saint Francis Xavier seemed a palace for its tidiness. McBride was careful to rub his shoes against a clump of grass before climbing the stairs lest he soil the runner on the whitewashed porch. He knocked and, as he waited for someone to answer, looked across the muddy road toward a neatly kept cemetery in the midst of the rickety world of the living. He knocked again and presently was greeted by a surly, ancient housekeeper, who kept him outside for a time as she examined him suspiciously. He showed her his identification.

"Father O'Rourke ain't here. Yiz'll have to talk to the curate, Father McDonnough."

"That will be fine, Ma'am."

"Wait in there. He'll see yiz in a minute."

She gestured toward an office off the hallway and shuffled toward the rear of the building. The pleasant aroma of soup floated from the kitchen, and he knew he was going to miss lunch again. The office was small but impeccable, suggesting the rule of an orderly but somewhat severe hand. *Funny,* he thought, *how one's working area speaks so vividly of his character.* McBride made a mental note to straighten out his own desk.

McBride focused on the large, majestic portrait of Pope Leo XIII until the lump went away—he had been thinking of the deceptive chaos in Tolan's office. He was still looking into the Holy Father's kindly eyes when the curate appeared from upstairs.

"Officer?"

McBride turned. Nathan noticed a button missing from the cassock just above the large priest's paunch.

"Father O'Rourke should be back by suppertime. He's visiting families down in the valley. We have all these poor districts in our province."

"No need for a pastor, Father. I'm only a policeman, not a lieutenant."

"I see. So, what can I do for you? Has one of my parishioners gotten drunk in town and beaten somebody up? Around here they seem to think the shortest distance between two points is a punch in the mouth. But I suppose you know that."

"It's about the Whalen girl."

"Do sit down, Officer . . . ?"

"McBride. Nathan McBride."

Father McDonnough sat at his desk and crossed his hands. "Have you any leads? That is what you call them, isn't it?"

"No leads so far, Father. You see, Mr. Whalen didn't report her missing until last night."

"Her mother came to us last night with howls and shrieks. I don't know what *we're* supposed to do in a matter like this." Father McDonnough opened his palms and displayed them to signify helplessness.

"I imagine she had no one else to tell, Father."

The priest remained unmoved. "I suppose."

"So I thought I'd start here," McBride continued. "Knowing it's a Catholic neighborhood, I thought you'd probably know more about the habits and associates of your parishioners than anyone else would."

Father McDonnough's eyebrows raised slightly.

"Officer, I cannot divulge the secrets of the confessional."

"I know that." McBride felt his intelligence insulted. "I believe I know what the problem is, Father. You think I'm a non-Catholic. Not so. I belong to Saint Canicus in Overbrook."

"Oh? Well, you see, your name. . . . "

"My mother liked Nathan. After a Brian and a Patrick and even a Francis Xavier, my father let her have her way. I have a degree in philosophy from Villanova, if that helps at all."

Father McDonnough chose to ignore the rebuttal. "I really don't know the Whalen girl well," he resumed. "Father O'Rourke is much closer to the family. I've been here only a little over a year."

"Does she have any close friends who may wish to speak with me?"

He thought for a moment. "As I understand it, Kathleen Whalen's father kept her from developing any deep or long-standing friendships."

"No confidants?"

"Certainly not in this building, Officer."

The chilliness of the curate's manner suggested more caution than McBride would have anticipated. It bordered, in fact, on hostility.

"Father McDonnough"—he chose his words carefully—"you must understand that the department is not interested in, well, the dirty laundry. But we're trying to establish a time frame, and to that end, Miss Whalen's customary activities are of paramount importance—her activities as well as you understand them, that is. Father, was Miss Whalen . . . er. . . ."

"They call her the grasshopper."

"The . . . uh . . . grasshopper?"

The curate arose, his swivel chair squealing behind him, and pointed out the window. "You see that long grass over there, Officer McBride, the plot on the other side of the creek?"

"I see it, Father." McBride answered, studying the acre of weeds and wild grass.

"She meets them there," said Father McDonnough, "hundreds of them."

"You're sure of that, Father?"

"Sure of that?" Father McDonnough's voice betrayed his intolerance for questions. "Would I dare say it if I weren't sure? The girl is trash."

"That's a serious allegation anywhere, Father. Especially here in Grundy's Gardens."

There was a definite scorn in his words as he turned to face McBride. A smudge on his cassock that looked vaguely like cigar ashes. "God's forgotten."

"I've seen worse, Father."

McBride had the feeling that the plump curate had a great deal of what was apparently required to rise in the ranks. Already he had the pomposity of an archbishop and the meanness of an old maid.

"Perhaps you have, Officer, but I haven't. I was told they were a challenge, these people. The church wastes its time and energy here. Take your pick, Officer. The hundred or so will be happy to tell you all about it."

Nathan refrained from saying anything grossly disrespectful to the inflated curate. He could not stand another minute in the rectory of Saint Francis Xavier. Nathan excused himself with muffled gratitude and stepped into the fresh air, wondering whether this investigation would be worthwhile or just another exercise in frustration. It had been an uninspiring start.

The quartermaster of the 2nd Regiment, 5th Pennsylvania Volunteers, had griped and groaned aloud when ordered to find a uniform to fit Private Ralph Ian Blakeley, but the colonel had been so encouraged by Ralphie's massiveness and eager, pliant character that the colonel's martial spirits had soared, and dreams of outstripping Theodore Roosevelt had blossomed as suddenly and wildly as had the lilac trees on the green. And so the quartermaster had cursed the colonel under his breath and issued orders to the corporal, who had muttered similar oaths all afternoon and well into the night before a uniform of Ralphie's approximate size had been found in a warehouse at Second and Edward streets. It had taken Ralphie some time to fathom the use of leggings, and the button at the neck of his tunic had refused to close without a struggle; but at last he stood proudly before his father in two-tone blue and khaki.

"Not bad, Ralphie," said Blakeley approvingly. "Not exactly the Khyber Rifles, but not bad in any case."

"He looks like a stuffed flounder," said his sister.

"Aw, Rosie, you're just jealous 'cause the suffragettes don't get to wear these duds. You gotta wear them dumb shirts an' ties," Ralphie retorted as he adjusted his neckerchief.

"Rosalie, my dove," Blakeley said as he rubbed his monocle with a linen cloth, "I presume you have a purpose for being here, other than to remind us of our barbarian hierarchy of values."

"Yes, Ian," said Rosie breezily, "I have a purpose for being here. My daily *raison d'être*, as it were."

Blakeley frowned. "It's not Ian to you, Rosalie, my darling. It's Father, or sir, or Dr. Blakeley—Pater, if you must—but not Ian."

Rosalie affected nonchalance. She sniffed a rose, her little finger projecting delicately from her grip on its long stem.

"In any case, Dr. Blakeley, there is a male outside who wishes to deliver a message. However, in light of your unsatisfactory management of his last crisis, he does not wish to address you in person."

"Victor is still pouting?"

Ralphie turned to his sister. "But how's he going to buttle?"

Rosie arched a brow distantly.

"What your brother means, Rosalie, is how can one be a butler and refuse to communicate with his employer?"

"I've no idea, Dr. Blakeley."

Ralphie turned to his father. "Should I hit him one, Dad?"

"Ralphie, you shall have to contain your hostilities until you get to the Indies. Show him in, Rosalie."

"Sir?" Rosalie crossed her arms.

"Rosalie, show the butler in. Then I suggest you join an indignant parade or something."

Presently Victor appeared, his coat still showing the stains of Snopkowski's potato and cheese filling, his face ashen with repressed righteous turbulence.

"What is it, Victor?"

"A message for you, sir," said Victor curtly.

"Very good. May I have it?"

The butler made no move to hand over the envelope. He had, in fact, tucked it in an inside pocket. Instead, he took one step backward and struck a graceful pose. *Here we go again,* thought Blakeley.

"Sir. . . ."

"Yes, Victor?" answered Blakeley wearily.

Victor held his pose and cleared his throat in preparation. Blakeley did a slow burn and cursed Rosie's duplicity. Victor did not wish to utter a syllable. She had as much as promised that.

"I've come to you, Dr. Blakeley, a suppliant," Victor began, gesturing gracefully with his left hand while his right hand grasped his lapel. "I looked upon the sun rising omnipotently, spreading its pastel hue over the river and lush, verdant horizon, and I said to myself, 'Victor this is it! This, this is your *moment.*' No longer would I suffer in silence. Never again would I subordinate my inalienable rights to the maintenance of dignity. And, above all, never—*never* would I expose myself to sanctioned vilification by attempting to rectify the erosion of our culinary standards."

With that Victor gestured with a flicker of the hand above his head. Ralphie stared at him, mesmerized. Blakeley struck a counterpose and asked that Victor get to the point.

"If it's about yesterday's kitchen incident, I was under the impression that the matter was settled."

Victor shifted from right hand to left and rearranged his stance so that his left foot was perpendicular to his right. "I've come here not about Snopkowski or to debate the appropriateness of the pirogi. I wish merely to establish an equitable framework for the future."

Ralphie leaped up. "Snopkowski splattered food all over him yesterday!"

Victor puffed up his chest. "May we discuss this in private, Dr. Blakeley?"

Ralphie started to laugh. "Full of cheese an' potato stuffing!"

"Ralphie," said Blakeley, weakly, "why don't you help your sister paint angry signs for this afternoon's suffragette march?"

"But," Ralphie grumbled, "she don't want me to. She says I can't spell."

"Well, threaten her or something."

Ralphie went out, muttering to himself. "Aw, that's no fun. She gets paint all over me."

"Don't soil your uniform," admonished Blakeley.

"It's been brought to my attention, sir," Victor resumed, "that the Quimbys' man, Gerald, has been granted another raise of five dollars monthly—his second in a year."

"Gerald?"

"Yes, Gerald. And I happen to know that he tipples."

Blakeley stroked his beard for a moment. "You tipple, too, Victor. In fact, you tipple quite a lot."

"And how, pray tell, do you know that, sir?" Victor flushed.

"Now, Victor, I'm willing to grant you two dollars per month."

"Four!"

"Three, and I'll overlook your having absconded with my Benedictine last night. It's no wonder you saw the sun this morning. Victor, it's been raining all day."

Victor gave a surly tilt of the head and sighed. "Three it is, sir," he granted. "But I'm a much better valet than Gerald."

"Three, and I want you to try to get along with Snopkowski. Speak with her or something. This open hostility is in very poor taste. That will be all for now, Victor. If you please, I'd like to read my note."

"Oh yes, the missive." He felt inside his coat for the envelope and handed it to Blakeley. Then he left grandly. "Good day, sir."

Blakeley waited until he was alone to open the letter. As he read it, he sank slowly into a chair and felt his stomach turning.

Ian Blakeley learned of the death of Captain Regis Tolan.

Eight

"What the hell is this?"

Hudson had just returned from his efforts at consoling Maggie Tolan. The question was rhetorical.

Fatzinger answered him anyway. "A missin' person report."

Hudson stared for a moment at the all-too-familiar folder. "When did it get here?"

"Vile you vass oudt," answered Fatzinger as he stuffed himself with Limburger and onion. "Some guy from City Hall brung it in. He says in dis precinct she got lost."

Hudson rubbed his eyes and waved at the air in front of his face. "Bones, what the hell is that daisy doing in your buttonhole?"

Fatzinger glanced at his chest. "Oh, dott! Dott's no daisy—dott's a sunflower. It ain't fer real anyhow. It's chust fer nice. At da seashore I vun it last summer. Dey bet me I couldn't ten punkin pies eadt. I showed dem by Christ!"

"Well, take it off. It's not part of your uniform." The guy from City Hall *would* have to meet Fatzinger, he thought. "What are you doing here anyway? I thought you were night shift."

"Yeah, but da sergeant says we need more guys on duty cuz o' the captain dyin' an' James leavin', an' I wanna become a detective."

Hudson tapped the top of his desk and contemplated such a hypothetical horror. "Bones, I never got to eat my lunch because I was out at Tolan's. Would you like it? Veal cutlet sandwiches."

Fatzinger was briefly pensive. "Weal cotlet?"

"Yeah, you know—Wienerschnitzel on pumpernickel with piccalilli relish."

"Und you vant I should eadt it? Yum-yum . . . " He looked predictably confused. "Vot's up?"

"Nothin', Bones." Hudson put his hand to his heart. "I just want you to spend the whole day in the back room straightening out the files."

"Dot's a woman's chob, dem files."

Hudson shrugged. "Suit yourself, I like Wienerschnitzel, too. The wife even packed a couple of apples this morning."

"Hokay, Lootenant, only I still wanna move up to detective pretty soon. I didn't all the vay to Philly come down chust to mess around vit leetle papers."

Eyes watering, Hudson quickly handed over his lunch. "Remember now, the file room all day. If I see you out here at all, the sunflower goes in the trash can. Clear?"

Fatzinger nodded and started toward the back office. Hudson waved his hands once again and sat down to study the report.

"She's wonderful rich, dis one." Fatzinger's scarecrow head suddenly appeared.

"Who?"

"The missin' lady." Fatzinger then finally left with that inimitable manure-kicking stride of his. Hudson shook his head at the futility of his circumstances.

Fatigue, the stale air in the room, and grief had caused his eyes to blur. He removed his coat and loosened his tie. *Fatzinger says she's wealthy, but how would he know* her *from a meat-packer's daughter?* . . . Jennifer Adrienne Figge, seventeen, Caucasian, slight build, light-brown hair, brown eyes, strawberry birthmark on left-front clavicle about one-quarter inch from deltoid. Figge. . . . Last seen wearing beige silk dress with light-blue fleurs-de-lis print, beige chapeau with light-blue veil. Figge. . . . Figge. . . . Disappearance estimated somewhere between City Line Avenue and Broad Street, presumably along Fifty-fourth Street. *Christ, that's at least seven miles, and they presume it's* my *precinct?* . . . Figge. Disappearance reported by: Hubert W. Dunsmore, coachman . . . coachman? Now how the hell did *he* know about a birthmark on her clavicle? Figge . . . Figge . . . Figge Farms, Figge Textiles, Figge Mining. . . . Good Lord, *that* Figge. This must have gone directly to City Hall. . . . Hudson swore he did not want to inherit Tolan's headaches, whatever amount of prestige might run concurrently with them. Lester Figge was a known power in the ruling class. A well-known power.

As he rubbed his temples, a round of laughter exploded in the area near the main doorway. Stanley Butterfield, his thick glasses perched atop a heavily plastered nose, waddled through the anteroom, led by the prissy Richard Cooper. Hudson looked up and grinned with satisfaction at what he'd done the night before. As Cooper stepped into Hudson's office, Butterfield kept his distance, lingering in the doorway.

"Speak up, Stanley," said Hudson. "I want to make sure it's really broken and not just another Patricia Madigan case. How did she put it? 'Nah, it was just busted.' I think those were her words. Right, Stanley?"

"I believe," stated Cooper, "that the profoundly nasal tonal quality and the discoloration under his eyes would indicate that my client's nose is indeed fractured."

Hudson nodded through spasms of laughter.

"I'm gonna zue yer azz off fer thiz, Hudsod. Dell 'im, Coober," shouted Butterfield. "You'll be bag t' walkin' a bead in zum nigger zeckshun bevor we're done with you."

"Oh, come on, Stanley. Since when do you sue a guy for punching you in the nose? Where's your pride?" Hudson's laughter was abating slowly. "You can't be serious."

Cooper sat down, crossed his fingers slowly and traded sickly smiles with Butterfield. "*We* have a roomful of my client's colleagues as witnesses to testify that you entered the tavern, found poor Mr. Butterfield, heaped verbal abuse upon him, and finally assaulted him."

Hudson sat back in his chair and gritted his teeth for a moment; then he turned to Butterfield.

"Why, you lying sack of snakeshit."

"Thad'z id! Thad'z whad he called me, Coober. Dake thad word down!"

At that moment Fatzinger, having heard Butterfield's howls, reappeared. "Vot's goin' on, Lootenant?" Hudson shooed him away toward the back room and got out of the chair to pace around, contemplating happy ways of handling Cooper and Butterfield.

"So that's how it is, boys. The newspaper crowd wants to show its solidarity."

"Actually, Lieutenant Hudson," Cooper responded with undisguised smugness, "we had considered a more grievous possibility. In light of your experience as a professional pugilist, three years as a walterweight—"

"Welterweight," Hudson corrected, though he knew the error was probably deliberate.

"Yes, a welterweight. A contender some years ago. I'm sure you realize we could make this a more serious charge, assault with a deadly weapon, say? To wit, your hand?"

"I see."

"But," continued Cooper, glancing again at Butterfield, "my client decided otherwise in view of the untimely passing of Captain Tolan. Clearly, Mr. Butterfield's magnanimity in this matter is most commendable."

"What am I supposed to do now? Kiss his foot?"

"Lieutenant Hudson," Cooper retorted, "we are not disposed to entertaining vulgarity, however desperate your state of affairs may be." Cooper was halfway out of his chair with moral severity.

Butterfield quickly seized upon his moment. "Thad'z all righd, Counzelor. The loodenand cand helb the way he dalkz."

"Yes, he can, Mr. Butterfield, yes, he can." Cooper clung fast to his angry god pose, his face flush with piety and concern. Hudson remained silent, folding his arms and sitting on the edge of his desk, waiting for the overrehearsed dialogue to burn itself out.

The storm had suddenly resumed, and irregular sheets of water now ran heavily down the surface of the tall front window. The soft, steady patter of the rain induced a deceptively tranquil atmosphere.

"All right," said Hudson with a grin, "so I don't have to kiss his foot. Where exactly *do* I have to kiss him?"

"Your levity continues to be inappropriate, Lieutenant Hudson."

"Go on, Coober," Butterfield chimed in ill-advisedly, "dell 'im where he's zuppozed d' gizz me. Hah!"

Cooper glanced sharply in the direction of Butterfield. "Lieutenant Hudson, do you think the door might be better left closed at this juncture? We seem to have drawn an audience." A crowd of patrolmen and clerical workers stood in the doorway.

Hudson again tapped idly on the surface of his desk. "No, I don't, Mr. Cooper. Leave it open. I can appreciate an audience as much as you do."

A clap of thunder rocked the room, but Butterfield did not hear it. His ambitions had soared high above the storm clouds. "I'b glad do hear thad, Hudsod. Dell 'im aboud our combromize, Coober. Go on, dell 'im."

"Compromise?" Hudson's fingers were still tapping.

Cooper's sanctimonious stare melted into his more familiar mealy smile. "Er, what my client is referring to is something of a variation upon the customary out-of-court settlement?"

"Well," said Hudson as he winked at a pretty stenographer, "at least that establishes the probable place and nature of the kiss."

She blushed and drifted away discreetly. He was getting anxious to return to his missing persons form; strangely enough, the business-as-usual had become attractive.

"All we want is an apology, Lieutenant," said Cooper.

"An apology. . . . " Hudson chuckled sarcastically.

"Yes, an apology. Is that so unreasonable?"

Hudson surveyed the audience and sighed. "I think I've had enough of this crap, Cooper. You'll get no apology from me or from anyone else in my precinct."

Cooper blanched. Butterfield's plastered nose twitched, and he had to adjust his glasses hastily. "You'll be zorry, Hudsod. Remember, we gabe you your chanz for an easy oud."

"Butterfield," said Hudson, pointing toward Stanley's nose with a letter opener. "if that ever heals, you'd better keep the patch on anyway. Because if it comes off and I see it, I'll break it again, and again and again. In fact, Butterfield, you'll never know what it felt like *not* to have a broken nose. Compared to you, a bulldog might consider itself John Drew."

Stanley slithered into a corner of the small office and eyed his attorney with stupid helplessness.

Cooper leaped out of his chair. "That's harassment!"

"How true, Mr. Cooper," said Hudson. "You're very perceptive."

"How can a police officer manifest such contempt for the law?" sputtered Cooper.

Hudson placed the letter opener on his desk and folded his arms. "I was sure you'd appreciate that, Mr. Cooper. It's something of a variation upon the Prometheus legend. Did you notice?"

Cooper's frustration was so complete that his lips had turned white. "Come along, Mr. Butterfield. We've matters to attend to. Obviously the lieutenant doesn't understand us."

"Oh, I understand you, Cooper. You're about as subtle as a cess pool. You'd like to dupe me into discrediting myself in public. You're feeling me out since you no longer have to deal with Captain Tolan."

Hudson contemplated a timely afterthought. "I now consider it my sacred duty to his memory that the Madigan incident not become clouded by your cheap manipulations. In fine, Mr. Cooper, *your* nose isn't untouchable either."

While Cooper's mouth dropped and his glasses fogged, another thunderclap rumbled through the neighborhood. Butterfield, finding it impossible to sink into the wall, inched closer to his attorney and poked him in the ribs. "Ledz go, Coober."

Cooper did his best to remain above it all, but in his haste he mishandled his overstuffed brief case. Its contents spilled across the floor. Hudson and the audience were particularly overjoyed at the sight of several very official-looking documents near a heavily-used spittoon.

"C'bon, Coober, you're maiging a vool of yourzelv!"

"Shut up, you fat incompetent, and help me!"

"I'b nod pudding my hands in that for anyone?"

"Then pick up my papers—the *dry* ones, you moron!"

"Thad'z id!" said Butterfield with finality. "I don'd have do dake thad. I'll vind a lawyer who don'd gall a guy names." With that he scurried toward the doorway.

Hudson, tears of laughter staining his tie, interrupted Butterfield's progress. "I hear the great frontier is starving for professional men like you. Maybe you'll be welcome in Butte, Montana. . . . The train leaves in an hour."

Butterfield proceeded like a chastised dog out the door and stepped into the storm, glancing over his shoulder at the grins of his auditors and relieved to be rid of his bumbling solicitor.

Hudson aided in the efforts to collect Cooper's papers and filed them neatly, if haphazardly, in the briefcase.

"I'm just trying to speed you on your way. We have more serious work to get done."

Cooper paused in his efforts to pick up his glasses. "You mean, like hanging suspects?"

Hudson spoke into the silence, following another thunderclap. "No, like checking out people who bribe and otherwise tamper with witnesses."

"You have no hard evidence to prove that, Lieutenant. You may be able to use that pack of fools on Butterfield, but not on me."

"Maybe not, Mr. Cooper," said Hudson, tapping again on his desk, "but we'll get you anyway, on something. We'll consider you our comic relief around here. Now get out."

Cooper bit his lip and summoned as much defiance as remained in him.

"You don't need any more comic relief around here, Hudson. You already have all the clowns in the police department."

Hudson gripped the sides of his desk just to be sure his hands were employed. "Clowns?" he seethed. "Cooper, it was precisely the use of that word that got your client's nose broken in the first place. Remember? . . . You've got ten seconds to hit the road."

With that Hudson started to count. Cooper grabbed for his briefcase. He watched the lawyer trotting out through the main office, and memories of Butterfield's cheesy journalism fluttered through his brain. *Justice is served in many strange ways,* he thought. Old Regis would be proud of him perhaps.

He called for Fatzinger, who reported in with a mouthful of cream cheese, liverwurst, and dark bread. "Bones, old boy, do you still want to become a detective?"

Fatzinger struggled to gulp down his food and nodded anxiously. "Dot's vott I chust told you, by Christ!"

"Good man. I like the self-assuredness in your voice." Fatzinger beamed proudly, his big red ears framing his face like the wingspan of a great bird. Hudson patted him on the shoulder. "Well, Bones, I have a little assignment for you, something to test your common sense and perseverance."

"Cheesuss. . . . " Fatzinger's tone was one of awesome discovery.

"I want you to be the tail on that lawyer who just left. You don't have to report every little thing he does, but be on the lookout for any infractions he may commit. Even if he just forgets to button his fly in public, I want you there to book him. Understand?"

"Yeah, fer anything I should book him."

"Right."

Fatzinger looked perplexed for a moment. "But, Lootenant, it's shtill rainin' oudt!"

"Get going, Bones, or you'll lose him."

"Vell . . . hokay," he said, taking another bite of his sandwich, "but I ain't sure I know vott he looks like."

"It's easy. He's carrying a briefcase and wearing a red-and-white-striped jacket, and thick glasses." Hudson's expression was triumphant. "Oh, yeah, you'll have to take your daisy off. You don't want to appear too conspicuous."

"Dot's right," Fatzinger thought aloud. He stuffed the sandwich into his mouth and fumbled with his artificial flower for a moment, then removed the sandwich to voice a very serious concern. "Don't I gotta get oudt of uniform? Like a plainclothesman I should dress up, huh?"

"Fatzinger, if you lose him, believe me, you'll never make detective."

"Oh . . . vell, hokay, Lootenant," agreed Fatzinger. "I'll catch dott horse's neck or my name ain't Wilmer P. Fatzinger, by Cheesuss!" He threw on his helmet, gulped down his sandwich, and dashed off, the sunflower still pinned to his uniform. Vaudeville, thought Hudson, would appreciate a team like Cooper and Bones.

The storm waned as the afternoon grew older. Hudson passed the next hour going over the Figge disappearance. Someone would have to talk with the coachman. Someone would have to get a quick profile of the girl. The area would have to be combed. He wished to heaven the city would give the department more telephones. And he wished that Lou James had flunked his physical for the Marines. At the end of the hour he wished he hadn't given Fatzinger his lunch.

He sent a patrolman for Andrew Sutton. Since Miss Figge was a debutante, Sutton would no doubt have her photograph, probably a tintype, in his files. Something else about her rang a distant bell.

Figge . . . what a silly name. They're usually silly names when one thinks about it, the rich, the golden. Bottomley, DePugh, Griswold, Smoot. . . . Not really dignified as a rule. You could laugh at them if you didn't know the power behind them. Like Borgia or de Medici. . . . Figge. . . . Two syllables. Not fig. Rhymes with Biggie. . . . He hated the rich. *Hated* them. Pampered-assed-knaves and harlots, and he needed no goddamn European intellectual to teach him that. . . . He liked the Sink. Really. The bums and winos were forthright; their survival gut-level, the exploitation less subtle.

McBride would probably like this case. Probably knock off a little plutocratic ass in the process. Maybe not. Lou James for certain, but maybe not McBride. They'd find something quaintly barbarous in James. McBride would be too deferential. . . . *Someone's probably dallying with Miss Figge right now, so she faked a kidnapping to add to the excitement. They're like that.*

Goddammit, he knew her from somewhere or other. A tintype's no good. We need to know about her moles and pockmarks. The rich must have them, too.

"You look as if someone's gotten into your bottle of whiskey again, Lieutenant." McBride woke him from his bitter thoughts, and he was privately grateful for that.

"Oh, I'm just . . . I was just, uh, thinking about Regis," he said, knowing that would cover all other questions. The somber look on McBride's face suggested that it did. Hudson perked up, strutted around the desk to his window and looked out.

"Now say something undisturbing. I'm counting on you, McBride. Before this day is over I intend to hear something in keeping with the promises of springtime."

Nathan smiled. "I guess I'm your man after all, Lieutenant."

Hudson stared ahead, a cool breeze causing his tie to ripple. "Remains to be seen, kid. Continue."

"I went out to Grundy's Gardens, expecting a bad time, and I got it for a while." McBride brushed away the yellow mud from his shoes. After leaving the rectory, McBride had gone directly to a tavern on the assumption that, second only to the parish priest, the bartender would be the most informed man in the Patch. "I couldn't have pried information out of that man with a can opener. I think he took me for an Ulsterman."

"You do look damnably English, Nate," joked Hudson, an Episcopalian himself.

Having washed his face in a basin of cool water, Nathan told of having expected the stiff upper-lipped anticipation usually encountered in these cases. Instead, he'd found a madhouse. Number Five lay at the extreme west end of the long row of lackluster dwellings, opposite a blacksmith's shop and adjacent to a couple of burned-out wooden structures of undetermined former use. Beyond Tinker Whalen's house, nothing was occupied any longer, and looking at the muddy road as it rose up, angled slightly, and then disappeared into a valley, Nathan guessed that Number Five must be the very end of the precinct, if not the end of the earth. Another hundred yards or so, he grumbled, and the Whalen case would have been someone else's problem.

To his side of the house, however, McBride had observed a great deal of activity. As he drew nearer, he had observed small clusters of shawl-draped old women and, craning their necks over the Whalen fence, one or two older men. From the house, Tinker's bellow could be heard above Ellie's unbroken keening and the intermittent shrieks of a younger woman. Instinctively Nathan had trotted the rest of the way but was stopped at the gate by one of the older men.

"I wouldn't go in there now, lad. When the Whalens have a family spat, ye niver can tell what's goin' to fly troo the air next."

Most of the listeners had almost choked with laughter, but some of the women on the outer fringe had quickly blessed themselves.

McBride had been enjoying the three-way repartee. But he still had had to see Miss Whalen alive and well in order to close the case. He had noticed a dark-haired young man in an army private's uniform standing, as obscurely as he could make himself, on the lawn behind a small vegetable garden, and guessed that that was the Italian so volubly in question. As Nathan had stepped through the gate, the man who had spoken to him had repeated his warning and gripped his arm so firmly that Nathan had found it necessary to show his badge.

"The police, is it?" Bird backed up a step or two. "Arragh, do ye mean they heard 'im all the way up the hill?"

"Cease yer prate," Mrs. Muldowney carped. "The police don't give a damn about the nize in Grundy's Patch. He's here for the girl, ye selly auld craycher."

"That's right, ma'am," McBride had said, gently inching toward the front door. "And I'm glad to see she's back."

"I still wouldn't go in there if I was you, lad," Bird had said once again.

Inside, Tinker could be heard shouting, "An Eye*talian* yet! Missus Pamphilio Di Ciori! My own dear Katie! Ah, Musha, what kind of a name is that to raise kids with?"

McBride had glanced at the young soldier, who had kept his arms folded and stared inscrutably at the ground.

"In my condition it coulda been a *Hindu* for all I care now!" Katie had screeched back, and Ellie's howls had grown louder. McBride had drawn a deep breath.

"Ye'd know it'd come to this in time," Bird had said philosophically.

"Ah sure," Mrs. Muldowney had answered. "Didn't she ayven do it with Mountain Fitzgerald, an' him a half-wit?"

McBride had let the air out slowly and opened the door, feeling something like a knight entering the dragon's mouth. A sudden hush had fallen over the household. Ellie had reached into her apron for her rosary beads and made for the outhouse, where she had resumed her keening. . . .

"That's a damn good brogue you have, Nate." Hudson obviously appreciated the tale.

"For an 'almost Englishman,'" McBride added. He was pleased to have cheered Hudson out of his doldrums. Then he started toward his desk to type up the report. Something suddenly occurred to him. "He was genuinely happy, you know."

"Who? Whalen?"

"Whalen. Beneath it all, he was immensely relieved. So were his sons. Sooner or later they'll all calm down."

"Yeah, but poor Private Di Ciori. If he's smart, he'll stay in Puerto Rico. I'd rather be a duck-billed platypus than an alien in that bunch."

Andrew Sutton arrived, toting a large portfolio. Hudson dismissed the patrolman who had escorted Sutton and realized that he'd neglected to specify which debutante concerned him when he'd sent for the files. As he opened the portfolio and aligned the stack of tintypes neatly on Hudson's desk, Sutton apologized for his tardiness, explaining that his wife had been ill of late and hence he was somewhat disorganized. Hudson could not help noticing the perfectly manicured fingernails and immaculate white cuffs which protruded from the arms of his well-tailored dress jacket.

"I just need one picture, Mr. Sutton," said Hudson with some embarrassment. "The girl's name is Jennifer Figge." Sutton's grooming conjured images of homes designed by Wheelock and Clay.

McBride's typewriter, never without malfunctions, became particularly aggravating in damp weather. His work slowed down in time for him to hear the missing girl's name. Sutton had, as was his practice, arranged the portraits in alphabetical order and, in a flourish, picked out that of Miss Figge. Hudson, almost against his nature, studied it admiringly; she was, under Sutton's skillful retouching, a vision of aristocratic loveliness—dreamy, almost celestial.

"Very lovely," he said, and Sutton agreed, both of them slightly above a whisper.

"But it's not the girl, Mr. Sutton. Her description says light-brown hair."

"Oh, yes," Sutton replied in his soft drawl, "that's a new pigment I've just started to use. It's quite effective, isn't it, Lieutenant? Notice the highlights. Very understated."

"It's very effective, Mr. Sutton"—Hudson sighed—"but I can't find Miss Figge from this picture."

McBride drifted closer to Hudson's desk, leaving his report at the third line. Hands in his pockets, he looked over Hudson's shoulder at the tintypes.

"I'm sorry to hear that, Lieutenant," said Andrew Sutton.

"What is your trouble, McBride?" asked Hudson, a bit irritated by the intrusion.

"Oh?" McBride blushed. "Well, the girl's name is Whalen, and I have no capital *W* on my typewriter anymore. The *H* sticks, and I haven't had an *L* since February."

"Just as long as you have an *F*. I'm putting you on another missing persons."

"Lieutenant," protested McBride, his tired feet nagging him. "One a day is an honest man's labor."

"That it is, Nate," said Hudson, handing the folder over.

Nathan looked at Andrew Sutton, who smiled back vacantly. He thought about the commission awaiting a college graduate, were he to enlist in the Army. Then he remembered the name. "Figge," he said, gesturing toward the folder, "I know who she is."

"I do, too," said Hudson, "but how about reminding me anyway?"

McBride sat down on a three-legged stool. "Do you remember a suffragette march last fall? We had to put extra patrolmen on the day shift because City Hall expected trouble. Very peaceful except for one incident, a girl who threw a rock at one of our men. You remember now? She missed and hit an old man instead. And when we brought her in, we decided to book her for obscene language and gestures, too."

"All covered up by headquarters. I remember it."

"Right. And it never made the newspapers either. As I understand it, Lester Figge has a large interest in all of them. Perhaps even control."

Hudson snapped his fingers. "It went even further. The suffragette ladies got madder than hornets because the papers refused to write up the incident. They thought they had a potential martyr issue. They even pleaded with the old man to press charges."

"But his family was bought off," said McBride. "It must have been some payment, too, because he almost lost the sight in one eye. So the suffragettes raised Cain about the papers for a while, but they were soon silenced. Another payment, I suppose." McBride's curiosity was suddenly piqued. He started to glance over the neatly prepared report.

"Then that rash of burglaries in November made us lose track of the whole Figge affair." Hudson scratched his ear for a moment. "We should have a file on her somewhere."

McBride shook his head. "It went down to City Hall and undoubtedly got misplaced."

Hudson turned to Andrew Sutton. "But we must have taken a mug shot, didn't we?"

Sutton shrugged his shoulders. "If I did, Lieutenant, I'm sure I'd remember. I never forget a face I've photographed. It must have been some other photographer in your employ."

"Are you sure, Mr. Sutton?" McBride knew when he looked into Sutton's frigid eyes that his tone implied suspicion.

Sutton shifted his gaze to Hudson after a moment of silence. "Lieutenant Hudson, I'm sure you realize, or at least you *should* realize, that my work for the city is only part of my overall practice. For a considerable time now, certainly well prior to last autumn, other people have been taking your mug shots. I am now engaged principally in your more serious affairs, such as photographing scenes and victims of homicide. For which, I might add, Dr. Blakeley pays me twice what the department does."

Officer Novak entered and placed another folder on Hudson's desk, the report on the deaths of Fred Bowman and his mother.

"Mr. Sutton," said McBride lamely, "I didn't mean to imply—"

"You may keep the tintype, Lieutenant Hudson," said Andrew Sutton as he quickly gathered the remaining pictures and replaced them in his large portfolio. His face was flushed with repressed turmoil. Clearly Sutton had nothing to say to McBride; diplomacy was left in Hudson's unfamiliar lap.

"Mr. Sutton, on behalf of this precinct—"

"Good evening, gentlemen," said Sutton as he picked his hat from a clothes tree and went his angry way, settling the matter abruptly.

McBride waited for the front door to slam. It closed with a crisp, rather military click. He awaited a sample of Hudson's famous broadsides. When that did not come, he decided to say something before his mouth became too dry to do so. "Lieutenant, I, uh, I'm. . . ."

"Oh, for just a tiny helping of that man's ego," said Hudson cryptically. "Have you ever in your life felt so awkward, Nate?"

"Pardon?"

Hudson got up and again surveyed the greenery outside the station. A blue jay fluttered busily about a hollow spot where the limb had been broken from the ancient apple tree by a December ice storm. He hoped the bird would nest there. "He has such a way of telling you off, that Sutton."

"Oh, I don't know, Lieutenant," said McBride, his own ego now experiencing a delayed reaction. "He seemed rather childish to me. We wouldn't play his way, so he took all his toys and ran home."

"To hell with him. He was stewing when he came in here. We were okay when he came up from Baltimore without a pot to piss in. Hey, take a look at that beautiful bluebird out there. Maybe he'll stick around. What the hell, he could choose less distinguished neighbors."

McBride, relieved at Hudson's laconic mood, went through the motions of admiring the bird. "Looks much better in blue than Fatzinger."

Hudson nodded and leaned against the window. "Didn't have a dime. Great reputation but debts up to his navel. He and his wife must have tried to buy out the whole South, and rumor has it, he arrived in Philadelphia just ahead of the sheriff. It was Regis who got him started here, with a recommendation from Dr. Blakeley."

"Human nature, Lieutenant. Our appearance brings back memories."

Hudson crossed over to his desk and picked up the tintype. "And speaking of memories, I'm almost *sure* that bastard took the mug shot. He was there expecting something prize winning to happen, and when they brought in the girl, calling us every foul name in the book, he was right behind them."

"Why would he deny that?"

"I have no idea, but I don't want you to overlook him."

"Lieutenant. . . ." Nathan wondered if he should take the next step. "I know this case is important, and I also know we're short of men."

"Go on." Hudson's face was indecipherable.

"Well, if it's all the same to you, I'd like to get cleaned up and pay my respects, very briefly, to Captain Tolan's family. I'll have the men comb the area and get started on the case in the morning. Devon's a long way from here, and I couldn't get much done tonight anyway."

Hudson looked somewhat torn between sentiments. "You're

probably right, Nate. It's really my case anyway. But if we lose this one, there'll be hell to pay."

At length he put his hand on Nathan's shoulder. "The viewing is at his home. You know how to find it?"

"I have the directions. Corner of Hopewood and Merion."

"Okay, Nate," he said, overlooking the Bowman report to stare at the lovely tintype. "I'll see you there later. Send Curran in on your way out."

Nine

Max Toberman was still unsettled, though the greater part of a day had passed since Fred Bowman had threatened to upset his entire scheme.

The nature of his work always forced him to employ humanity's errors, perverts like Vincent and Arthur and half-wits like poor Fred. In the end having to rely on such creatures always rendered his position insecure. He fully realized that sooner or later the other two, like Fred, would have to be disposed of. It was both frightening and demeaning to be forced into such abominable associations.

He now called himself Max Toberman. Circumstances had been the same in Austria and later in England, and in both instances he had barely eluded the authorities. The percentages were not in his favor the third time around. He did not want to have to abandon his research and his equipment and to change his name again. It had taken too long to reestablish himself this time. He was too close to completing his research now to permit the dregs of the world to jeopardize it.

He tapped an exotic cigarette on his desk, wondering. Could he trust Vincent not to bungle it this time or would Arthur and the fat man decide to do things *their* way again? He was convinced that it was Arthur who had engineered the entire performance of last evening. Arthur had grown weary of Fred; that was obvious if one understood the twisted Arthur: Fred was no longer amusing.

Totally aware of Fred's morbid fascination with the contents, Vincent chose to look the other way, allowing the little moron to abscond with the parcel. That meant Toberman's having to involve himself—because Arthur was conveniently opiated—in affairs that were more properly delegated to Vincent and his ilk: brutal, messy matters.

It gave Toberman the chills to think of it. Vincent had seemed to *enjoy* his labors so. The club across the defiant old woman's face after she had spat at him, Fred's pitiful groveling. . . . Someday the fat man would turn on Toberman, in a fit of excitement or, more probably, at Arthur's instigation. Theirs was an odd love-hate relationship.

Toberman hated Arthur even more. Pale, effeminate, disdainful Arthur, the perfect voyeur with a flair for the dramatic, made Toberman truly uncomfortable. Arthur would overturn the boat in time . . . given time.

Snuffing out his cigarette, he summoned his nurse. "Get me Mr. Hartleigh."

"I believe Mr. Hartleigh is"—she fished for a word—"preoccupied."

Toberman removed his glasses and rubbed his eyes. "Get him anyway."

She curtsied hesitantly and went off to Arthur Hartleigh's room. In the time that Arthur had been there, as a live-in patient so to speak, the nurse had obviously not got used to him.

Toberman thumbed through his latest case study and placed it securely in his wall safe. The files were swollen, reminding him of how much had been accomplished during the past year. Awaiting Arthur, who would surely waste as much time as possible before coming down, he rearranged the studies into alphabetical rather than chronological order and set aside the last ten for further study. As he closed the safe, he poured himself a glass of brandy, and sat at his desk.

"You might offer me some of that." Arthur Hartleigh entered, dressed in a smoking jacket and slippers. Toberman could assess the dilation of his pupils from across the room.

"I haven't asked you here for social purposes."

"That's too bad." Arthur yawned. "I'm in a rather sociable mood."

In his middle thirties, Arthur had the constitution of a man over sixty. Facial eruptions, dozens of them, bespoke the chemical factions doing battle deep within him.

"Sit down, Arthur. I've only a moment to spare."

"You're very splenetic."

It always annoyed Toberman that both Arthur and Vincent always simply took his expensive cigarettes. Both had long forgotten that they were in his employ. "You've drugged yourself again when I need you."

"It stimulates my imagination. You ought to try it yourself." He struck a match, holding his little finger some distance from the flame, and inhaled deeply. "These cigarettes are vile," he pronounced. "Their odor pollutes the air."

"You'll never be able to assist Vincent this evening."

"Don't be a silly boy." Arthur laughed. "It's a very simple matter."

"That's my point exactly, Arthur. I wish it to remain a simple matter."

Arthur sat back and blew a large puff of smoke into the air. For a time the only sound in the office was the ticking of a clock near the door.

"Vincent and I should know how to take care of your affairs by now, Dr. Toberman," he said finally. "We are, after all, quite experienced at our trade."

"I want no improvising, Arthur," Toberman said firmly. "You are to dispose of the parcels as I've instructed you."

From the start Toberman had fed him, clothed him, kept him in opiates, even permitted him to bring in Fred Bowman as his plaything, merely because he was the sort needed to procure specimens. He had been derelict in that regard as well. And now this ingratitude.

"Arthur," he said in a tenuously controlled voice, "have you ever seen your fellow grotesques after the drugs are no longer available to them? Have you ever seen them writhing, alternately burning up and freezing, their mouths parched like salt beds, their skin crawling as if beset by cannibal ants, gushing from every orifice and begging for death? Have you?"

A nervous tic appeared in the corner of Arthur's mouth. He appeared to have some trouble placing the cigarette between his lips. "I . . . I've heard such tales," he muttered.

"They are not fables, my friend." Toberman selected another cigarette. "I can prove that to you if you wish."

Arthur was silent; he wrung his hands and mused. "Your Judas goat leading the pitiable samples of nature to your laboratory, your fat assassin, your test tubes and case study forms—it's all very crisp and scholarly for you, isn't it? But you have your fun after all, I'll bet."

Toberman thought for a moment.

"To be sure, Arthur. To be sure." He lit his cigarette. "You'd better get dressed. Vincent will be here presently, and he shall require your assistance."

The War Department, wrestling with the problem of preparing for war after the war had begun, and slightly troubled by the Surgeon General's report that one-third to one-half of the American troops would probably die of yellow fever if landed on Cuban soil during the summer, had decided upon a deliberate, if ingenuous, plan of campaign. What had been rumored for weeks had been confirmed by a spokesman for General Nelson A. Miles: First, Puerto Rico would be taken; secondly, a force of of regulars would land at the eastern end of Cuba to organize the insurgents and assist in their efforts against the Spanish; finally, when the American Army was fully prepared, a frontal assault would be made on Havana.

The plan was not entirely without merit; the capture of Puerto Rico could be executed with little risk, and the ambitions of the native Cubans for independence guaranteed their good faith. General Shafter, however, had found his volunteer army as sluggish and unwieldy in the Florida heat as his own three-hundred-pound frame. The inadequate port facilities and lack of a well-planned highway system in the Tampa Bay area, plus the absence of professional officers, had rendered the massive force hopelessly behind schedule. General Miles was en route South to give the matter his personal attention.

The Reverend Richard T. Hopkins, now free of the irritating Whittingham affair, joined others of his calling in railing from the pulpit against the Papist menace in the hemisphere. Before a gathering of two hundred severely righteous men, women, and children, he described in horrifying detail the imminent vision of Pope Leo XIII and his cloven herd assuming control of Washington. Borrowing freely from Dante and using generous portions of Increase Mather, he described the desecration of our national shrines and monuments and the substitutions of icons, saints' bones, and decadent art, the death of the English language and the forced rebirth of Latin, the baronial privilege of cowled monks in the deflowering of

American virgins, the conscription of firstborn sons into the Roman priesthood, and the transformation of patriotic societies into convents wherein young women were to be trained in all the lecherous arts to gratify foreign churchmen. He reached his peak by exhorting his congregation to give liberal sums for the conversion of the childlike natives of Cuba and other subjects of the soon-to-be-vanquished Vatican hordes at our doorstep. Lest the message be taken lightly, he concluded with images of the burning of Protestant ministers and officers of the Daughters of the American Revolution for heresy. As in his past two sermons, the Reverend Hopkins collected more than six hundred dollars with pledges of more than one thousand more. A limp Mrs. Whittingham, supporting herself on her daughter Betsy's arm, left before the service was over, but those who remained were treated to ham and baked beans.

The headlines on the evening paper dealt with the war, and the Reverend Hopkins' sermon, along with others of like nature, was mentioned on page five. Much of the second half of page one, however, was devoted to the disappearance of Jennifer Adrienne Figge. After her description, a brief biography, and mention of her possible whereabouts, the story announced the offer of a substantial reward for pertinent information. Affixed to all that was a lengthy report on the arrest and subsequent suicide of Piggy Spaganoli and a tirade against the gross incompetence of the police department.

The rains had flooded the small streams running parallel to the tracks, and the Seashore Express was even tardier than usual. From his private coach Lester Figge glared at the hedgerows and white picket fences which curlicued the rolling New Jersey countryside and grunted something to the effect that *his* railroads tolerated no such interference. Julia Abernathy Figge, her ankles propped upon a hassock after several days in the hot sand had swollen them, motioned to the valet to refill Mr. Figge's gin and quinine water.

A seizure more than a decade ago had left Lester Figge with an eerie trademark: his face had frozen into a cocksure smile, and only the inflection of his voice suggested anything of his prevailing humor. To strangers he remained untranslatable, sinister, even on those rare occasions when he wished not to be. After an interminable series of tests, thousands of dollars in medications, and one painful effort at surgery, the greatest medical talents of two continents had thrown up their hands in defeat. And so Lester Figge had grown accustomed to his embarrassment. Sometimes he even enjoyed the way the impenetrable stare affected his competitors.

He accepted the drink with a surreptitious nod and another grunt and continued to gaze out the window. The countryside gave way gradually to the outskirts of Camden; red-brick industrial buildings, their faces blackened by smoke from an endless stream of locomotives, stood like rotting teeth in the twilight. He watched as the buildings closed in and floated by, obscuring the horizon for a moment until the train climbed over the city to traverse the Delaware. Drops of gin and a twist of lime splashed over his silken vest, but he ignored the obsequious Oriental valet and opted instead to follow the progress of a distant three-masted schooner far below as the coach shivered on the long, narrow bridge. His attention shifted to a tugboat making its way through a muddy channel with a chain of anthracite barges astern. His spirits quickly improved. The war had brought favorable times to the coal market.

Alighting from his coach at Suburban Terminal, he was taken aside by a very nervous aide and notified of his daughter's disappearance. When questioned why a day had passed, the aide mumbled something feebly about his having hoped to get the matter settled on his own, that Miss Figge had been his responsibility, that he'd wished to spare Mr. Figge a lot of unnecessary worry. His voice trailed off as Lester Figge, glancing over his shoulder at the approaching Julia, signaled him to remain silent.

Julia, exhausted by the journey, drifted off to sleep shortly after leaving the noise of the city; however, she would probably retire at once and sleep soundly until morning. He draped his coat over his shoulders to ward off the chilly drafts finding their way through the carriage floor. Now and then he would turn, after listening to Julia's soft, peaceful breathing, and study her for a time. Jennifer had done well in the luck of the genetic draw. She had Julia's high cheekbones and small frame; both looked forever as if they'd just smelled something foul. Aristocratic from their proud, thin waists to their long, tapering fingertips, they sometimes reminded him of figures out of a medieval romance. But the similarities ended there; instead of Julia's flowery nature, Jennifer had all his own damn-it-to-hell and more. That was precisely why he felt more deeply for her than for anyone or anything else in his big, avaricious world.

When his four-horse carriage rumbled under the archway and

pulled up after completing the half-circle to his front door, another two hours had gone by and night had begun to fall.

That evening, when he kissed Julia good-night—she had supped lightly with him after all—Lester Figge experienced an odd feeling of tenderness, and he wondered in passing if Julia shared it. When she was comfortably settled, he retired to his study to consider the welter of possible answers to Jennifer's most recent adventure. He ordered a cup of hot tea and perused her diary, searching for names or other clues. Probably she was well aware of his access to it and too cunning ever to put in anything very substantial. Nothing but gingerbread pronouncements on fashions, schoolwork, high school proms, holidays. . . .

Principally he believed it a hoax, another one of Jennifer's many attention-getting maneuvers: well-feigned illnesses when she'd neglected to do her hated math assignments, prolonged bouts of adolescent melancholia that used to throw Julia into fits of despair.

The moonlight which spilled through the broad window behind him was vivid for a change, and the massive reproduction of the Bayeux Tapestry encircling the room was more starkly brutal than usual. His mind wandered from Jennifer's picture, painted last summer in Rome, to flashes of his most determined enemies, which he summarily dismissed and thence to the richly colored figures on the wall. He found himself focusing on the awesome Norman knights, riveted to their armor-plated steeds, and on the smaller Saxons at ground level, writhing in pain on the tips of the long Norman lances. He felt a sudden twinge of queasiness in his stomach, a sensation he was loath to acknowledge, and rang impatiently for another cup of tea. Three bells meant tea. He rang a fourth to amend the order to gin.

He got up and crossed to a small table between a bookcase and an easy chair and picked up an old gilded photograph. Three smiling children dressed in Sunday clothing were posed against a background of a lake and a hillside of pine trees. A note at the bottom read "Forest Haven, 1888." That summer, as he was convalescing in the central Jersey place after his surgery. . . . The two boys, uncomplicated Lothar and the incurably restless Leyland, had since gone their ways for a while: Lothar to Idaho to run the Figge lignite mines, Leyland to travel the Continent with his latest passion, the Romanian countess who admired his paintings. Then there was Jennifer. . . . While Lothar stood at attention with passive dullness and Leyland puffed out his chest with heroic determination, the little girl extended a defiant tongue toward the camera. Julia had wanted the photograph destroyed or at least locked away in a safe with the other family secrets. Lester Figge would have none of it. The picture was granted an expensive frame and given a place of honor in the room where he did his most important thinking.

The valet entered, somewhat haggard from the pressures of close confinement with Mr. Figge for the last few days, and set the gin and quinine on the table. Lester Figge hated the little bastard. Couldn't stand any Oriental. Hated their mincing ways. Sneaky little devils, especially this one. Never looked the master in the face. He picked up his gin, failing to notice the valet's sudden attention. Something was happening outside.

He bade the valet good evening and, in an effort to appear occupied, scooped up the evening newspaper. But the valet, his overly ingratiating smile never fading, drifted behind the desk and peered out, straining to see through the clump of dogwood that shaded the far reaches of the estate.

"What is it, Eng?"

"It look like fiah, Mr. Figge."

"*What* the hell . . . ?" He put his glass down and rushed to the window. Off in the distance, where the trees were densest, a small flame danced in the breeze.

"Maybe only bonfiah," suggested the valet.

"Bonfire, my ass! That's down at the stable."

He fled the room and in a matter of seconds had run down the stairway and out the door. The valet observed the gin and quinine still untouched and, with an acrid giggle, sipped it delicately. Behind Figge, doors along the hallway opened with uncertainty in response to his heavy footsteps. Slowly the servants gathered and followed, but with considerably more deference to the shrubbery than their master displayed.

Figge ran across the gravel drive and through the ornate patterns of Julia's prized white rosebushes. He struggled over the soggy knoll behind the bridle path and shortcut his way through the woods.

Ten minutes passed before the servants reached the stable and found the master. Near the trough, between a hitching post and the fence which surrounded the yard and a large haystack, he stood like one petrified.

The flames from a torch flickered in heavy ripples, throwing black curls of pitchblende smoke into the moonlight and seeming to make the head of Jennifer Figge blush. Firmly impaled on a tall shaft, it stared with openmouthed surprise.

The Five Sorrowful Mysteries droned on, led by the diminutive white-thatched priest who knelt at the casket. The steady stream of gawky mourners, who had moped through the front room where Regis Tolan lay in state, had broken file and taken to various crannies at the start of the benediction. During the eulogy the police had followed pickpocket Felix Wellington with their eyes as he moved about the periphery of the crowd until at length he'd found a space to kneel with both hands in plain view.

The gathering was rather a social crazy quilt. Nearer the casket were Maggie and the children—minus Father Kevin, who was doing missionary service in China, and minus Kathleen, whose cloistered order would not permit her to leave. Behind them, some fingering rosaries, others staring with quiet reverence, were Tolan's closest relatives and friends. Most evident among the latter were the fire marshal, Congressman Garvey, an Italian grocer, the president of the Ancient Order of Hibernians, a German beer distributor, and Ian and Sophia Blakeley. The third wave consisted mainly of his fellow officers; Lou James was very impressive in his blue, cardinal, and gold Marine uniform. On the fringe were faces familiar only to the police, people like Wellington, whose grief was equal to the sincerity of the others. None of them had reformed or wished to reform; they were simply reacting to the loss of an old and honorable adversary.

Nathan McBride struggled to appear absorbed in the prayers, but the young woman kneeling in the front row near Maggie had his attention. The roses and carnations decking the room made it seem to him part of her natural milieu. Would she look up, if only for a second or so, and perhaps exchange a moment of recognition? She had entered quietly, and it seemed to Nathan that she had attracted little attention other than his own. After the customary brief prayers at the coffin, she had said a few soft words to Maggie before taking her place for the rosary. Her hair, wisps of which could be seen beneath the dark-gray bonnet, made the breast of a robin seem as drab as a

November Monday, and the pink and white of her cheek brought memories of summer sunrise. He watched her as she knelt, sobbing for a moment, then drifting into feminine resignation.

"Get your eyes off her and say your prayers." Lou James nudged him on the elbow. "Besides, I saw her first."

"Yes," Nathan whispered, "but you have to go off and make the hemisphere safe for Protestantism. Who is she?"

"Aidan Tierney, the captain's favorite niece."

"Lovely name. . . . Do you know her?"

Lou nodded and looked into Nathan's uncertain smile. "Met her once, around Christmastime, I believe."

"Do you think she remembers you?"

"Of course." Lou's tone implied, good-naturedly, the silliness of the question. He paused as the little priest announced the transition from the Crowning with Thorns to the Carrying of the Cross. "I'll introduce you if you promise not to make a fool of yourself."

Both becoming aware of the Gothic expression of an old woman in the next room, affected the deepest piety as the priest intoned the Our Father. In that fashion did Nathan McBride hang mesmerized, mouthing ten Hail Marys and a Glory Be to the Father until, at last, the priest announced the fifth Sorrowful Mystery, the Crucifixion, and, ever so briefly, Miss Tierney glanced directly at him and he saw the tears. For what seemed a very long time he looked back, hoping he didn't look too dull in his rote recitation, thankful that Lou, resplendent in his new uniform, was going far away, hoping that she hadn't noticed his conversation and so thought him boorish and irreverent, wishing he'd remembered to splash on a bit of cologne or something. . . .

Then she turned away, and he fell to wondering whether the time was propitious for such an introduction. He felt his mustache wilting and his knees weakening. The warm glow from a set of votive candles nearby played delicately on her features. He forced himself to concentrate on the priest.

The ceremony ended, and those gathered rose quietly to their feet. The fringe element stole away without comment. Felix Wellington, seeing Lieutenant Hudson at the door, raised his hands to signal innocence and passed by with a wink from Hudson. In the shuffle of increasingly vocal mourners, Hudson, who had arrived late, was trying to get McBride's attention. But Lou James was already leading the somewhat passive McBride toward the kitchen for the traditional shots of whiskey. There, Lou reasoned, he could introduce Nathan to Aidan Tierney casually and effectively.

"But . . . she's not coming back *here*, Lou. The ladies will stay out in the living room."

"I know that, Nate. We're not going all the way. We'll just take our whiskey and stand in the doorway where we've a clear advantage once the crowd spreads out. I know how to stage these things. Look, there's Dr. Blakeley. Now *he's* a suave one for you."

Nathan barely noticed the neat bearded man in the blue suit and the trim, handsome woman with him though ordinarily, having heard so much of Dr. Blakeley, he'd have been anxious to meet him. "Yes, Lou, but I think your strategy is way off. She doesn't look the type to drift back toward all the drinking men."

"Sure, Nate," Lou pronounced, "go over and stand at the coffin, looking stupid and obvious. That's the way to do it."

"That isn't what I mean, Lou." James had a way of making him feel just hatched from an egg. "Maybe we'd just better forget about it."

"To thine own self be true, Nate. I'm going in for a nip."

Lou disappeared into the throng convened around the table laden with bottles of rye and pitchers of ice water. The custom of toasting the dead, which was older than mythology, had never seemed correct to Nathan, but then, he reasoned, neither was his irresistible romantic urge in the midst of a wake.

Deciding to follow Lou into the kitchen, he wended through the cigar smoke and still-subdued voices and found him at the table arguing playfully with a Navy veteran of the Civil War. The old salt was holding his own, telling Lou that the high-buttoned blue tunic made him look like a tuba player for the Salvation Army.

"See if I bring you a native girl now," answered Lou. "After that remark you'll be lucky to get a few stale cigars."

The old salt laughed and drank a toast to Lou's safe return. Nathan poured himself little more than a finger of rye, drowned it in ice water, and stood by rather listlessly. Lou noticed him and asked about his progress. Nathan shrugged.

"You know, Nate, for the precinct's coolest customer, you're looking pretty transparent right now."

"How's that, Lou?" Nathan's flat grin remained unsteady.

"You'd better get on with it soon. With a name like hers, the church will get her if you don't."

Nathan looked through the doorway. The glimpse afforded him by the milling crowd revealed her speaking with the little priest, and he didn't scoff at Lou's cynical comment. "Hmm. . . ."

"Drink up. I'll show you how a Marine liberates an island," Lou said with disturbing silkiness.

Once they were out of the kitchen, they were spied by Lieutenant Hudson, who had paused to speak with the Blakeleys.

"Miss Tierney?" Despite his choice of a questioning tone, Lou James' voice was firmly controlled. She turned, and Nathan felt certain that this all was a mistake. He now had to force himself to look directly at her; she was even more enchanting up close. In the back of his head were thoughts of Cyrano wooing Roxanne on behalf of her dull-witted suitor.

"Miss Tierney," Lou continued, "you probably don't remember me. We met last December, the day after Christmas I'm sure, at Harrison's Skating Rink. Lou James?"

Her polite smile expressed more confusion than cordiality. Nathan's reaction was one of unexpected relief; down deep he was pleased that his own Cyrano had made no profound impressions.

"Oh, yes . . . Mr. James."

"I know what the problem is, Lou." Nathan could hardly believe the sound of his own voice. He had slipped into the dialogue, and his flow of words sounded confident. "You weren't in uniform then. Miss Tierney remembers you in civilian clothes, and you were probably bundled up like a Russian at that."

"That's very true," answered Lou James. "I think I even had a scarf over my earmuffs. Right out of Currier and Ives."

"Oh, yes, of course." She smiled genuinely, apparently happy to have made the connection. "And how is Miss Peterson?"

"Miss Peterson?"

"The girl who was skating with you all afternoon."

"Miss Peterson. . . ." James made an effort to recall the name of his companion on that day. "Please forgive my thoughtlessness, Miss Tierney. This is Detective Nathan McBride of your late uncle's precinct."

Nathan reached forward and touched her hand gently. "I really wish it could have been under any other circumstances, Miss Tierney."

"Mr. McBride, I've heard quite a lot about you from my uncle. You're the one they call the Psychiatrist."

Nonplussed for the moment, he nevertheless responded, "Only in an ironic sense, Miss Tierney, I'm certain."

Lou James showed his teeth at the well-studied humility of Nathan's reply.

"Really," she went on, "he thought a great deal of you." Her eyes were not quite the blue of the sea as one might well expect. In this light they reminded him of the young woman in Chaucer's "Miller's Tale," "as black as sloes," and he liked that. "He said he was glad you'd been assigned to his precinct. He used to say it was nice to see that the Augustinians had at last gotten over Martin Luther and were producing something worthwhile for a change."

"Your uncle was a very charitable man, Miss Tierney, an unusually kind man."

Hudson and Blakeley left Sophia for the moment and came over to interrupt. After a brief exchange of amenities Hudson took Nathan aside, leaving only Blakeley to impede what Nathan presumed, ruefully, would now be Lou James' progress. But Hudson's words swung Nathan's eyes away from Aidan with astonishment.

"They found a body in Fairmount Park this evening, Nate. It looks like the Figge girl."

"Did it have a strawberry birthmark?"

"On the left front clavicle about one-quarter inch from the deltoid," recited Hudson. "It's a good thing, too, since we'd have had a helluva time identifying her without it. The body was headless."

"Good God."

"We're expecting a lot of noise out of this. The tally is now ten disappearances since last autumn, and four who've turned up mutilated since the Masterson tramp last March."

"What are we supposed to have done, Lieutenant? We can't put a tail on every potential victim in town. We're undermanned as it is."

"I know. . . I know. . . ." They stepped aside for a moment to allow the little priest to make his way into the kitchen. The sound of the men's voices dropped rather suddenly into a more somber murmur. "And I'm afraid we're going to be even more understaffed now."

"How so, Lieutenant?"

"You've heard of Dr. Ian Blakeley no doubt."

"Of course. Isn't that he chatting with Lou and Miss Tierney?"

"Well"—Hudson leaned against a grand piano that had been pulled out of the living room to make space for the casket—"City

Hall wants to make a big move to keep the papers off its back as much as possible, however embarrassing to the department. So they're bringing him into the case. Personally I don't go for it. It makes us look like a pack of dunderheads, but there it is."

Nathan looked at Dr. Blakeley and studied him cursorily. He was somewhat shorter and rounder than Nathan had pictured, but nonetheless regal. "I think I like the idea, Lieutenant. Let him go chase our monsters for us."

"There's a hitch, Nate. The commissioner, bless him, insisted that the department not be severed—please excuse my use of his words—from the case, so we're putting one man on with him. Naturally the department will make available all records, evidence, or any assistance Dr. Blakeley deems necessary. It should be interesting from here on."

"Should be." Nathan's eyes were again fixed upon Aidan Tierney.

"Good. I think it's time you two got together then."

"What?"

"Look, Nate, the way it's going now, I think Regis would have made the same decision. I can't do it now. I've got a station to run. Lou would have been the most likely choice, but he's out. Frankly, I think you'll work well with Blakeley."

"I don't know, Lieutenant. I think I'm pretty inexperienced to play in the same league with him."

"Young man," Blakeley interjected. He had inched close and was suddenly in the conversation. "I am totally convinced that we shall be an unbeatable team."

Hudson took the cue smoothly. "Your inexperience may be an asset, Nate. Dr. Blakeley likes to do things his own way."

"If you say so, Lieutenant." Nathan had no choice anyway.

"I do hope you don't object to my eavesdropping, Detective McBride, but I've been most concerned that you would see the logic behind all this. I've been briefed on your record, you understand, and I must say I find it most suitable."

Nathan took one more look at Miss Tierney. She was looking back at him. He brushed aside all presentiments. "Actually I'm flattered. I realize that I'm just enough and no more, but it will be a great experience to work with you, Dr. Blakeley."

"Splendid."

"Better get some rest," said Hudson. "You'll have to get started early in the morning."

"Oh, yes," said Blakeley with a cheery smile, "we shall need the pale head."

Ten

Angie Sutton scrambled from beneath the faceless young man. Her husband stood awestricken. She sprang from the bed totally unclothed, but for some jewelry which flickered in the candlelight, and flailed wildly at him. "Yew done this on purpose, yew sonbitch!"

Andrew Sutton's face was white with shock. "The wife is not the master of her own body, but the husband is."

The young man hastily picked up his trousers and backed into a dark corner to put them on. Sutton, intent upon Angie, scarcely noticed him. She put her hands on her hips and jutted her body forward to flaunt her nakedness. "Now don't give me none o' yer Bible-thumpin' shit, Andrew," she yelled, reaching for an empty bottle beside the bed.

As Sutton dodged the shreds and slivers of glass that ricocheted from the bourbon bottle shattering on the wainscoting, the young caller saw an opportunity. Still barefoot and semiclad, he made a dash for safety, knocking Sutton to the floor as he bolted through the doorway.

Sutton rose slowly to his feet and planted himself inside the room. Angie, her companion gone, started to shiver.

"The bridegroom is the one to whom the bride belongs," he whispered.

"What . . . what're yew gonna do?" she whimpered, grasping a bed sheet and holding it before her with sudden modesty.

"Turn away from your sins," he said, removing his broad leather belt, "for the kingdom of heaven is near."

"Oh, Andy," she pleaded as he raised the belt, blood running from the cuts on his face where many tiny pieces of glass had struck him.

He stepped forward.

He brought the belt down across her shoulder with such force that she fell onto the dresser, scattering bottles of perfume and boxes of sachet.

"Don't, Andy. Stop it!" she screamed.

He struck her again and the bed sheet fell from her hands as she grasped the fleshy part of her thigh.

He hit her again, and her body twisted across the bed, where she was helpless against his uncontrollable anger.

Charlie Hudson stiffened his body and haunched his shoulders as he walked nearly empty streets in the chilly night air. The station house was approximately halfway between Regis Tolan's wake and Hudson's home.

Now that the disappearances were in the hands of Ian Blakeley, the precinct could focus its energies on the burglaries, which had been somehow relegated to obscurity despite the howls and protests of every merchant in the district. But he'd lost another man. Maybe a good case could be made for Curran now. City Hall couldn't be *that* obtuse, though poor Regis swore it could be—now Charlie Hudson had the reams of evidence to prove it.

As he rounded the last corner, he noticed the full moon and wondered if there were anything to that old rigmarole about tides and vapors.

The first going-off-duty shot removed the chill. He opened his collar, propped his feet on the desk, and poured another. Tomorrow would be another long day and, besides, his wife would raise the dickens when he came home—it was already what she considered an unrespectable hour. The precinct personnel took no notice of him; it was presumed that, like Captain Tolan, they would now see him there at all hours. He wondered if he'd be promoted to captain now. It *would* assuage the wife somewhat.

Oh, what the hell. . . . City Hall will no doubt say either *a promotion* or *new manpower. They'll see their chance to nail me to the wall anyway. . . . He tossed down his whiskey.*

He replaced the bottle in the lower left-hand drawer of his desk and prepared to go home. As he was saying good-night to the desk man, Fatzinger entered the lobby, struggling to keep a very woebegone Richard Cooper on his feet.

"Bones, you did it! I'm proud of you!"

"I got dis chicken shticker on tree, maybe four counts, by Christ. Shtand up, Cooper!"

Cooper stared at the desk sergeant and raised his index finger feebly. "Your Honor, I ob . . . object. This, this is a most heinous zample of entrap . . . ment."

"Better let him sit down, Bones. If he falls, he'll claim we roughed him up."

Fatzinger released his grip on Cooper's collar, and the lawyer slumped into a chair.

The desk sergeant laughed. Fatzinger looked as if he had just caught a prize fish; he beamed with intemperate pride.

"What are the charges, Bones?" asked Hudson.

"Vell, as iss evident from hiss shmell an' appearance," Fatzinger asserted, "he'ss full o' schnapps, an' doot vass in public, by Chesuss!"

Cooper protested, "I used to be a wine, wine taster. It's my present avo . . . avoca . . . hobby."

"Intoxicated in public," noted Hudson. "Yes, that will certainly hold water."

"An' shpeakin' o' vater," said Fatzinger, "I caught him defacin' property. Against the shteps o' Mr. Heester's loan shop he vass, y'know, urinatin'." Fatzinger shook his head in disbelief. "Yeah, peein' on the *vindow too* he vass."

"Atrocious!" Hudson snapped. "Mr. Heester will no doubt have something to say about that. This will look just terrible, Mr. Cooper."

"You have no evidence t' sport that, Hudson."

"Do you want us to go back and take samples, Cooper?" Hudson grinned. "Anything else, Bones?"

"Yeah, wavin' his thing in front o' that lady over there."

Hudson looked to his left and saw a rather dour young woman in gaudy velveteen, propped against a wooden pillar. "Is that so, Miss?"

"You betcha it's true, Lootenant, 'cause she vass holdin' him up venn he did it against Heester's place, by Christ."

She shrugged her shoulders. "So he couldn't make it to my place. Does dat make me an accessory?"

"Either that or a witness. Take your choice."

"Hey, I don't even know da jerk. Of *course*, I'm a witness."

"Good."

"Yeah, an' den he resisted arrest an' called me a name," Fatzinger shouted. "An' me a preacher's kid!"

Cooper looked at the girl, mumbled something about collusion

and frailty-thy-name-is-woman, then tilted into unconsciousness.
"Derr'ss vun more charge, Lootenant," added Fatzinger, now encouraged beyond endurance. "Cavortin' wit a known prostitute cuz dott's vot she iss. I betcha she'ss in dott pitcher book. Take a look chust vunst."

"Don't bother, Lieutenant," said the young woman. "It's not a very flattering shot. Much as I tried, I just couldn't look like the Gibson Girl."

"Well, miss," said Hudson, signaling a uniformed man to deposit Cooper in a cell, "I'm sure you'll be a wonderful witness. We'll be in touch."

She left, and Fatzinger told Hudson his tale of having followed Cooper to a tavern at Sixty-ninth and Calvert. After an hour it had become chilly, so Fatzinger had entered and taken a remote table to have knockwurst and sauerkraut and a piece of chocolate cake. When at length the girl had found Cooper, even Fatzinger had known it was only a matter of time, so he had gone outside and tried to appear inconspicuous for the next two hours, even directing traffic for a short time but mostly walking around the block repeatedly.

Finally, Cooper and the girl had left just as Fatzinger was about to go in for another piece of cake. He had tagged along till the incident at Irwin Heester's office.

"It vass all pretty easy, like shooin' flies on a frosty mornin', Lootenant. Chust common sense like you sez."

Hudson sat back, folded his arms, and smiled. "Excellent work, Bones. I thank you, and the department thanks you."

"Yer velcome, Lootenant. Now maybe I can become a detective, huh?"

"A detective? . . . It's a bit soon for that, Bones." Fatzinger might be happier in another precinct.

"Vell, maybe anudder two or tree veeks. I kin vait. Boy, oh, boy, venn I tell dem *dat*, dey'll trow *some* party for old Fatzinger up in Ebenezersville, you betcha!"

Hudson had a third shot of whiskey before going home that evening.

On April 29 the Spanish Admiral Pascual Cervera, commanding a fleet of four armored cruisers and three destroyers, departed from the Cape Verde Islands for some unknown destination to the west. The U.S. War Department's intention of starving out the Spaniards by blockading Cuba was commonly understood; hence, all substantial evidence supported the assumption that Cervera was bound for Santiago, on the southeastern coast of the island, to assist the Spanish soldiery there. Yet the press vociferated about the threat to the entire Atlantic coast, finally convincing many citizens that Cervera was destined for Boston, New York, New Jersey, or Washington itself. Predictably the sensation mongers in Philadelphia did their best to drum up images of the *María Teresa* and the *Cristóbal Colón* sailing up the Delaware to bombard Chestnut Street. Admiral W. S. Schley's flying squadron, however, was setting out for Caribbean waters to hunt for Cervera.

Nathan McBride turned the page and sipped his coffee, scanning advertisements for Listerine tooth polish, Victor gramophones, and Procter and Gamble lye soap. He rubbed his eyes and slapped the side of his neck to brace himself. The evening had been late but inspiring; he had asked Miss Tierney if she would permit him to escort her home, and to his amazement, she'd agreed. She'd seemed pleased, in fact. Soaking his feet in a basin of warm salts, he flipped another page, seeking the score of yesterday's game with Boston, until he realized that rain had caused a postponement.

With a yawn he perused a feature on the new Spanish governor of Cuba, General Ramón Blanco, who in November had replaced the "executioner," Captain General Valeriano Weyler. The public was warned against the naïveté of expecting less than barbarism of Blanco in his treatment of American prisoners.

Pouring more coffee after tightening his bathrobe against the morning chill, he made note of the coming visit of the allegedly wicked Mrs. Leslie Carter in *Du Barry* and wondered whether Miss Tierney would enjoy the theater. The small clock on the mantel chimed six times, and he knew that he was lagging.

Wearily he turned back to the front page and sought the more immediate news. He had made a pact with himself, after his first year on the force, to ignore the police and crime reporting until he'd had a chance to gather himself. Through half-open eyes twenty minutes previously he had come across the name "Figge" on page one but successfully evaded it. Now he ran his eyes down the columns quickly. Most of it told him what he already knew. Some of it told him what he knew to be untrue. All of it typical of crime coverage. He yawned again.

And then he noticed the supplementary item: Lester Figge had offered a reward of thirty thousand dollars for information leading to the arrest and conviction of Jennifer Figge's murderer.

Damn it, he thought, *Pandora's Box. Every crackpot on the East Coast will probably turn up over this.*

As Nathan's buggy sped across the countryside toward the Figge estate, Ian Blakeley, after a hearty breakfast of kidneys, jam, and tea, retired to his laboratory, where the body of Miss Figge had been deposited by the police. It was a very delicate matter, this autopsy; it would have to be over with by late afternoon. Pressure, apparently initiated by the mother of the deceased, had been brought to bear upon the authorities to release the body posthaste. After securing the door behind him, he donned his rubber apron and gloves and moved the stretcher into position under the hot lamps.

When Nathan arrived at the Figge estate, a police photographer was already at work. He asked the whereabouts of Andrew Sutton, and the photographer muttered something like the "Dixie Darling" not feeling up to it this morning. Staff people considered Sutton a prima donna, and he dropped the issue. Sooner or later Dr. Blakeley would want Sutton, and it would be his unhappy task to fetch him. The Dixie Darling: Nathan liked that.

The constabulary had had the foresight to cordon off the area and to leave the head as it was, impaled. Nathan observed the photographer circling around the blood-soaked shaft, clicking his portable Kodak intermittently. He recalled an advertisement for one in some catalogue or other. The sun was brilliant in a rare, unclouded sky; thus accurate, if grotesque, detail in the photographs.

He looked up, finally, at the head, striving to appear detached in his awe. Nothing he had read, or heard of, or had seen, nothing ever again would be so starkly, so horribly fascinating.

The hollow eyes seemed to fix his with a look at once insipid and hypnotic. Dark blood in the corners of the mouth and in the flared nostrils stood out against the translucently white skin. Blood had crusted the long light-brown hair. Most of the hair was now matted against the shaft, but some of it flickered absurdly in the breeze against Miss Figge's forehead.

He asked the photographer to take some shots of the deep ruts in the road leading up to the stable. In the buggy, on the floor, was a large leather satchel with a special rubber lining. He pulled it from the cab and, for the first time, paid attention to the crowd that had gathered at the ropes. There was very little noise. Nathan played the dubious role of supporting actor to an inanimate object. He slipped his hands into a pair of heavy gloves.

After the photographer had finished his work at the fence, Nathan placed the satchel on the ground near the head. He climbed to the top of the overlapping, weather-beaten logs, stretching his arms toward the long, thin shaft. But he could not reach the head.

The crowd murmured, then quieted down as he again stretched upward and forward as far as he dared. The head was still beyond his grasp. This time the crowd oohed in strange delight.

He climbed down and asked the photographer for assistance. "I just take pitchers," answered the photographer.

Nathan cursed the photographer, Dr. Blakeley, Lieutenant Hudson, and the head itself. The long shaft had been nailed into the oaken post in such a way that detaching it without severe damage to the head was impossible. Nathan had sickening visions of loosening it, the head waving to and fro on the wobbly shaft, and being catapulted into the ever more excited crowd.

As he argued with the mulish photographer, a stableboy appeared with a crowbar. Nathan held the shaft, awaiting tensely the moment it would come loose. Dr. Blakeley's orders were explicit: The head must be gotten to him precisely as found. The stableboy moved the crowbar cautiously.

"You gonna do anything to old Hubert, Officer? You know, the coachman."

"Just question him for now, son. He was the last one to see her."

"He doesn't know nothin' about her."

"Do you?"

The stableboy grinned. "Everybody around here does, except old Hubert. All he knows is what he's heard from us."

Nathan readjusted his grip on the shaft as the last of the nails came under attack. "I'm not sure I'm following you."

"Look, Officer, Miss Figge was always doin' somethin' she wasn't supposed to. When she knew we knew, she had her own ways of keepin' her secrets, if you know what I mean."

"I suppose I'm following you now," said Nathan.

"An' if she'd ever come anywheres near old Hubert that way, I swear he'd break out in boils, honest!"

The shaft came loose. The stableboy dropped the crowbar and helped McBride lower the shaft to the ground. A hush fell over the crowd as Nathan grasped the long hair as gently but firmly as possible. When he had disengaged the head, he placed it in his black satchel and locked the bag tightly. Perspiration blanketed his face, and his shirt stuck to his back.

The crowd began to disperse. Nathan thanked the stableboy and put the satchel in the cab. The photographer had finished his work and, after watching the goings-on with the head, went to put away his equipment. The smells of the stableyard seemed to grow stronger in the breeze drifting up from the birch trees by the stream.

"You got the picture of the road?"

The photographer was bent over his fastened cases. His face darkened, and he nodded.

"Good. Now take one of each carriage in the stable, making certain you include the wheels."

"But I just put everything away!"

"I'll bet you wish you hadn't," said Nathan. He understood now why Dr. Blakeley put up with Andrew Sutton.

"But," the photographer groaned, "it's dark in there, an' my flash powder's almost run out."

"Just don't start any fires when you use what's left."

"It *stinks* in there!"

Nathan sighed wearily. "If you go up to the house, I'm sure one of the servants will lend you a clothespin."

He left the photographer to sulk and removed a smaller case from the buggy. A thought crossed his mind as he watched the remaining youngsters hanging about in a group, so he locked the cab before pacing over the grass to the dirt lane. His stomach still felt slightly queasy.

The ruts in the muddy lane were five and one-half inches deep according to his measuring tape. A very heavy buggy, it appeared. When he discounted the clumsy photographer's footprints, one set led up to the shaft, evidently rather small and wide, flat probably. Most of the prints unfortunately had been obscured by intruders. The feet looked to be about size seven; the photographer's were much larger.

Nathan looked up at the charred fence post where the pitch-blende torch had burned itself out overnight. The flat-footed murderer was bold. Having gained access on a service road at the far end of the estate, he blithely carried out his demonic fantasy. The road began over the creek in a covered bridge, coiled snakelike uphill, through acres of wavy alfalfa, past an eighteenth-century storehouse of heavy logs and massive stone. A long distance to travel with impunity.

He took his glass and studied the ground. There had been no other wagons on the lane. The right foreleg of the horse pulling the heavy buggy had a worn, cracked shoe.

Ian Blakeley felt under his rubber apron for his pocket watch. Twelve thirty. He covered the body and jotted the last of his notes. The oppressive heat from the big lamps was relentless. As he flicked them off, he unstuck his perspiration-soaked collar, shed with relief the heavy apron and gloves, and rested for a moment in a deep chair. His monocle had become clouded again.

The air in the laboratory was stale. He arose to open the windows and drew in a deep breath, refreshing with the aroma of new-mown grass. Knowing the morbid nature of his subject, he'd planned his laboratory as a basement operation, close to the earth, just to keep his own sense of continuity alive.

After this morning's examination that was even more essential than usual. His notes were a terrible litany of man's potential for cruelty. Miss Figge had been burned, branded actually, on random areas of her body. But Blakeley had seen that before, most recently in a simple extortion matter. What had taken him by surprise was the thorough dislocation of all of Miss Figge's limbs. Almost as if she'd been racked. . . . Heretofore, he'd only read of such things.

Blakeley had discovered something potentially rather sensitive. No more than three months past, he estimated, she had had illegal surgery—abortive surgery. It had been a skillful operation, but the telltale scars of her experience were physical evidence of her cavalier code of ethics.

He'd found evidence of her spirit as well. Scraping beneath her fingernails, he had found traces of human skin the texture of which did not match her own. Miss Figge had not gone out meekly.

Finally, and to his confusion, the deceased had *not* been sexually assaulted. He rubbed his eyes and cleaned his monocle. Most disturbing. . . .

He checked the fingertips out of a purely historical curiosity. They were swollen but unopened.

The rack plucked one's bones and joints asunder. Blakeley recalled that it had been introduced in 1420 by the Duke of Exeter, just before the reign of Henry VI, and rarely left idle throughout the fifteenth century. Then, under Henry VIII, Sir Leonard Skevington had brought to the Tower of London the Scavenger's Daughter, related to the rack, which crushed the victim until blood seeped through the nostrils . . . and out of the fingertips.

Blakeley wondered how sophisticated and historically accurate the killer's methods were. He would need the head to be certain.

And why the gratuitous decapitation and display? It was as if the killer had grown weary of his total anonymity. How else explain the matter of Miss Figge's consummate degradation: her head on macabre display and naked remains bound against a tree in a park? The fiend had done everything short of wrapping her up in a great pink bow.

A demanding knock on the door broke his concentration. He closed his note pad and buttoned his collar before moving to open it. As he approached, there was a second, more irritable knock. He pulled the latch hastily.

"A gentleman to see you, sir," uttered Victor imperiously. "He has a parcel for you."

"In a black satchel?"

"Indeed," answered Victor peevishly. "I offered to carry it to you, but he would not permit me to touch it."

"That's fine, Victor. Show him in."

"I want to speak with you today, sir," said Victor, still standing rigidly in the doorway.

"Victor!" growled Blakeley, his monocle fogging up, "if you do not show the gentleman in immediately, I shall tell Snopkowski that you wear theatrical makeup!"

"You wouldn't!" gasped Victor.

"I shouldn't bet my hairpiece on that if I were you."

Victor bit his lip and put on his best martyr pose. "As you wish, sir."

As the butler's angry footsteps faded down the hallway, Blakeley opened the wall safe and removed a bottle of Amontillado. He kept his best wines out of Victor's reach. While waiting for McBride and the satchel, he glanced once again at his notes. Miss Figge had been dead, he reckoned, for approximately thirty-eight hours before his examination of her remains. That would fix her time of death at about five o'clock the day before yesterday. The killer had waited until the park was deep in shadow before placing the corpse where it was bound to be discovered. That must have been after seven; he had time to get out to the Figge estate by about nine or ten. The head had been severed cleanly, either by the hands of a physician or by a guillotine. Unless the killer had the skill of Torquemada's inquisitors, her agony had ended quite sometime before.

And what had caused a full day to pass before the body had been disposed of? he wondered.

"Dr. Blakeley, I'm sorry to have taken so long." Nathan McBride, very wan, stood in the doorway, flanked by the sullen Victor. Nathan did not wish to elaborate. He had been very sick as soon as he had got to an isolated section of the highway.

"Don't apologize. I quite understand that it's been a beastly morning for you."

"I won't deny that, Doctor." Nathan placed the satchel on a stool near the corpse.

"A glass of Amontillado, Detective McBride?"

"Thank you, no," said Nathan as he knelt to unlock the satchel and open it for Blakeley's convenience. "I'm afraid it would make me sleepy."

"Nonsense, it will awaken your circulatory system and give you an appetite."

Nathan had wondered about the taste of Amontillado ever since he'd read the Poe tale as a boy. "Do you insist?"

"I insist."

"Then who am I to argue with a doctor?" One of the locks had jammed, and Nathan continued to struggle with it.

"Splendid." As Blakeley poured, he noticed the butler still present. "That will be all, Victor."

"But, sir," Victor grumbled, "I've not finished discussing my problem."

"We shall discuss it later. Detective McBride and I have more serious business right now."

"But I was here *first*," sulked Victor.

"Yes, of course. . . ." As Blakeley contemplated the often odious

Victor, he tried to dismiss a thought with tantalizing possibilities. After a very brief struggle, he yielded happily to temptation.

"Yes, of course. Now do be a good chap and help Detective McBride."

"Very good, sir." Victor's voice sounded especially mellifluous as he knelt beside Nathan, who had despaired of unlocking the satchel and had begun to pull on the strap.

"Perhaps," Victor suggested, "Officer McBride would prefer to hold the satchel whilst I extricate the strap?"

Blakeley set his glass upon a laboratory table and rubbed his hands anxiously. "It would be much simpler if all three of us took part."

"Oh, good fun, sir!" chimed Victor.

"Yes. . . . Now hold the satchel, and Detective McBride and I shall tug the strap loose. I fear we shall have to break the lock."

Victor held the satchel while Nathan and Blakeley strained to break the lock. Puffing, Victor rocked back and forth on one knee. "Warm work, sir," he said with a silly grin.

"Hello—be careful now. The contents are fragile," grunted Blakeley.

"Yes, be careful, Officer McBride," Victor said officiously. "The contents are fragile."

Nathan looked at the butler and forced a smile.

In another moment the lock snapped, and the leather bag came open. Victor peered through the opening, blinked his eyes, looked away to think about it, glanced again at the pale head, turned pale himself, and fell backward into a deep swoon.

"Capital!" Blakeley beamed as he beheld the prostrate Victor. "Come, my boy, give me hand with him. I expect he'll be bloody heavy."

"Is he all right?" Nathan was not quite prepared for Blakeley's whimsy.

Nathan took Victor's feet, and they lifted him with some effort. He felt like a saturated sandbag.

Blakeley remarked, as they placed Victor on a stretcher adjacent to the corpse, that at such times he regretted the absence of Ralphie. "There. He should be quite comfortable for a while."

They finished their glasses of Amontillado. Blakeley expressed a desire for fresh air, so they strolled the sunlit grounds until they reached the riverbank, where Blakeley paused to study a school of bass. Nathan apprised him of the evidence and of the hypothesis involving a flat-footed man in a heavy buggy. Blakeley exhorted Nathan to visit the site in the park to check for similarities.

"This is the first time we've had any scientific evidence other than mere mutilation. Nice work, Detective McBride."

Nathan was truly flattered. "Thank you."

"Does it make you hungry?"

"Hungry? The evidence was encouraging, but certainly not appetizing."

"The fish. Looking at them, I mean."

"Oh. . . ."

"Chubby, aren't they? The picnickers upriver feed them well. They seem to thrive upon rubbish."

Nathan had, once again, missed breakfast. It was now past one o'clock. He focused on the particularly large fish darting to and fro in search of water bugs and imagined it in a pan of hot butter. His stomach had settled some time ago. "Yes, it does."

"I can't abide fish chowder as a rule. Howbeit, our cook has a way with such fare, and that seems to be what she's decided she wants today. One seldom argues with old Snopkowski."

"I like fish chowder, Dr. Blakeley. I like it especially with thick slices of bread."

"Whole wheat?"

"Oh, yes. . . ."

"Then let's go, my boy. I've been growing weaker with each step."

When they reached the house, the servants were abuzz already with word of Victor's comeuppance. Snopkowski evidenced her delight with a Cheshire cat grin. At the sight of Blakeley and Nathan, who she immediately decided was an identical twin of some actor whose photograph she'd seen, she warmed up some freshly baked bread and apple pie and ladled out two bowls of fish chowder. "You good-lookin', but you even skinnier dan him," she said, pointing at Blakeley. Nathan savored the chowder; his ideal woman would look like Aidan Tierney and have the talents of the dowdy Snopkowski.

"This ought to reinforce you this afternoon as you walk in the park," said Blakeley, his mind now on his own afternoon's labors.

"Actually," said Nathan helping himself to another two ladlings from the antique silver tureen, "I don't think I'd mind walking the

Black Forest after this." Snopkowski served the apple pie personally and seemed pleased with Nathan's appetite. His slice of pie was somewhat larger than Blakeley's.

"How is Victor?" asked Blakeley indifferently.

"He go for bed. You not see dot yonko till da cows come home." She waved a large, meaty hand in mock disgust.

"In bed?" Blakeley was concerned about that evening's preparations. Sophia had invited another crowd of bores.

"Do you have any plans for dinner, Detective McBride?"

During the long ride to Blakeley's, Nathan had been trying to formulate some means of persuading Miss Tierney to go to dinner that evening; knowing that it was unwise to move so quickly and obviously, realizing that he would not have time to see her in any case, he said no. "I find myself dining rather peripatetically since I took this job, Dr. Blakeley. Good food and I have become ships that pass in the night."

"That's dreadful, my boy. Worse than that, it's unwholesome," Blakeley said into his tea.

"It's a pain in the neck. Sometimes I think I should have become a restaurateur."

"Well then, how does escargot followed by roast duck sound? We shall open some bottles of Châteauneuf du Pape, unless Snopkowski insists we serve one of her own wines instead. She gets touchy about that at times."

Nathan accepted, and Blakeley warned him that he would have to tolerate the Snobys. The essential things, Blakeley stressed, were not to laugh at Mrs. Snoby's bird calls and not to appear too ill-at-ease when he found her son Willard staring at him most of the evening.

"Mrs. Snoby's efforts have always made me wish I were scheduled to perform an autopsy or something."

They spoke of England, the war with Spain, and Philadelphia's weather. Blakeley already knew of Nathan's readings in literature and metaphysics, his speaking knowledge of French and German and reading knowledge of Latin, Greek, and Italian, his weakness in mathematics and odd facility with pure sciences, so the conversation stayed away from personal matters.

As the teapot cooled, Nathan's mind was straying to his afternoon's labors and Blakeley grew more anxious to return to his laboratory. He had a brief but important matter to attend to which involved the head, but he didn't think Nathan was prepared to discuss that sort of thing at lunchtime. Blakeley was, however, gladdened by the brief conversation; Nathan's breadth of knowledge and interests had been affirmed. Beside being essential to the effectiveness of their investigation, Blakeley could not abide a dull associate.

After lunch they parted company, Blakeley to his scalpel and test tubes, Nathan to check the wagon tracks in the park.

Given the variance of soil texture and the influence of the warm sun, the tracks were reasonably similar to what Nathan had found at the Figge estate. More interesting than that were the marks of a broken horseshoe on the trail just above the slope where the corpse had been left to lie. He took his glass and scrutinized the land, rechecking the tracks where a surface cover of dust had developed within the mesh of ivy.

Under the foliage he found not only the set of flat-footed prints he'd hoped for, but an added set of prints that stood out with brazen clarity. Someone with more natural foot contours and expensive shoes. Splotches of blood marked the trail from the carriage to the tree onto which the two men had tied Jennifer Figge's remains. Nathan measured the distance between footprints from the tree to the grooves in the trail and rejoiced that the killer had at least forsaken the security of concrete. By his calculations the flat-footed man was tall, almost six feet, and his companion, whose stride extended only about two feet from shoe to shoe uphill, was of medium height. Despite the mud and damp ground, the two had carried the corpse a great distance, perhaps for only dramatic effect, propping it against the nearest dead tree stump.

Rummaging on his hands and knees beneath the bramble bushes, he found a broken wineglass, a moldering boot, a torn pulp magazine dated sometime last summer, a workman's glove of like age, and two recently discarded cigarette butts.

Blakeley must have some means of determining the brand of a cigarette. Nathan scooped up the butts into his handkerchief. There was no trace of the discoloration the storm of two nights ago would have caused. Both less than a quarter inch long, ground out before being tossed into the bush; neither had a trademark.

In a modest way something of a profile was starting to develop. While carrying out the sordid errand, each man had smoked a cigarette. There wasn't time for one man to have smoked two. Perhaps to avoid a brush fire, which would have attracted premature attention, the cigarettes had been snuffed out, but they had been dropped in a logical, if inconspicuous, place.

The killers wished to taunt them; megalomaniacs, he thought. The Figge girl's body had been trussed up with the same kind of thong that had been tightened around the Whittingham girl's neck. Simple rope wouldn't do them. No one could have started a fire on these sodden grounds. They were dangling ephemeral hints and *laughing* at their pursuers. Even the poorly shod horse was probably part of the macabre charade, he mused. "Any luck, Nathan?" Hudson stood on the trail atop the rise with a uniformed officer.

"A little, Lieutenant," he answered, scrambling up the hill.

Hudson extended a hand to help him over a ditch running beside the trail. "I had to get out of that station house. With old man Figge offering a reward, we get a loony an hour."

"I was afraid of that," said Nathan, brushing off his trousers.

"Nate, have you ever met the Majestic Lady? The one who claims to be a clairvoyant countess?"

"Oh, yes, Mme. Natalia Cheever," he said. "Have you ever met the fellow with the intuitive dog, John Stanklow from Pittsburgh?"

"No. I'll have to get used to all this now. The countess bent my ear for an hour before I realized she's missing her marbles. So I left her back there with Fatzinger. Someone should take that priceless conversation down. I don't imagine we'll be able to read the report if he writes it, or understand it if he has it typed."

Hudson leaned against a tree and lit up his short cigar. The patrolman eased down the hill to check the cord around the restricted area. "What've you got?"

Nathan showed him the cigarette butts and offered his assumptions. Hudson listened intently, nodding at times, staring off mostly. He seemed particularly taken by the measurements.

"I thought you might like that, Lieutenant. I think that flat-footed man is rather heavy, but I'm not sure if he's muscular or just fat."

"You're doing well, Nate," said Hudson, puffing on his cigar. "Think how easy it would be to follow their tracks in snow."

"I wish to heaven they were dumb."

They looked down in silence at the patrolman chatting with a guard at the foot of the hill. Hudson pushed himself away from the tree and stretched his arms.

"How many did Jack the Ripper score? Six, was it?"

"Six."

"It's getting close."

"Well, Lieutenant"—Nathan sighed—"I'd like to think that we are, too."

Across the city, at that moment, Max Toberman was uncontrollable in his fit of anger over Arthur and Vincent's defiance of his orders. Their latest bit of whimsy, he swore, would be their last.

As Nathan soaked in a hot tub and wondered if his pin-striped suit would be appropriate for the evening, Blakeley arrived at the last of his afternoon's labors. As the Figge hearse pulled out of his drive, he stroked his beard and felt a twinge of uneasiness. His thorough analysis had proved that the girl had indeed been racked to death. The rack could take hours, even days. At such moments he always wanted very badly to be gentle with those around him.

He sipped a cup of tea with Sophia. For a brief time, in an attempt to puncture his reticence, she pursued the matter of Victor's sudden illness, then spoke of Ralphie, who was on his way to Florida. Blakeley finished his tea, kissed Sophia on the forehead, and went upstairs to rest. Damnable case, he thought. Damnable how you couldn't help bringing them into the house.

There was one blessing, he reminded himself, remote as it seemed now: This chapter would deal with a most unusual multicide. He had the feeling that whatever they'd uncovered was but a fragment of the complete mosaic and that the eventual answer would bring with it a whole new series of the hues and patterns of madness. As the floor creaked beneath his footsteps, he searched his memory for a precedent and had the tantalizing thought that it was not far away. Sleep successfully evaded him when he had stopped his pacing and lay in bed.

Eleven

Nathan reined up his horse and came to a halt in the driveway. The muscular roan stallion was a further bit of extravagance and something for which he knew he had to be grateful to Hudson. That morning, true to Hudson's promise, the horse and buggy had been left outside his modest flat along with the rubber-lined satchel. If the left wheel squeaked somewhat and the seat was rather rickety, the convenience still bordered on luxury.

As a servant led the horse away, he drew in a deep breath of lilac from a lavender grove on a nearby hillock. A gentle river breeze promised to put a tang into the evening.

How tranquil it was, he thought, how pleasant the pastoral setting, so removed from the mean, contemptible world of the streets. He felt a little like Orlando in the Forest of Arden, wandering through a temporary Green World. The geraniums and rhododendrons were blooming in pink and white splendor under an early-evening sun.

His attention was drawn to a glittering horseless carriage parked in the driveway some distance from the stable. He stopped on his way to inspect it, noticing gravel on the lowest step nearby. Mostly he had seen such vehicles as they chugged over cobbled streets. The rich smell of leather told him that it was probably new; he guessed that the odor of fuel would take over in time. Deep maroon with intricate gold trim, the machine bore an insignia which read "Winton, Cleveland, Ohio." He gathered it was worth his yearly salary.

Deciding that it was an unpleasant waste of time to admire what he could not afford, he proceeded up the steps and tugged on the heavy bronze knocker. As he awaited an answer, he looked once more at the vehicle, imagining himself driving it up to Miss Tierney's door on a Sunday afternoon. It was a tantalizing vision. A servant answered and showed him in.

The sun shone through the stained glass windows, over the geometric beams, and played lightly upon the chandeliers. Nathan walked through what seemed to him a medieval great hall. The servant led him to a waiting room and prepared him a rare glass of cognac. In a sense, it reminded him of his visit to Saint Francis Xavier's rectory, nevertheless being in every way more agreeable, of course. For some reason he had expected a series of skeletons and diagrams of the alimentary canal like the rectory's religious plaques; instead, he found busts of Shakespeare and Molière and paintings after Sir Joshua Reynolds and Gainsborough.

He perused the heroic portrait of Commodore Keppel. It was an excellent copy, the naval hero stepping ashore after the wreck of his command, brave in the midst of the stormy sea and crags. The replica of Gainsborough's portrait of Mrs. David Garrick was equally precise. Not a pretty woman, really, at least by modern standards. Her mouth was a bit too full, albeit sensuous, her nose a trifle too long. But her eyes—they pierced and invited, with well-controlled passion, the artist's hand had captured the ageless essence. The words of an almost-forgotten tribute came back to him: "For where is any author in the world/Teaches such beauty as a woman's eye?" He had no reason to fault his memory, though what—and how—it summoned up sometimes mystified him.

"They've fallen into disfavor with the avant-garde, you know." A charming vision in ivory and lace had appeared in the doorway. Her richly modulated voice seemed incongruous, coming from such a delicate person.

"I'm Sophia Blakeley." She extended a finely shaped hand. "I've been ordered to keep you company, so you must put up with me for the time being."

The appropriate answer came to mind: "I shall tell my grandchildren of the evening I spent with Gainsborough, Reynolds, and La Gioconda. I'm Nathan McBride."

A servant appeared with a tray. Sophia took a glass of Burgundy from the girl's tray.

"I've just been admiring your horseless vehicle, Mrs. Blakeley. Like everything else here, it's in impeccable taste."

"Oh, it's not ours, Officer McBride. Ian doesn't care for technological improvements on that scale. The machine belongs to Mr. Sutton."

"Andrew Sutton, the photographer?"

"Yes, and though I don't suppose he'd like my disclosing this, he seems to be in a terrible mood today." She lowered her voice to an intimate level and drifted over to the window to watch Blakeley escort Sutton to the horseless carriage. As she passed by, he detected a new subtle eau de cologne.

"He's probably unhappy with Dr. Blakeley for permitting a department photographer to work on the case," said Nathan. "Actually there was no alternative."

She pulled the drape aside and peered out while Nathan looked over her shoulder. "It appears to be more than that. Something of a psychic tension exacerbating whatever immediate difficulties he's encountering," she speculated. "There are unusual scratch marks on his face, too. On Mr. Sutton such flaws are conspicuous."

Sutton, clad in white smock and goggles, was waving his arms about, trying to make a very lasting impression on an unreceptive Blakeley. Most unlike Sutton was the cigarette between gloved fingers, creating a small wisp of blue smoke near his head.

"I suppose, Mrs. Blakeley, he's acting rather cheeky, as you'd put it." Nathan bit his tongue after he said that. It sounded terribly presumptuous.

"Poor fellow, he's been here for at least the past hour, trying to put his fingers on his actual grievances." She seemed to have taken no offense. "Look at him, challenging the wind, as it were."

"Perhaps if *I* said something. . . . "

Nathan listened to the chugging of the vehicle and watched it make its way past the screened window. "I wasn't aware that Mr. Sutton had a horseless carriage. It's very . . . eye-catching, isn't it?"

"It's new. I believe he's only just purchased it."

Nathan had the feeling that the purchase had occupied the morning hours when the matter of the Figge estate was being attended to and that the Dixie Darling had concocted a tale of genteel illness. Once under way, the machine accelerated well and soon disappeared through the main entrance.

In lieu of roast duck, Snopkowski served something called galupkis, little patties of ground meat and rice wrapped in cabbage leaves and flavored with tomatoes and sauerkraut. And rather than detract from the intended effect by having Châteauneuf du Pape, the company sipped Snopkowski's own dandelion wine. While the Snobys regarded all of this with well-studied disdain, Nathan found himself in a delicious utopia. So, apparently, did the Blakeleys, for they offered no hint of apology for the heady redolence of the galupkis or the drab, uninspiring bouquet and color of the wine. Snopkowski herself made a rare dining-room appearance to oversee and to see that Nathan suffered a third serving. When he made a feeble effort to beg off, she stopped him in mid-gesture: "You don't go noplace, you skinny bummas, till you eat dot!" All in all, he ate nine of the little patties, together with two heaping side dishes of potato pancakes and sour cream.

When Nathan finally looked up to see Willard Snoby staring at him, he nearly burst out laughing. Willard was wearing sauerkraut on his tie and tomato stains on his collar; his knife and fork were forgotten in his hands as they rested placidly on the table edge.

Twelve

Jillian Ranshaw's apprenticeship in prostitution had been spent in the upstate coalfields. It had been of about one and one-half year's duration, and it had involved chiefly the company store manager, who had threatened to terminate Buck's credit, the rent collector, who had served notice of their impending eviction, the constables, who had arrested Buck for being drunk and disorderly much too often, and the mine foreman, who was fed up with Buck for the same reason and had actually fired him for a day.

One day in the early spring of 1897, wearing a new dress and more makeup than ever to conceal the black eye given her by Buck the night before, Jillian handed the train conductor an extra token and drifted off to sleep, knowing that when she awoke it would be in Philadelphia, where she could do forever what she'd learned to do so well with the mine foreman.

Memories of Buck faded rapidly. Thoughts of her two children hung on stubbornly awhile, but they, too, faded into fragments of a former life and became lost amid the waves of faceless, nameless bodies constituting her working milieu. She had taken a room in an old hotel on Arch Street, not far from the riverfront, where customers were plentiful. With the war a feverish new pace came to the dockside; the multitude of merchant seamen from the world were flush with money and heightened needs. She found her niche within the open quadrangle at City Hall, establishing as her own a section of the entranceway facing Broad Street. The territory had not been ceded without a struggle; a few of the older professionals had to be driven off; memories of the poverty Buck had forced on her weighting several well-placed kicks gained her sole possession of the prized ground. Jillian inherited the sailors, the noonday businessmen, the weekend college boys, occasional society figures. She labored nights and days, synchronized with the tedious workings of the city government, and threw herself into her profession with great energy and imagination.

If pressed to explain her dedication and vigor, Jillian would have admitted to enjoying her work. She would probably have blushed and bitten her lip demurely, turned curt, then feisty, then sulky, but at length she would have confirmed her *joie de guerre* with a blunt quip.

"I should be chargin' you by the ton. It's a good thing fer you I don't have a weigh scale at home." She looked with customary aloofness at the obese man who, entering the quadrangle and, glancing about at the assortment, had spotted Jillian through the light fog.

"I don't want to go to your place," wheezed the fat man. "I have my own."

"That'll cost you extra fer my lost time."

"No matter."

Taking a second look as he tossed away the cigarette, she decided to double her unspoken price anyway. He was fat enough for two. She wondered whether the fog or his own heat clouded his glasses.

"I don't do nothin' with no women, " she warned, just in case he was representing some aberrant society matron or the like.

"I'm sure I've no idea what you mean," he replied as he lit up another cigarette.

She decided to go along with him. Though repulsive, the fat man had an aura of wealth about him. She envisioned something difficult but lucrative.

"Youse lead the way," she said, rearranging her flowered bonnet as he plodded before her in his heavy frock coat.

They crossed the quadrangle over the oily-wet bricks and walked along the row of shops that led to South Street. The humid air was still hot, scarcely a breeze mollifying the evening. As she listened to the deep rales emanating from his chest, she contemplated the horror and stimulation of having a customer die in the midst of the act, wondering just which emotion would prevail should such an exotic matter occur. She put the thought aside as they approached a carriage parked in an alley off Edward Street. In the dim light from a nearby streetlamp, Jillian could make out a cadaverous-looking gentleman at the reins.

Her quartered remains were discovered in a garbage can by an old scavenger, who died of apoplexy on the spot. When the police were summoned from the Nineteenth Precinct to collect the old derelict's body, they found the open receptacle and summoned Dr. Blakely in accordance with departmental directive. He, in turn, determined that Jillian had been racked—as had the Figge girl—but with a machine refined well beyond the ordinary medieval instrument. Most of Jillian Ranshaw's history, up to her final rendezvous, had been compiled by Nathan at Blakeley's suggestion. He then dispatched Nathan to the coal region. The profile of the victim could prove immaterial, but he could ill afford to leave any stone unturned.

In the three weeks since Nathan first sank into the deep leather chair in Blakeley's den to allow Snopkowski's heavy cuisine to settle as they collated their data and hypotheses, the weather had become oppressively and permanently hot. Even the most upright and fashion-bound of the city's gentry took to shirt sleeves by ten in the morning, and the ladies opted to shed at least one petticoat weeks before it was ordinarily considered permissible. The summer promised to set uncomfortable new records.

Rear Admiral W. T. Sampson and Commodore W. S. Schley had succeeded in blockading Admiral Cervera's fleet in Santiago Harbor, or they were about to blockade it, depending upon the relative conservatism of the tabloid one read. It had been determined, at least, that the battleships *Oregon, Iowa,* and *Texas,* the cruiser *Brooklyn,* and the yacht *Gloucester* were in the American force, and in addition to the *María Teresa* and *Cristobál Colón,* the Spanish naval assemblage included the potent *Almirante Oquendo* and *Vizcaya,* and the torpedo destroyers *Furor* and *Plutón.*

Lou James reportedly had been engaged in combat training in South Carolina for an eventual Marine landing in Cuba. But in a letter to Lieutenant Hudson Lou complained of his assignment to a gunboat patrolling the Atlantic coast from Cape Hatteras to Provincetown. Important as it was to the defense of the eastern seaboard, he'd discovered a digestive aversion to salted meat and a propensity for seasickness, and he protested vehemently.

Ralphie, meanwhile, had written that the climate along the Florida Gulf Coast was insufferable in the winter uniforms that the Army had issued, neglecting to replace them with lighter ones. On the other hand, Ralphie had arranged a happy relationship with a cook and he expected to be reassigned to a commissary soon. He also included a comment on the effects of the Army diet of sausage and beans upon his system; Sophia refused to acknowledge this, ignoring Blakely's amusement.

* * *

After her young visitor and the ensuing whipping with Andrew's belt, Angie Sutton had become subdued. She was genuinely frightened this time; the look in Sutton's eyes had had hints of lunacy. It was relatively easy lately to maintain a more somber pose; for the past two and one-half weeks the city had been paving the street in front and Angie had struck up a close acquaintance with the laborers. To keep Andrew at ease, she kept her bourbon intake to one pint a day and restricted her entertainment to the daylight hours. To mystify him even further, she had put on her most demure habiliment, a black and gray tailored outfit, and had accompanied him to church services last Sunday.

Sutton had attracted the interest of Dr. Blakeley and, to a greater degree, Nathan McBride. Both remarked the odd coincidence of Sutton's facial scratches and the flesh under the fingernails of Miss Figge. Though Blakeley had been unimpressed at first by the obvious signs, the tests on the cigarettes found in the park confirmed that they were Ateshians, the same brand Andrew Sutton had been seen to smoke. Still reluctant to put much faith in such flimsy, circumstantial evidence, but somewhat piqued by Sutton's undue wrath, he suggested that Nathan look deeper, beyond Sutton's neatness, avarice, petulance, and religious fanaticism.

Nathan recalled Sophia Blakeley's reference to Sutton's apparent psychic tension as he traced the new suspect's steps to Castleman's Livery Stable. He had not wished to visit the place again since Captain Tolan's stroke there. He located Sutton's old buggy, no longer needed, in a corner of the yard. It was heavy, weighted with lead for negotiating mud and snow. Sutton's tired old horse was there as well, and its right front hoof, according to Castleman, had had a broken shoe at the time of the sale.

Castleman seemed nervous. The wheels of the buggy showed traces of yellow clay, similar to that in the park, embedded in the grooves worn into the overburdened tracks and caked onto the rear axle.

No wonder, thought Nathan, the Dixie Darling had been unavailable that morning. Evidently he'd had a busy time of it.

Nathan was convinced that he was on to something. He did not like Sutton personally and knew it would be easy to inflate the value of such circumstantial evidence. He knew also the awesome temptation of the Figge reward; ever since Dr. Blakeley had promised him one-half of it, he'd felt himself growing overanxious. The prospect of fifteen thousand dollars at age twenty-seven was mindboggling to someone whose earning would probably fall short of one thousand each year for the next decade.

His one glimpse of Angie Sutton took him by surprise. He expected a severe-looking frump, but she bore a resemblance to Miss Tierney—from a distance at least. But the comments he picked up from the neighbors, and in more graphic terms from the road workers, regarding Mrs. Sutton's life-style, ended the resemblance abruptly. The thought of contending with that even caused Nathan to feel a begrudging sympathy for Andrew Sutton. It also lent support to the argument that the killer or killers had a burning hatred of all womankind. When he hurried back to the livery stable to question Castleman again, the horse had been sold. Castleman, annoyed at having to answer the same inquiries once more, soon admitted that he could not remember one goddamn nag from another and added that he had better things to do than to waste time playing Pinkerton man.

Nathan thanked him very civilly for his cooperation and cited him for breaking the sanitary code. Castleman had always been negligent in keeping his sidewalk free of manure.

Aidan, no longer Miss Tierney to him, enjoyed the theater and *Du Barry* beyond Nathan's expectations. The evening was all the more delightful since Blakeley had given him the tickets. Sophia had gone so far as to express her uneasiness at being in the same city with a strumpet-at-large like Mrs. Carter, much less watch her portray an even more infamous strumpet. Blakeley had laughed, and Nathan understood that was the expected form of the time.

As the days grew warmer, so also did Nathan's ardor grow. At times he resented the demands of his work on the time he wanted to spend with Aidan. On rare occasions he found it possible to meet her in the late afternoon as she departed the school where she taught and would accompany her home. They would take the longer route, through their favorite park, and stay awhile in a grove where a small stream ran quietly and the air was rich with the smell of blossoms. Blakeley had promised him more theater tickets to a new play by George Bernard Shaw, *The Devil's Disciple.* Blakeley was delighted that Nathan and his lady friend so enjoyed the arts, certain he could not make use of the tickets himself—if not because of Sophia's reservations, then probably because of his book in progress. Nathan marveled at Dr. Blakeley's indefatigability.

Meanwhile, he had to be content with the occasional long walks and Sunday picnics in the dell. Their moments together had to be widely spaced to maintain propriety. He managed to effect one great novelty, however. Aidan went along with him to the baseball park on Saturday, and although she had confused the game, the teams, and the final score, she seemed to enjoy herself immensely. Pittsburgh won the game easily, but Ed Delahanty went four for four. In the sixth inning, the Pittsburgh shortstop, Honus Wagner, made an unassisted double play. Nathan, in the process of explaining it, unconsciously addressed Aidan as Kitten. She showed no profound reaction to the name, probably thinking it a slip of the tongue; he stammered for the next two innings anyway. It was too soon for cute little names. He got the idea during that pleasant evening at Blakeley's, when Sophia, after too many glasses of dandelion wine, confessed with a giggle her nickname for Ian. He reciprocated in joviality. With that, Sophia had suddenly repaired to her bedroom.

Aidan was not without competition. Since Nathan's first visit to the Blakeley estate Rosie had forsaken her suffragette uniform for more feminine couture. She seemed actually to be attempting to emulate Sophia. Blakeley was delighted with the change. She showed Nathan more civility early on than she was wont to show her father's visitors; subsequently she had fallen into her best pouting pose on his more recent visits. One evening, as Nathan approached the driveway, he found Rosie seated beside the road. Alighting from his buggy, he discovered that she had, she claimed, turned an ankle. As he picked her up and carried her in his arms, she let out a terrible groan and proceeded to swoon. He placed her into the cab and drove up to the main door, glancing at her often enough in apparent worry to notice her eyes slightly open. For the first time in his life he felt old. While Sophia blinked with quiet amusement over her shoulder, Nathan followed her, carrying the limp Rosie all the way to her boudoir.

Charlie Hudson rejoiced briefly that the city, showing unusual common sense, had at last seen fit to promote Curran to detective's rank. Along with that, two men had been transferred from a South Philadelphia precinct because they could not learn to speak Italian. McBride had been replaced, Lou James also, and Pat Curran was a seasoned veteran. Life was temporarily glorious.

Then, one by one at first, then in swelling numbers, the loonies—a multitude of the befuddled, the swindling, and, worst of all, the well-meaning—floated through the outer office and into Hudson's cramped little working area with tidings of varying credibility in response to the Figge reward. Before Hudson threatened to demote anyone who failed to screen the crackpots, he wasted a total of thirty-two investigative hours.

A rabbit-toothed little fellow from Spring Garden, Ignatz Hezekiah Sweat, claimed to be the Figge girl's secret lover for the past two years and even presented forged documents purporting to prove that they had been married in Maryland two months ago. Mr. Sweat was convinced that Lester Figge had murdered his own daughter upon discovering their relationship. Hudson had Sweat remanded to the county prison for attempted fraud. Jennifer Figge-Sweat indeed! Hudson agreed the hyphen admitted of more intelligence hidden from plain sight than he had imagined.

An obvious homosexual named James Berryford Saxon claimed to have seen Miss Figge struggling with someone outside the club in New Jersey in which he was appearing as a magician and master of ceremonies. A summary investigation showed that the description of the alleged assailant fitted Saxon's manager, who had refused to allow him to perform his imitation of the disturbed Mrs. McKinley.

A Mrs. Hosek from Passayunk insisted that the veil of Saint Veronica had manifested itself on her living-room wall, just between the portraits of Jesus and the late Mr. Hosek, bearing a bloody inscription accusing her next-door neighbor, Mrs. Shapiro.

Finally, Hudson listened for a time with some credulity to the statements of Franklin Darrent of Southwark, whose careful study of the crimes infused his confessions with plausibility. His knowledge of relatively minor details even prompted the lieutenant to bring in a stenographer and witnesses. Then, just as Hudson was about to send for Nathan McBride, Darrent, growing more excited, also confessed to having blown up the *Maine*. Saxon, Mrs. Hosek, and Franklin Darrent all were turned over to medical authorities for observation.

For sheer peculiarity, though, few matched Mme. Natalia Cheever, the Majestic Lady. Ever since the lieutenant had assigned Fatzinger to interview her, Bones had been hopelessly smitten. He had even given her his prized sunflower. While Hudson scratched his head—the two seemed truly flattered by each other's attention—

others in the station found it reason for coarse merriment. Poor Fatzinger, oblivious to the gibes and laughter of his colleagues, took to writing poetry and even to using mouthwash.

John Stanklow's dog, Joseph, still unable to detect the mysterious odors of sin, left his characteristic mark under the desk before Hudson returned to his office. Stanklow, embarrassed but undaunted, left a Bible on Hudson's desk as a gesture of appeasement. But he uttered some learned profanity when Hudson had kicked Joseph into the street. The pressures born of his new responsibilities and the unremitting heat of the city had begun to fray Lieutenant Hudson's nerves. He hated animal abuse.

Life was not without its little rewards, however. When things seemed to approach the unbearable point, Hudson could always open the file on Richard Cooper for laughs. He estimated that with haggling and plea bargaining and eventual probation, the little jerk would be screwed to the wall for at least a year. With luck it might be longer than that, because Cooper, fool that he was, had decided to represent himself. One could not ask for a dumber attorney.

When the word came in that there had been a shooting in Grundy's Patch, the lieutenant decided to investigate it himself. He seized the opportunity. Affairs like this and the bludgeoning of that Bowman family were welcome relief from the bedlam in his station.

Thirteen

One year ago to the day Irwin Heester had purchased the old Henderson Building on the corner of Forty-ninth and Berkshire with an eye toward converting its twenty cramped offices into thirty-five tenement flats. On the evening before work was to begin, as if by act of divine retribution, a storm had come up and lightning had struck Irwin's building. Among the other terms of the sale which he had neglected to fulfill was the installation of a lightning rod atop the roof, although he swore to the insurance company that lightning had had nothing to do with it. Irwin was convinced, or at least he howled repeatedly, that it had been the work of an arsonist—one of the many deadbeats of his ledger—and for months he had steadfastly refused to have the eyesore razed.

Finally, after exhausting every ploy to sell the building and after receiving his third citation from the city, Irwin had acquiesced. It would take money to clear away the debris, but he had found a company that was willing to do it at cost in return for some vaguely worded promises: The Fergus O'Farrell Construction and Demolition Company. The Gouger thrived on immigrant companies; they were so easily double-talked.

Satisfied that he had made the best of a bad situation, he ordered them to begin work. But thinking about it at breakfast, he had the gnawing realization that he'd overlooked something. He put on an older suit and a pair of scuffed boots and hopped on a trolley, having left his poached eggs and tea untouched. His wife ate his breakfast.

Having disembarked one block from the building, he cut through an alley and approached the workers unnoticed, surveying the operation from within a crowd of idle onlookers. Just as he'd expected, there was the flatbed wagon already laden with the least damaged timber from the basement.

"Where the hell do you think you're goin' with that lumber?" he shouted at the wagon driver.

"Right over yer arse if ye don't git outa the way," answered the driver.

Irwin shouted for O'Farrell and refused to budge. The wagon driver jumped down from his seat and rolled up his sleeves.

O'Farrell glanced at Irwin and squinted with minor annoyance. "Oh, it's yerself, Mr. Heester."

"It is, O'Farrell, you crook, and I'd like to know who told you those logs could be toted away."

"Why, you did, Mr. Heester," said O'Farrell, swabbing his forehead with a bright-red handkerchief as he barked an order to some men.

"I couldn't have," snorted Irwin. "As you can see, they're perfectly useful logs—all of them."

"Mr. Heester"—O'Farrell grinned—"didn't ye read yer own contract?"

"Of course I did." Irwin flushed. "I wrote it, didn't I?"

"Well then." O'Farrell pulled a folded document from the hindpocket of his trousers and opened it up for Irwin's inspection. "Ye'll recall, Mr. Heester, page two, paragraph three, line six, which states: 'All salvageable and salable materials to be recovered from the property of the party of the first part shall automatically accrue to the party of the second part.'"

"What?"

"That's meself, ye see. The Fergus O'Farrell Construction and Demolition Company."

Irwin grabbed the document from O'Farrell's hands. O'Farrell's broad grin never slackened. He signaled the wagon driver to proceed as Irwin scanned the page, his lips moving a mile a minute.

"I couldn't have written that," Irwin insisted. "You've forged this!"

"It's a notarized copy, bucko," answered O'Farrell in a calm voice. "The *law's* on me side in this instance. Ye know, ye really ought to be more careful with the King's English," he advised, just to rub in a bit of salt.

"You've cheated me, you immigrant sons of bitches," he protested, to the delight of the crowd. "You knew that contract was a mistake!"

"Now, Mr. Heester," said O'Farrell with obvious satisfaction, "ye wrote it yerself, an' what was a poor ould immigrant to do but sign it?"

The crowd of scattered workers cheered gleefully. Irwin's face turned white. A worker grabbed O'Farrell's arm and pulled him aside. Irwin demanded to know what was going on. O'Farrell waved him away with a short gesture.

In the basement, under the stairway, in an area where the storage bins used to be, one of the men had found a body.

To the police the worst thing about the discovery of the shopgirl's remains was the effect it had upon the residents of the district. Aura Lee Darcy had been reported missing one week before. Her condition was not unlike that of her unfortunate predecessors, ghastly but as expected.

One day previous, the body of the dishwasher Susan Beckwith had been discovered, the president of the First National Bank of Philadelphia nearly stumbling over her down the front steps of his home.

Irwin reacted predictably. Horrified at first by the effect the corpse could have on the property values, he soon created some vague form of association with the bank president and was beside himself with his new and dubious prestige. While the bank president remained reticent, Irwin told all of his encounter with the menace hovering over the neighborhood. In his excited recollections the facts changed shape; soon it was Irwin himself, not the laborer, who had happened upon the body of young Miss Darcy. Until the police had put a clamp on him, reminding him that he would have to swear to his court testimony, he recounted each morbid detail to everyone he met.

The neighborhood was gradually slipping into a state of panic, certain ones arming themselves with knives, small arms, and hatpins, locking their daughters indoors after six, and organizing vigilante patrols. Within a week West Philadelphia had become unsafe for strangers.

All this naturally delighted the yellow press. The war with Spain had crested, and for a time had eased into sameness. The series of easy victories since Manila Bay grew monotonous, and the matter of conducting the war prosaic. The dailies had been relegated to a preponderance of material relating principally to the far less glorious question of financing the war effort. After a squabble on Capitol Hill, Congress had decided to float a bond issue of two hundred million dollars beyond the fifty million appropriated in March. There was talk of higher internal duties on stamps, beer, and tobacco, to which the public, save the members of the Ladies' Temperance League, had responded with chagrin. Admiral Cervera, bottled up in Santiago Harbor by Admiral Schley's flying squadron, was lying low for now. Rumor had it that the troops in Tampa would soon be deployed against the Spaniards at Siboney, El Caney, and San Juan Hill. A romantic new figure, the Philippine insurgent, Emilio Aquinaldo, piqued the imagination of some readers. But to a large extent the conditions abroad had created a climate ideal for the exploitation of a local sensation.

To its credit this time, the press made few attempts to manipulate the facts. Stanley Butterfield was still writing obituaries and advertisements for foot plasters, and his colleagues had learned something of a lesson from his embarrassment. There was one reporter, a young woman who wrote for a ladies' periodical, who tried repeatedly to solicit an interview with Irwin Heester. Hudson's warning had been clear and impressive enough; the Lieutenant had told Irwin that a perjury charge awaited if his lies should follow him to court, and the repercussions could even involve investigation of his lending practices. Much as it pained him, Irwin remained silent in the face of the young reporter's obstinate efforts.

Nor did the writers dwell on popular myths to any great extent. The foreign menace issue was old hat. Germany, like most of Europe, recognized the imminent American success against Spain and took pains to establish warmer relations with Washington. As stimulating as it might have been to suggest evidence linking the West Philadelphia butcher to a Spanish plot, such action was unnecessary. The facts were sensational enough.

Try as they might, the police were unable to prevent macabre facts from leaking out. The number of victims, counting the Misses Darcy and Beckwith, was up to seven—not including the missing and presumed dead. The details of mutilation and torture had become common topics on the street corners and over fences. Indelicate as they sounded, even in hushed voices, the tales were told and retold, each time with new distortions. The dailies did their best to keep the stories on neighborhood lips, featuring the Butcher at every opportunity.

When the name of Dr. Ian Blakeley was dropped by a senile clerk in City Hall, they focused their attention on him. They demanded to know what inadequacies of the police department had necessitated his employment, how many tax dollars were being squandered on him, and why a man with his reputation had so far failed to stem the flow of events. Almost immediately cartoonists pinpointed his features and satirists captured his crotchets and epicurisms.

The district was further agitated by the Bowman murders, which the press claimed were connected to the other crimes. Hudson insisted they were unrelated. He much preferred Lizzie Borden to Jack the Ripper and he wanted no confusion. Lizzie was manageable.

Nathan McBride was weary of his routine. The frustration of getting nowhere, or worse yet, seeming suddenly further away from the solution, was almost overwhelming at times. Whenever a body turned up, he would arrive on the scene before Blakeley. According to their agreement, Lieutenant Hudson would leave the preliminary investigation to him while the city patrolmen kept the press and the public out of his way.

Nathan returned to Philadelphia late Saturday evening after a fortnight in the coal region. Dr. Blakeley felt that something of value could be got by looking into Jillian Ranshaw's unhappy history. He guessed that Blakeley was searching for some common denominator in the victims' backgrounds that made them either more receptive to the Butcher's inducements or more satisfying to his purposes. Whatever the intent, the journey, in retrospect, seemed more academic than useful. As the train had rumbled homeward through acres of white birch and linden, Nathan looked out at the bright-green hills and wondered whether his was the seat Jillian had occupied on her last train ride. The scenery was exhilarating before the mountains of Schuylkill County gave way to the duller farmlands to the southeast, and bored by the barns and cornfields, he looked back on his annoyingly inconsequential encounter with Buck Ranshaw. He had traced Buck to a seedy tavern in the next town. Buck, who had always harbored some poorly defined resentment against the law, had picked up a poker and threatened to beat Nathan senseless; Nathan had had no alternative but to subdue him by force. After dodging a series of wild-eyed swings of the poker, he had brought Buck down with two well-placed left hooks and a right cross. Awakening a short time later, for Nathan had been careful not to hit him too hard, Buck had been only slightly more cooperative. While the tavern crowd did its best to ignore the whole affair, Buck had shouted, "She was a slut, wasn't she? She got punished for sluttin'!" In a primitive way, Buck's summation had been apt. As he massaged his bruised knuckles and closed his eyes to rest for the last hundred miles of the journey, Nathan's weary thoughts revolved among the five murders of which he was aware. Downbeaten, on his return he found himself almost uncaringly assuming the burden of two more investigations in two days.

Nathan would notify Andrew Sutton and oversee the photographing of the scene and subject. At such times Sutton's flashy new vehicle proved a blessing, tending to draw attention away from their labors and keeping the morbid onlookers to a minimum. There was still no thaw in their relationship, however. In fact, their mutual resentment grew every time tragedy inflicted them upon each other. Furthermore, the photographer had not been eliminated from the detective's list of suspects. For the most part Nathan and Sutton communicated in simple uninflected sentences.

Nathan would check for blood and other stains, clothing fibers, fingernail scrapings, footprints, and any articles unconsciously discarded at the scene. Then he would sketch a floor or ground plan of the scene and interview the shaken and often nauseated person or persons who had happened upon the body. By the time Dr. Blakeley arrived, Nathan had the essentials of the investigative report completed. Both soon recognized the futility of most of it since the remains had always been transported from another place.

The pressure was affecting Blakeley, too, although so far apparent only to Sophia and Snopkowski. The former noticed his restiveness, the latter his lack of appetite. They had seen this before on similar cases—though Snopkowski did mutter a long skein of epithets when informed that he had not touched her specially prepared meat loaf last evening. "Eats like bird, goddamn," she had pronounced.

The scarcity of good light in the basement of the old Henderson Building rendered clear detail in Sutton's photographs of Aura Lee Darcy an impossibility, but the pictures of Susan Beckwith, taken the day before, were good. The morning sun had shone brightly upon the bank president's front steps. It was of little consequence in any case; the pictures, the interviews, the diagrams, everything else at the discovery sites, would be useful only if and when they got the Butcher to court. For the moment the broken bodies told Dr. Blakeley everything immediately useful.

Later in the day, however, Blakeley suddenly realized that the sites had provided him with something more substantive after all. Indeed, they forced him to his first conclusion.

He set the reports down and reviewed them in chronological order, paying particular attention to the places of discovery: Masterson, riverbank; Poole, rubbish heap; Wittingham, abandoned building; Figge, public park . . . and riding stable on own estate; Ranshaw, garbage can on skid row; Beckwith, front steps; Darcy, demolition site. . . .

The Figge discovery had, of course, been deliberately sensational, so much so that he had almost begun to think it an isolated case, perhaps even a ghoulish imitation of the Butcher's work. Such heinous phenomena were the usual by-products of bizarre crimes, especially in the wake of publicity. Now he saw it as an important link in the macabre chain, a formal but premature announcement. Contrary to his and detective McBride's earlier opinions, he no longer regarded it as a gesture designed simply to taunt them. He now believed it a mistake on the Butcher's part. It had brought not only Blakeley himself into the case, but also a great deal of notoriety, and so had broken the carefully planned pattern. He felt certain there would be other, bigger announcements in the future unless a break in the case were to come their way, since the Butcher had for some reason put himself into the position of having to top himself.

The damned thing kept slipping in and out of Blakeley's brain, tantalizing him. There would be more of those quiet, unsolved disappearances as well, less dramatic, but equally frightening, little valleys amid the awesome hills.

That was it. . . . The pattern almost reminded him of the structure of a Shakespearean tragedy—a series of smaller peaks all leading up to an inevitable climax. That, of course, would prove the Figge incident an error: too melodramatic, too soon. It was almost as if the Butcher—as Blakeley, unconscious of the press' influence on him, had come to use the term for the collective—were involved in an internal struggle over how best to terrorize the district. The Butcher was a two- or three-headed monster; that very divisiveness could be the chink in his heretofore-perfect armor of invisibility.

He returned to the nuts and bolts of the case. The earlier disappearances, the still-unaccounted for like Deanna Grayson, dated back, before the Masterson girl, well into the winter. Presumably they had been disposed of efficiently, perhaps by the use of lye or acid or just into well-isolated grave sites. Then Masterson and Poole turned up, relatively undramatically, but nevertheless discovered. Whittingham, too. Her body, like the two previous to hers, had been placed where one might or might not happen upon it. No advertising, mind you, but neither had there been a great effort at concealment. Bodies thrown into the river are bound to be washed ashore sooner or later.

Since the Figge death the pattern showed an increasing exhibitionism. Jillian Ranshaw's remains had been stuffed into a garbage can in a locale where derelicts were known to rummage; surely she had not been there long before that unfortunate old chap had encountered her.

But the last two cases had confirmed an even more important suspicion. Blakeley sipped a glass of cognac and concentrated on the Beckwith and Darcy reports.

Who would know, he asked himself, not only that the gutted Henderson Building was due to be demolished that day, but also that the bank president made it a practice to get up early on Sunday morning and walk to his office because he appreciated the quiet of an empty building? Not just someone from the neighborhood, but someone intimately familiar with everything going on, someone who walked among its citizenry and retained random pieces of intelligence. The Butcher knew just where and when to leave his victims and how best to elicit his desired response. Since the Figge murder, Hudson, for one, had begun to think that his precinct was only a convenient dumping ground for the human debris wrought of crimes committed elsewhere in the city. But Lieutenant Hudson was unflagging in his paranoia these days, and for good reason; the newspapers had been hounding him since his enlistment of Blakeley had become known. West Philadelphia, like it or not, was the proper place of venue, and the Butcher had been aptly named.

Blakeley opened the window and looked out on the green. Shadows had begun to creep across the lawn, and there was a welcome breeze from the river, cooling the twilight atmosphere. He watched a family of squirrels as they busied themselves around a chestnut tree. Across the river he saw the lines of carriages moving along the drive, and he thought of taking a walk in the hour before sunset. He often did his best thinking on an evening stroll.

He had given the worn Detective McBride the night off. Nathan and his young lady would have liked to go to the concert, Blakeley thought he'd overheard him say. So they would, and he rather envied them. Both the music and the young lady would help pick up his spirits, or at least blow away some of the cerebral fog. The symphony, as he understood it, would feature the massive Wagner overtures, appropriately enough, considering the martial temper of the age.

Sophia was painting in her studio when he found her. From the blush upon seeing him, he suspected that it was his long-promised portrait on which she was working, but since she made no move to cover it, he discovered that it was a picture of Ralphie in uniform. She missed Ralphie; the watery corners of her eyes said so. And she was worried. From his last letter they had learned that Ralphie, despite his awkwardness on horseback, had joined the Rough Riders. Colonel Roosevelt, apparently impressed by Ralphie's size, had decided that he looked the part so well that his inadequacies could be

put aside for the moment. It was well understood that the flamboy-
ant Roosevelt would have his men in the thick of it when the action
against the Spanish garrisons became a reality.

Blakeley kissed his wife on the cheek and poured some tea.

"It's quite good," he said. "Quite heroic, I'd say."

"To an extreme," she agreed, smiling her own satisfaction.

"Bit of a change for you, isn't it? The technique, I mean." He
studied the lines that were slowly taking shape on the canvas. "It's
almost Pre-Raphaelite."

"Do you think so?" She stepped back and looked on with him.
"It's unintended if so."

"Probably."

"Do you think it appropriate, Ian?"

"Oh, yes, quite so." He nodded. "Ralphie certainly deserves bold
lines and strong tones."

She put her brush and palette aside, seated herself on a divan in
front of the wide doors that opened up on the green, and sipped her
tea.

"Forgive my saying this if it disturbs your vanity, Ian, but you look
rather fatigued."

"I feel rather fatigued," he acknowledged.

"I wish you'd take a rest for one evening. Get out of your laboratory and read a silly novel or something."

"I was just about to take a stroll by the river. Will that do?"

"No. It's only an extension of your work, and you know that. You
shall think yourself into the grave. Read a silly novel instead."

"I've read them all, darling," he claimed. "I do believe I could re-
cite one in my sleep by now."

"I've a new one by George Moore," she said, showing him a book
that had been lying on the divan. "If you lie down, I shall read to
you."

Sophia, in spite of her propriety, had always been the subtle
temptress. With some difficulty he stifled the urge to give in. He
could not afford the distraction just now. He promised her a cruise
home to England when this loathsome case was over, kissed her
again, this time on the forehead, and started out the door. But he
paused before going on his way, turned, and reminded her that he
loved her. She smiled and threw him a kiss. What a grand lady, he
thought.

The yellow roses were in beautiful bloom. So were the asters and begonias. The air was refreshing, and the murmur of the water as it rolled against the river bank put him at ease after a while; but his mind remained preoccupied by the case.

There had been no sexual attacks on any of the victims. The idea had disturbed him for some time. It made no sense at first, and it also eliminated as suspects a large sector of the criminal population. There were extensive records of sex criminals at police headquarters. Blakeley had gone through the records, picture after picture and history after history, at least three times. The motives of sex criminals were usually easier to pinpoint and their propensity for repeating their offenses rendered them more identifiable than homicidal maniacs. They, on the other hand, came from nowhere. In any event, the sex theory had flown out the window for good after his completion of tests upon the Darcy girl this day.

It was never possible to prove unequivocally that a prostitute had been sexually molested; hence, the remains of three of the victims had been useless in that regard. But the others, eliminating the Whittingham girl, whose condition when discovered had made such an assessment impossible, showed no evidence of having been abused in that manner either. For a time yesterday Blakeley had feared there would be more confusion, for the customary smears taken on Miss Beckwith's body had given evidence of recent sexual contact. He had been about to review the department records for a fourth time when finally her young man, under Lieutenant Hudson's pressing interrogation, had all but admitted to having had intimate relations with her shortly before her disappearance. They had been betrothed for some time, the tearful young man had whispered, and had been planning to be wedded later in the month. Poor fellow, he was barely holding onto his sanity, and Hudson had hated to have to put him through it.

Blakeley sat on a bench near the river, lit up his pipe, and watched a sea gull diving for its dinner. It was somewhat unusual to see one there, so far inland, in the evening. Often, when he awoke, he would observe the birds sporting on the bank in the early hours and he would presume there had been a storm at sea. The gull soared for a moment, then rose with an updraft and dived abruptly into the water. It did so repeatedly, and he wondered at its patience. Then his attention was drawn to a dead fish that was bobbing inertly in a tidal pool, attracting swarms of parasites. Nature was not always reassuring.

Children at play, in their efforts to assume a role more menacing than the next, had taken to calling themselves the Butcher. Blakeley's enemy had taken over the roles previously held by Indians and Western outlaws. Wasn't it a simple matter, he thought, to make oneself into a folk hero?

"Dr. Blakeley, may I speak with you?"

The voice was far from hostile, but it startled him anyway. "What the deuce?" he muttered before realizing that there was no cause for alarm. "Oh, I'm terribly sorry," he hastened to add.

"It's I who ought to apologize, Dr. Blakeley. I haven't been able to meet you in a more orthodox manner, you see. So I've taken the liberty of disturbing your meditation, with the fervent hope that you're too much the gentleman to order me off your estate."

"Of course, I wouldn't order you away from here," he reassured her as he got out of his seat on the bench. "You observe no barricades around us, do you, Miss . . .?"

"Meredith. Adam P. Meredith," she replied with a smile.

"Eh?" He had a vague recollection of a Mr. Meredith who had been leaving messages for him here and there, but he'd had no opportunity to answer. She was radiant in the rosy twilight, wearing a summer dress of lacy tangerine which emphasized the raven's-wing ebony of her luxuriant hair. *If this is truly a female impersonator,* he mused, *he must be the greatest one since Edward Kynaston.*

"I'm the Mr. Meredith who's been trying to find you."

"Do, do sit down, Miss, er, Mr. Meredith."

"Thank you."

They took seats on opposite ends of the stone bench. She could sense with amusement his uneasiness. The temptation to leave him in that state was considerable.

"Actually, it's Allison Patricia Meredith, Dr. Blakeley. There's nothing very mysterious about me at all, I assure you."

"I'm quite certain," he answered with guarded relief, "that I knew that the moment I saw you." He noted that Miss Meredith was herself nervous; she gripped her small shapeless white handbag as if she were kneading dough, and when she spoke, there was a discernible quiver of the lower lip.

"For some time now," she proceeded, "I've been mulling over just how best to approach you. I considered any number of simulations, the best of which was to pose as a graduate student in criminology who was hoping to write a paper on your homicidal recidivist percentages theory. I wisely calculated the probability of your seeing through that."

"Pun intended?"

"Of course."

"It's been so long, you know, since I wrote the book that you might have gotten by," he said modestly.

"*Now* you tell me."

Across the river in a park set in the natural grove between three small escarpments, a band started to play some popular music; ragtime, they called it. It wasn't *Lohengrin,* but it helped relax the mood for the time being.

"That's not very remote really. Last week a fellow came here shortly after breakfast one morning and announced himself as a distant cousin of Mrs. Blakeley. His North Midlands accent was quite good, too. In fact, we almost took him in. Claimed to have seen action against the Zulus in southern Africa."

"An impostor?"

"A reporter."

"Oh?"

"Now, *Mr.* Meredith, what is the nature of your business here?"

"I, perhaps I should begin at the beginning."

"Do."

"You see"—she spoke carefully—"I had hoped to be involved in the war effort. In fact, I'd been counting on it ever since the *Maine* went down."

The tempo of the ragtime music picked up behind Miss Meredith's speech, and she became increasingly agitated as she spilled out a tale of great professional disappointment. They repaired to an isolated gazebo a few acres away to escape the distracting rhythms of the band. As they strolled along the path that led up to the gazebo, through a row of hedges that faced the river, she explained that Frank Norris and all the others who were considered good at her trade had been sent to the tropics. At the last minute the editors had reneged on their promises, claiming that a war zone was certainly no place for a lady.

"Forgive me, Miss Meredith, but I'm afraid I must agree with your editors, in this instance at least."

"Horsefeathers, Dr. Blakeley." Her tone was determined. "I grew up in a family of very manly gentlemen, my father and six brothers. I can certainly take care of myself."

"War zones, Miss Meredith, are not necessarily the milieu of gentlemen," he said with sobriety.

"I hope you don't think me too forward when I say this, Dr. Blakeley, having just met you for the first time, but we are embarking on a new century in just a little more than a year and a half, and tired attitudes like the one you've just expressed are bound to be re-examined in the next era."

"To be sure," he concurred somewhat patronizingly and in a tone she could not possibly misunderstand.

"You miss my point, sir. I am a talented woman being swallowed up in the conventional views of my superiors. I should be corresponding from Cuba on significant matters right now, instead of having to wheedle some compassion out of you."

He was reluctant to abet such latent paroxysms within the kind of world he had loved for so long. Bernard Shaw's enlightened women were nothing novel to him; in her own gentle way, Sophia had always been one of them, and in a manner much less ameliorated, Rosalie was truly a creature of the New Dawn. But Blakeley was, despite his inherent tolerance, determined to hold the line on some things.

"My dear lady," he averred, "whatever your vision of the future—and I'm certain it is quite sophisticated—I cannot condone the presence of an estimable young woman in a combat zone. Your editors' objections are, therefore, sustained."

She deprecated his sentiments. "Frankly, Dr. Blakeley, I'd feel a great deal safer in the tropics amid the sabers and Gatling guns than I do here in Philadelphia these days."

"Which, finally, brings us to the matter of your business here."

"Yes."

The sun was declining rapidly, and the band in the park had lapsed into a pleasant waltz. The breeze coming up the river was now downright chilly, but she declined the use of his coat.

She explained her interest in him. With the war coverage out of the question, she had turned her attention to the ever more celebrated case of the West Philadelphia Butcher. When it had become sorely evident that the police would not permit her to solicit the cooperation of Irwin Heester and other background figures, she decided to go directly to him.

"Have you ever heard of *McClure's Ladies' Journal?*" When he shook his head negatively, she went on. "My editors may be rather stodgy and counterproductive at times, but they are not of the same cut as the yellow dailies. We do not thrive on panic and sensation. Nor do we seek our scapegoats and whipping boys."

"It all sounds rather pristine," he offered facetiously. In the distance Blakeley observed the gull feasting on something, perched atop a tree stump on the riverbank.

"Relatively, at least," she responded in all seriousness. "Our readers, you see, are much less inclined to wallow in muck."

"But doesn't that seem a bit of a *non sequitur?* This case, of all the recent goings-on, is surely a matter of muck. Indeed, great portions of the details are unprintable, even in the less conservative sheets."

"You shall simply have to trust in my ability to work with the English language." She looked directly into his eyes. "Look, Dr. Blakeley," she pressed on, "you must realize that you are a rather fascinating figure in your own right, an urbane genius who enjoys worldwide esteem but who lives in a rigidly conventional life-style. There will be no need to concoct any satirical overtones or the like. I do not doubt for a moment that our readers shall love you."

"Granted," he replied matter-of-factly, "but I fail to see how they'll love the story, however skillfully you may phrase it."

"In all respect, sir," she countered ("sir" made him feel older than he felt or wished to be), "they don't have to love it to read it. I'm certain you don't literally love the dissection of a corpse, though it may tell you what you must know."

"Well taken, Miss Meredith, but what *must* they know?"

"May I remind you that all the victims are young women? The Butcher has molested no men, no older citizens, no children, thank God. Somewhere in there, I'm sure, is a message for my readers, who are in the main women of my age."

"If anything, I should expect it could be stated rather simply: Be more discreet in your choice of companions."

"That's blunt," she proclaimed. A sudden gust of wind caused her hair to come undone, and some of it fell to her shoulders. "Perhaps we can find out something of the mind of the sex fiend that we still don't know. There are many platitudes and very few words of substance to date. We learned nothing at all from Jack the Ripper, you know, save the fact that illicit love can be dangerous. Perhaps this is our chance."

The wind became chillier and whirled through the gazebo with determination as the shadows started to cross the green. The band was now playing "After the Ball."

On the way back to the house, he inquired about her choice of a nom de plume. She answered that women readers still tended to grant more credibility to authors with men's names. "Rather like the career of George Sand," he remarked, to which she only shrugged noncommittally. One negative factor was her not evidencing so far a sense of humor. Their main concerns being grim, a sense of humor was imperative. Maybe that would appear when his cooperation relieved her tension.

Not exactly the chronicler he'd have chosen for the record of his finest hour, he mused. Perhaps she would keep him on his toes; with such a conscientious Boswell in his shadow, he could ill afford to do anything ridiculous or self-serving. He wondered just how she would rate in Sophia's perceptive eye. Certainly Ralphie would have appreciated her.

The early-morning session with the bank president, Mr. McIver, was only slightly productive. He hurriedly escorted Nathan into his office on the pretense that he spoke more clearly over a second cup of coffee and locked the door with the admonition to his subordinates that he was not to be interrupted under any circumstances. It was not that he was unwilling to cooperate; he simply did not wish to draw any more notoriety than had already come of his melancholy discovery. He answered what he could, tapping his fingers nervously on the desk. The coffee went from tepid to cold.

The only testimony Nathan believed Dr. Blakeley would consider useful was the name of McIver's physician. Blakeley was interested in establishing a common denominator in the habits of those who happened across the bodies of the victims. He explained that he believed there were traces of a pattern to be found there. Nathan failed to see how Mr. McIver's story would turn up anything worth their while.

McIver, a stocky little gentleman built somewhat along the lines of Blakeley himself, took great pride in his constitution. McIver lifted a heavy leather chair off the floor by gripping its leg at the bottom. As Nathan expressed his fully anticipated appreciation, the banker added that he'd once been capable of lifting much heavier weights. He still made it a practice to swim three miles a day on his vacations in Atlantic City. Accordingly he never needed the services of a family physician. In fact, he had not had to seek medical attention since the day he'd dropped a chair on his foot while performing his favorite routine at a lodge meeting ten years ago.

Thus, it had come as quite a shock when, returning from a business appointment one evening last winter, he had become dizzy and had experienced a shortness of breath. Despite McIver's protests, the coachman had rerouted the carriage to an office he'd spied near City Line Avenue. Luckily, the doctor had been in. McIver recalled that the doctor had been a smallish man, lacking in warmth and a bit preoccupied by other matters, but thorough and competent. The doctor had diagnosed nervous fatigue and ordered McIver to soften his daily regimen. He had suggested that certain taxing work be put aside until Sundays, when it could be divorced from the other stresses of the busy weekday office. Dr. Max Toberman, a foreign fellow, and McIver still visited him for monthly checkups.

Nathan thanked him and, out of courtesy, left through a side door. The little banker had been surprisingly likable.

It was still only midmorning as Nathan made his way along the river drive back to Dr. Blakeley's home.

The morning was still pleasant, at least in the shade of the trees that lined the river drive. The heat was rising rapidly. He slowed the horse's pace and plodded along to the sound of the birds. The drive along the river was dotted with whitewashed stones and decorated with mulberry bushes—very soothing.

His thoughts soon returned to the past evening. The Wagner overtures had been overwhelming. The orchestra, expanded by extra brass and strings, had been so powerful that as the carefully paced "Procession" built up to its awesome climax, one could feel the skin grow taut on the cheeks, as if taken by a centrifugal force.

More than that, in the heat of the moment Aidan had reached for his hand and gripped it with excitement. At her door sometime later, after ice cream and conversation, he had kissed her good-night. Not for long, he recalled, but in a manner more passionate than heretofore: Nathan knew he was in love to the depths, and the feeling was comfortable. Aidan had been more beautiful than ever before in her dress of light green and rose. The night had been good to him.

* * *

Some miles away Lieutenant Hudson was sitting at his desk listening to a bizarre tale.

As Nathan entered the Blakeley driveway, he slowed to notice Sophia riding her favorite chestnut over the well-maintained rise. Dr. Blakeley had commented that she usually rode more often whenever he was buried in a serious case such as this one. In the mornings, sometimes accompanied by Rosalie, she took the lane that ran parallel to the river, then turned onto a path that wound through the woods at the eastern end of the property and found its way circuitously back to the stable. She reined up and waved at him as he guided his rig through the open gate. Near the main entrance she caught up with him.

"Have you had your breakfast, Nathan?" she asked.

He had not, except for a cup of coffee, but his face showed uncertainty.

"Don't worry," she added, "Dr. Blakeley has eaten all the kidneys and jam. Snopkowski will be more than happy to prepare some bacon and eggs."

"In that case I'm famished," he responded.

"So am I. I've been on this beast all morning. I'll meet you in five minutes."

She rode away toward the stable. He selected a hitching post under a large tree to keep his horse out of the sun. The day promised to become oppressive; the sky was overcast and the air still. Mrs. Blakeley's ability to control that huge animal almost mystified him; her fragile appearance was deceiving.

Snopkowski was in a grouchy mood when he found her in the kitchen. The irregularities of the domestic schedule, Dr. Blakeley breakfasting at six thirty and the others at ten, had been quite enough, but when Victor had suggested that she had overcooked the lobster last evening, she had settled into a state of aggressive preparation. Nathan's efforts at conviviality were met with a series of surly grunts. Sophia entered, shed her riding helmet, allowing her hair to fall freely about her shoulders, and ordered breakfast. Snopkowski grumbled that they would have to settle for sausages instead of bacon and then waddled off to her sacrosanct kitchen. Sophia resigned herself to sausages.

"Do you like them with your fried eggs, Nathan?" she asked. He answered that it made no difference. He was hungry enough to eat the table.

"Have you met your new associate?" she asked.

"Associate?" He wondered, with distant hopes, whether Sutton had been replaced. "No, I haven't." Sutton's work was the best he had seen.

"She's most attractive."

"She?"

"Yes. She writes for one of my favorite magazines. If you play your cards properly, you may become the darling of every young woman in the country. She's especially capable of piecing together vivid profiles."

"Hmm. . . ." He sipped his coffee and was pensive for a moment. "And if I play them badly, I suppose she'll make me look like a three-headed toad."

Sophia laughed cheerily. "Oh, I trust you'll handle her with prodigious charm, Nathan."

Snopkowski entered with a plate of buttered toast. Sophia asked her why Victor was not serving breakfast. When Snopkowski did not answer, Sophia cleared her throat and repeated the question.

"Dot yonko," the cook said eventually with a dismissing gesture. "He spill chicken grease on his pants goddamn."

"And how, pray, did that happen?" Sophia asked suspiciously.

"How I know?" the cook answered with an enigmatic smile. "Maybe he should wear apron. Goddamn clumsy bummas."

Snopkowski went off chuckling to herself. Sophia sighed and bit into a piece of toast, and Nathan did his best to cover a grin. When she looked up, the two broke into laughter.

"Why, may I ask, has Dr. Blakeley chosen to let a journalist in on our business?" Nathan asked at length. "It seems to be something of an about-face."

She paused and looked slightly wary. "You won't be angry with me, I hope, if I tell you the whole truth?"

"Of course not, Mrs. Blakeley." He knew it would be next to impossible to be angry with her.

"It was my doing," she said. "I met Miss Meredith at a lecture last week and liked her proposal, so I arranged a meeting last night. I handled it with consummate tact, if I may say so."

Snopkowski interrupted Sophia and whispered something into her ear. Sophia nodded but looked puzzled. The cook turned to Nathan.

"Why you no come eat poor Snopkowski food no more? You look skinny goddamn."

"Every chance I get, Mrs. Snopkowski. I promise."

She waddled back into the kitchen, shaking her head and muttering to herself in broken English. Nathan wasn't sure she believed him.

"It must have been bothering her," Sophia commented. "She's very touchy about her art."

"So I've noticed, Mrs. Blakeley. It's written all over the butler's uniform."

A short time later, when they had just about finished their breakfasts, Dr. Blakeley entered, bristling. In his hand, rolled into the form of a small cudgel, he carried a copy of the morning newspaper. Sophia greeted him with a peck on the cheek and repaired to the kitchen, claiming to have to mediate the Slavic strife. Behind Blakeley strode a young woman looking weary; when Nathan observed Sophia wink at her in passing, he presumed that this was his new associate, Miss Meredith. He stood up until the young woman was seated, then resumed eating his breakfast.

Blakeley slammed the newspaper down and told him to read page three. There was a column describing Nathan's presence at the Wagner concert last evening attached to a cartoon depicting Blakeley as Nero fiddling while Philadelphia burned. Nathan glanced at it, smiled, then looked for the results of the baseball game with Washington.

"Doesn't it rankle you, my dear boy?" Blakeley removed his monocle and stiffened with indignation.

Then it dawned on him that the police must grow accustomed to unfair treatment. He'd neglected to introduce Nathan to Miss Meredith, and he hastened, apologetically, to do so.

"I'm afraid, Detective McBride, that I must beg your indulgence," she said. "I am fully aware of my rather disheveled, haggard look this morning. I'd hoped to be much more presentable for our first meeting."

"Permit me to observe, Miss Meredith, that you look quite fresh for one who's been trying to keep up with Dr. Blakeley. He's worn me to a frazzle in the few weeks I've known him. The proper adjective for his pace is manic."

"Tommyrot, my boy," Blakeley objected amiably, "you merely wish to discourage Miss Meredith from tagging along."

"Actually," she uttered at length, just to break the ice, "I'm particularly worn out from the lack of sleep. I spent the night poring over the files on your case."

"Hardly the most appropriate bedtime reading, I should think," said Blakeley.

"No, but I knew I had a lot of catching up to do. I'm grateful you entrusted them to me."

Nathan disliked overly assertive young women, and the thought of having to tolerate one for the duration chafed his composure considerably. He had not said a word for the past minute or so, but he had felt keenly the sting of her aggressive tongue.

"Did you like the section on the pale head?" he asked icily.

There was a long, painful silence. Miss Meredith looked at Nathan as if she could happily throw him into a pit of mad dogs. Nathan, meanwhile, spread some marmalade over a piece of toast while Blakeley looked on nervously.

"Well," he began awkwardly, hoping to make the best of things, "I, er, suppose that's as good a cue as any for what I'd wished to brief you on this morning." The air in the room seemed to be growing close, though the windows were open. "I seem to have gotten too caught up in the external pattern. I'd all but overlooked the recent departure. It occurs to me that, since Figge, the murderer has refrained from moving organs from the bodies. The skin, of course, is still being taken from here and there, but the other surgery has stopped."

Nathan glanced at Miss Meredith. She betrayed no timidity. Apparently she was determined to give him no such satisfaction.

"I noticed that," she said, somewhat hoarsely, "in the autopsy reports."

"In a way," Blakeley continued more easily now, "it makes me tend to rule out our earlier theories on cult murders, if you will recall our having played around with human sacrifice and so on."

"Would a doctor fit the picture?"

Blakeley got up and paced around the table. "I've thought of that, and it certainly would narrow the field conveniently. But I don't think our man—or woman, I might remind you, since there's a very delicate touch to some of this—has to be quite that good. A medical student cannot be ruled out."

This time Miss Meredith winced, Nathan noticed. Blakeley was too absorbed in his thoughts to be distracted.

"I picked up the name of a doctor this morning in my conversation with the banker McIver," Nathan said.

"Really?" Blakeley was thoughtful for a moment. "That may indeed be useful."

In his days as a practicing physician some years ago, it had occurred to him how much information he received from patients in their efforts to relieve anxiety. They would talk of anything unrelated to their medical problems. He and his colleagues had often joked about their kinship with the barkeepers on Fleet Street; he could have published a tattle sheet of his own.

He apprised them of his interest in establishing a list of those in a position to know where best to leave the bodies for dramatic effect and of why he considered that important. Nathan quipped that they should question every newspaperman in town in that case. Miss Meredith's natural color seemed to be returning as the talk mercifully turned away from what it had been moments ago. Clearly fascinated by Dr. Blakeley's mind, she jotted notes on practically every word he uttered.

Nathan recounted his conversation with McIver, especially the matter involving the doctor.

"What was the physician's name?" asked Blakeley.

"A foreign name, German or Austrian." Nathan checked his notebook. "Dr. Max Toberman. His office is at Fifty-fourth and Calvert, near City Line Avenue."

"We must check up on him," Blakeley thought aloud, "if only for the sake of thoroughness. Perhaps the county medical association would be the best start."

Victor entered, dressed in a new uniform and wearing his customarily aloof expression.

"A phone call for you, sir. Leftenant Hudson. He wishes me to announce," Victor relayed stiffly, "that he has a hot one for you."

Blakeley excused himself and rushed off to his study to take the call. As he passed by Victor, the butler complained sotto voce about Lieutenant Hudson's forwardness and indelicacy. Blakeley either did not hear him or simply chose to ignore him. Victor huffed and strutted off to his favorite corner of the house, where he was less likely to be put to work. Lieutenant Hudson's telephone call had come through just as Victor was about to call the gentleman on Smedley Street who supplied him with gin, and he resented the intrusion immensely.

"I knew when we came up with this one that you'd be interested," the voice on the other end of the line squawked. The telephone always made one sound like a laryngitic tenor.

"Have you got our man, Lieutenant?" Blakeley asked with guarded anticipation. There had been so many blind alleys.

"Could be, Dr. Blakeley, could be." Hudson's tone was enthusiastic. "This one has to be the archetypal loony. We picked him up for defacing a church—Saint Brigit's on Market. That was Regis Tolan's parish, you may recall. Anyway, this character was smearing blood all over the statues and altar and running naked up and down the aisles yelling 'decadence' when the priest walked in and grabbed him."

In the dining room the awkward silence was broken only by the sound of Miss Meredith pouring another cup of coffee, this time with cream and sugar. Nathan's fork tapped unconsciously against a plate as he wondered just how Andrew Sutton could possibly fit the new picture as Dr. Blakeley had painted it.

Hudson's tale bordered on the grotesque. Blakeley listened in awe as the lieutenant proceeded to tell him why the suspect was something more than just a bewildered vandal. The Furies that beset this creature were especially vicious.

He had slipped into the church by the rear entrance and slit the chicken's throat while kneeling before the twelfth station of the Cross. In front of the tenth station he had shed his clothing, and as the chicken had clucked and flapped about in his grasp, he had raised a lighted votive candle and drank of the chicken's blood. Then he had skipped up the aisle and over the altar rail, still waving the chicken. The priest subdued the suspect finally by the sudden introduction of a heavy ciborium to his head—but not before Zoltan Mroszek had marked virtually every statue in the church with his tormented message.

Aside from causing old women who had lingered after eight o'clock mass to suffer possible strokes—convinced they were witnessing a case of demonic possession—the police had not considered him of any permanent gravity. When one of the old women had calmed down, she thought she recognized him. Within an hour, while Zoltan was being taken off to Hudson's precinct station, Officers Scarpatti and Fletcher had been shown into Zoltan's sleazy room. An excited Mrs. Leibowitz had been entrusted a pass key by the landlady.

"You'll never believe what they uncovered there," Hudson announced with exuberance.

"A lot of bedbugs, I'd venture," answered Blakeley, trying to mask his own excitement.

"That too. My men say the smell almost blinded them. But it seems this guy keeps an album on anything related to the Butcher: newspaper clippings, magazine articles; he even has photographs of the Poole girl."

Blakeley blinked his eyes at that.

"But get this," Hudson went on. "He's written poems about the Butcher. 'Songs of Joy' he calls them. He claims the Butcher's been sent by some higher authority to cleanse our pernicious society."

Hudson's men had rushed off to Zoltan's tenement because they'd remembered it as the site of the Bowman murders. One of the patrolmen who had been there on that morning, Officer Novak, had confirmed that Zoltan lived one or two stories up from the Bowman flat, adding that he was considered a strange, essentially harmless creature with no connection whatsoever with the deceased. They had regarded him, one of many derelicts in the area, with more pity than suspicion despite the hysterical urgings of Mrs. Leibowitz.

Expecting no more than evidence pertaining to the Bowman case, the officers had checked the room for a blunt instrument or perhaps a few previously unnoticed stains, ignoring the ubiquitous piles of paper and other samples of Zoltan's literary frustrations. But Mrs. Leibowitz, more encouraged than ever, had insisted that they go through every scrap of it. Her officious carping had all but driven them away. When for the third time she had reminded them that she was a taxpayer, and that, according to her son the law student, meant they were on her payroll, they had decided to humor her.

While Scarpatti was thumbing through Zoltan's unfinished novel on bohemian life and reading portions aloud for Fletcher's amusement, Fletcher had opened the album. "If this don't beat all hell, Scar," he had muttered as Scarpatti gaped at the album.

"We've got him in a straitjacket if you'd care to have a look."

"Have you got his poetry, too?" asked Blakeley.

"That and the photographs of Samantha Poole. It seems he knew her for a long time. We found hundreds of little ditties written to her too. He called her his 'unkind' Samantha. Some of her pictures have been stabbed at with a sharp instrument. Probably a pen. It's as if the sight of her put him into a frenzy."

"I'll be there in less than a half hour, Lieutenant. Please don't let the newspaper chaps get wind of this yet."

"No fear of that," said Hudson. "I wouldn't give them the wind that comes down from the outhouse." Blakeley laughed as he hung up the receiver and wished Hudson had used that comment on Victor.

Just as Miss Meredith was about to make a comment on the exceptionally fine taste shown in the selection of furniture and decorative objects in the Blakeley house, hoping to relieve the tension that she had somehow created, Snopkowski entered again and tapped Nathan on the shoulder, summoning him abruptly from his thoughts.

"You come eat supper here tonight. I make beefsteak and oysters. Some French stoff, too, maybe."

After the large breakfast he had just concluded, the thought of food was less appealing than usual, but he knew that reticence could mean disaster in his so-far rapturous relationship with the cook.

"Beefsteak and oysters," he considered, "that sounds like something Henry the Eighth would have enjoyed. Is this an official invitation?"

"Huh?" The comment, the inspired question seemed thoroughly to have baffled her for a moment. She glanced suspiciously at Nathan, her imperious smile summoned up to relieve his indecision. "Snopkowski tell you come for supper, you come."

"If you insist," he said with a chastened smile.

"You, too," said Snopkowski, turning her large moon face to Miss Meredith. "You so skinny a butterfly knock you down."

Nathan was beginning to wonder if Snopkowski would not be satisfied until her world was populated with bulbous creatures out of Breughel.

"Thank you." Miss Meredith blushed.

"I make borscht, too, You like dot?" she asked Miss Meredith, who looked with confusion at Nathan.

"I'm afraid I've never tasted it, but," she added hastily, "I'm sure it's quite good."

"You betcha," Snopkowski averred.

"Have you ever had it?" Miss Meredith asked Nathan, thinking to establish some sort of grounds for agreement.

"No, Miss Meredith, but I know what it is," he said. "It's a soup made of red beets and spices. It's served hot or cold and sometimes as a meal in itself. It sounds delicious," he declared as Snopkowski looked on proudly. Miss Meredith's head was nodding uncertain agreement. He could not resist the temptation to throw one more jab.

"I don't think you'd care for it, though. It looks like blood."

"Blood!" howled Snopkowski as Miss Meredith's jaw dropped. "Dot's funny goddamn! Always you joke with poor Snopkowski! You funny bugger," she said, rubbing his head with her great meaty hand.

Snopkowski went off to the kitchen, alternately laughing, shaking her head, and repeating the word "blood" as Miss Meredith stared at Nathan with such fire that he could almost feel it on his skin. She was about to unravel a very unladylike stream of epithets when Dr. Blakeley entered.

"Victor wasn't joshing, my friends," he said. "Lieutenant Hudson's suspect certainly is a hot one."

Fourteen

The diminutive little priest had not wished to press charges. Frankly, he preferred to have the whole pathetic affair played down and would have been more than satisfied if that poor fellow in custody could have been made to pay for the cleaning of the church carpet. He was especially concerned about the wax that had dripped from the votive candle onto the thick rug which ran between the sanctuary and the altar rail. He always stressed great care when training the altar boys in how to snuff out the candles for that reason and was not certain how he would explain those blotchy stains to them without having to describe all that had happened. And he didn't wish to do that. Hudson pointed out that judging by the defendant's apparent circumstances, the chances of his paying such damages were minimal. The little white-haired priest looked chagrined for a moment, then said he would have to consult his superiors in that case. Looking at the little priest, Hudson wondered how he had been able to subdue a man in such a turbulent state. He considered it a good indication of what a physical wreck Zoltan Mroszek must be.

Before he had become so agitated that it had become necessary to put him, raving and hallucinating, into a straitjacket, Hudson had checked Zoltan's arms for needle marks. Finding none, he deduced that Zoltan's addiction was probably to an oral drug, such as absinthe or belladonna, rather than to cocaine or morphine. Certainly he was beyond the limits of an ordinary drunk. The visions and other hysterical symptoms suggested the coming of delirium tremens, and Hudson knew it would be some time before anyone could question Zoltan on a serious basis. If he survived, that is; he looked to be on his last legs from malnutrition.

Blakeley arrived, according to his word, in less than a half hour after what had been a very uncomfortable ride in Nathan's buggy. Besides the cramped arrangement, there had been the inexorable tension that obtained between his two colleagues to keep matters unpleasant. So, with a sigh of defeat, he had decided simply to brief them on what Hudson had told him.

While Nathan sought out a shady spot for his horse, Blakeley and Miss Meredith entered the precinct station. On their way up the steps Blakeley recognized the little priest as the one who had said Regis Tolan's requiem, and he tipped his hat as the priest went on his way. Inside, Mrs. Leibowitz was berating a long-suffering Lieutenant Hudson for his refusal to pay her the Figge reward immediately. She had turned in the West Philadelphia Butcher. No goddamn crooked cops were going to cheat her out of it. No, sir. Her son in law school would see to it that every last one of them lost their badges. And if they forced her to say it, things have come to a damn pretty pass when an ailing old woman has to do their work for them. A lot of good it did to pay your taxes when the cops let every immigrant pervert run loose to cut up young ladies.

Blakeley interrupted her by introducing Miss Meredith hastily to Lieutenant Hudson and asking to be shown the man in custody. Mrs. Leibowitz noted his black satchel and sprang out of her chair.

"You must be the man with the reward," she declared sweetly. "I'm Mrs. Leibowitz."

"No, Mrs. Leibowitz," groaned Hudson, "this is not the man with the reward."

"Oh," she said, and the toothy smile disappeared. "Then what are you doin' here?"

"I beg your pardon?"

"I turned in the West Philadelphia Butcher, and this bastard won't give me my reward," she snapped, pointing a finger at Hudson. "Well, I'm just gonna sit here till you do. And I don't give a fart who likes it."

She sat down and folded her arms. Hudson looked at Blakeley and shrugged. Nathan entered and joined them.

"Suit yourself, Mrs. Leibowitz," said Hudson. "Shall we go, Dr. Blakeley?"

"Yes. Thank you."

As Nathan passed by, Mrs. Leibowitz glowered at him. "You cops are all alike. Yiz probably wanta keep the reward for yourself, so yiz can drink it all up."

He tipped his hat and excused himself. Spying Fatzinger in the file room, he suggested that Bones keep out of her way. "The heat does dott, dey say," Fatzinger explained as he nibbled on a strongly scented pig's knuckle.

Hudson led them through the long, damp jail corridor. The studious look in the young lady's eyes answered his unasked question for him. She seemed to be making a mental record of everything. Far from frightened, she appeared excited by the rare privilege afforded her. He knew she wasn't Nate's new lady friend. If she were not a nurse whom Dr. Blakeley had brought along, he reasoned, then she would have to be a reporter or the like. Now, he asked himself, why the hell would Blakeley do something like that?

"Quite a mess, isn't he, miss?" Hudson asked as they peered through the bars at Zoltan. It was the same cell in which Manfred

Koch had been detained. "Have you ever seen someone in the rams before?"

"No," she whispered after some hesitation. The uneasy tone of her voice as she gazed upon the twitching figure in the straitjacket told him that she was certainly not a nurse.

"How long has he been twitching like that, Lieutenant?" Blakeley asked.

"Not long, Doctor. We put him in the harness just before I called you."

Blakeley entered the cell and opened his satchel. Zoltan leered at him through glassy, terror-stricken eyes as he poured a tumbler full of a colorless liquid from an unlabeled bottle. "This may taste somewhat potent, Mr. Mroszek, but it won't hurt you." He held the tumbler under Zoltan's nose until Zoltan recognized the aroma of the liquid.

"What sort of medicine is that, Dr. Blakeley?" Miss Meredith inquired. Hudson and Nathan exchanged informed glances.

"It's known variously, Miss Meredith," said Blakeley as he put the glass to Zoltan's mouth and helped him gulp it down. "I suppose one hears it most commonly referred to as moonshine. It's one hundred and fifty proof alcohol."

"With that stuff you could anesthetize a panther," Hudson observed.

"Oh, yes, of course," said Blakeley as he spread Zoltan's eyelids apart in order to examine his pupils. "It would probably cause the average person to go blind or worse, but it will have no such effect on one in this chap's condition. Principally I keep it around to sterilize my instruments."

"But," she continued, "shouldn't you be keeping him away from alcohol? That is what put him into this horrid state, isn't it?"

"To be sure." Blakeley put a stethoscope to his ears and listened to Zoltan's heartbeat, fitting the instrument through the neck of the straitjacket. He listened to Zoltan's breathing and determined that there seemed to be no danger of his lungs collapsing. "And we shall have to detoxify him, of course. But not so suddenly as all that. Without pacing his withdrawal properly, the patient could even cause himself to die of exhaustion."

"I see." She nodded.

"Do you notice? He's calming down already," Blakeley pointed out. "Soon I expect we can have a word with him."

"Thank you for the drink, Doctor," Zoltan chortled. "As a rule, I never touch strong spirits, being a rather abstemious individual as you may observe."

As Zoltan broke out in short, maniacal laughter, Nathan mentioned that he had seen him before. He was not well known in the neighborhood, but he had been around for a few years. That, mused Blakeley, answered the question of how this particular suspect would know the neighborhood's habit patterns, especially when Nathan recalled that Zoltan had often been seen in Nellie's Tavern.

"What do you think, Dr. Blakeley?" asked Hudson.

Blakeley folded his stethoscope and put it away, considering a welter of factors at once. His chief doubt was that the suspect had the physical strength to commit the crimes, much less the clarity of mind that some of the ghastly business required. He also doubted that Zoltan would possess the necessary instruments. Above all, he doubted if Zoltan's hand had ever been steady enough to perform the surgical mutilations. But there was no reason to discount his being part of the whole business.

"Certainly we can't afford to dismiss him. He may very well be in it somehow. And if he isn't, letting him go now that we've seen his condition would be tantamount to murdering him."

"I hate to be the bearer of bureaucratic tidings," quipped Hudson, "but City Hall frowns on our adopting the town's rubbish. The best we can do is keep him in the drunk tank."

Nathan looked over Miss Meredith's shoulder to see what she had been working so diligently at ever since they'd come to the cell. Instead of taking notes on the activities around her, she was sketching the suspect. In the stark light from the coal-oil lamp, Zoltan's sunken eyes and sallow complexion were almost spectral. Nathan had to admit, begrudgingly, that she had captured his eerie qualities.

"I don't think we can do that," said Blakeley. "Not if we ever expect to get any useful data out of him. For one thing, I'm not quite certain as yet whether we must treat him for delirium tremens or for narcotic poisoning. He looks to be somewhere in between."

"*Imbécile!*" shouted Zoltan in French. "*Comment savez-vous? Vous n'avez pas la science m'aider. Vous devez être plus attentif à votre putain!*"

Nathan knew by the blush of Miss Meredith's cheek that she well understood what the suspect had said. Blakeley looked as if he wished to strangle Zoltan.

"What did he say, Nate?" Hudson asked.

"He said," answered Blakeley, "that I should have become a veterinarian or something of that nature. He doesn't think I can fathom his complexities."

"From the look of him," Hudson snorted, "he may have a point there. He's not far from being something the zoo might want."

"*Merde,*" muttered Zoltan, "*vous êtes idiot aussi, et amoureux des cochons!*"

Nathan was grateful that Hudson understood no French. Addled or not, that comment, if Hudson had even an inkling of its translation, would probably have been Zoltan's last utterance. Blakeley was preparing to level a verbal broadside, for French was only one of the eleven languages he was at ease in, when Miss Meredith shocked everyone by stepping forward.

"*M. Mroszek,*" she began evenly, eschewing the more offensive singular number, "*je soupçonne que c'est votre désir nous enfreindre. Mais il n'en faut pas essayer. Vous succédez vraiment. Vous êtes assez offensif sans artifice.*"

"*Formidable!*" Blakeley expressed approval. Nathan looked on with an admiring grin.

"All right," Hudson looked at Nathan, "now what did she say?"

"She just said, loosely translated, that someone as creepy as he is need not work so hard at being offensive."

Zoltan was silent for the moment, apparently considering his next effort to shock his auditors. Despite himself, Nathan's attitude toward Miss Meredith was gradually changing. Blakeley pondered his next move. Hudson still wondered what exactly Miss Meredith was doing there. He also wondered why the suspect had chosen to speak in French rather than in Czech or Hungarian.

"We must keep him in storage somewhere," said Blakeley. "I should not wish to draw attention to him before he's well enough to submit to our probing."

"I don't think you can prevent that," said Hudson. "You've seen Mrs. Leibowitz. She'll be knocking on every newspaper door in town just as fast as her broom can carry her."

Nathan rolled a cigarette and leaned against the bars of the cell. "What about giving him an alias for the time being?" he suggested.

"He's been anonymous enough so far. Maybe we can call him Snodgrass or something and have him admitted to the hospital as any old wino might be."

"But what about Mrs. Leibowitz?" asked Blakeley.

"That should be the least of our tasks, Dr. Blakeley," Nathan offered jovially. "Her delusions are obviously symptomatic of dementia praecox."

Blakeley put his hand on Nathan's shoulder. "Excellent move, Officer McBride. Excellent."

Hudson beamed proudly. Nathan was a product of his and Regis Tolan's training. "If he gets any smarter, Doctor, we may want him back." Blakeley even noticed the germ of an appreciative smile registering on Miss Meredith's face.

"Lieutenant Hudson, do you think one or two of your constables might cart the suspect off to Good Samaritan Hospital for me—inconspicuously, of course. It's near my home, and I can watch him closely there."

"I'll do better than that, Dr. Blakeley." Hudson smiled impishly. "I'll even have Officer Fatzinger clean him up first."

As they departed the cell, Blakeley thanked Hudson for his cooperation and remarked that he had saved them some valuable time by his quick reaction to the affair in the church.

"Time," muttered Zoltan. "'And Time, a maniac scattering dust,'" he intoned, "'And Life, a Fury slinging flame.'"

"That's from Tennyson, I believe," Nathan mused.

"Yes," answered Blakeley, "*In Memoriam*, part fifty, to be exact. I should love to find out who he really is. This chap seems to live in a zone that teems with fear and self-loathing."

"Better yet," added Hudson, "*what* he really is."

Zoltan's eyes popped open and looked like billiard balls in the stark light. "I," he declared, "am a dicky-dong."

Nathan thought it must have been particularly uncomfortable for her when that creature accused Miss Meredith of being Dr. Blakeley's whore.

After having had to listen to Mrs. Leibowitz for the past ten minutes or so, Fatzinger actually welcomed the opportunity to clean up Zoltan Mroszek. Having picked up a water pail and scrubbing brush, he dashed off to the jail, leaving her in midsentence. Mrs. Leibowitz continued to sit in a chair near his desk, because, she contended, as a taxpayer she owned this goddamn seat just as much as anybody else in Philly. She punctuated her carping by jabbing her umbrella in the air. Hudson cursed the fact that the precinct possessed only one straitjacket.

"Mrs. Snopkowski will no doubt hate you, and she shall probably put me on a diet of hardtack and salted beef should you fail to appear for dinner this evening," Blakeley told his colleagues.

It was now after noon, and the sun was scalding as they stepped out of the station house. The doctor hoped there now existed between them an unseen flag of truce. But he wished to let them know he pictured one there.

"Now see here," he demanded. "I've been looking at and listening to your silly bickering since this morning, and I must say that from the start I've seen nothing amusing in it. On the contrary, it strikes me as pettiness itself. I must inform you that you are both with me for the duration and you might find it a singularly miserable task should you persist in this pointless animosity."

They had not expected such directness and were taken aback.

"I was unaware that any such hostility existed," Miss Meredith replied primly.

"We are entirely amicable," Nathan averred, "in our fashion."

"I deal in facts, Detective McBride, not amenities. Furthermore, I am not naive. I can see that you've both got off to a poor start. Some of that, admittedly, is of my doing, and I shan't be satisfied until I've settled it."

The sun was beating down on all three of them unmercifully. In their brief visit to Zoltan's cell, it had made an uninvited appearance and presaged more thunderstorms. Nathan wished to get out of it at all costs.

"Dr. Blakeley"—he swabbed his brow with equal impatience— "personally, I see no profound reason why Miss Meredith and I should enjoy each other's company. Under the circumstances, we should all be contented with mutual tolerance and an unimpeded working agreement. In all due respect, sir, the spheres have not existed in harmony since the discovery of Neptune, and you cannot mediate the ineffable hostilities of two natural antagonists."

For a while Blakeley was pensive, but the beads of perspiration which showed themselves on his neat little beard betrayed his well-feigned restraint. "Well said, Detective McBride, but you shall still have to coexist, beginning with this afternoon. Now run along, and remember Snopkowski's spleen if you elect to be tardy this evening."

He realized that his victories were small and begrudging these days.

Chantal de Rohan was born in the village of Langres, famous as the birthplace of M. Diderot. Like the incomparable *philosophe*, Chantal was also the product of respectable bourgeois parents. The de Rohan vineyards, though not vast by French standards, had held a place of honor for generations, and the winemakers of the province of Champagne had long coveted the black grapes so ably cultivated by Étienne de Rohan. Had the winds of political history not taken a fateful shift, the life of Mlle. de Rohan would surely have been one of ease and propriety.

On the sultry morning of July 19, 1870, three weeks after having delivered the lovely child, Mme. Solange de Rohan, beloved wife of M. Étienne de Rohan, breathed her last. The village of Langres was solemn for a while, and the funeral heavily attended by weeping, dark-clad neighbors, but Étienne de Rohan's period of mourning was soon left to him alone. For later in the day on which Mme. de Rohan had passed on, war had been formally declared against Prussia and the entire nation buzzed enthusiastically with cries of *à Berlin!* Preparations for this most delicious of all victories had been made many months previously. In the following September, however, the defenses of Napoleon III at Sedan buckled under the pressure of Bismarck's overwhelming forces and the Emperor himself was taken to Wilhelmshöhe in Germany in ignominious captivity. As the French armies retreated south, Prussians tramped through the province, burning the de Rohan vineyards along with the mills and anything of value. Late one evening in the spring of 1871 the despondent M. de Rohan sat in the master bedroom of the house and put a pistol to his head.

With the small fortune gone and debts to be paid, creditors soon attached themselves upon the moribund estate like a host of desperate saprophytes. There was M. Ogier, the banker, who wielded a handful of papers as proof of a loan agreed to when the extra acre had been added to the western corner of the vineyard, and M. Bonneau, the tax collector, who insisted that the past quarter of the land assessment had not been paid. M. Villemain, who was the spokesman for the vineyard workers, presented a statement of the hours his men had worked without recompense. Even Père d'Aubignard of the village church presented documents to assert that the late M. de Rohan, in his great charity, had agreed to underwrite the remodeling of the rectory.

Amid the chaos and wringing of hands it was Chantal's indomitable grandmother who took it upon herself to make muddy waters clear. Paying off the creditors by distributing furniture, china, and silverware—no one dared haggle with Grand'maman de Rohan—and dismissing the last of the servants, she fled with the infant to Paris, where a brother operated a small publishing house.

After a winter of great hardship it became necessary to flee once again. In January France was humiliated by the Federation of German States and forced to sue for peace. By March the Paris Commune, finding itself in possession of arms after the German siege, rose up against the central government, and the city was racked with violence and hunger. So desperate was the population after ten weeks of the Commune that stray dogs and cats had vanished from the streets, and it was rumored that children were also unsafe among the starving Parisians. Grand'maman de Rohan, alarmed less by what she saw than by what she heard, prevailed on an influential gentleman whom her husband had once befriended and who had successfully accommodated the young fanatics. Through him she managed to make her way through the barricades and out of the troubled city.

The little girl grew tall, bright, and bilingual under the kindly, if uncompromising, direction of the old woman. Grand'maman had chosen Philadelphia for much the same set of reasons that had inspired Blakeley, and for fifteen years she had found modest prosperity as a private tutor of French language and literature. And then the gallant old woman had passed on after a long illness. Her life, as Chantal put it in a letter to a distant relative in Poitou, had been a tribute to the survival of the fittest.

The history of Chantal de Rohan for the next few years was equally obfuscated as Nathan tried his best to piece it together for Dr. Blakeley. Left without support and, as the de Rohan family curse would have it, indebted to two doctors and one mortician, she had abandoned her dream of becoming a language instructor to find work in a shirt factory. Soon the eyes of the factory owner had fallen upon the tall girl with the auburn hair and soft, elusive accent, and he had made her a proposal that was at once shocking and alluring.

"You see Lil over there?" He had pointed through his office window toward a surly, sleepy-eyed girl of about Chantal's age, who sat idly drinking coffee as the others bustled about her.

"How do you think she got them rings she's wearin'?" he had asked rhetorically.

"I've never asked her, Mr. Gross," Chantal de Rohan had answered flatly.

In retrospect, the tasks she had performed on that evening had not been at all so unpleasant as she'd expected. The gentlemen had been for the most part tidy and courteous, not at all like M. Gross.

Grand'maman's tutelage had ensured that Chantal would always be a lady of gentler mien. She had learned early that it was better to disguise her mastery of English and to affect a very light, almost ephemeral accent. From her readings of Corneille, Lesage, and the great Molière, she had become acquainted with the art of conducting delicately risqué repartée, and her customers were obviously appreciative.

When the debts had been paid and she had established a money reserve, Chantal had begun to think again about her career as a language instructor. She had, after all, accomplished her short-term goal. It was then that she caught Mr. Gross in a blatant case of fraud, and she complained vigorously.

"There are, I'm sure, authorities who would be intrigued by your means of stimulating commerce. And you know that, Mr. Gross."

"Bullshit." He sniggered. "Who the hell would take the word of a common chippie like you? I'm a respected businessman!"

"If I were you"—she blanched at his arrogance—"I'd get used to speaking in the past tense. There are some rather uncomplimentary terms for men like you."

He did his best to appear unmoved by her threat.

"What if I raise your ante?"

"You couldn't raise it enough to repay what you've withheld from me over the last six years," she charged. Her experiences had given her a quickness much beyond her twenty-one years. "No, I think it's time we parted ways, Mr. Gross. One cannot reasonably expect you to change the mean habits of a lifetime. Cheating is as much a part of you as the gravy stains on your necktie."

His half-smile gave way to a sneer, and he slapped her across the face.

With that motivation, Chantal de Rohan proceeded to do something most unladylike—the only truly vicious act of her lifetime. Through a passing acquaintance with a rather shady creature, she arranged for Gross to encounter three former pugilists one evening as he left the factory. Later it was difficult for her to maintain her composure when she received the report of his broken cheekbone and three broken ribs.

That was in the summer of 1891, and she was anxious to change her life-style. Four years behind her peers, Chantal was very nervous about returning to school. The thought occurred to her that the percentages were in favor of her past's catching up with her, and she knew that she could never bear the shame of exposure. She confided in Lil, the dour young lady who had, in a way, given her dubious career its beginnings.

"Well, Jeez," said Lil, "it ain't hard to make money if you're ambitious!" Chantal would feel her dream defeated were she to return to Langres in less than the finest of style.

Lil too had had enough of the likes of Gross. She introduced Chantal to a toothless crone in a bright red wig and preposterous red boots named Thomasina Roach, who tried immediately to change Chantal's name to Cherry.

"Chantal's okay as names go, Frenchie, but—"

"Don't call me Frenchie." Gross had called her Frenchie.

"Well, what the hell, it's better than that name you got now. Yer real name sounds like 'shanty' or 'cattle' or somethin'."

"Not if you know how to pronounce it, Mrs. Roach."

"It's the customers I'm thinkin' about. They like names they can remember. Now"—she turned to Lil—"that's a good monicker you got."

"Ah, well," said Chantal with finality, "I was told we could talk business on a serious level, but. . . ."

As Chantal reached the door, the crone interrupted her without pausing to look up from her solitaire. "I ain't said no yet"

"No matter. I've said it for you."

Chantal sensed that she was winning the game of silly preliminaries. The hag had accurately assessed her potential and wanted her in the stable whatever her name. It was a simple task to appear exceptionally salable opposite poor Lil. She could almost hear the word "class" playing in the mind of the avaricious crone. Mrs. Roach removed the strong cigar from her lips and looked up. She smelled of penny perfume and stale perspiration.

"Okay, but you won't make half as much out on the street. Yiz can bet yer haughty little ass on that."

The old Mansion Hotel had fallen on hard times during the past decade, principally as a result of mismanagement and a lack of imagination. Its most recent ownership, however, had found a new source of revenue. Since the Centennial Exposition in 1876 the city had become more popular as a convention site, and the summers had brought hordes of business and professional men eager to enjoy the fruits of distance and anonymity. The crusty Thomasina Roach had established her business there, alternating between the fourth, sixth, and ninth floors of the old hotel to avoid easy detection. The locale had been generous. Chantal de Rohan, though feminine as ever, had settled into her profession with resignation, if not happiness. By the time seven years had passed there was little else to do, and the money was admittedly easy. Though Mrs. Roach was no more honest than Gross had been, the working conditions prevented her efforts at wholesale cheating. Thus, Chantal had prospered in a manner seldom dreamed of in the more legitimate pursuits.

There had been only one difficult time a little more than three years earlier. In spite of her expertise, Chantal had discovered one day that she was with child. Somewhere along the way she'd been careless. But Mrs. Roach had been well prepared for such emergencies, and the problem had been soon solved by a doctor who had an office near City Line Avenue and Fifty-fourth Street. Chantal did not care much for him; he was cold, distant, and, she thought, a Prussian. But he had been efficient, even if there had been some unfortunate aftereffects.

On that afternoon in the summer of 1898, as Zoltan Mroszek was being admitted to Good Samaritan Hospital under the name of Alvin B. Porterfield, Chantal and her associates were entertaining some affluent gentlemen in a suite of rooms on the fourth floor of the Mansion Hotel. The windows were open, and the overhead fans running to check the oppressive heat. Chantal followed her usual strategy of remaining removed from the main activity for a while, waiting for someone to discover her. It was a tactic that never failed her, but it used to aggravate Thomasina Roach to distraction.

"Get in there an' move. What the hell are yiz waitin' for?" she nagged. "Looka that one over there. Nobody's took him on yet."

"Which one do you mean?"

"The one in the dark-gray suit," she pointed out. "Over there fannin' hisself by the window."

"But he's so fat!" Chantal exclaimed.

"What the hell—they're *all* fat," clucked Mrs. Roach. "They come from the brewmasters' convention, fer Chrissake!"

"Very well then," said Chantal, "but this will cost a lot more than the usual."

"Suit yerself." Mrs. Roach chewed on her cigar. "Maybe you'd rather work the streets, where the Butcher can get you."

"Such compelling torment," said Sophia, her eyes fixed upon a gaunt, cadaverous figure in regal habiliments. Her voice was almost a whisper. "Unappetizing, but almost awesome in its vision."

"Prophetic, do you think?" asked Blakeley.

"Entirely possible, Ian," said she. "The fall of the monarchs is believed in many quarters to be imminent, everywhere save the British Empire, of course." But it was the technique that most held her attention. "Do you notice the dark lines which separate the crown from the awful, moribund face?"

"Excellent form as agent," he pronounced.

"Yes. . . . The only fact that gives me pause"—she looked away from the painting and toward him—"is the question of whether the distortions are intended or merely technical sloppiness."

That, he acknowledged, would, of course, be a germane consideration. He sipped his after-dinner cognac and studied the painting. The sickly little king was surrounded by legions of busy, antlike creatures, workers presumably, whose zest for activity underscored his own corrupt condition. There were no symmetrical values to the painting, no really measurable dimensions. Like the others that Detective McBride had found rolled up in a dusty bundle behind Zoltan Mroszek's dresser and brought along for whatever they were worth, it seemed almost amorphous in its design. Blakeley was rather startled by Sophia's positive reaction; her tastes had always run far afield of this kind of art.

"Would you call him talented?"

"Purely and simply," she replied without hesitation. "I only hope this disturbance is not the total source of his power."

"It's been a gold mine of information for me, you know," said Blakeley, gesturing toward the picture. "One can detect, just at a glance, the hallmarks of several personality disorders. Mostly, it appears to be a classic case of rejection that he's channeled into a messianic world view. One gets the feeling, however, that he does not wish to punish the whole of humankind, only the authority figures. One could almost piece together the mind of an assassin, but for the undertones of compassion. See there how he's given a subtle hint of sadness to the king's eyes, like one whose time has come but not entirely of his own doing."

"We are more ignorant than evil, in other words," she summarized.

"Yes, decadent by habit more than by nature."

They paused to restudy the work, somewhat mystified by their own interest.

"Truly talented?" he repeated just for the sake of continuity.

"Ian, my darling," she answered, "I wish I could paint like him."

"But," he offered, "I thought you detested the new schools. You've always regarded them as charlatans."

"The charlatans, yes." She drifted away from the easel and sat on the divan to sip her cognac. "This poor fellow has had no opportunity to become one of them. It's their whining, self-righteous manifestos that have always repelled me. He, on the other hand, simply practices it. He's not only the best of the lot, but he's the first one I've seen that one can honestly call an artist."

Her evaluation reinforced his own. Blakeley had neglected to inform Sophia of all the facts about Zoltan Mroszek, and he was aware that her praise would surely have been qualified were she to know that she was complimenting a suspect in the Butcher case.

Dinner had been exquisite. With Victor once again confined to bed—this time with a bee sting—Snopkowski's spirits had soared. The care that she had lavished upon the ratatouille had almost suggested she was in the midst of a victory celebration. The only discordant note of the evening had been repeated each time one of

Blakeley's colleagues had ventured to speak. It had been clear not only to Blakeley but to all in attendance that the frozen stare of the other at such moments signified a modicum of icy tolerance at best. There had been one anxious moment when Blakeley had all but expected to see the mushroom sauce in Detective McBride's lap as Miss Meredith passed it to Rosalie.

"What am I to do?" he asked.

"About what?" She was still staring in fascination at the strange picture.

"About Miss Meredith and Officer McBride. Their enmity is stubbornness personified."

Sophia smiled. "For all your scholarship you seem to be a trifle deficient in chemistry."

Certainly neither party seemed inert, he conceded, although the chain reactions that had so far occurred had been singularly self-destructive. But yes, there was potential there for something good between them. A small consolation. He felt he was entering a desolate land, and he wanted to pass through it in congenial company if possible.

As they relaxed in Sophia's studio, a terrible event was taking place in Charlie Hudson's precinct.

Hattie Rau set out with grave reservations to make the rounds of her small chain of pet shops. Though aware that the Butcher roamed the district, she also knew that it was foolish to expect the help to feed the animals and to clean the cages properly. She dropped in on her three properties at different hours of the evening. Thrice in the past five years negligence had cost her managers their jobs; good pets were expensive, as well as hard to come by. A poorly bedded-down setter, for example, could easily become skittish, even hyperkinetic, and lose its value in no time.

That evening she had endeavored to enlist the escort of her son. But poor Oscar was all worn out after his long day at the horse races in Jersey and his evening with those ne'er-do-well friends of his at Nellie's Tavern. Hattie had excused him with a terse comment. Before leaving this time, however, she had taken a large gulp from Oscar's whiskey flask and had slipped his .45 Colt revolver into her purse. She had never tried to fathom precisely why her son possessed such a weapon, but Hattie had no wish to become the Butcher's oldest victim. As she was leaving the house, she had expressed that fear to Oscar. He flopped into an easy chair, laughing. Oscar's sense of humor was morbid.

Hattie's first stop, on Cedar Street, was satisfactory save the continued weight loss of the rhesus monkey and the listlessness of the pregnant cat. Hattie rejected an offer of a cup of tea from the manager, Mr. Stevens, in order to move on to the store on Ramsey Road. She proceeded up Fifty-first, and the "belt," as Oscar called it, from the whiskey flask had been appreciated in the chill that was starting to permeate the night air. She wondered if Stevens had detected it on her breath.

About three blocks from the Ramsey Road shop Hattie Rau became slowly aware of the presence of someone or something in her vicinity. The streets were relatively deserted by ten o'clock, this Friday night having offered no particular excitement, and the Butcher had curtailed most of the normal pursuits of summer evening. She started to feel clammy under her dark-brown dress and heavy corsets. Oscar joked about her Butcherphobia, as he called it, but she knew she wasn't imagining this. *The business be damned,* she thought—and added an epithet for herself for having ventured out that night.

She turned down Dobrin's Alley, and the footsteps followed, louder, echoing between the empty buildings. At the end of the murky alleyway Hattie turned left on Fiftieth Street to take the short route home.

The footsteps were still there, tapping behind her in the darkness.

A fog had come up from the river, blurring the streetlamps and blanketing the moon. As she turned to look around, she thought she could see a gaunt figure leaving the alley and drifting toward her in the mist. Sweat ran from beneath her bonnet, and she could feel her heart pounding.

She started across the road; but as she stepped from the curb, her ankle gave way, and Hattie sprawled into the street. She swore aloud, and panic set in when she realized that she could not run for her life. *They say he quarters his victims,* she heard herself whimpering. The ankle felt broken.

Hattie got up slowly and crouched against a wall. The steps were uneven. He seemed to be limping. Her ankle throbbed with pain, and she could feel herself losing control. Her fingers trembling, she opened her purse and gripped the revolver as the footsteps drew closer. She wanted to call for help, but that might simply rouse his anger. So she hid behind a stoop and waited.

Waited.

He came up the street, brazen as life, and soon approached the building where Hattie had taken refuge. As he came out of the mist, she raised her revolver and aimed. A shot rang out, his head jerked backward. He fell to the ground and rolled into the gutter.

Hattie Rau lowered her revolver and screamed at the top of her lungs.

Nathan coaxed his weary horse onward. Since the evening at Blakeley's had concluded somewhat earlier than usual, he thought he might drop in on the precinct station before eleven. He was as fatigued as the horse but certain that he would not be able to sleep in any case. The past few weeks had oriented him to a more spartan regimen than he'd been used to under Captain Tolan. He believed he was slowly catching up to the indefatigable Ian Blakeley.

It had been a strange day. After depositing the frigidly mute Miss Meredith in the early afternoon, he had moved on to Zoltan Mroszek's furnished room. The stench had actually made him dizzy for a time. How could someone fall to such depths? Still further, he had marveled at the suspect's ability to survive in such an environment. To make matters worse, Mrs. Leibowitz, having vented her spleen upon Fatzinger, had come home to discover Nathan at work. As he rummaged through the filth and trash, she had continued to carp without pausing for breath.

At home by five, he had scrubbed with ferocity until his skin reddened, and he had daubed himself with a somewhat pungent cologne. Not for Miss Meredith; the relationship hardly inspired amenities, even in a gentleman.

He had to admit, however reluctantly, that she'd looked handsome that evening. At the risk of hyperbole, she was, in fact, beautiful: white gown with blue lace and something of a sparkle to her eyes. Of course, she *had* had a lengthy rest while *he* had been groping through the garbage. Then he'd caught himself thinking unbecoming thoughts and chastised himself mildly. Not her fault, of course. During the ride to Blakeley's he had tried once again to make small talk, if only for the sake of appearances. So he had asked her in passing where she'd learned such fluent French. "In France," was the cordial reply, and for some reason that had alienated him even more. The remainder of the journey had been spent listening to the chatter of the birds in the trees along the drive.

The warmth with which Sophia had greeted him and the reception accorded his findings in the suspect's room had been gratifying. Blakeley had received them eagerly, complimenting him, evidently impressed by the insights they would afford him. Nothing else of any real value had been uncovered, however; Mroszek's room was cluttered with papers, empty bottles, and food scraps.

Even Rosalie had been rather civil for a change. She had pouted in his presence of late, as if to elicit a shaken reaction which, to her dismay, had never occurred. The delicate balance of that relationship also called for a cool head at all times.

And of course, the food had been superb, with Snopkowski hovering nearby now and then. He was not yet certain just how Mrs. Snopkowski regarded Miss Meredith, but somewhere between the elaborate salad and the steak and oysters he had thought he sensed a hint of approval in her sharp old eyes. What scintillating qualities of Miss Meredith's personality had eluded him? As he sipped his Liebfraumilch, he had probed his mind for possible errors of judgment. Finally, he had concluded that the cook was merely registering her appreciation of the young lady's hearty appetite. Perhaps, Nathan mused, she'd have survived in the combat zone after all. Certainly, she could at least eat like a soldier.

Lovely, though, very lovely. . . .

The meeting after dinner had been more of a briefing over cognac than a sharing of thoughts. Blakeley clearly was tired. Mostly he had wanted Nathan to remember that doctor on City Line Avenue mentioned by Mr. McIver, whatever diversion Mroszek might have created. Nathan had decided to pose as a patient in the morning and had been given a set of plausible symptoms of stomach troubles in case Dr. Toberman should prove suspicious.

On the way home a curious, somewhat disturbing thing had happened. The wine and the heavy food had combined to make Miss Meredith drowsy. In the silence of the cab and the steady rhythm of the horse up front she had fallen asleep. Actually, Nathan had recognized, her assignment for the following day was the more taxing one. She was to get in touch with the immigration authorities and try to develop a profile of Zoltan Mroszek beginning somewhere in Europe. That, he believed, should prove to be a disjointed tale. Dr. Blakeley could certainly concoct some Chinese puzzles when he wished to. Nathan had glanced over at her briefly to observe the determined bobbing of her head as she struggled to resist the temptation of sleep. *She may not like me,* he'd thought, *but she certainly must not be afraid of me.*

The small buggy had made its way into a bank of fog as the drive wended along a broad section of the river. He had checked his pocket watch, squinting at it in the dim light. Ten o'clock. Too late to call Aidan. Blakeley had insisted on his acquiring a telephone in order to improve their lines of communication. It had been subsidized by the department, but only for the duration of this case unfortunately. Besides saving working time, it had made it easier to keep his relationship with Aidan healthy despite their many days apart.

He had wished the fog would lift. The lights along the drive were spaced far apart, and they were not the brightest to begin with.

His thoughts had been broken when he felt something brush lightly against him. Miss Meredith had fallen asleep, and in the closeness of the cab her head had come to rest on his shoulder. Nathan had debated with himself for at least a mile the question of whether to awaken her. Although it was certain to embarrass her upon awakening, his awkwardness had soon passed, and he had enjoyed having her there, breathing softly and smelling of a delicate sachet. Deep within him lurked a feeling that Allison Meredith was not all bad. It was entirely possible, though probably farfetched, that she was even capable of vulnerability and tenderness. One thing he'd had no strength to deny: Something about being seen with her inflated his masculine vanity.

When they'd arrived at her door, Nathan had awakened her gently and, saying little more than good-night, had escorted her to the front steps. The blush of her cheeks had been discernible even in the darkness. He had simply nodded with a smile to assure her that everything was fine, that her little slip would be forgotten.

That, he knew, had been an episode Adam P. Meredith would surely omit when the story was written.

Within the hour he was at the station house inquiring after Lieutenant Hudson. The desk sergeant informed him of the shooting and directed him to Fiftieth Street near Dobrin's Alley, where a crowd had gathered. He parked his rig and waded through the somber onlookers, observing on his way a fragile old woman seated on a stoop, dazed and silent.

"Better step gingerly, Nate. There's a lot of blood around here, and you don't want to soil those nifty duds," Hudson said. He wished he'd gone home hours ago, leaving this mess to Pat Curran, but a damned report had held him up.

Nathan spied some ugly maroon splotches on the sidewalk and on the front of the brownstone building. The old lady was rocking back and forth on her haunches, draped in a blanket.

"Did she have anything to do with this, Lieutenant?"

Yes, she *had*. Hudson regretted his sharpness, added that an ambulance was on its way for her, and told him to look at the body. Nathan tugged at the canvas sheet, carefully avoiding contact between the bloodstains and his gray linen suit. The victim's face was frozen with horror and surprise. A gaping hole lay where the nose used to be.

Nathan replaced the canvas and turned away, sickened. He was still not used to it, the pain and brutality which had become so much a part of his milieu.

"You know him, Nate?"

"Not personally, but I think so. He looks like someone I've seen in the neighborhood, at Nellie's mostly. He looks like Oscar Rau, but under the circumstances I wouldn't want you to take my word for it."

"Well, I'll be. . . . " Hudson shook his head. "And she thought it was the Butcher. God." The old woman looked so desolate and alone there in the midst of the strangers. It was not difficult to piece together the probable chain of events. Oscar Rau was a harmless playboy, a practical joker.

"You and Blakeley have got to catch that son of a bitch, Nate. This is only the beginning."

Fifteen

The next morning was cooler than usual, after a night of thunderstorms that contributed to Blakeley's state of restiveness.

"I say, Victor, you must learn to observe the rules here. Can't you see I'm at work?"

Blakeley had taken a rare moment to get back to his book and was making a statement on Thomas Neill Cream, the physician who had been executed earlier in the decade after a criminal career that had included abortion, blackmail, bigamy, arson, and multiple murder. Rather pithy, too, he thought until Victor had entered without knocking, looked over his shoulder, and grunted disapproval.

He tried to recall the nature of Victor's latest problem and at last remembered the bee sting. "Have you any trouble sitting? I believe that *is* the site of your difficulty?"

"I bear it," Victor answered nobly.

"Good. Now what else is on your mind this morning?"

Victor looked momentarily sheepish; then he started to burble. Blakeley wondered whether he hadn't better change the lock on the liquor cabinet again.

"I shan't raise your salary again, Victor. Nor will you receive another day off, no matter how long you sulk." Blakeley was obviously curt this morning. "If that is the issue, you may soak your bottom in the river all morning, provided Madame has nothing for you to do."

"There is a . . . person to see you," Victor said finally, collecting himself. His tone suggested a sense of deviltry, unusual for Victor. He was acting as if he'd just uncovered some family secret of vastly silly dimensions.

"I suppose you remember that my mornings are reserved for private work," he said tersely, and Victor's grin became even more foolish.

"Now see here, Victor"—Blakeley arose and pointed with his monocle—"I'm losing valuable time whilst you bandy nonsense." Realizing that the dialogue could go on forever, he sighed and paced toward the window. The sun was bright and warm as he stood bathed in it.

"Oh, very well then," he said finally, "show him in."

Victor was gone for a moment, reappearing with a vividly painted lady whose appearance gave Blakeley a bit of a start.

Victor, predictably, took that to mean untimely recognition and gave him a disturbingly knowing smile. Blakeley did not know whether to growl or to remain, as best he could, unaffected.

The butler struck a rigid pose. "Miss. . . . " He looked at the young woman and fumbled about. "Uh. . . . "

"Walker," she said. "Lil Walker. You know, as in *street*walker?"

It was no doubt her customary quip, but Victor drew back and stiffened even more. Blakeley, for his part, loosened up after the saucy retort. But he was thinking at the same time how best to extricate himself from the situation when Sophia got wind of his incongruous visitor. And he knew she would, for Victor was already champing at the bit to let it out.

"Er, Miss Walker," Victor intoned and strode off in his gooselike manner.

How strange they look in the morning light, Blakeley thought as he studied her. *How pale and out of place, like aliens in the authentic world.* He was not quite sure how to receive her.

"Won't you sit down, Miss Walker?" he began hesitantly.

She thanked him and did so. Her perfume was much too strong. Called something outlandish like Flora Mato Grosso, no doubt.

"Tea?"

"Yes, please."

Whatever he knew to the contrary, he'd always entertained the stereotype that prostitutes drank nothing other than hard liquor. He poured and offered some milk and sugar, which were politely refused.

Thoughts of the past victims fluttered in his mind, and he soon found himself feeling uneasily compassionate. With a little scrubbing, he thought, she would be far less unnerving.

"The butler left us both at a disadvantage, it would appear."

"Yeah, he took one look at me and asked no questions. I'm sorry if this puts you in a bad position, my coming here, I mean."

"Not at all," he lied.

"I have this friend, you see, and she disappeared yesterday with some fat guy, and I read where you're on the case, so I got this guy to take me out here to tell you about it."

"And"—he chose his next words cautiously—"she was engaged, your friend, in what enterprise?"

"Oh." She smiled nervously. "Chantal was, is, a . . . highly specialized entertainer."

"I see."

She sipped from her cup of tea, then put it down. "Hey,

Doc"—she looked up uneasily—"got anything you might put in this besides cream or sugar?"

He poured some Napoleon into her cup and listened closely as Miss Walker seemed to relax. She spilled out her testimony; speculation, too, about the fate of her friend, Miss de Rohan. The fat man she mentioned seemed a coincidence, for in his delirium Zoltan Mroszek had alluded recurrently to some sinister man of the same description, a fat, sweaty person with an asthmatic wheeze. She opened a pack of Sweet Caporals and smoked a cigarette. She referred several times within one breath to Miss de Rohan's "class." He presumed that the term, as Miss Walker employed it, meant some quality which had set Miss de Rohan apart from others in her field.

According to Miss Walker, Miss de Rohan had always worked within the confines of their establishment, either the old Mansion Hotel or at the resort where they were sometimes transported for holidays and weekends. Cautious by nature, probably because of her origins and diligent upbringing, she had never gone off with anyone except for a very high fee. Never in the eight or so years that Miss Walker had known her had she failed to return before dawn. It was, she added, therefore a certainty that she was officially missing, and the prospect of foul play hung heavily over her history. In a way, Blakeley was a trifle disappointed by the timing of this most recent announcement, for he knew it would cast a strong doubt on the value of Zoltan Mroszek as a suspect. He could sense no hysteria in the disorderly young woman who sat before him puffing on her cigarette and sipping from her teacup. A bit uneasy perhaps, in her unnatural surroundings, but Miss Walker showed no hint of impetuosity. Mroszek couldn't, after all, have done anything ghoulish while strapped into his bed, babbling incoherently about Cynara and frightening the nurses. Blakeley took heart, however, at the realization that Mrs. Leibowitz's dreams of a reward would also have to fade. That would be only proper, he felt, considering the presumptuous article he'd read in the morning paper. Some misguided reporter had taken her claims at face value and had asked where the police were hiding the Hideous Hungarian, a term coined, undoubtedly, by Stanley Butterfield.

Miss Walker was clearly disdainful of the fat man, and Blakeley was willing to accept her as an unacknowledged authority on human nature, giving its due her long acquaintance with people at their, well, nakedest. The fat man, said she, was of the lowest caliber, a foulmouthed boor whom Miss de Rohan would doubtless have ignored were she not in desperate need of money. Chantal had been, y'know, addicted to morphine ever since Thomasina sent her to that doctor when she was in trouble.

"Thomasina?"

"My, uh, manager," she explained.

Ten o'clock. Early to be going home. Andrew Sutton had left his house shortly after seven, hoping to take advantage of the bright morning sun as he photographed the famous Eleonora Duse.

It was her first and probably only visit to the city, and her manager had asked that she be placed before the various landmarks to emphasize the degree to which great art transcends all national boundaries. But the availability of sunlight was always so uncertain in Philadelphia. True to his word, the manager had presented the beautiful actress by eight o'clock at the front steps of Independence Hall. Sutton had always heard that theater people customarily slept beyond noon, their lives being lived after decent folks had gone to sleep.

What a glorious work of God she was, that woman. Once again he'd felt the mixed emotions that always came to him when he worked with subjects like her: beauty of form, corruption of purpose. Sutton swore that with prosperity he would never again photograph an actress. It was much too taxing on his conscience.

The sun, when it had appeared, had been bright enough, but the sky had been full of clouds, and whenever it had seemed he had the perfect pose, the perfect background, the perfect light, a shadow would invariably reappear. Frustrating.

And then by nine thirty the manager had informed him that Miss Duse was looking weary after her long journey from San Francisco and had refused, for the sake of his client's reputation, to permit any more pictures to be taken. Realizing that he'd already got more publicity than he'd had in months, judging by the size of the crowd gathered around them, Sutton had offered no protest. He had folded his equipment carefully, and as still others milled about his vehicle, he had packed it into the storage area. Sutton had designed the trunk to fit his specifications when ordering the machine.

Jehovah had been good to him that morning. Through Blakeley

he had met a producer months ago, and the producer had, in turn, introduced him to the inner circle, and the assignments following had been of the sort to perpetuate themselves. There would be time, he thought, to catch up on other work after developing the morning's photographs. Then perhaps he could prevail upon Angélique to join him in evening prayers. It would bode well for her progress.

Alighting from his horseless carriage, he looked up and thought to himself that there could have been at least another hour of productive work had the manager not been so temperamental. The actress herself had been cooperative, docile, in fact, and he wished now that he'd said something, rather than merely acquiesced. Too late. But the sky was truly grand. It was not the kind of day to bury himself in his darkroom.

"Angie," he called out. Surely she must be up by now.

He let the front door close and called again, and again there was no answer. Placing his materials on the living-room floor, he followed the undefined noises he thought he'd heard. Soon he was hurrying through the front rooms and up the stairs two at a time to the second floor.

There, in the bedroom, was Angélique with two gentlemen.

Unfortunately Miss Walker could not remember the doctor's name. Her friend had been reluctant to discuss the matter, but she had had the feeling that the physician—a greedy bastard, Miss Walker called him—fixed Chantal de Rohan on drugs forever. But Miss Walker was certain that he operated within the area.

"She used to disappear every now and then and come back with this dull look in her eyes. I know he ain't too far from us right now."

"I see." Her story had been depressing but valuable.

She theorized that the fat man might have lured her companion away by leading her to believe he could offer her some of the opiate, which she had been taking in ever-increasing quantities lately. That seemed plausible.

Blakeley excused himself, leaving the bottle of Napoleon at her disposal, and telephoned Officer McBride. Dr. Toberman was beginning to seem much more than a background figure. But there were other, more salient matters. The description of the fat man was his first solid testimony, and Blakeley was excited now over his chances of snaring the Butcher. And he knew deep down that it was the Butcher, or at least a party to the conspiracy he'd learned to call by that name.

He did not think he had to tell Miss Walker that it was already too late to save her friend. Almost twenty hours had passed since her disappearance. If their suspicions were accurate, the best they could hope for was the remote chance that she'd escaped on her own. He was grateful that she had come to him with her story. It showed that someone had faith in his ability to catch the fiend. For a while he'd been questioning that himself. Now he could smell an opportunity, and he was anxious to put his plan to work.

"Blakeley here. Is that you, Officer McBride?"

"Yes it is, Dr. Blakeley."

Nathan had been sitting in silence for the last half hour. The telephone had rung once before on that morning. That time it had been Maggie Tolan. "Nathan," she had said in her light brogue, "Lou's dead." My God. . . .

An unexplained explosion aboard the gunboat *Portland* off the North Carolina coast had taken the life of Sergeant Louis Gardell James and three sailors. It had not been a combat-related death, purely accidental, apparently the result of some gunnery mate's carelessness. Lou had not even had the chance to go down in action—the final insult, if anyone understood Lou. Maggie Tolan—it was the first time he'd heard from her since the captain's passing—had spoken gently out of deference to his close ties with Lou. Nathan told Dr. Blakeley. He had to tell someone.

"I am truly sorry, Nathan." It was the first time Blakeley had used his first name, but the novelty went by unnoticed. "I met Sergeant James once. At the Tolan wake, I believe. An estimable young man."

Nathan pulled himself together. He wanted to get to work. "I suppose there's been a turn in the case."

"There is. How did you know?"

"Intuition," he said facetiously. "Something tells me we've got another one missing."

"Yes we have, only this time we've got something else involved—something quite promising."

He brought Nathan up to date on the events of yesterday, referring to Miss de Rohan by a quiet euphemism, uttered somewhat uncertainly and giving his visitor a chuckle. Miss Walker was within listening distance, having begun to float around the study in evident awe of the books. Although she could not read, the bindings were impressively colorful.

Max Toberman sat at his desk, jotting down the last items of his report. The more data he recorded on Number 262 the less satisfied he became. The subject had not lasted long enough, and according to his timetable, this test had been an important one.

The burning had lasted one hour and thirty-six minutes before the first spell of unconsciousness, the incisions two hours, seventeen minutes, the dismemberment only thirty-three minutes. Total length of experiment: nine hours, twenty-nine minutes. Eventual cause of expiration: shock. One could never anticipate the durability of a morphine addict; if the nerves had been dulled by drug use, the heart had also been taxed.

He put his notes in the safe, feeling weary after the long night of work. He rubbed his temples and sat down to look at the morning paper before seeing the first of his patients.

There was no mention of the victim this time. That kind was rarely missed. But the prostitutes, though easy enough to come by when an experiment was due, were becoming less useful with each encounter. Their soft, wasted bodies afforded him no true test. The next one must be younger, stronger. If only he could find a creature with the strength of a man and a woman's threshold of pain.

On the front page, below the war news, was a story about Blakeley's newest suspect, some wretched fellow from skid row. Toberman found it amusing. The Blakeleys of this world were old playthings to him.

"I take it you still want me to visit Dr. Toberman?" asked Nathan.

"Oh, yes, of course." The probability of a physician's being involved in the case was greater than ever now. "And I want you to pay particular attention to his office. Note the distance between the window and the safe. Should there be any records worth our interest, they'll be there, I'd wager. And if you can, get a sample of his hair."

That last request sounded unusual, but Nathan understood its importance. In the paucity of evidence uncovered so far, there had been alien hair follicles found on the Beckwith and Darcy remains, and they had matched. According to a microscopic examination, they were those of a person whose hair was turning from dark brown to gray. Andrew Sutton had been ruled out—his hair was still sandy, if thinning. Nathan would wait for Toberman to turn his back and hope to find a stray piece of hair on his coat.

"Nice place you got," observed Miss Walker after Blakeley had hung up the telephone.

"Thank you," he answered as he fussed momentarily with some pipe ash that had fallen onto his desk. He was considering how best to approach the subject of her friend's chances. She poured one more drop of Napoleon into her teacup and looked pensive. He realized that this was actually her nighttime, but he nonetheless felt slightly uneasy. The mere thought of one drinking such potent spirits at this hour made his stomach twitch. She seemed to be staring into the cup.

"I seen a lot of the old ones go that way. Every day your habit gets bigger, an' you know you've got to sell bigger. Only one day your body ain't up to it, and worse yet, nobody wants to buy it no more," she thought aloud. "What the hell's Chantal got to lose anyway?"

Her world and his were at far extremes of the spectrum, yet she was permitting, indeed welcoming, him into hers for a glimpse of its loneliness. She was saying things about her inner feelings that he knew she would be loath to unveil to others of his class. She went on lethargically, admitting that she'd really come because she wanted someone to get the Butcher.

"It's gettin' so bad a lady don't feel safe on the streets at night." She laughed as she got up to leave. "He won't be hard to spot in a crowd, y'know. He's wider than any two guys you've ever seen. And he has these scratches on his cheek—kinda faded, but you can see them if you look. It's as if somebody really scraped the hell outa him about a month ago."

That, he informed her, thinking of the flesh he'd found under the fingernails of the Figge girl, was valuable information. As she lit up another cigarette, he thanked her for her cooperation and rang for Victor. Sooner or later, he knew, Sophia would appear, and his life had been complicated enough as of late.

Victor entered and looked at the Napoleon with flaring eyes. Usually it took him much longer to respond; Blakeley suspected that he'd been at the keyhole this time. What he'd hoped to *witness* was something upon which Blakeley did not wish to speculate. Victor stared at the bottle with obvious scorn, the discovery distasteful that Blakeley had been drinking with a painted lady at midmorning.

Miss Walker obviously delighted in such moments. After strolling back to Blakeley, she craned her neck and pecked him on the cheek. He stared at her like one unsure of his next breath.

"Remember"—she giggled—"if there's ever anything I can do for you, you know where to find me, Doc."

Victor trailed behind her, glaring over his shoulder at Blakeley as he left. Shortly thereafter, as Blakeley was doing his best to sketch a plan of attack for this latest effort against the Butcher, he heard angry footsteps in the hallway. He was endeavoring to put himself in the Butcher's place, asking himself where he would deposit the next remains if he wished to elicit the most horrified response, when Sophia entered his study, followed by the tight-lipped Victor. Her face was almost ashen, but she wore a determined, if eerie, smile.

"Busy this morning, are we?" she chirped.

"Um . . . a bit," he acknowledged warily.

Victor was standing in the background, rigid with self-righteousness. Blakeley eyed him with a promise of retribution. "You, you odious creature," he roared. "I've seen higher motives in the slums of Khartoum!"

Victor smiled. *"Suaviter in modo, fortiter in re."*

Smooth in manner, strong in deed.

Blakeley knew it well; it was the motto on his family's coat of arms. He picked up a lead figurine he used as a paperweight and bent it with his bare hands.

Victor fled.

Nathan McBride pulled up before the Sutton home. Blakeley had asked him to drop by on his way to Toberman's office because he'd been unable to get through to Sutton by phone. It had not been a serious matter; Rosie was, in Blakeley's words, stumbling into young ladyhood, and he wished to arrange for some tintypes of her to be taken. But he had been unable to get through because, he presumed, someone else was on the line exchanging useless information. Nathan had agreed that Sutton should be aware of their intentions since a photograph of the Butcher caught in the act of depositing the *corpus delicti* would be incontrovertible proof of guilt, and he had added diplomatically that the recognition would be good for Rosalie.

Those party lines were a damned nuisance. His own ring was three longs and a short, and some palm reader on his line had three shorts and a long, and Central could never seem to get the two straight. Central always seemed to him a putty-faced person made of wires and finger-smudged tin. No meaning, no gender; just function and nasal interrogation.

Sutton's vehicle was parked in front of the house, and Nathan settled his horse and buggy directly behind it. When the sun hit the polished metal, it gleamed like the surface of a lake at eventide. He tarried for a moment to inspect it, still wondering how much it cost and asking himself whether he'd ever have the opportunity to find out.

The walk from the newly paved street to the front door was lined with neatly trimmed hedges, and the walk itself meticulously groomed. The flowers separating it from the foliage were colorful and evenly spaced. Had he not known Sutton's address, something would have told him that he'd found the house. Had the circumstances of his life been better, it would have been easy to appreciate the pleasant morning in such a setting.

There was no answer when he knocked the first time. Not even a bird or an insect broke the eerie quiet. He looked around and knocked again, this time more deliberately. The window was half open, and through a space between the curtains he could see Sutton's equipment on the floor.

Well, thought Nathan, *the hell with him. Blakeley can try the telephone again if he really wants to deal with Sutton.*

A noise, something like a steady groan, disturbed the quiet. It was faint at first, tempting him to blame his imagination, but it persisted. He put his ear to the opening, and the noises became more discernible. *Sutton, are you in there?* No response.

"Are you in there, Sutton?" he repeated, louder this time, and was answered by another groan. That was no delusion, he knew immediately. It had all the characteristics of a death rattle.

He found the front door unlocked. After entering the vestibule, he stepped over the photographic equipment set down where the front room abutted the hallway. Moving cautiously against the wall, he eased himself slowly, gradually, into the center of the house, listening closely to the tortured sounds. They grew fainter and less frequent, making it increasingly difficult to detect the source. The house was exceedingly close; for some reason no air circulated in the meticulously kept rooms. There was no hint of violence; not even a single fragile *objet d'art* had been overturned. But one could sense violence after a time. It tended to hang in the atmosphere like something acrid and forbidding.

Another groan. Nathan darted up the stairs, pausing at the second floor to look around for signs of activity. Down the hall there was a door ajar; it was the only signal of anything strange since he'd encountered the equipment on the floor. Nathan drew his revolver and hugged the wall again, eventually reaching the end of the corridor, where the open door offered him the only possible answer. He held his breath and entered with a sudden move.

Sutton, glassy-eyed and mouth agape, sat at the foot of the bed. In his hand was a common scissors, still red in spots where the blood had not dripped off.

Good Lord, there were three bodies.

One lay flat on the bedroom floor, grasping his throat where it had been cut. Another was seated on the floor, propped against the wall, eyes fixed oddly upon his naked feet, wounded many times in his arms and chest. On the bed, totally nude, Angie lay dying, her labored breaths coming very erratically. How the emerald-green ribbons with which she'd bedecked her hair accentuated the blood on the sheets and pillows.

Nathan was seized by compassion—something only a few weeks ago he never thought he'd feel for Andrew Sutton. But in that time he had learned much about the melancholy circumstances of Sutton's life. It had been obvious that Sutton would one day drop in unannounced and discover his young wife paying homage to her overwhelming drives. The insatiable Angélique-Marie Sutton—whose uncanny likeness to his own Aidan Tièrney gave him chills—had finally broken Andrew Sutton's reserve. Fatally. Her arms, which had been waving slowly and aimlessly, as if grasping for uncertain help from her prostrate position on the bed, went limp, and the groans ceased.

Nathan put away his revolver and took a cautious, almost delicate step toward Sutton. He remained apparently oblivious to Angie. He was slumped there with shock and fatigue from realizing what he had done.

"Sutton," Nathan spoke softly. "Sutton, can you hear me?"

Save for the unusual spasms of Sutton's cheeks and the tears running down his ashen face, he was a statue. Patches of blood stained his clothing and caked his hands. He had been seated there for about a half hour, Nathan guessed.

"Give me the scissors, Mr. Sutton. I'll take you where you can rest for a while."

He could not be sure whether the abrupt jerking of Sutton's eyes meant that they were actually focusing upon him. Nor could he be sure how Sutton would react to the sight of him. He might be seen as a harbinger of comfort or simply as one more man in Angie's bedroom. He wanted to call the precinct station, but he knew he had to get the scissors out of Sutton's hands first.

Nathan coaxed him, careful not to alarm him. Sutton was at that moment as dangerous to himself as he was to Nathan. Above all, he knew he could not afford to let Sutton run loose. But he was averse to the thought of using force; Sutton had already suffered enough, and his energy had probably been sapped by all that had gone on before. He looked totally spent, but for those eyes, which kept twitching mechanically.

"That's it, Mr. Sutton, give it to me. You won't need it anymore."

Sutton seemed to be loosening his grip on the scissors. Nathan thought he noticed the eyes beginning to clear after another few minutes as Sutton gradually got up.

Just as Nathan thought he'd got his way, the eyes began to shine, and Sutton made a sudden dive at him. Taken off-balance, Nathan strove to restrain him with an armlock, but Sutton slipped out of it and struck at him with the scissors. Nathan felt a burning in his shoulder and gritted his teeth. He felt himself propelled across the room, tripping over one of the bodies, as Sutton, with unnatural strength, threw him against the wall. He fell to the ground, his head striking the corner of the dresser.

When his head cleared, he was on his knees and Sutton was gone. His own blood ran down his sleeve and covered his left hand, mingling with that of the body he touched. The back of his head felt even worse. That cut made his eyes nearly cross with pain.

Getting up and shaking his head, he called out for Sutton, then mumbled curses. Through the bedroom window he saw Sutton cranking up his vehicle and climbing into the carriage. Even from that distance and with his vision clouded, the bloodstains on Sutton's clothing were prominent. "You can't make it," he cried, but Sutton was insensible. There was no time to run down through the hallways and stairs. Not far from the window there was a drainpipe leading to a rain barrel. He shook his head again and blinked his eyes, trying to summon enough clarity of mind to undertake what he knew to be the only possible way to capture Sutton.

As the machine rolled away and gathered momentum, Nathan gripped the pipe and prayed that it was fastened securely to the side of the house. As he swung himself onto the outside, he almost screamed with pain; he could feel the flesh in his upper back tearing where the scissors had entered. It seemed he would fall unconscious to the ground.

But the darkness passed, and he lowered himself as gracefully as possible to the level of the first floor. His foot touched a windowsill. It was none too soon, for at that moment the drainpipe gave way. He was able to land on his feet as he fell. A crowd was gathering on the corner across the street to witness what it must have believed to be a burglary.

Nathan knew the neighborhood intimately. He knew that Andrew Sutton would have to drive almost fully around the circular street. There were few side streets wide enough for horseless vehicles, most of the roads in this section having been planned long before the advent of such machines. If he were Sutton, he reasoned, he would gamble on making it down Webster Place and hope that the street would not narrow too much where it approached the creek. Not unless he wanted to find Nathan waiting for him, in a much less humane frame of mind. The cut behind Nathan's head seemed to grow more painful by the minute, and the uncertain grumbling of the gathering crowd only piqued his anger. He could sense its sublimated ugliness becoming concentrated upon him. He dashed through the backyard and followed a run-down lane that wended through a clump of foliage and terminated where the street met Webster Place. People from the crowd were following him. Webster Place was the only corner wide enough to negotiate in a horseless carriage. It had to be there if he was to capture Sutton at all.

The vehicle held the road well, accelerating quickly over the brick surface and disappearing beneath the elm trees at the curve. Nathan ran for all he was worth, cutting through a briar patch. But the sting of the thorns tearing his trousers was lost in his other pains. In rising desperation he spied Sutton's vehicle turning down Webster Place, still many yards from the small rise he was attempting to climb. The ground was muddy from the early-morning rains, and he could feel his shoes losing traction in the yellow clay.

Sutton had slowed briefly when his front tire hit the curb and swerved to avoid a stationary milk wagon. Nathan could hear the chugging of the machine as it quickly built up speed. He leaped over a ditch and hurdled a broken wagon abandoned by some child at the roadside. Onlookers turned with amazement to stare after the wounded figure running feverishly down the street. Members of the crowd who had followed him from Sutton's house could be heard shouting well behind him. He kept his eyes on the vehicle. He thought he was gaining ground. He wondered in passing how Sutton, in a state of terror himself, could drive with such control.

Sutton turned around to look for Nathan and, seeing him still running with determination, started to panic. The vehicle's progress became suddenly wobbly as Sutton temporarily lost his grip on the steering mechanism.

Encouraged, Nathan put on a burst of speed and gained on him as Sutton struggled to secure command. Soon, with exhaustion setting in, he was beside the vehicle and smelled the heady fumes it threw off as Sutton looked back at him with fiery eyes. He grasped the rear bumper with his left hand, and using it as a leverage, pulled himself forward. As he hooked his right hand around to grip the leather padding where the cab joined the body, Sutton started to flail wildly behind himself with the scissors.

Nathan evaded the blows and placed his foot firmly upon the running board, throwing himself into the cab as the scissors missed his face by a fraction and tore into the upholstery. The street was narrowing, and the bend near the creek was not far away as he lunged at Sutton and wrested the scissors from his hand. The machine started to sway and rock as Sutton released the steering mechanism to grasp Nathan by the throat. In his fury he was uncommonly strong. Nathan had to hit him twice before Sutton's hands finally let go. His third blow knocked Sutton unconscious. The vehicle had slowed only slightly and was coasting toward the bend. Nathan tried to regain control.

Sutton's body had fallen forward, and Nathan could not grip the rod. For the first time it occurred to him that they both were in danger of going over the side. He struggled to pull Sutton off the mechanism, the wind through the open front smelling of creek water. Pedestrians dashed for safety as the machine rolled wildly over the dirt road.

He tugged at Andrew Sutton as the bend came up before them, deciding to get both of them out of there. Then the vehicle hit a rut in the street, swerved abruptly to the left, and Nathan felt himself tumbling helplessly, hurled through the air as the beautiful maroon and gold Winton rolled over and landed in the creek.

For a moment—he could not tell how long—Nathan lay motionless in the mud on the creek bank as the crowd caught up with them and gathered at the bend to gape. His quarry lay a few feet from him in the water, his body pinned from the waist down under the vehicle. On its side, wheels spinning purposelessly, it steamed where the creek ran over the heated engine. He dragged himself through the rocks and mud to inspect Sutton.

There was a gurgling sound which he took at first to be the sound of the water lapping against the shore. Blood welled from the man's mouth, and Andrew Sutton died.

Nathan had another attack of pain, this one in his leg as he struggled to get to his feet. The crowd was dense as he looked up toward the bank, and he could hear vague murmurs of astonishment. Feeling inside his coat, he pulled out a badge and held it up.

"Police Officer," he mumbled as he felt himself drifting into blackness.

$\mathfrak{S}$ixteen

"Vit all the fancy ladies I've had it fer good, by Cheesuss." Fatzinger bit into his sandwich of fried scrapple and chowchow relish on rye and munched with determination. "I'm goin' back up to Ebenezersville next time. Maybe the vimmen don't all like pansies shmell, but you don't gotta give their trinkets back eeder, you betcha."

Fatzinger had been grumbling all morning. Mme. Cheever, to whom he had pledged his troth only a fortnight ago, had been apprehended the evening before in the act of shoplifting. For weeks he'd been the recipient of a number of gifts. Now he had to return the pocket watch, the tiepin, the two rings, and the fourteen pairs of summer underwear. Hudson had permitted him to keep the bottle of cologne in his locker because it tended to dampen the odor of Bones' lunch pail. Worse yet, Mme. Cheever, appearing before the night sergeant, had claimed to be the wife of Constable Fatzinger just before she had overturned a waste can and pitched a bottle of ink at the sergeant's head. And that morning she had called Fatzinger a peasant and had sworn to go on a hunger strike. Until the czar's agents freed her and put Hudson to death for his insolence.

"Vot iss a red-blooded man to do?" He sighed. The secretary smiled cordially and continued typing.

He poured some buttermilk into a cup and drank absentmindedly while others busied themselves around him.

"Yah," he said, "I'm goin' back to Ebenezersville, back to my first an' only woman, Strawberry Knockelknorr. Now dott's vun hell of a sow, by Christ. A good fella can't go wrong vit dott vun. Biggest tits in six counties."

The secretary stopped typing and turned pale.

"Fatzinger, get in here." Hudson's voice was trenchant. He wanted Bones to identify some more articles. The case had already demanded far too much attention. "What do you know about these lemon-yellow shirts?"

Reporters had been harassing Hudson all morning. There was more than enough to fill the pages of the later edition, but they wanted more, and their obsessive tactics had eroded his small reserve of patience. Each one used the same ploy. They feigned interest in the Hattie Rau case, which, though tragic, was cut-and-dried. Then they got to the matter truly interesting to them, the mysterious European suspect in the Butcher murders. Where was he? Who was he? Why couldn't they have a look at him? Hudson shrugged and finally announced that he had never heard of this sinister suspect of theirs or of the Mrs. Leibowitz who claimed to have seen him. He suggested that Mrs. Leibowitz was a woman with a morbid sense of humor who had gulled them all. Undaunted, three of the newspapermen still sat outside his office.

"Real nice shirts, Lootenant," Fatzinger replied. "How come yer askin'?"

"Well, Bones," he said, placing a hand on Fatzinger's shoulder, "aside from the fact that they're stolen, they're your size, and we found them in your locker, I can't think of any reason to ask. But I thought I would anyway."

"In *my* locker?" His tone was one of astonishment.

"Under a box of junk."

"Cheez," Fatzinger mumbled, "she must o' shlipped dem in venn I vasn't lookin'."

Hudson banished Fatzinger to the file room for another day and sat down to compose a letter to Lou James' family. The news of Lou's death had left him so drained that he'd even found it difficult to be angry with Fatzinger and the reporters. He had been trying all morning to find the words.

Lou James had been with him for five years until that stupid war broke out. Together they'd handled hundreds of crimes, large and small, even settled a tavern brawl or two. Lou was a little the way his son would have been, the one who had not made it into his ninth year. Influenza had taken Charles Alfred Hudson, Jr., just as whimsically as the accident had taken Lou. But he knew he couldn't say that. Writing letters was far from being one of Hudson's strong points. He decided to leave it to Nathan.

What a goddamn cursed precinct this is, he thought. *Death and grief should be printed on its letterhead under the city's insignia.*

There was a minor commotion outside. Word had just come in that something dramatic had occurred over on Webster Place and the reporters were bolting for the doorway.

"Why then are you giving me that insipid look?"

Toberman had had a last-minute turn of mind, deciding not to incinerate the body of Chantal de Rohan as originally planned. Something had inspired him to try a much more pointed method of disposal. He had just informed Arthur in incontrovertible terms.

"Is it because you shall have to shun your drugs until later in the evening?"

"That, too," answered Arthur brazenly.

"And?"

"It seems to me," he went on, "that for someone who's been bitching for so long about my so-called penchant for the dramatic, you're rather daring all of a sudden!"

"You have my instructions, Arthur."

Arthur huffed and slammed the door behind him.

Just how long he would be able to put up with those two deviates, Toberman did not know, but he smiled when contemplating their elimination. Philadelphia was becoming wearisome anyway.

When he awoke, the morning sun burned brightly through the window, forcing him to blink the room into focus. There were ghostly figures near the foot of his bed, and a crucifix on the wall startled him just a bit as its image clarified. He was propped up. His body ached everywhere.

The figures took on color and form as a sharp pain in his back snapped him into wakefulness. He heard Blakeley's voice.

"You may leave now, Sister. Thank you."

A stiff-looking nun in a very large hennin floated out of the room. When she had gone, Nathan discerned Miss Meredith's presence as well.

"Is it morning?" Nathan asked.

"It is Sunday, June the twenty-first, and we are experiencing the beginning of the summer of 1898." Blakeley smiled. "I decided to put you out for the night because we had a lot of work to do on you."

Nathan tried to disguise his anxiety. "How much?"

"Oh," he said offhandedly, "that was quite a nasty wound below your shoulder, and the filthy creek water didn't do it much good. The risk of infection had us a bit occupied for a time. You really should take better care of yourself, my boy. The knee is merely sprained. And you have a bump on your noggin. All in all, you could have got worse than that on a rugby field."

"I take it that will be all, Dr. Blakeley," Miss Meredith broke in. Nathan knew by the circles under her eyes that she had been there as long as Blakeley. Even so, she remained disturbingly attractive.

"I just dropped by with some information for Dr. Blakeley," she said. "I'm so glad to see you pulling out of it, Detective McBride."

"Thank you."

She wished him well and left.

Blakeley proceeded to open the curtains to let in more sun and raised the window. The air was brisk and, in light of Blakeley's prognosis, refreshing. But Nathan's head still felt as if he were underwater, and yesterday's episode still had him unsettled. He had been told when he had joined the force that perhaps in one case out of eight a policeman has to kill a man. Something had usually gone wrong in such incidents, the instructor said. Something had gone wrong yesterday, Nathan knew. Had he not put away his revolver, had Sutton been too addled to be deterred by the sight of the weapon, Nathan could at least have stopped him with a leg wound. Later, when Nathan's recovery was imminent, he knew Lieutenant Hudson would have to remind him of that. What the hell do we issue those things for? he would ask. Killing a man left a very vile taste.

"Does Aidan know what happened?"

"Your young lady? Oh yes, she's been notified." Blakeley's tone was restrained. "By Lieutenant Hudson, I believe. Do you know that Alvin B. Porterfield, also known as Zoltan Mroszek, is at the other end of the floor? I wanted to keep you two within walking distance in case I had emergencies at the same time."

"If he's been bathed and deloused," Nathan said half-jokingly, "you could've put him next door. I'm a heavy sleeper."

A student nurse muddled through the doorway, carrying a tray, while a nursing sister screeched in the background. Zoltan Mroszek's presence on this floor of Good Samaritan Hospital had put many nerves on edge.

"Am I permitted to drink some coffee?" asked Nathan as the girl went out.

"Anything in moderation. We've not removed your stomach," he answered heartily and handed him a cup.

"Aidan does know everything's all right, doesn't she?"

Blakeley really wished Nathan would get off the subject. Miss Tierney had been apprised of all that had transpired, but she had thus far made no appearance. Blakeley had no desire to get into that issue—it was much too likely to trap him into passing judgment—so he lied.

"She was considerably relieved to know that you were out of danger."

"That's good." Nathan sipped his coffee. It was weak but welcome.

"You shall probably be out of commission for a time. Had he used a knife rather than a scissors the wound in your shoulder would have been deeper. All joking aside, it is severe enough. Not to mention the possible concussion and other bumps and bruises. In fine, a week or so."

"I'll be up and about by the middle of the week," Nathan said with confidence.

"A week to ten days," Blakeley amended.

Nathan was looking depressed enough. Blakeley, perhaps sensing that the time would never be better, showed him a copy of last evening's newspaper.

"You might as well know you've become a celebrity," he said as unconcernedly as possible. "The press has decided you're the closest thing we have to Colonel Roosevelt."

Oh, no. . . . With the absence of war news they'd found the chase exciting—involving as it did a detective, once a university athlete, and a horseless vehicle. The added fillip of sexual intrigue enhanced the episode. Prominent local photographer, having just posed the great Duse, discovers his young wife in an indelicate position with two strange gentlemen. The reporter made the picture clear enough but chose his words judiciously. The multiple murder, presumably in the heat of uncontrollable passion, the wild chase, the daring efforts of the young detective, the fatal conclusion—had it involved someone else, Nathan would have found it interesting reading. There were righteous commentaries on the natural mental collapse of the aggrieved husband and a maudlin treatment of the fallen wife as the writer lapsed occasionally into a style reminiscent of an earlier period. And here and there Nathan was taken aback when the reporter presumed to know what had gone on in *his* head as the melodrama was unfolding. The incident was all the more unusual because Andrew Sutton's was the first death involving a horseless vehicle recorded in the city.

Nathan's own unwanted celebrity status had come when the commissioner's niece—the same one who had hired Fatzinger—provided the newspaper with his life history and a photograph from the personnel files. A particularly fine artist had reproduced Nathan's features with great detail, and he stared at himself for a moment before putting the newspaper aside.

"You know," he mused aloud, "last year I saved a life. I had to jump from a bridge to pull a little girl out of the Schuylkill. It got a few lines on the fourth page. Just look what happens when you take one away."

"To your credit you did not go out shooting frantically when it looked as if he'd make it to freedom. You jeopardized no life other than your own."

Nathan did not wish to recount just how sickened he'd been on the evening before by the sight of Oscar Rau. Nathan could not have aimed to kill, he knew deep within him, had Sutton threatened to massacre the entire community. He had serious doubts about his own ability to continue in this profession. Latin teachers lived much saner existences. He thanked Blakeley, however, for his support.

"Not at all. You're going through normal pangs of guilt. Frankly, I'd be rather disappointed in you were you to react otherwise."

They went on to a second cup of coffee, and as Nathan's haze cleared, he noted the fatigue in Blakeley's eyes; the strain of the challenge was showing.

Some miles away on Blakeley's estate, Snopkowski was walking through the woods in search of wild mushrooms. She sought something to perk up Blakeley's appetite, case or no case, goddamn, and remembered the raves of satisfaction when once he'd tasted her mushrooms broiled in Sauterne and butter. She served it as a first course on whole wheat toast. Later she would serve creamed mushrooms and spinach with the lamb chops. "Dott should fixink his belly," she swore, "no matter what dott Butcher bugger does next time."

She padded in her cloth slippers over the rise and down the hill where the riding trail ran through a cluster of mountain laurel. It was a good time of year for the wild things, with most of the shrubs in bloom and the woods alive with small animals. There was bound to be a wealth of fresh vegetables to be uncovered this morning. She hummed a tune that had been heard in few places other than the village in which she was born sixty-eight years ago.

"Dere you are, you little mushrooms. I see you goddamn."

Near the trail, in a line which ran through the laurel to a small open patch in the cherry orchard, she spied the plump little buttons. It was a damn good thing Madame was a good rider, she reasoned in so many words. Otherwise, the best of the mushrooms might have been trampled as the big stallion made the tight curve.

She stepped over some deep ruts, oblivious to their strange presence on either side of the narrow lane, and proceeded to cover the bottom of her first pail. Moving steadily away from the riding trail toward the orchard, she paused to taste some blackberries from one of the bushes growing beside the drainage ditch, nodding her head with satisfaction. It was a little early, but they were just about ready for picking. Then Snopkowski's imagination started to take over. Dinner would begin with some very rich mushroom soup and end with blackberry cobbler. . . . No, the blackberries could wait another week. Dessert that evening would be Schwarzwälder Kirschentorte made from their orchard's own cherries. *If dott's no vorrkink, den poor Snopkowski's givink up an' kookink only bean soup, goddamn.*

She filled her first pail from a cluster of mushrooms behind one of the blackberry bushes and, grunting, moved off through the long grass on the periphery of the trees. Again she spied a bountiful crop in a damp section and knelt to pick as many as she could in as short a time as possible.

Snopkowski was deathly afraid of snakes and did not care how many times she'd been told that garters and grass snakes were harmless. They couldn't be any good or they'd walk around instead of crawling, she swore. After the first time she'd encountered one, a baby black snake, she had not gone near the woods for more than a year. There were skunks out there, too; sometimes on summer nights she could smell them. *Prob'ly Veektorr's friends.* She grinned.

For a fleeting moment she wondered if she'd dare slip some bad stems into Victor's mushroom soup. Nothing lethal, she thought with a giggle, just enough to give him the runs.

"Jezu," she muttered. The deeper she continued into the orchard, the more plentiful the big juicy buttons seemed to become. There had been just enough rainfall to keep the shaded areas moist, and the sun had broken through the trees for only a brief period daily around noon. She had visions of many other tasty delights to come throughout the week as she crawled around the trunk of an aging elm tree and plucked at the ground with steady determination, ignoring the footprints which had tramped before her in the same direction. There were dandelions, too. Snopkowski would make more wine for the winter, she decided, smacking her lips.

She stopped abruptly and remained frozen on hands and knees. . . . Before her eyes was a human foot. It lay upright, protruding from the deep grass. It was dainty, not unlike a child's, but in the brief minute or so that Snopkowski felt in control of herself, she observed that it was attached to a long, slender adult's leg.

Wojku!

Mushrooms scattered through the orchard as Snopkowski's pail flew into the air, accompanied by an unearthly shriek.

In light of recent events Zoltan Mroszek was no longer a plausible suspect, and Nathan asked what they were going to do with him.

"Now he is not totally without merit in any instance. If he is not directly involved in the affair, I am still of the suspicion that he bears some relationship to our concerns. His troubled dreams, for example, continue to revolve around the mysterious fat man. My visitor of yesterday made much the same allusion, and while I'm sure there are scores of innocent obese gentlemen, the coincidence remains too strong to ignore."

"Is he making any progress?" Nathan inquired referring to Mroszek.

"Surprisingly, yes. No deep-rooted drug addiction. His delirium may be purely traumatic, and he's suffering from severe malnutrition. As we mend the body, so we hope to strengthen the mind. I'd venture we'll have his head cleared by the time you leave here. If nothing else, he's been a prodigious fund of psychological data; the poor wretch is virtually a walking id."

The student nurse reentered with a breakfast tray; she was now griping about the reporters in the waiting room. The head nurse had ordered her young ladies to be on the alert. After placing his breakfast before him, she paused to stare at Nathan.

"What's the trouble, miss?" asked Blakeley, thinking she'd seen something irregular in his patient.

"Are you really the guy that killed that madman over on Webster Place?" Her eyes were like large coins as she addressed Nathan.

"No," he answered soberly, "I sell rugs for a living. But keep the reporters out of here anyway."

She looked at him quizzically and left.

"I'm going to have to move you to another floor, Detective McBride. At this rate I'm afraid you'll attract attention to Mroszek."

Nathan understood, but the pain of his dubious popularity kept him speaking in a monotone. Enough was enough.

"How can they be so certain that Sutton was mad?" he asked. "One would expect many men to crack under the strain of *his* married life."

"Yes, but there have been subsequent discoveries which have given more, should we say, color, to the tale."

Blakeley was helping himself to a piece of toast and a slice of bacon.

"Such as?"

"Sutton, it seems, had kept copies of all the photographs he'd taken of the Butcher's victims. When the constables unearthed them in his darkroom, the household was already swarming with newspapermen. You can read about it on page three."

Nathan's fork paused in midair, and he turned away from his griddle cakes. Why, he asked, would Sutton do such a thing? Voyeurism?

"No, not really, Nathan. The pictures were being collected under the heading 'wages of sin.' I presume he intended to produce a photographic morality piece for young women. Only the unfortunate prostitutes had been included, of course, none of the honest girls. Morbid, yes, but no doubt he thought it a creditable venture, given his religious severity. You may recall our excitement over Herr Koch's store of medieval torture devices and how we jumped to conclusions at that time? It's much the same kind of farfetched circumstantial evidence. The press, naturally, want to think that Sutton was in with the Butcher."

A breeze came through the open window, disheveling briefly Nathan's usually fastidious hair. *He must be of the sort that heals readily,* Blakeley mused with some degree of wishful thinking; the investigation could not proceed very well without him.

"Do you have any pain?" he inquired.

Nathan shook his head and poured some honey over his griddle cakes, still eating without enthusiasm. If he had truly wished to kill, he said, he'd have gone off to the Marines with Lou. It would take time for those wounds, the ones born of strangely conceived guilt feelings, to mend.

Blakeley knew the feeling. Thirty years ago, while a young captain serving in India, he had been waylaid by three Sikhs as he departed the post to deliver an urgent message to General Sarsfield. In the process of driving them off, he had had to kill one and paralyze another. With the realization that the Sikhs had had no interest in

his military dispatch and probably were more concerned with showing ill-advised bravado, Blakeley had become violently sick to his
stomach. Here he was, he had reflected ironically, a pampered
Kentish dandy who purported to be enamored of the healing arts,
killing and maiming young men on their native soil! The memory of
that episode still gnawed at him. All in all, he reckoned, Detective
McBride was holding up well.

"In any event," he said cheerily, trying another approach, "you
must admit the papers are treating you well for a change. You might
as well enjoy it while it lasts. You shall remain a celebrity, at least
unti the war gets lively again."

Nathan smiled back and started to eat more easily. The breakfast
of griddle cakes, bacon, fried eggs, and grape juice looked tempting.
One of the reasons Blakeley favored Good Samaritan Hospital was
the old German nun who oversaw the kitchen. She was only slightly
less dedicated than Snopkowski, if considerably less imaginative.

A ruckus outside the room broke his thoughts. Blakely opened the
door and saw Lieutenant Hudson eddying through the reporters.
Presently he stopped to face a small round man with thick bifocals
and a dark mustache.

"Your paper must be pretty hard up for writers, Stanley," Hudson
was heard to observe. "I understand they had you posing for car-
toons only yesterday."

There was laughter, followed by a high-pitched retort uttered
with forced good humor. Hudson made mention of a broken nose,
bringing more laughter. The lieutenant's manner appeared relaxed
as he came into Nathan's small private room.

"Ready to get back to work, Nate?"

"Just as soon as I finish breakfast, Lieutenant."

"Good," said Hudson dryly. "I'm afraid it's a bit premature to plan
your retirement." He handed Blakeley a note and crossed to Nathan's bedside to shake his hand. Nice work, he commented, then
cursed Nathan good-naturedly for taking undue risks while the precinct was undermanned.

Nathan answered that it was about time someone brought some
positive attention to the precinct. But the easiness was short-lived;
Blakeley was visibly shaken by the note.

"Nathan," he asked, "whom would you assess to be the best burglary artist in the city?"

"Owen Ward-Lattimore," Nathan answered promptly, looking toward Hudson for corroboration.

Hudson nodded. Owen Ward-Lattimore was old now and spent his days feeding pigeons in the park, but none of the current crop could dream of surpassing him. He was, so to speak, the dean of breaking, entering, lifting, and escaping.

"I should like to meet him posthaste, Lieutenant." Blakeley's face was grave and ashen. "Posthaste," he repeated.

Allison Meredith sat at her typewriter and stared at her hands, telling herself once again that her mind could control their quivering if only she could concentrate long enough. Her task had been minor enough, a tersely worded statement for the press which had been dictated for the most part by Dr. Blakeley, but she was already at work on her fourth draft. The words simply would not come—they should have presented no challenge, even at the start of her career. Though her apartment was cool, her mouth felt as dry as alum. When she poured a glass of ice water, her attention was again drawn to the unaccountable weakness in her wrist.

She put the glass down to catch a breath of air, wanting to attribute her nervous state to fatigue. Or perhaps she'd merely caught a cold.

It was, after all, the kind of thing Nathan MacBride had been hired to do. Dr. Blakeley had selected him for his strength and agility, she deduced. . . . Certainly not for his charm. Why then, she wondered, had she stopped on the way home to visit a church and thank God for Nathan's deliverance!

The old man sniffed the tobacco with a connoisseur's detachment and looked up without registering yes or no.

"It's Miner's Extra, bejaysus. Ye'll find no better plug from here to Ohio," Tinker averred.

"I dunno," the old man commented. "I'm a Bull Durham man meself."

Tinker scoffed. "That's fer the likes o' that lad with the hole in his nuts. A lady's man like yerself needs a stronger chew."

Reluctantly, but with affected generosity, he handed the old man another plug and waited for a response. Ellie was good for another ten minutes or so, he knew. Once she got started with her prayers she was hard to interrupt, mostly because the task of maneuvering her bulk up from the kneeling position was so great especially after the five-flight climb to Father McDonnough's room. Tinker looked on with waning tolerance as the old man considered his proposal. He had averred that Flyin' McBride was housed on the floor.

"All right, lad," said the man at length, "but we'll have to make it look good. Here—help me outa this wheelchair."

Tinker eased the old man onto the floor, then stepped behind the huge frond and signaled him to howl like a soul in hell. In a second the policeman snapped out of his daydreams and bounded across the waiting room toward the wheelchair. Tinker made his way into Nathan's room.

"Hey," he announced to the astonished figure in the bed, "I know ye."

Nathan had been lost in an Émile Zola novel that Miss Meredith had brought him while on her way to Dr. Blakeley's an hour ago. Her kindness was almost as puzzling as her tight-lipped concern. In any case, the mess Nana had made of her tawdry life had got his mind off his own melancholy for the moment.

"I thought I recognized ye when I saw yer pitcher in the paper, but now I'm sure." Tinker's eyes were big as he scrutinized Nathan. "Ye're the one I talked to about me daughter. Remember? We were sure she was carted off by the Butcher, an' she only run off to get married!"

"Yes." Nathan sighed. "I remember. But what the hell are you doing here?"

"Oh," he said nonchalantly, disposing of his chew to bite into an apple from the basket of fruit on the dresser, "where there's a will there's a way."

Perhaps because Tinker evoked a rare, pleasant memory of the past few months, Nathan was not chagrined to see him.

"Have some fruit," he said facetiously.

"Don't mind if I do," Tinker answered, stuffing his coat with peaches and oranges. "Ye know," he said, "ye're quite the lad."

Nathan gave no response. God how he wanted no more fanfare.

"I'm not talkin' about what ye did the other day, bucko," he went on to Nathan's surprise. "That was a fine thing too, of course. But I think ye really showed yer mettle when ye come in an' faced down the Whalens that day."

"Pardon?"

"Bird Martin, damn his tongue, has always said he'd rather dive naked into a barrel o' vipers than come near the Whalens when a squabble is under way. Especially when Katie's got her ass up. She's more dangerous than big Michael ever was. Bird still talks about it, ye know, but not to me of course."

"How is the family doing nowadays?" Nathan inquired earnestly.

Tinker summarized his wretchedness ever since the boys went off to war and left him at the mercy of those two cursed harridans. His life had turned so sour at home that he'd even gone back to working on the railroad just to get out of the house.

But Nathan was pleased to discover that his hunch had been correct; the Whalens no longer despised Private Di Ciori. Tinker now regarded the little Italian as a martyr of sorts and predicted for him a life expectancy of two years after returning to dear darlin' Katie. Nathan laughed at that, but Tinker saw something in his eyes.

"There's sadness in ye, lad. Why?"

"Aches and pains, I suppose, Mr. Whalen. I got bounced around like a football."

"The divil ye say. It's more than that," Tinker suggested as he dropped his apple core into a waste can. "There's pain in yer soul, there is."

"I wasn't aware of that," said Nathan lightly. "Perhaps I should talk to the doctors about it."

The knobbly little man scoffed at the suggestion that doctors were good for anything other than overcharging for pills and double-talk. Nathan wished to drop the subject, but Tinker persisted in his analysis. His perception was remarkable; idleness, Nathan speculated, must breed amateur psychoanalysts.

"Never get down on yerself, lad. The world will be more than pleased to do that for ye," Tinker pontificated. "If ye keep that in yer head, ye'll always have at least one friend, an' he's someone you can count on too."

"What makes you think I'm down on myself?" he asked naively. "You don't even know me." Nathan was disappointed by his transparency; he had thought his acting to be good enough.

"Haven't I lived all these years by me wits? I can see, can't I?"

"Yes, but—"

"There are lots of things the wags in Grundy's Patch will tell ye about ould Tinker Whalen, but ye'll niver hear them call him a fool. A man doesn't live a life of ease the way I have unless he's a damn good student o' human nature. I can read people's eyes. I can tell in a minute how they feel about themselves an' that's how I manage to have them support me. No, sir—I'm *niver* wrong."

"I . . . I see."

"Ye're quality, lad," said Tinker, moving toward the door. "Ye're made o' good stuff, so get better soon. Ye niver can tell, ye know. If me daughter drives that poor Eyetalian to the grave, I'll need a new son-in-law just to kape her off me back."

He left with a wink of the eye and strutted in his bantam-rooster fashion past the bewildered and red-faced guard, leaving Nathan somewhat dazzled but not at all sorry to have seen him. Giving a sign of victory to the old man in the wheelchair, Tinker retraced his steps back toward Father McDonnough's room and puffed out his chest. Now and then—but not often—he went out of his way to help someone along. That, too, would make a grand story in the Patch Saloon. Tinker got thirsty just thinking about it.

Near the priest's room he heard a slight commotion and put his ear to a door. Someone was knocking on the wall and shouting vile comments at Father McDonnough. Tinker opened the door and looked in.

"Mr. Porterfield, please settle down," urged one of a team of nurses who were attempting in vain to bathe a wild-eyed patient. "You'll hurt yourself."

Tinker noticed that the man was partially strapped down to the bed. With his free hand he was pounding on the partition, taking almost manic delight in his taunts.

"Now thou art truly a man of thy vows, my dear cleric," he howled, "naught remains to tempt thee!"

"Mr. Porterfield, we shall have to gag you," threatened a nurse. No one had noticed Tinker's presence in the doorway thus far. He stood mesmerized by the bizarre-looking man on the bed. Somehow, in a rare lucid moment, Porterfield had ascertained the indelicate nature of Father McDonnough's wound.

Ellie was frozen with fear. Tinker took her arm.

"Let's get out of here, darlin'. It's a nuthouse we've come to, I'm thinkin', an' no hospital at all."

He guided her to the top of the stairs and paused once to look back toward Nathan's room. *It's a good thing that boy's on the other end of the floor,* he thought. *This end must be reserved for lunatics.* They started down the stairway, and Ellie began to howl and blow her nose. At the turning of the third floor Tinker stopped to look at the most beautiful Irish girl he'd ever seen. She was climbing the stairs on the arm of a friend. Her hair was the color of the wild rose and her eyes as dark as coal, and Tinker caught himself staring at her just as Ellie turned to see him. As they proceeded down the stairs to the sound of Ellie's wails and accusations, Tinker wondered what a lovely girl like that was doing with such a dumb-looking escort. *No accountin' fer taste. . . .*

Lester Figge emerged from his period of mourning.

"Get me Blakeley," he told his secretary.

Since Jennifer's death he had become reclusive and, for a time, lethargic. While his competitors extended their personal empires by riding the prosperous waves of the war effort, he had remained at Devon in an easy chair not far from the liquor cabinet. His only deliberate act since that shocking evening had been the offer of a reward. Now he was determined to reactivate his vast machinery. He had sent Julia abroad to convalesce; her sniveling was depressing. He had summoned his advisers and reaffirmed his intention to get a piece of the Cuban sugar and tobacco wealth that they knew to be forthcoming. His anthracite mines were ordered to meet higher quotas to take advantage of his contract with the Navy, and extra laborers in the Figge textile mills strove to satisfy the need for military uniforms. Now he was intrigued by the rice and rubber interests in the Philippines and was about to set out for Washington to discuss the subject with some of his close friends in the Senate.

But first, there was a little matter to attend to closer to home.

"It's not that I'm unappreciative, mate," Owen Ward-Lattimore contended, "but I'm not so agile as I used to be. Why else do you think I retired?"

Through Felix Wellington, Hudson had tracked Ward-Lattimore down in a small park on the north end of the city, and Nipper Doyle had delivered him to Blakeley's estate shortly after one o'clock.

Lieutenant Hudson had quipped that Blakeley would probably understand Owen's mind, since Ward-Lattimore had been known throughout most of his career as English John. The old fellow seemed to be affecting an especially heavy series of Britishisms in Blakeley's presence.

"But you're still the best we can come up with, Owen," Nipper Doyle answered. "Now don't let us down. We've been bragging about you to Dr. Blakeley all morning."

"I'm fully aware that you're pulling my leg, Officer Doyle. My ego begs me to let you go on. Why don't you tell Dr. Blakeley about the time I absconded with the payroll at City Hall in January of 1872?"

"Was that really you?" Doyle asked. He remembered the incident well, though he was only a beat patrolman at the time. City Hall had been reluctant to report the actual sum of the payroll lest the public discover the degree of bureaucratic fat that it contained. "We thought it was you at the time, but, as usual. . . ."

"I *earned* that, gov'ner," he insisted. "I had to spend three hours on a window ledge outside the Bursar's Office in the January winds. It took me days to thaw out."

"Well, this operation will present no such a challenge, Mr. Ward-Lattimore," Blakeley hastened to add. "It should be cakes and ale for a professional like you." Ward-Lattimore considered the proposal. In the distance they could hear Snopkowski banging her pots and pans and cursing in Polish. Blakeley was sincerely grateful that she did not have a faint heart and was happy to hear her letting off steam.

"What is it again?" asked Ward-Lattimore. "You want me to lift a typewriter?"

"Yes. It's quite important to us."

"Is it a special typewriter?"

"No." said Nipper Doyle.

Ward-Lattimore scratched his ear. "Why?"

"Because," Blakeley answered, removing a note from his desk, "we wish to determine if it was used to type this."

The old man's lips moved as he scanned the note. It was a brief statement, scoffing at Blakeley's efforts to unravel the mystery of the Butcher and inviting him to guess where the next victim would be discovered. The arrogance of the message was downright chilling.

"Gawd," whispered Ward-Lattimore.

"Now you're starting to see"—Blakeley spoke with urgency—"why we must track down the typewriter. This note was pinned to the body of a dead girl by the man or men the press have dubbed the West Philadelphia Butcher. Her body was deposited on this property sometime last night."

"Pinned?"

"Yes, look here." Blakeley turned the note over to display some brown stains where the paper had been in contact with blood. Ward-Lattimore grimaced.

"I'll get you your typewriter, Dr. Blakeley, or the world can say that English John was only a figment of the imagination."

"Thank you, Ward-Lattimore," said Blakeley earnestly. "Have some tea, if you will."

"Owen," said Nipper Doyle, patting him on the shoulder, "pull this one off, and all is forgiven."

Victor appeared, carrying a nightstick. He had had it in his hands ever since Snopkowski's terrible discovery. He had been especially hysterical over the body's having been discovered so near the spot where he hid his gin. He had been there only a fortnight before.

"Telephone for you, Dr. Blakeley," he proclaimed. "Mr. Figge."

Blakeley excused himself and went off to his study, uncertain about his attitude toward this call. He knew Lester Figge only by reputation, and despite the common denominator of their interest in the Butcher, he had serious misgivings about their ability to commiserate.

"Blakeley here."

"We've never met, but I'm sure you know who I am." The voice was self-assured but not unpleasant. It was also much deeper than Blakeley had imagined.

"Indeed I do, Mr. Figge, and I presume this is a matter of some importance."

"It certainly is. Otherwise, I'd have left it to one of my men to take care of."

"Go on then," Blakeley said guardedly.

"First, I thought you'd like to know that the reward for my daughter's murderer has been doubled."

"That, sir, is not now and has never been my main concern in the case." Blakeley's tone was gentle.

"Of course," said Lester Figge, obviously unconvinced. "All the same, it will give you, Officer McBride, and Miss Meredith more incentive. I'm sure of that."

"Oh? You're aware of Miss Meredith?"

"Blakeley," the voice snorted, "I'm aware of every step you've taken since the day you got on the case. I can tell you what color necktie you wore last Wednesday and what you ate for lunch. I can also tell you that so far your investigation has not been exactly a model of efficiency."

"I do what I can, Mr. Figge," Blakeley answered frigidly.

"I don't have time to debate that right now. I've got to go out of town. But before I do, I want to leave you with another incentive."

Blakeley inquired, cursorily, what that might be.

"I'm giving you three weeks to find that animal who desecrated my daughter. If you haven't done so by the end of that period, Blakeley, you're a dead man."

Figge had, Blakeley understood, felt impotent when his offer had failed to produce the Butcher, and now he was striking back at the world. But understanding failed to dull the sting of what he'd just heard. Blakeley was determined not to let Figge think he could be bullied.

"Do you think," he requested, "that I might have that in writing?"

"What?" The voice was clipped.

"What you've just said."

"You'll receive a notarized copy in the morning." Lester Figge sounded a bit self-conscious, but Blakeley could not be sure. "On it there will be stipulated the terms and amount of the reward. As to the other matter, well, you'll just have to take my word for it."

"That's not very sporting of you," Blakeley chided.

Lester Figge hung up with a loud click.

When Blakeley returned to the porch, he saw that Officer Doyle had already taken Owen Ward-Lattimore off to brief him on his assignment. They would probably have to consult with Lieutenant Hudson, who knew the neighborhood.

Miss Meredith was certainly to be commended for her efforts of yesterday. It might have been the realization that the temporary loss of Detective McBride had weakened their team quite a lot, motivating her to greater exertion. In any case, having traced Zoltan Mroszek back to his schooling in Budapest—an academic background surprisingly impressive to both investigators—she had gone on to look up Dr. Toberman's records.

Finding nothing of substance in the immigration files, Miss Meredith had communicated with the county medical society on the pretense of researching an article on the breadth of specialization among the Commonwealth of Pennsylvania's physicians. That, of course, was taking a chance; misrepresentation could have brought the hounds of hell upon her, but she'd proceeded with insouciance. Again the files on Max Toberman were sparse.

After returning to the immigration office, Miss Meredith had proceeded to collect information on a mysterious endocrinologist who had practiced in Vienna under the name of Maxim Nikolayevich Tobrensky and a surgeon named Maximilian Tauberfeld who had worked in London. Both files were incomplete, and both had been stamped "deceased." Although she had returned limp and discouraged by her apparently fruitless labors, Blakeley considered significant Miss Meredith's conclusion that Toberman was untraceable

If, after all, Dr. Max Toberman did not actually exist, he had asked her, then who the devil was that? What sort of creature was that who practiced medicine out there at Fifty-fourth and Calvert? There had to be something special to be found by going on to investigate this chap. There was, for one thing, the coincidence of a Russian in Vienna and a Viennese in London. There was the scientific anomaly of a surgeon who was well versed in endocrinology. There were the obviously falsified documents and the ubiquitous mysteriousness of the man. No, he had insisted to Miss Meredith, it was thorough, professional work. She was quite capable in his judgment.

Judge not, lest ye be judged, she had jested with a warm smile, and he'd appreciated that. A sense of humor after all.

Restless, if exhausted, after his long night's watch over Nathan, he shook off Figge's ultimatum and tramped down the dirt lane toward the cherry orchard in hopes of dredging up something useful. His hopes were farfetched, he knew, but thoughts often came to him in moments of solitude and once, on an island near Charleston, he had solved a murder by what had amounted to communicating with the dead. The memory made him uneasy, and he had never answered with readiness any questions on the subject, but it had lent personal credence to his thesis regarding the fallibility of science.

The afternoon sun beat down upon the dusty lane, forcing him to remove his coat as he drew nearer the cherry orchard. He caught himself longing for the autumn when all those trees would deliver themselves of a panoply of colors, and that damn blistering sun would finally give in. The thought of not having this bloody case over and done with by that time gave him a very disagreeable twinge.

Toberman's documents had not been exactly falsified; it seemed more a matter of their having been shuffled or, better yet, endowed with inherent confusion. Somewhere in the miasma of international, federal, state, and local paperwork, the real Max Toberman, whoever that was, had managed to render himself in effect a nonperson. Seen objectively, it was as comical as it was perverse. If, for example, the suspect were one and the same and Toberman could be traced back to Maxim Nikolayevich Tobrensky through Maximilian Tauberfeld, he would have to be more than a century old! Toberman himself must have chuckled at that when the files were so arranged.

Curse him. He's in on this business somehow. Blakeley was almost sure.

The section of the orchard in which the body had been found had been roped off, and a policeman was standing guard in a shady area. Swabbing his brow, he nodded to Blakeley and passed a comment about the heat. Peering into the deep grass, Blakeley could see the imprint left by the remains of Chantal de Rohan.

This latest episode, with its impudence and scornful message, left him all but drained. The Butcher had already threatened his way of life by coming so near, and he knew he would have to take measures to protect his household. Blakeley's interpretation of freedom had always been broad, and security had never been a matter of real concern to him. Lieutenant Hudson had suggested the assignment of a police detachment to his property, but Blakeley felt that to be rather extreme. Besides, he knew the department had no men to spare.

The carriage had entered the estate through the east gate and had made its way silently over the forty acres downhill toward the house. The tracks were not difficult to follow; the shade from the maple trees lining the road beyond the orchard had prevented the sun from drying the surface. The footprints were also easily distinguishable in the shaded sectors and bore marked similarities to those found by Detective McBride in the park and on the Figge estate. That was especially true of the flat-footed prints. All that kept him from confusing them with Snopkowski's equally uncontoured markings was the habit the old cook had of waddling about in her bedroom slippers. How often Sophia had grumbled about *that* practice.

More than to the flat feet, however, Blakeley's attention was drawn to the tracks of the carriage, which had left deep ruts in the damp ground on both sides of the riding trail. The horse's hooves showed no irregularities this time, but the depth and dimensions of the wagon wheels were identical. Blakeley remembered how this had once set them to wondering about the part Andrew Sutton may have played in the crimes. A great deal of logic had been wasted on that affair; but the one salient angle had been overlooked, and that oversight now hovered over Blakeley like a persistent storm cloud. Instead of a heavy wagon, they should have been looking for a heavy man.

Now, if Miss Meredith has performed her task well, and he had no reason to expect otherwise, the long easy period of the fat man would soon approach its crisis.

Harry Hackett read his dime novel in the waiting room and shifted his legs nervously as Aidan Tierney visited Nathan and apologized trimly for her long absence. In her gray dress with black lace she brought Nathan uncomfortable images of a wake or funeral, but her finely cut features were in themselves an affirmation of life. She had waited, she said, until she was certain he was out of danger, not wishing to get in the way of Dr. Blakeley and the others who had better reason to be there. Nathan accepted her explanation eagerly. In the joy he felt at seeing her he failed to recognize the care with which she had selected her words and the effort behind their delivery.

Seventeen

"Now, don't give me any of that 'Gov'ner' crap," Hudson snorted. "I happen to know you come from Scranton."

Owen Ward-Lattimore bristled a bit but maintained his characteristic immovability. They had never been chums. Hudson had once sent him up.

"You've no feeling for showmanship, Leftenant," he accused with a half-smile. Ward-Lattimore had never worried much about that kind of disclosure. Whether one wished to comment upon it depended on the romantic or prosaic nature of one's soul.

"You can bet your ass on that," Hudson returned.

They were studying a blueprint of Max Toberman's office. Later the suspect's ledgers would be audited. Nipper Doyle was obviously enjoying the little skirmishes.

"I say," the old burglar asked somewhat churlishly, "isn't this a bit out of your realm, Leftenant? So far from the Sink, I mean."

Hudson sat back in his swivel chair and suggested they get on with their business. "And I wouldn't scoff at the Sink if I were you," he added. "It's where most of your friends and associates are. It's also where you belong, Owen."

"Ah, yes"—Ward-Lattimore smiled serenely—"but I couldn't feed the pigeons there. And the ladies are much lovelier to look at up north."

Calvert was quite an old street. Toberman's office, like most of the edifices along that row, had been there since early in the century and still retained the steep, narrow, ivied look of the post-Colonial period. Three stories high, the building sloped back toward an alleyway and joined the property next door by means of a high red-brick fence. The distance between the two buildings was short, about fifteen yards by Hudson's estimate, comprising a walkway, lawn, and small, circular flower garden in the middle.

"Nice place," Ward-Lattimore jested. "One would think I'd have seen it before."

"You probably have. You've probably hit it before," Hudson grumbled.

Ward-Lattimore fingered his silvery beard pensively. "Half a mo, gentlemen, I do believe I have."

"You did?" asked Nipper Doyle

"When?" asked Hudson.

"Oh, must have been twenty years ago. Not Toberman's but the place next door. The bloke was a jeweler as I recall." The old fellow beamed at Hudson with much self-satisfaction.

"Is that all?" Hudson derided. "One would think you'd knocked off the White House."

"Who owns it now, Charlie?" Nipper Doyle asked Lieutenant Hudson.

"An eccentric named Statler bought it a few years back. It's an antique shop now, old-fashioned lamps mostly. He must have independent wealth because the place is closed more often than not."

"A shame." Ward-Lattimore shook his head in mock disgust. "It's never been a convenient business fencing antiques."

Closer scrutiny of the blueprint showed the building to be deceptively wide. In the fashion of the bygone era everything had been made to appear smaller and tidier than reality. What had been a living room facing the street now served as the waiting room. Toberman's office occupied the greater part of the first floor, what used to be the dining room and kitchen. Since it faced the alley, that seemed to be the most propitious point of entry, although it was virtually certain that the windows and back door would be tightly secured.

"It can't match the security at the National Savings and Loan Building," Ward-Lattimore said.

"That was the heist I ran you in for," Hudson gladly reminded him.

"But you didn't prevent me from getting in, did you?"

The old burglar was reminded once again that the typewriter was all that he was authorized to remove from the office. There was still no hard evidence linking Toberman to anything more serious than illegal immigration. The bad press had already been more than the department would stand for.

"Come along, old boy," said Ward-Lattimore to Nipper Doyle. He tipped his hat to Hudson and strode regally out.

Aidan had chattered nervously for the past ten minutes, and the word "ambivalent" had been her most recurrent term. He had never heard of this Harry Hackett, once her beau, who had reentered her life. Nor had he expected, among the welter of possible reactions to his wild adventure, that she would reveal this side of her personality.

"I cannot have children by a violent man," she said.

"If there's a violent man in this room, I've failed to notice him," he said. *What the hell is she trying to say?* he wondered. At the moment he could not have been violent. His wound throbbed.

"I've done a lot of thinking in the last few days, about us, that is," she went on. "I've made novenas."

"Have you consulted professional help?" he asked dryly.

She flashed a reprimand. "That's what I'm trying to say, Nathan, and you've said it for me. The work you do, all this viciousness and degeneracy, it makes you cynical. You may not want it. It's not your fault, but it makes you cynical."

"And, if I were an undertaker," he countered, alluding to Harry, "I guess that would make me a nicer guy."

"It would make you . . . normal."

"Oh."

She had brought him a bouquet of flowers, affording herself an opportunity to fuss with something. She fussed with them as he looked on. Someone safe, respectable, and affluent somehow had been reinstated. It was, more than anything else, humiliating, and he felt as used as a worn-out hole-infested shoe.

He had no answers left.

"Repeat that story, miss," Hudson asked. "I want to be sure the stenographer didn't leave out any details. You can appreciate, of course, the gravity of your charges."

He wanted to hear the story once more, chiefly to be certain that none of the important facts would be altered. It was the kind of case that could bring a world of wrath down upon him unless it was airtight. The girl seemed stable, however, and he had to admit that her presence in his office was something of a dream come true. The stenographer appeared slightly less ill-at-ease as the tale was repeated.

"What was the purpose of your being there?"

"As a volunteer, I, I performed a number of services. Clerical mostly."

The girl was fighting back tears, but she went on with spartan determination. Her work had been shared with two others in volunteer service, typing, keeping files, seeing to correspondence. Hudson poured another glass of ice water. She sipped it demurely.

"Had he ever indicated previously that he was interested in you in that way?" he asked her.

"If he had, Lieutenant, I wouldn't have been there alone, I assure you."

"Of course." He spoke softly. She was young and obviously rent by conflicting emotions. What she was saying was so hateful to her personally that at times she seemed to gag on the words.

"You're certain," he asked once again, "that we have no witnesses? No one at all who might have overheard anything or perhaps saw you leaving his office in a disheveled state?"

She shook her head and sighed.

"How did you explain your torn undergarments to your parents?" he inquired.

"I, I said I snagged myself when I was walking by the neighbor's fence. To be sure they'd accept that I . . . tore my dress and petticoat in the same place."

"Did they believe you?"

"No"—she sobbed—"I don't think so."

It was her family's incredulity that had finally convinced her that she had nothing to lose by reporting the assault. He supposed that she could not bear to think that they believed she had lost her virginity by her own consent and that she had dreamed up such a feckless tale to cover herself.

It was not the best possible evidence. No witnesses against a man of such stature in the community, an assault reported more than a week after the fact, the kind of complaint that a defense attorney could turn into a bowl of oatmeal in court within minutes, the kind of charge that young girls are wont to level for hundreds of spurious reasons. There was one encouraging factor, however, among the many weak links. The girl had said that her assailant had mentioned at least three other volunteers whom he had engaged in similar rites.

He summoned Fatzinger, who was about to go off duty, and asked him if he'd like to be involved in a very celebrated case.

"Yeah, sure, Lootenant," he answered willingly, "as long as after supper I can shtart!"

"Fine, Bones. Just be sure you don't get so involved in your food that you forget. I want you to pick this man up and book him for rape."

He showed Fatzinger a photograph of a zealous-looking young man in a black suit and wrote down an address. While Bones studied the picture and scratched his head, Hudson glanced over the stenographer's notes. She was a prim young woman who was still emotionally unprepared for most of the sordid testimonies she had been forced to hear. But her work was impeccable, and she was also much pleasanter to look at than the frumpish old senior secretary.

"But," Fatzinger stammered, "diss here's a preacher!"

"It certainly is, Bones. His name is Reverend Richard T. Hopkins, and we want him for at least one, and if fortune smiles on us, four, counts of criminal assault."

"Vell, if dott don't milk da bull," Fatzinger swore. Hudson smiled, while the young stenographer blushed a deeper shade of sunburn.

"I'll fix dott toadshtool, by Cheesuss," muttered Fatzinger as he stomped resolutely out the door.

Hudson opened his bottle of bourbon and laughed so loudly that he drew stares from all directions.

Controlled by the nation's favored sector, the dailies had grown dizzy with their own power over the minds of the public and their ability to manipulate even the federal government. Like a pampered child, the more influence the press accrued, the more it felt it had to have, and in its own internecine competition the role of ethics had dwindled to the status of an et cetera.

There was, nevertheless, on the staff of the Philadelphia *Record-American* one writer whose reputation for honesty and integrity remained essentially unblemished. His clear head and sense of proportion made him something of an anomaly in the medium. Despite Blakeley's natural skepticism, Miss Meredith argued convincingly on behalf of George Fenwick, eventually persuading Dr. Blakeley to do business with him.

Fenwick had had nothing to do with the satire and other journalistic tomfoolery that had surrounded Blakeley since his assignment to the case. It was said of Fenwick that he never put his name to a column or story without first having double-checked all his facts and sources. A gentlemen of the old school, Miss Meredith called him. He was not known to omit qualifying details or to play games with sensitive issues. Even Regis Tolan, who had grown to despise all forms of journalistic life during his thorny career on the force, had been known to utter occasional words of respect for George Fenwick.

The *Record-American,* in spite of itself, had actually gained prestige by his presence on its pages, and the editors had long ago despaired of bullying him.

Thus, the tale of the fat man had had to be written carefully. There were no remote contradictions or ambiguities by the time

Miss Meredith had completed her last draft, and the press releases had been pared down to the basic truths. Her decision to give the story only to Fenwick had been based on two important considerations: First, Fenwick's name would inspire even broader coverage in the long run; secondly, Toberman, if he bothered to read newspapers at all, no doubt read Fenwick.

Nathan McBride was also a reader of the *Record-American*. Unaware of Blakeley's strategy, he had turned to check on yesterday's game with Brooklyn before looking at the front page or the editorials. He wondered how Blakeley ever could have compared the hospital's cook with Snopkowski; it was something like comparing a ragweed to a carnation. Of course, Aidan seemed to have taken his appetite with her when she went off with her undertaker friend.

Her timing could not have been better. He tormented himself with the thought that if he were not feeling so weak and inert, he would probably have shown more anger. Had he told her what he really thought—that she was a shallow excuse for a human being—he would have felt less humiliation somehow.

Harry Hackett's part in the drama had not required an explanation. Aidan's guilty smile as Hackett entered, looking well dressed but awkward, was all that Nathan had needed to see. Hackett must have promised her champagne breakfasts, handmaidens, sprawling lawns, and a house in Rosemont. Something like that. Undertakers could aspire to such things. Policemen were indeed optimists if they could look to a future out of debt.

And then he caught himself thinking cheap thoughts and indulging in self-pity, so he focused briefly again on the newspaper. He sighed and glanced briefly at the cityscape view from his window. It was fittingly gray and unpleasant.

Probably, after his near disaster, she had simply decided that it was better to be on the profitable side of death, he reasoned. Undertakers never run short of merchandise, as they say. The worst thing about her visit was the restlessness that followed; with his heart pounding there was no chance of getting the sleep that Blakeley had ordered.

The most degrading thought was that he had been simply rejected for a more lucrative offer. It was like choosing a more fertile plot of land—she was just as cold and insensate as that. *McBride,* he chastised himself. *You sound like Troilus wailing over Cressida, and the whole affair only began a few weeks ago. . . .*

Fat Man linked to Butcher, the by-line article read. George Fenwick's column came as a sudden awakening from his gloomy daydream.

> Sources close to Dr. Ian Blakeley say authorities are seeking an obese man in connection with the so-called West Philadelphia Butcher case. In a statement given expressly to this reporter early in the afternoon, Blakeley confirmed that fibers of cloth found in the briars of a rosebush on his property match those found earlier in the investigation by Det. Nathan J. McBride at a site in Fairmount Park. McBride, the subject of considerable publicity lately after his daring seizure of a demented murderer, is a member of Blakeley's task force. The Blakeley estate this morning yielded the latest in a series of mutilated victims, all of them young women, in a case that has been as baffling as it is gruesome.

Nathan's jaw fell as he read on. Blakeley had released to the press a reasonable composite of the suspect as evidence thus far collected would indicate. It was a bold maneuver—unexpected, despite its inherent logic.

According to Blakeley, the suspect was quite heavy—well over two hundred pounds, no more than five feet five inches tall—judging by the depth and dimensions of his footprints. He suffered from chronic *pes planus:* flat-footedness. The other distinguishing feature was prominent scratch marks running vertically along his right cheek from below the eye to the jaw. This conclusion had been reached through a determination of the texture and amount of skin found under the fingernails of one victim's left hand. The presence of hair follicles in that same analysis suggested that he was also clean-shaven as of one month ago. Had he grown a beard subsequent to that time, it would be no more than one-half inch thick and dark brown in color. The ratio of gray follicles further indicated that the suspect was in his late thirties to middle forties and might or might not be balding. He was a habitual smoker of Ateshian cigarettes, and his breathing was marked by a sever bronchiectatic rale, more commonly known as wheezing.

Neat. Very neat, thought Nathan. Using the press to our own advantage for a change. It was a desperate move, he recognized. It was an exciting tactic and he applauded it.

Thank God for briar bushes and fingernails.

A nursing sister with a cheerful countenance entered carrying a tray. She was the first one he had seen who did not look as if the world around her were populated by fornicators and aborigines.

"Good evening, Mr. McBride," she greeted him. "Are you comfortable?"

"Yes I am, Sister. Thank you." Actually, he still felt as if he'd been trampled, but he was anxious to get out and wanted no one to misinterpret that. "Pleasant evening."

"It promises rain, I'd say," she corrected, her smile never diminished.

"If you say so, Sister," he hastened to agree. The ladies had very short fuses. "What have you got on the tray?"

"Your medicine," she chirped.

"It looks like a rather large dose."

"About six fingers are Dr. Blakeley's orders." She removed a white cloth from the tray, revealing a fifth of Irish whiskey.

Nathan blinked his eyes.

"I . . . believe you have me confused with Dr. Blakeley's other patient, Mr. Porterfield, on the other end of the floor."

"Oh," she gasped, "please don't mention Mr. Porterfield. The head nurse may overhear you. He puts her into a terrible snit."

She proceeded to pour a glassful of whiskey as he folded his newspaper and sat up.

"The sun hasn't gone down yet," he persisted.

"Well, of course not, Mr. McBride," she countered with a smile. "It's the longest day of the year."

"I know that."

"Don't you want it?" She handed him the little glass. "I've always thought policemen *liked* whiskey. At least they preferred it to warm milk."

He looked into her ruddy, round face and smiled.

"Is that my only choice?"

"I'm afraid so, Mr. McBride." She seemed used to Blakeley's irregularities.

"All right, Sister," he said, putting the glass to his lips, "as you say, who are we to argue?"

"But we've got a bounty on our heads!" Arthur's voice was shrill, and he was pacing around the room. "How the bloody hell do you *expect* me to react?"

"Sit down, Arthur."

"I shan't sit down!" he declared. "I've had quite enough of you and that swine I've had to work with! How could you *not* expect them to spot him? He's like a rhinoceros with a criminal mind. You might as well have run an advertisement in the mail!"

"Above all else, I despise repeating myself, Arthur. Sit down."

There was finality in Toberman's lightly accented words, and Arthur felt a familiar buckling in his spine. He sought out a remote chair and sank into it.

"That's much better," said Toberman. "You could have overturned something in your aimless meandering."

"You have"—Arthur hesitated—"you have such a way. . . ."

"A way of what?" Toberman inquired wearily, Arthur's voice having trailed off in midsentence.

"Of making one feel terribly inadequate," said Arthur, burying his face in his hands.

"Frankly, Arthur, I don't think you needed any help from me in that regard."

"You see? *Another* reproach." He jumped up and waved his hands frantically.

"Sit down," Toberman commanded, his tone even and his eyes humorless.

Arthur Hartleigh paced a step or two more, stood frozen under Toberman's stare for a moment, then snuffed out his cigarette. Beads of perspiration dotted his face despite the coolness of the morning air. He had had a bad night; the surfeit of blemishes attested to that.

"You'd get nowhere without me, you know," he fired back weakly.

"You, my boy, are a recipient of my charity these days. I've kept you in opiated comfort for weeks now and your contribution to my efforts has been minimal, however one measures it. What exactly *do* you do to earn your keep? You find subjects, which no doubt satisfies some deep-seated carnal need in itself, and you assist the other deviate in ridding us of odds and ends. You've gone downhill, Arthur. I fear your brain has turned to curds and whey. I must cut down on your dosage." That, of course, was the most frightening threat imaginable.

"That was harsh."

Toberman never moved. "That was mild," he said. The implication was obvious.

"It isn't painless, Max," Arthur answered after a period of silence, "dealing with you. You're so . . . chilly. It wouldn't reduce your power, you must realize, were you to show less contempt for us."

The clock in Toberman's study ticked monotonously, and he smiled with genuine amusement. He studied the wretched Arthur: sunken eyes and eruptive skin, a foul rag and bone with a seething, impotent resentment, the nadir of the human condition with an acid tongue.

"That, too, is no facile matter," he answered. "Two classic bores: the one a fat, sweaty error of nature with nothing to recommend his existence on this planet but his insatiable penchant for cruelty, the other a cowardly textbook of perversion and dissipation. Now I ask you, who in this world can love a necrophile and a homosexual?"

"We've been useful to you, regardless of how you may feel about our proclivities. Justice demands that you be concerned for our safety now."

He looked into Arthur's frantic eyes. Red-rimmed and bleary, they described a private world of terror and self-loathing. Toberman smiled once again and drifted mercifully away toward the windows, complaining of the smoke in the air.

"How, how do you propose to handle Blakeley?" asked Arthur unsteadily.

"Blakeley." Toberman shrugged. "I've seen a hundred like him. Narrow, conventional minds and Victorian propriety make them eternally predictable. This desperate new wrinkle of his, publicizing his progress. And the poverty of his findings!"

"That's easy for you to say." Arthur bristled. "He's not on your trail yet."

"You think the description in the newspaper fits you?"

"If they've made so much of Vincent's footprints, do you really think they've totally overlooked mine?" Arthur's petulance gave way to a sinister smile. "Or yours for that matter. You do recall the Figge girl?"

Toberman grunted and poured two cups of tea. He looked on with disgust as Arthur tried to raise the cup to his lips with trembling hands, spilling tea down the front of his bathrobe. He turned away because something about Arthur in the morning always nauseated

him. From the window he could look down at the traffic and dismiss
for the moment his aggravating company. Horses trudged wearily
along Fifty-fourth Street, pulling their cabs, beer wagons, trolleys,
burdens of produce and fish. Those that stopped along his road usually transported more genteel merchandise.

"Do you remember that simpleminded fellow who used to assist
you, the one we finally had to get rid of?"

"You mean Fred Bowman, my private fool?"

"Yes, that one. He used to eat human organs for your amusement, didn't he?"

"It kept him happy. He was useful, too, up to a point."

"A gastronome of the old school." Toberman chuckled, still peering out the window. "How did you ever get him to do that?"

Arthur Hartleigh forgot briefly his pressing fears. He sat back in
his chair and crossed his legs, blowing smoke into the air. He had
the unusual habit of hooking his right foot around his left ankle in a
pose that would have been uncomfortable for most men.

"After I left the circus, I was with a carnival for a time. It was
somewhere in Indiana, I believe, or one of those ungodly bland
places, that his hag mother joined us as a fortune-teller. She was
nothing out of the ordinary, a toothless old finagler such as one
finds by the thousands in fairs and the like, so after a year the management decided to let her go. That was in Pittsburgh, I think. Well,
the crone had an ace up her sleeve. She offered her son, whom we'd
only known by the title Poor Fred, as a geek. Do you know what that
is?"

"A subhuman creature in a cage. He eats live chickens, doesn't
he? I believe their employment is illegal now."

Toberman seemed interested. "But what about human flesh?"

"Ah, that was an easy step," Arthur replied with a smug grin.
"Much as he'd always appreciated the attention of the gawking
crowds, Poor Fred was always aware that he was not quite right, you
see. So I told him about the mountain tribes of southeastern Africa
who eat the enemies they've slain. I had him believing that certain
organs would make him stronger, others more intelligent and,
above all, less grotesque in appearance. He was partial to liver, I believe!"

As Arthur continued to laugh at his own cleverness, Toberman
turned around to face him and spoke evenly, coldly.

"You should have taken yourself more seriously, Arthur. Perhaps a few hearts in your own diet would have made you less squeamish by now."

The laughter stopped abruptly, and Arthur's face flushed. Once again he had been set up and made to look foolish. More than anything else, he sought reassurance from Toberman that the danger of his discovery would pass and he could retreat to his room and dose himself heavily with cocaine until the whole wretched business was over.

"You *do* know what to do, Max? How to get us out of this?"

"Vincent shall be furloughed for a time." Toberman sat down and glanced long-sufferingly toward the ceiling. "It's as simple as that. He has relatives in the Harrisburgh area who can put up with him until Blakeley and the police have found some other crumbs to feed the public."

"Is that all?" Arthur's tone was disparaging.

"What the devil did you have in mind, Arthur?" Toberman's patience was gone. "Are you prepared to eliminate him yourself?"

"But . . . that doesn't seem very—"

"Get out of here, you whining, foul-smelling coward," Toberman shouted.

Arthur jumped out of his chair, backed away toward the door, then stopped in the center of the room. His eyes jerked in spasms of fear, and his face turned ashen.

"You can't treat me like an animal," he protested feebly. "I won't stand for it! Even if you despise me, you need me! Who brought you all those young girls? Who saw to it that they were taken and disposed of just as you've wanted? It certainly wasn't you, and it certainly wasn't Vincent. All he knows is the excitement he feels in the presence of pain. He wouldn't know where to begin if you relied on his mind! And what exactly do *you* do, now that I think of it? All of those tortures and mutilations—what are they aimed at? You play God with Vincent and me. You do none of the dirty work, and for what? You're probably nothing more than the rest of us. You're simply more sanitary!"

During his tirade Arthur had almost backed into Vincent, who had entered unnoticed by either party. Toberman had come around his desk and was approaching Arthur Hartleigh menacingly, but now he stopped.

"Sit down, both of you," Toberman commanded.

Vincent gave both of them a sinister smile. "You know, Arthur," he said as he shoved him into a chair, "you should never ask questions. You should only enjoy your work as I do. Life's too short for all that complicated stuff."

Toberman ran his hands over his hair, collecting himself. The heat was starting to rise from the street below, and the study was becoming uncomfortable. It was shortly after nine o'clock, and his patients would be arriving presently. He opened his cigarette box and carefully offered one to Vincent, ignoring Arthur for the time being. Vincent picked one up and slumped with his characteristic groan into a deep chair not far from the box, which Toberman had placed at the front of the desk.

"I'm going to give you something of a paid vacation, Vincent."

He outlined his plan, moving discreetly away from time to time, allowing the fat man to snatch a few more cigarettes from the silver container. They were a special brand, a rare blend of Turkish, Virginian, and East African leaves.

Vincent's larcenous nature had never permitted his passing them by. Though it annoyed Toberman, he let it all go unseen. Actually Vincent picked up any number of things as a rule; it was one way to succeed in the antique business. He winked at the pouting Arthur when Toberman turned his back and pocketed a handful of the little white cylinders.

Toberman proposed a period out of town and offered him fifty dollars to ease whatever hardships his travels might present.

"When am I supposed to come back?" Vincent asked as he counted his money. He had shown no signs of gratitude, although none was expected.

"It won't be long. I'll send for you."

"He gets a summer in the countryside, and we've got to bake in the city. Pretty unfair arrangement if you ask me."

"Who the hell's askin' you?" snarled Vincent. "You been a bad boy, Arthur, talkin' back to Dr. Toberman like that." He turned to Toberman. "You want me to make him apologize?"

"No, just get him out of here. Put him to bed before you leave. He pollutes the air."

Vincent took Arthur Hartleigh by the collar and, wheezing from the mild exertion, led him out the door. Toberman waited until their footsteps had faded before checking the cigarette box. There were quite a few missing. He smiled and sat back in his chair.

* * *

The cheerful nun fluffed up his pillow and straightened his bed-clothes while á student nurse placed his breakfast before him. After downing the six fingers of Irish whiskey, Nathan had slept soundly all night. No, there was no discomfort in his back or shoulder, or at least none that he would yet admit to. The sun was shining brightly, and he asked whether he'd be able to get outside later in the day.

"That is, Mr. McBride, as I'm sure you must realize, up to Dr. Blakeley," she said.

"I have, that is I had, a friend—a very good friend—who was in the Marine Corps, you see, and he was killed about a week or so ago. It was a freak accident, not a war casualty."

"Sergeant James," she observed.

"Yes, Sergeant James. Actually, he was Corporal James in the service, but he always said it was a matter of months before he'd be a general. Did you know him?"

"In a manner of speaking." She blushed. "He used to court at least three and probably many more of the young nurses on our staff." She added rather coyly, "Mother Superior used to say, good-naturedly, of course, that he was the most charming philanderer in Philadelphia. But she really wouldn't appreciate my repeating that." The little old nursing sister put a finger to her lips, swearing him to absolute secrecy.

"I was hoping to go to his funeral today," Nathan intimated.

She looked indecisive. "At this hour it's hard to predict how Dr. Blakeley will react to that. Indeed, it's always hard to predict Dr. Blakeley."

Bones Fatzinger gulped down his buttermilk and bit into another slice of liver pudding with chili sauce on raisin bread, pressing laboriously on to the next paragraph as Lieutenant Hudson fumed in the background. The morning newspapers had featured Officer Wilmer P. Fatzinger as the perseverant minion of the law who had single-handedly, and against terrible odds, broken the case of the Carnal Clergyman, as someone had dubbed it. Hudson cursed himself for his whimsical decision to send Fatzinger after the Reverend Hopkins. The humor had backfired: Bones had called the press to inform them of what he was about to do; the reporters had arrived at the parsonage just in time to see Fatzinger confronting Reverend Hopkins at the door, charging him with fraud, conspiracy, misrepresentation, and "vitt da leedle girls diddlin'."

Afterward Bones had concocted an inflated tale of horror, suspense, national security, and great detective work. He had also mentioned that he was attached to Hudson's precinct and, incidentally, worked closely with Flying McBride. The Reverend Hopkins, almost speechless with shock, had, of course, retained a battery of lawyers and had gasped countercharges of false arrest and religious persecution.

Fatzinger concluded his perusal of the morning paper, set his buttermilk down, cleared his throat, and reminded Hudson that there was still an opening for another detective on the staff and that this was his second major arrest, "countin' dott shtupid lawyer."

"What?" Hudson was livid with frustration. The commissioner had already called to demand an immediate explanation, and he had had none. Not enough to satisfy even the worst moron in City Hall.

"Bones, if you ever bring that up again, I'm going to break your instep! Get back to the file room, and don't come out until next winter!"

"But"—Fatzinger groaned—"the newspaper fellas are comin'. How are dey supposed to find me back dere?"

"That's the idea, you imbecile! If you utter so much as a peep to one more reporter—"

"Aw, cheez," Bones complained, "I vass only doin' it to impress Strawberry Knockelknorr. Dere's lots o' guys up dere in Ebenezersville dott vandt a piece o' *dott* cow, by Christ."

Hudson gritted his teeth and snapped his pencil in half, looking very much as if he wanted it to be Fatzinger's neck. Bones jumped up and trudged, in his own manure-dodging fashion, back to the file room, muttering about Hudson's unromantic soul and his disregard for freedom of speech, "vunn o' dose inaudible rights endured by our Creator."

A few blocks away, however, unbeknownst to Lieutenant Hudson, a young woman from Reverend Hopkins' staff was sobbing out a story of lust and unpleasant surprises, while her parents listened with growing nausea.

Eighteen

Thinking about it later, Blakeley realized that he'd probably granted Nathan permission to leave the hospital out of sheer exhaustion. The nights had been sleepless, and the days hard to endure. That morning a representative of the Figge Enterprises home office had delivered Lester Figge's signed statement of conditions. The contract was succinct but thorough, and although the matter had slipped his mind in the excitement of yesterday, he could not help feeling like a Russian roulette player after having signed his copy of the strange agreement.

The agent, a small, nervous man whom Blakeley assessed to be a lower-rung attorney, had smiled mousily before making a hasty exit. At the time the Figge ultimatum had still not made that deep an impression, for Blakeley was completing his analysis of the machine Owen Ward-Lattimore had taken out of Max Toberman's office the night before.

"It's not the one. It's not the bloody typewriter!"

Blakeley had been looking for a typewriter with a brand-new ribbon and a B that was slightly out of line in the upper case. This machine had a ribbon that had been used for some time, and it had no uneven letters at all. There was absolutely no connection between this instrument and the letter on Miss de Rohan's body.

"Damned fiend has us jumping like hares with his decoys and cruel taunts," he had thought aloud.

"Now see here," Ward-Lattimore had chided him, "what with the kind of bob you medical chaps make, I'm quite sure our man has more than one typewriter at his disposal."

Doyle had suggested that the levity was a bit out of place.

Blakeley had rather resented the association but realized that the comment had been intended principally as a jocular sedative. Having practiced his kind of felonious art for so many years, Ward-Lattimore no doubt had a set of nerves sheathed in cast iron. Blakeley had, despite his own shakiness, returned the jest in kind. It was commonly understood, he quipped, that a good burglar could earn twice in a month what a physician would see in a year and work only when he cares to. Damned profitable way of life.

Ward-Lattimore concluded the difference was the superior intellect and candid posture of the burglar.

The operation had not been without its minor rewards. Ward-Lattimore had encountered no obstacles to speak of as he'd insinuated himself through the rear of Toberman's residence. Like pie and ice cream, he had described it. As he felt his way along the wall according to Lieutenant Hudson's blueprint, he believed that he'd detected the hollow sensation of a false wall under his fingertips at fifteen paces between entry and desk. As he'd inched his way along the back wall, he swore he had detected the presence of a safe. Ward-Lattimore had smelled the distinct odor of chromium and lubricating oil behind a bookshelf. For what other reason would one smell such a combination in a doctor's office? His immediate response had been to weigh his chances of getting it open. He had concluded that that, too, would have been an elementary task.

"Well, why the hell didn't you do it?" Doyle had questioned him with obvious exasperation. "If it were city property, you'd have had no serious qualms."

"I couldn't, gentlemen, really," Ward-Lattimore had insisted. "There was someone stirring in the neighborhood."

He had not been certain whether the voices he'd heard were coming from overhead or from the next room, but they had not been far away. The voices, alternately muffled and clear, had been those of two men who were arguing bitterly. One of the men had a high, piping, effeminate quality and was clearly distraught. Ward-Lattimore also thought he'd heard mention of a fat man in tones which suggested both fear and hatred. Blakeley had wondered whether the voices could have been coming from a chamber behind the false wall.

"Entirely possible, gov'nor. I don't think they were actually within the building, now that you mention it."

"But you can't be sure?" Blakeley had asked.

"I can be *reasonably* sure."

"Could you," Blakeley had inquired, "describe the other voice, Ward-Lattimore?"

"It was considerably steadier than the first one," Ward-Lattimore had answered. "Definitely in command of the situation. I'd assess his age to be roughly the same as your own, Dr. Blakeley. There was just a touch of a foreign accent. Quite fluent. Only there was that laborious hint, ever so slight, which tends to signal one that it's a second language being spoken."

Doyle had reminded Blakeley that Owen Ward-Lattimore was also a master of disguises, including many foreign accents—anything to facilitate entry and escape.

Blakeley had asked the logical question. "German?"

"Could have been," Ward-Lattimore had replied thoughtfully. "Or perhaps Eastern European. There was a heavy reliance on consonants, plosives especially, and an occasional voicing of the vowels and diphthongs. An even, rather aloof tone. Of course, as I've said, the voices were rather far away."

"Could it have been Russian?"

"A fifty-fifty chance, Doctor," he had answered, considering the query obviously academic.

Less than an hour later, as Blakeley approached Nathan's room, a severe, exact-looking nun, the head nurse on the floor, approached him. If ever human form could have emerged from its stony environment, this was it. She smelled of phenol and coal tar and gnashed her teeth as she spoke.

"The sisters and I have uncovered your deception. Proceed no further, for we have found you out." She stiffened even more. "Your Mr. Morcheck, or whatever, is merely a piece of fiction."

Her arms were folded, indeed welded, into a position of entrenched opprobrium, putting him on the defensive.

"Last night he tormented poor Father McDonnough so," she alleged, "that he got out of bed and went into Morcheck's room to administer a well-deserved thrashing. Only the efforts of two large orderlies saved your Mr. Morcheck from serious injury. As for poor Father McDonnough, we've had to transfer him to isolation."

"I shall have a word with Mr. Mroszek, Sister Remegius."

"It had better be brief, Dr. Blakeley," she huffed. "We want him out of here today."

"But," Blakeley said haltingly, "where are we supposed to put him?"

"That, sir, is no affair of ours."

"But. . . ."

The carriage eddied through the winding dirt road, made its way

over a somewhat steep rise, and found Lancaster Avenue. Blakeley
glanced over at Nathan, thinking he might see a touch of fatigue. A
trifle pale, perhaps, but not of the sort to suggest debilitation. True,
he had been favoring the bad knee as he walked, and his arm still
rested in a sling.

The heat at noon was oppressive despite the shade of the carriage.
It seemed as if the air was not circulating quite enough. Blakeley
had hailed a cab, which had turned out to be a rather poor excuse
for a hansom. The rites at the graveside had been brief and touching, led by the same little white-thatched priest who had presided
over Regis Tolan's funeral and whose church Mroszek had vandal-
ized. It had never occurred to Nathan that Lou was a Catholic. In
fact, the association of Lou with anything of religious gravity
seemed incongruous when he thought about it. A Marine Corps
honor guard had been present, and a bugler had played taps after
the customary firing of the salute. There had been a brief stir of excitement as mourners recognized Nathan, but the crowd had been
generally somber and respectful. Lou James had, like Captain Tolan
before him, collected many friends and acquaintances.

The carriage rumbled over the cobbled roadway and encountered
occasional ruts, at which times Nathan winced inside but retained a
granitelike pose for Dr. Blakeley. More than ever, he wished to get
back to business. It was important to him that this state of depend-
ence and worthlessness come to an end. In a far corner of his mind
he had feared that he might shortly become inert and mired in self-
pity; he realized that there was no room in this business for weak-
lings.

The street broadened as they traversed the several miles from the
cemetery into the city limits. Nathan counted the neatly trimmed
lawns and brightly painted houses, the apple trees and whitewashed
fences and put aside his dreams of romantic life on the outskirts of
violence. His thoughts returned to Aidan.

"Look there—up ahead."

Blakeley had broken the long silence. Nathan craned his neck and
squinted into the sun to observe a small carriage directly before
them on the busy street. It moved drunkenly along the outside lane,
bobbing and weaving like a stunned fighter, eventually turning toward the curb. Nathan shouted to the driver to take notice, and
their cab slowed down.

The small carriage moved in an arc over the sidewalk and stopped there, its rear half blocking the street. There was an immediate and angry response from the drivers whose cabs were forced to halt abruptly and form a lengthy single line down Market Street.

"Let's have a look," Nathan suggested, his eagerness to rejoin the world ever apparent.

By the time they'd hopped out of the cab and rushed to the scene a crowd was gathering near the small carriage and the advance guard was gawking at something in the driver's seat. When they approached, Blakeley and McBride came to a sudden halt as a large figure tumbled out of the vehicle to the ground. The onlookers were abruptly silent.

"Open his collar, Nathan," Blakeley shouted as he hurried back to their cab for his medicine bag.

But their efforts were in vain. When Blakeley returned a few seconds later, Nathan was shaking his head to indicate that nothing could be done for the man. Blakeley put aside his medicine bag and looked temporarily weary. It was just one more nagging frustration. And then he took a closer look at the departed.

Nathan could not have opened the collar had it made a difference. The man's hand was almost invisible under flabby jowls as he clasped his own neck in a steely death grip. The face was like a full moon frozen into a look of horror. The eyes bulged, and the tongue protruded. *My God,* Blakeley gasped to himself, *this is our fat man!*

"See the marks on the cheek, Nathan? And the color of the hair?"

"Yes, and the small flat feet. . . . Fascinating, Dr. Blakeley."

"It certainly is."

On the sidewalk, just above the shoulders of the corpse, Blakeley spied a burning cigarette. He picked it up and snuffed it out.

"Did he take a stroke?" Nathan asked.

"He has all the markings of a coronary attack, although a stroke is not out of the question."

The crowd was growing in size, and soon it was pressing them. But several patrolmen had been summoned by the excitement and arrived in time to restore order. Nathan was studying the body and directed Blakeley's attention to some burns around the dead man's lips.

"If those aren't cold sores, Dr. Blakeley, then I'd suggest they're in an unusual place for a burn."

"They *are* burns."

He studied the fat man's puffy, livid face and put his magnifying

glass close to the lips. The burns were *very* recent. They were not
the sort caused by exposure to the sun. They were, in fact, only
minutes old. There were similar markings on the tongue, little blis-
ters growing even as Blakeley studied them. "Now that's curious. · . . ." He picked up the cigarette and sniffed it cautiously. It
was not an Ateshian, but it was a unique blend.

"The chap's been murdered, Nathan," he said with a touch of
surprise in his voice, "and for the first time in all these months a set
of high cards has finally fallen into our hands."

He put the cigarette butt into a piece of cloth, folded it, and
dropped it into his medicine bag. The tests would have to be run later. The murder weapon was an ingenious choice: a little cigarette,
harmless enough in appearance, but saturated with chlorine gas. In-
haling the toxin directly brought on almost instantaneous circulatory collapse. It would have been a perfectly executed homicide; almost anyone else would have surmised that he had suffered a heart
seizure, common to such obese individuals.

The crowd started to murmur recognition; some knew who Blakeley was, others Nathan. But the grotesque state of the fat man on
the steaming sidewalk created the greater stir. Nathan recognized
two of the patrolmen, Roberts and Flannery, and asked them to
keep the onlookers several feet from the corpse. Then he felt inside
the dead man's coat until he'd found a wallet.

"Vincent Eliah Statler," he read to Blakeley from the dead man's
identification card. He thought he had heard that name before.

"I've no doubt who he is," Blakeley mused. "What we must
confirm is whether he is, in fact, our fat man.

"Why don't we call in your recent visitor?"

"I, er"—Blakeley blushed—"don't believe she'd be all that easy to
find. I believe we should let Mr. Mroszek have a look."

An hour later they were in the emergency room of Good Samaritan Hospital. The nursing sisters, believing they were dressing the
groggy Zoltan for his discharge, had scurried about officiously. The
chagrin on the face of Sister Remegius was profound as the orderlies
presented him to the obviously concerned authorities.

"That will be all, Sister Remegius." Blakeley smiled coldly.
"Thank you."

After she had flown off, two of Hudson's men took Zoltan Mroszek by the arm and led him to the stretcher on which lay the shroud-

ed body of Vincent Eliah Statler. A small section of the emergency room had been set aside and enclosed in off-white drapes.

Zoltan Mroszek's incoherent babbling ceased as he ogled the corpse for a moment, blinking his eyes and letting his jaw hang open. Blakeley and McBride studied him closely, watching for any signs of recognition.

When the murky haze cleared, Zoltan Mroszek's knees buckled, and he looked as if he were about to faint. Then he struggled to get away from the dead man. Mroszek's face broke into a sweat, and he started to rattle about clubs and broken bodies.

"Take it easy, Mroszek," said Hudson. "He can't hurt you now."

"Murderer . . . murderer!"

"The murderer of all those young women. Is that he lying on that stretcher?"

"I, I don't know . . . I don't know!"

"Now, don't get excited," said Blakeley very softly. "You're not in any danger. We're here to protect you."

This time the glassy eyes darted back and forth from one police officer to another. His past had given him little cause to suspect anything better than hostility from anyone wearing such uniforms.

"We have him quite under control, as you can see. Now, what *else* do you see?"

Mroszek's mind, poised always in a state between sleeping and waking, was, as Blakeley had so often testified, a dark pit of mystery and sublimated thought.

"They were pleading for their lives," Mroszek muttered under his breath. "It was pitiful."

"Who were *they*? The young women? Were they young women?"

"No—no young women. Only the old gypsy."

"Who was this gypsy woman?" Blakeley pursued.

He grasped Mroszek by the shoulders reassuringly as he questioned him. Mroszek's eyes were heavy-lidded and his breathing spasmodic. His voice was dulled by exhaustion, and for a time he recited lines from Dowson.

"Not now," Blakeley interrupted. "You shall have your days of wine and roses quite soon, but first you must help us. Mr. Mroszek, we need your mind, your magnificently creative mind. Now, who was this gypsy woman you speak of?"

"The crone." Mroszek smiled stupidly. "He killed the crone. Her idiot son also. He scattered their brains across the floor. My God, it was messy."

"The Bowman case. . . ."

Hudson stopped again. More witnesses had come forward to testify against the Reverend Hopkins a few hours ago. He was beginning to sense that this was at last the day when Fortune would stop treating him like an unwanted child. He asked bluntly whether Mroszek had ever heard of the name Bowman, and Mroszek stared back at him vacantly.

"Have you ever heard of the Bowman murders?" Blakeley repeated. It was clear Mroszek would speak to no one else.

"Yes, he slaughtered them. The fat man. He and his friend slaughtered them."

"Are you certain?"

"Certain."

Apparently Mroszek's memories became more vivid at that moment, for he began to wail as he drifted over toward the stretcher, shouting obscenities at the corpse from a safe distance. Hudson's men, Tully and Bergenhoff, struggled not to laugh at the pathetic man.

Hudson was still dumbfounded. He glanced back at his men, who quickly snapped into more earnest poses, then looked at Dr. Blakeley.

"Dr. Blakeley," he roared, "I thank you and the department thanks you."

"Hmm. . . ." Blakeley observed Sister Remegius, who had slipped through the drapes as Mroszek was raging at the dead man. "Your gratitude, albeit most appreciated, is a trifle premature, Lieutenant. Your star witness is also, unfortunately, your *responsibility*. I fear your vicissitudes are only beginning."

Sister Remegius stood in her characteristic posture: arms folded, head thrown back, face frozen into a cheerless Gothic gaze. Like every other institution in civilized history, the hospital had its casual, politically distracted titular rulers, whom no one had ever heard of, and its one unifying fanatic. The eyes of Sister Remegius could pierce the flintiest trespassers.

"Not here, Sergeant Hudson."

"I'm, uh, *Lieutenant* Hudson." He attempted to correct her.

"Mr. Morcheck will spend not one single added evening under the roof of this sanctified edifice. I stand before you like a rock in this cause."

"Sister Remegius, meaning no disrespect, naturally, I suggest your apprehension with regard to Mr. Mroszek—"

"Don't patronize me, you petty bureaucrat."

"Sister, you don't seem to grasp the seriousness of our problem."

"Seriousness," she snarled. "There is no seriousness in your entire fiasco. First, you bring a dead man, already reeking with the first stages of decomposition, into a hospital where he may contaminate the others. Then you endeavor to inflict that other beast upon us after we've already served notice upon Dr. Blakeley that we shall have no part in his scheme."

"Well," grunted Hudson, "what the hell are we supposed to do now?"

Sister Remegius' lips tightened in pent-up fury. Mroszek was seated now, babbling in what sounded like Hungarian, under the watchful eyes of Tully and Bergenhoff.

Blakeley answered finally. "I certainly can't take him home with me. I don't suppose you'd care to take him back with you, keep him in an isolated cell perhaps? I shall see to his medical needs, of course."

"Not unless you. . . ." Hudson's voice trailed off as he was about to make a comment about the inadequacy of policemen as nurses; a devilish grin fell over his face. *Dott's really rotten, Lootenant,* he could hear Fatzinger say. *Diss guy shmells like a soldier's sock, an' I gotta be his nursemaid. Cheesuss. Now, Bones,* he would answer with great satisfaction, *you mustn't speak so disrespectfully of our star witness.*

"What do you think of that alternative?" Blakeley inquired after Hudson had been silent for a time.

"Never let it be said," Hudson replied with mock resignation, "that the police department is unwilling to make necessary adjustments."

Mroszek was carted off to his room to be dressed and returned to the precinct lockup. A surprisingly cheerful Lieutenant Hudson left to make arrangements for Vincent Eliah Statler's transportation to the city morgue. Blakeley took Nathan aside to speak with him privately.

"How are you feeling, Nathan? How exactly, I mean. No double-talk now."

Nathan was pensive for a moment as he took a good look back at Blakeley.

"If I told you I was all prepared to chase another motorcar, you could have me committed to the cell next door to Mroszek. But I'll wager I don't feel much worse than you do right now."

Blakeley sighed and sat down on an empty stretcher. It seemed to him as though he'd not slept since the day the department had handed him the damned case. But really it was only a little more than sixty hours. Reluctant as he was to press Detective McBride back into service, he knew he had no choice.

"I wonder if you'd do me a favor."

"Of course."

"We must seek Miss Walker's cooperation. She should be capable of making a positive identification of our fat man. I should like you to find her and take her to the morgue."

"Very good, Dr. Blakeley," said Nathan, checking his pocket watch. "She ought to be up and around by the time I get there."

"Fine. I'd do it myself, you see, only Sophia would undoubtedly misunderstand." Blakeley laughed. "Then too, if I don't soon go to bed, I believe I will hallucinate like Mroszek."

Nathan directed the cabdriver to Blakeley's estate and quietly paid him in advance for his labors since he realized that Dr. Blakeley would be into a deep sleep by the time the cab got home.

Knowing, for example, that his ability to control the reins would be suspect for at least another few days, he had to hail a second cab for himself. And when the afternoon sun hit him with full force, he was reminded of how much energy he'd lost. When the dizziness abated, it became a comforting reminder that he was, after all, alive. While the wooden wheels rolled noisily over the brick roadway, he felt the stabbing pains and ruminated once again upon his romantic foolishness.

But the memories passed when he looked out the window and observed the many delightful young ladies who strolled along Market Street under delicate parasols. They became more numerous as the cab approached the center of the city, and, for a fleeting moment, he felt slightly grateful. There were many, many fish in the sea, as his father used to say.

His contentment, however, was short-lived, and in a moment—after glimpsing a lovely red-haired girl in a green dress—he felt that gnawing emptiness once again. He had not yet admitted to himself that so many women would seem to resemble Aidan.

The cabdriver bore an air of artificial unconcern as Nathan alighted and paid him. As the horse's hoofbeats joined the clamor of the busy street, Nathan realized that the driver had worn that look since he had advised him of the destination.

The lobby of the old Mansion Hotel was as shabby as he had expected. The walls wore a patina of soot and cigar smoke accumulated over several generations. The floors had not been swabbed with any determination since the last rainy day. But the absence of cigar butts and newspapers suggested that someone had at least made a cursory effort at maintaining respectability. The floor around the spittoons was especially grimy, as were the areas nearest the sand-and-concrete ashtrays. The walls were decorated with nudes reclining on tawdry backgrounds. The Mansion seemed eager to publicize its main attractions.

A surly desk clerk motioned with his head toward the elevator and grunted the number of the room where Nathan would find Lil Walker. When the rickety little box creaked to a halt, he got off quickly, breathing a sigh of relief. He counted the numbers on the doors until he'd found the room. He vowed to take the stairs on his way out, however much the pain in his knee might annoy him.

The state of the hallway was similar to that of the lobby: cosmetic measures inadequate to combating the general shabbiness.

The large man who opened the door was rather dark, perhaps a mulatto, judging by his sallow cheeks and clinging hair. The loud, almost brazen hue and tailoring of his clothing suggested a shadowy association with the principal type of commerce of the floor.

"She ain't seein' nobody. Come back in a hour."

"She'll see me."

"What makes you think so?"

"Because I'm a cop. And because I'll turn you into a three-headed frog if she doesn't."

He looked Nathan over, seemingly confused by the incapacitated form and the easy aggressiveness.

"You don't seem to get it, Clancy. She ain't ready fer visitors. Now, go chase yerself, like a good little boy."

"I told you to move on," said Nathan.

The dark man assessed Nathan, paying special attention to the sling and the labored walk, but Nathan was aware of that. When the punch was thrown, Nathan was ready. He dodged it, and the man's fist struck the doorway wainscoting with a loud crunch. Nathan drew back and sank his foot into the dark man's crotch, holding his breath while he listened nervously to the groans and coughs as his attacker slumped to the floor. Staying on his feet had been, in retrospect, purely a matter of Providence.

Back into the world, such as the world was.

"A great watchdog he is. Looka that."

Miss Walker appeared in a very thin negligee. He felt ill-at-ease; under the circumstances, he was clearly an intruder. Her heavy makeup was caked on in areas where it had been applied twenty-four hours ago, and she smelled of sleep and stale alcohol. Nathan moved away from the dark man, who still writhed on the floor, and fumbled around in his coat for a police card.

"I've been told to look you up, Miss Walker," he said.

"Yeah, well, it's a little early."

"I know, but I'm here on what you might call extraordinary business."

She surveyed him approvingly and waved her hand in the air nonchalantly. "Don't worry about yer condition. Excuse me, conditions. I know all the latest techniques. We're real sophisticated around here."

"That's not what I'm talking about, Miss Walker."

"Y'know what?" She shook a finger perceptively. "I know you. I know who you are. I seen yer pitcher. Yer Fly—"

"I'm Detective Nathan McBride," he said coolly. The name the press had given him had never seemed fitting. It had brought him more aggravation than anything else.

"Yeah. . . . "

She excused herself and shifted her attention to the dark man, who began to show signs of collecting himself. Nathan was debating his next move: whether to kick him in the head before he got up or merely to subdue him with a drawn pistol.

"Lazarus, get the hell outa here," ordered Miss Walker. "You know you ain't supposed to be here when I'm receivin'."

"I wanna bust his tail!" roared the dark man as he struggled to his feet.

"This here's Flyin' McBride!"

Lazarus beat a hasty retreat, pausing only to retrieve his gaudy straw hat. Nathan suddenly understood that there was little he could do to suppress his unsought reputation.

The police card had finally appeared from somewhere deep within his vest pocket, and he hastened to present it.

"Miss Walker, I'm here on police business."

She sat on a divan, lit up a cigarette, and draped her arm over the back. In the sunlight her negligee was even more revealing. It was, essentially, invisible.

"Police business," he repeated.

"Yeah, yeah," she replied, rather unsettlingly. "Listen, Flyin' McBride, fer you it's on the house. I mean, you're workin' with Dr. Blakeley, an' he sure as hell ain't comin' around here, even if I *did* make it plain as day that he can drop in anytime. An' Chantal *was* a friend o' mine. Y'know what I mean?"

Miss Walker was not altogether unattractive, after a tinsely fashion. In the hours he'd spent lying in that hospital bed after his encounter with death, Nathan had often regretted that he had not spent enough time in the celebration of life. Pristine infatuations, such as the one he'd just been through with Aidan Tierney, had been too much his style.

Too early or something.

"It's too early or something, Miss Walker," he said with a polite smile, but she did not seem to catch his meaning. It had not been his intention to hurt Miss Walker's feelings, any more than he had wished to scare off her bodyguard. The matter had become entirely too involved.

"Look," he explained softly, "I'm sure the delights you offer are estimable. That's as obvious as the pigeons on your windowsill. But I wasn't kidding. I'm really here on police business."

"What kinda police business, fer Chrissake?"

She sprang out of the divan and rested her hands on her hips. Her attitude had changed abruptly, and he suspected she now wished her bodyguard were still here and all prepared to throw him out.

"We want you to identify someone for us. Dr. Blakeley and I believe we have your fat man."

"Where?"

"In the county morgue. His name is Vincent Eliah Statler."

"Well, why the hell didn't you say so?" She ran off to get dressed. "Insteada comin' in here an' roughin' up Lazarus an' lettin' me make an ass o' myself?"

He sat down on the divan and shook his head.

Nineteen

The conflict with Spain became suddenly popular again. The war
fever, dormant for the past several weeks, made a strong recurrence
as reports began to trickle in from Cuba. Even the public's dissatis-
faction with the taxes levied to maintain the expeditionary forces
was smothered in a renewed wave of national pride.

The First Division, under Brigadier General Kent, moved at last
on San Juan Hill; the Second Division, headed by Brigadier General
Lawton, first took the village of Siboney and then moved on El
Caney, lying to the north of San Juan Hill. In a matter of days these
previously insignificant little sectors of the island became as familiar
to the man on the street as the city of Santiago had been for the past
month. The strategic mountains, in particular, took on romantic dimensions in the American mind. The Cavalry Division, now dis-
mounted, took Las Guásimas, on the road to San Juan, and then
moved to assault Kettle Hill and later San Juan. This division, led by
Major General Joseph Wheeler, became the center of journalistic
attention, for in its ranks were two of the war's most illustrious
figures: Colonel Leonard Wood and Lieutenant Colonel Theodore
Roosevelt. Their First Volunteer Cavalry Regiment, which the
newspapers were now calling the Rough Riders, was to be found
wherever the action was fiercest.

Sophia Blakeley soon refused, for the sake of her own sanity, to
read or even hear of the military reports. She knew that Ralphie,
through the kind of roundabout factors that had always been part of
his existence, was with Roosevelt. And Ralphie was such a very big
target.

The struggles over El Caney and San Juan Hill were vicious. The
Spaniards, their backs to the wall, sensing that this was to be the last
vestige of their once-proud empire and uncertain of their fate under
the liberated Cubans, held onto their positions stubbornly. And this
time the statistics had a greater ring of war's reality. Out of his
thirty-five hundred men Lawton's Second Division lost four hundred and forty in killed and wounded before El Caney fell. The village had been heavily fortified in the time it had taken to organize
the assault. The attack on San Juan Hill was equally desperate; the
American troops had to proceed across broken country and through
a rough scrub in the face of withering fire delivered by a concealed

enemy. The toll among both officers and men was especially heavy in this operation, one brigade losing four commanders in succession before the twelve hours of fighting came to a close. By the time American troops finally gained control of all the heights commanding the northern and eastern sides of Santiago, the casualties had mounted to a hundred and twelve officers and fourteen hundred and sixty men killed, wounded, and missing.

With Spain quickly approaching the moment when its government would be forced to sue for peace, the American public began to hear news of a different, even more dreadful enemy which now threatened to annihilate the entire military force on the island. Soon the words "yellow fever" had started to enter saloon and street-corner conversations with more frequency.

"What can I do for you, Mr. . . . ?"

"Heester—Irwin Heester. You remember me, don't you? They found one of them dead girls on my property."

"Oh, yes, of course, Mr. Heester. Do sit down, please."

He had already seated himself in a chair on the other side of her desk. Miss Meredith's comfortably furnished office was small, and fresh flowers added femininity to the polished wood and file cabinets.

Affairs had gone badly for Irwin Heester of late. First, he'd allowed himself to be humiliated by old Fergus O'Farrell. When word of that got around the district, two other clients had presented the Gouger with lawsuits. One involved a matter of usury, and the other a contractual fraud. Although it was not yet a foregone conclusion that Irwin would lose either case, the charges against him had cut deeply. Moreover, the Gouger had retained an attorney, not the best in town, relatively inexperienced actually, but the fee was low.

"Coffee, Mr. Heester?"

"Uh, okay, but I use milk and sugar."

His tone suggested an inordinate respect for the cost of the accessories. She fixed him a cup of what the Viennese call *Schale Gold* with generous heapings of sugar, and when she had removed her glasses, he added some more milk.

Beginning with the death of the fat man, Allison Meredith's energies had been particularly absorbed by the case, creating a large

backlog of all her other assignments. Recently her editors had taken
to calling her at 6 A.M. to demand that equal attention be paid to
McClure's Ladies' Journal. Yielding to them because she had no
crisp alibis, she had spent 4wo days earlier in the week on the Delaware River wharves covering the arrival of several dignitaries of the
European fashion community. For the most part they were boorish,
petulant, and wearisome, and a buyer from o.e of the local department stores had propositioned her repeatedly until his wife had
chastened him by dropping by unannounced. There had been one
exciting moment when a merchant vessel arrived with what had
been rumored to be a battalion of Spanish prisoners of war—but it
was only a shipment of grapefruit and bananas from Barbados. The
sun glancing off the water had been merciless, and despite her best
efforts to remain in the shade, Allison Meredith's face had taken
quite a burn. Freckles remained on her nose and cheeks, giving her
something of a gaminlike quality. Heester eyed her somewhat uneasily, turning over his next line. She wore a lacy dress of mauve
and smelled of a light sachet; her fresh appearance and penchant for
tidiness rendered her almost an alien being in his arena of commerce.

"That's a nice purple dress you got on," he observed.

"Thank you," she said, holding out a tray. "Would you care for a
gingersnap?"

Heester scooped up a handful and stuffed several of them into his
mouth.

"I guess you're surprised to see me."

It was difficult to understand him through the wad of gingersnaps.
Politely, but without warmth, she repeated her request for an explanation.

"Well," he resumed, after gulping and sucking his teeth, "the way
I figure it, you owe me."

"How so, Mr. Heester?"

"First off. . . ." He paused to slurp his coffee. "I agreed to give
you that interview, remember?"

"I remember."

"Yes, I did, and it was a bargain in good faith. Nobody can say Irwin Heester's a welcher. No sirree."

"Almost nobody," she reminded him, but the reference to his current lawsuits slipped by unnoticed.

"Number two," he went on, waving his fingers before her eyes, "you and your associates gypped me outa some first-class advertisin', sort of."

"Indeed, Mr. Heester, your choice of words—"

"You'll have to make allowances for my background, Miss Meredith. I don't usually do business with fancy ladies the likes of you. Maybe 'gypped' ain't the best word. Let's just say I got a raw deal from all you cops." He was leaning on her desk now, smiling with exaggerated confidence.

"I'm not a police officer, Mr. Heester. I'm a writer. And I'll thank you to remove your elbow from my desk."

"I didn't come here to argue, Miss Meredith." Instinctively, he backed off, but his smile remained. "With your connections, I wouldn't dream of gettin' on your wrong side. It's Allison, isn't it?"

"It's miss," she retorted, "and I wish you'd get to your point. As you can see, I'm quite busy this morning."

He dunked a gingersnap into his coffee and consumed it greedily.

"The point is, I cooperated, and now I think it's about time you and your associates did somethin' for me."

"What?"

"After all, I did find that *corpus delicti* for you, and got nothin' but abuse for it. Not only that, but you oughta see what happened to my property's value when word of that got around. It might as well be quicksand now as far as those superstitious bastards in the neighborhood are concerned. And all because I tried to be an upstandin' citizen."

Miss Meredith was doing a slow burn. She was not used to such language, nor did she appreciate the mess he had made of her desk.

"It goes without saying, Mr. Heester, that my associates and I are most appreciative of your exemplary conduct in this matter. It will serve as a paradigm of behavior in these troubled times. As, I'm sure, it would be highly recommended to all civilized people on this globe to emulate your impeccable table manners. Now, if you please, I'm afraid you'll drip some of your wet gingersnap into my typewriter if you continue to crowd my little work area."

Once again he withdrew, but this time his smile seemed to droop. He was not certain, but he felt reasonably sure he'd been chastised.

"That's right," he reasserted, "upstandin'."

"Mr. Heester"—she flashed a quick look directly at him before sipping her coffee—"you have two minutes to tell me what you want before I telephone my associates. They'll arrest you then and throw you into solitary. I shall say you broke into my office."

As she spoke, she realized that she had learned something of Dr. Blakeley's capricious sense of humor. The look in Heester's eyes and the perspiration on his forehead told her that the lessons had been useful.

"Don't call them!"

"One minute and forty seconds."

"I bought a new piece of property," he hastened, "a butcher shop. It used to be Easterley's Meat Store, up near Castleman's Livery Stable, where Captain Tolan dropped dead. Easterley tried to branch out, you see, and he was into me for hundreds, thousands maybe, so I foreclosed. It's only fair—I gave him a month and a half."

She reminded him that he'd just used twenty seconds and picked up the telephone.

"Well, I was wonderin'," said the Gouger, "bein' as this here's a butcher shop, you might use your influence or even your feminine wiles to get Flyin' McBride out there on Wednesday, the day I open it, bein' as it's called a butcher shop. Get it, a *Butcher* shop?"

"I get it, Mr. Heester."

"We could get the newspapers to come out, and I know there must be somebody who could draw his pitcher stranglin' one of our butchers. Just for a joke, of course. Nobody can say Irwin M. Heester ain't a great kidder. No sirree."

"It sounds like an excellent piece of public relations."

Heester failed to recognize the irony in her voice.

"Yeah," he rambled on, "I'd pay him for it, naturally. We got a sale on chicken livers that day. I'd be willin' to cut him a percentage. Just on the chicken livers, of course—the other stuff's too damn expensive! Them wholesalers won't let a man make an honest livin'."

She smiled to herself as she contemplated the absurdity of the situation.

Though a thaw in their relationship was developing slowly, correspondence between Detective McBride and herself was still, unhappily, restricted to business and guarded civility. The total of their words exchanged during the past week would not fill a page, and this creature imagined her selling Nathan an incredible bill of goods.

She still held the telephone in her hands and seemed poised to use it at any moment.

"Mr. Heester, either you're crazy or stupid or both. Certainly you are the most insensitive person I've ever met. I doubt, sincerely, whether it's at all possible for either of us to communicate with the other."

He sat up in his chair, obviously taken aback, and sputtered for a time before collecting himself.

"Well, the same to you, lady," he said at length with a scowl.

"I think it's time you found your way back to the hole you've crawled out of. Your two minutes are more than up."

"Hey—listen, you." He jumped out of his chair. "Your Flyin' McBride oughta be flattered. I coulda gone after Blakeley hisself. Maybe Colonel Roosevelt!"

Allison started to laugh. The Gouger shot back charges of fraud, unfair bargaining, and character assassination and threatened to bring in his attorney.

"Who . . . who *is* this pettifogger?" she asked between spasms. "Perhaps we should prepare ourselves for him."

"Cooper!"

The name was familiar. In her hours spent around the precinct station, Allison Meredith had learned to appreciate certain figures of comic interest, like Stanley Butterfield, Mrs. Leibowitz, Bones Fatzinger, and above all, Richard Cooper, Esq. *"Cooper,"* she repeated, and her laughter now overflowed and reverberated among the file cabinets and book cases.

"With hysterical women like you writin' for the public, no wonder the country's as confused as it is." Heeter stomped out of her office.

Sophia Blakeley rested her head against a pillow on her easy chair and closed her eyes. The studio was almost blissfully silent. More than once during the past week she had wished they'd never left Kent. How pleasant were the dreams of tea, horse shows, receptions at court, dress parades, the Savoy, idle chitchat on art and books, even the more serious discussions of colonial matters in India and Africa.

Since the death of the fat man, Ian had been working almost around the clock, appearing only for supper and then running off to his study or laboratory. He was convinced that he and his colleagues had rounded the corner, but there were more mysteries to unravel. That in itself was nothing new; she had seen him equally absorbed in the past. It was the least of her problems really.

The war news grew more jubilant by the day while the casualty lists mounted ever so quietly. The former enjoyed an honored place on the front pages, the latter were secreted away in a corner of the lost and found section, almost like a sinister afterthought. No one appeared to be concerned about the grim side, a necessary evil in the quest for national identity.

Sophia was honestly frantic about Ralphie. It was a harsh certainty that the big, bumbling, lovable dolt was chasing about that silly little island amid the cannonballs and all the other ordnance. Probably he was volunteering for messy assignments that he, in his reckless fashion, regarded as fun. She envisioned him galloping on his imaginary steed up that hill they called Don Juan or whatever.

Snopkowski's first reaction to her fright, a prolonged period of banging pots and pans, had finally passed, and Sophia was reasonably certain that that would be the end of it. But there had followed an even lengthier period of shouting and cursing, and once again Sophia was grateful that she understood no Polish. Anyone who had chanced upon Snopkowski's territory had been assaulted with verbal barrages that Sophia was sure were audible across the river in New Jersey. The kitchen had become a scene reminiscent of a siege. The whole affair gave Sophia a terrible headache. At last Ian, who was home for a brief recuperative visit, had prevailed on Snopkowski to spend a week or so in bed.

"You tink I scared?" she had said, glowering. "I no scared o' dott Butcher yonko, goddamn. He come around dis place again, I ringink him neck like I kill a cheekum!" With that Snopkowski had demonstrated her defiance by squeezing a large piece of sausage as if it were appended to someone's shoulders.

"That's very true, Mrs. Snopkowski, but—"

"You tal dott to Veektorr, too! I no puttink op wit nottink outa him needer, dott sonumbitch!"

When Snopkowski had finally been pacified, Sophia had endeavored to assume control of the kitchen. Her new command was far more challenging than anticipated. The tasks should not have been intimidating; she had, after all, read all the recipes long regarded as certain to please the English palate. The lamb had, however, been overcooked, the goose undercooked, the kidney pie had been rendered to sawdust, and the Yorkshire pudding had closely resembled oatmeal. The ham and Cheddar had been very much like effluence from a chemical plant, and the roast duck akin to a cat trapped in an oven. Poor, *dear* Ian. He had striven valiantly to disguise his disappointment. She had known after the sixth day that dinner was no longer something he awaited eagerly. Only the sherry, which she had not had a thing to do with, had met with his total approval. The toll on her ego, had not many other worries preoccupied her, would have been catastrophic. Sophia had long believed Snopkowski to be overindulged.

The matter of Ralphie's safety had, however, overshadowed all other matters.

Olga Wojdzekevicz seemed to Ian the distaff counterpart of Ralphie, the sum total of inordinate attention to bodily development. She reminded Sophia of the miller's daughter in Chaucer's "Reeve's Tale," grown to twenty or so—a well-rounded wench, blue eyes clear as glass, buttocks broad, with breasts round and high—not at all the sort to be portrayed in more polite literature.

But her cooking was supposedly as superb as her English was poor, and she *was* Snopkowski's favorite niece. So it was formality when at last Sophia had relinquished her position to young Olga. Sophia had hated the kitchen anyway. The odious Victor had felt annoyingly free to drop in unannounced, offer his stuffy advice, and abscond with unguarded ingredients, generally making a nuisance of himself. Thinking about it now, Victor should be held most responsible for the lamb, the goose, and the duck fiascos. There had been moments recently when Sophia had even wondered whether Victor had not been enlisted—or more probably duped—by Snopkowski into a nepotist conspiracy. Rosy-cheeked Olga Wojdzekevicz, only recently delivered here by a crowded freighter, had seemed to arrive just in time. It was all rather curious, thought Sophia.

It had been a time of terrible ignominy for Sophia all in all. Lady Blakeley had often warned Sophia, in the days of her courtship, that Ian was an incorrigible collector of things. Nowadays he seemed to collect people with much the same nonchalance with which he had brought stray animals to Blakeley Manor in his childhood. Nathan and Miss Meredith had met with Sophia's heartiest approval. That wretched Zoltan Mroszek fellow, however, had been quite another thing. Mroszek was the last straw, she vowed. When, after days of heavy feeding and detoxification, the miserable creature had returned to something resembling normality, Ian had mentioned Sophia's avid interest in his work.

"*Quelle oeuvre?*" he had inquired in his grammar school French, as Fatzinger looked on in bewilderment.

"Your paintings, of course," Ian had answered.

"*Mes peintures?*"

"*Oui, les peintures que les gendarmes ont trouvés dans votre chambre derrière le bureau.*"

Mroszek had thought for a moment before breaking out in his derisive laughter. It seems he had won those paintings in a dice game in Prague several years ago. The artist had since passed on—run over by a horse that had broken away from a beer wagon. And Mroszek was not even certain that the late artist had not stolen them himself.

"*Mon cher docteur, votre épouse est très innocente.*"

It took Ian days to confess that experience, and then only after hours of prodding. Running his fork absentmindedly through the ham and Cheddar, he had forgotten his decision to spare her feelings and had passed a comment about Mroszek's progress, and that had inspired her to force the issue.

"Yes, I'm afraid he said that."

Much as she had tried to appear only mildly amused by her own misguided enthusiasm, it had been impossible for him to miss her seething displeasure.

She rubbed her temples and tried to dismiss her headache by insisting to herself that it was there only because of psychosomatic reasons as readily ignored as nurtured. On the floor, beside her chair, lay a copy of the morning newspaper, filled with more frenzied dispatches from the combat zone. Chills ran down her spine. Lately she had begun to think of the great conflict with Spain as one great danse macabre .

The war had brought more unexpected complications into Sophia Blakeley's life. With its end imminent and the glorious victories receiving more attention with every issue of the yellow press, the Philadelphia suffragettes had suddenly decided to capitalize on the current events by conducting a march of protest. Wandalee Hinch, the self-appointed commandant of the local effort, had decreed that a meaningful point could be made at this juncture in history. According to Mrs. Hinch, it was both callous and shortsighted of the federal government to spend the lifeblood of American manhood merely to liberate those illiterate savages in the West Indies, while American womanhood still remained in unconscionable bondage. The dear, courageous ladies, Rosalie in particular, had never seemed to grasp the honorable concept of temperance in all matters. Ian had warned Philadelphia's womanhood in unmistakable terms of the danger inherent to such gatherings while the Butcher still remained at large. It now seemed terribly irresponsible of Wandalee Hinch to ignore his words.

Throughout the evening, ever since Sophia had told her that her participation in tomorrow's demonstration was unthinkable, Rosalie had been whining about her mother's unforgivable *treason.*

At the moment Rosalie was pouting in her room. Sophia was contemplating an abrupt outburst of her own, something to take the petulant Rosalie by surprise and perhaps give her something real to sulk about,

There was shouting and exultation from the direction of the vestibule. Sophia swore that this would give rise to the headache of her lifetime. The whoops and yells made her think the war had come to the banks of the Schuylkill.

"Ralph Ian Blakeley, you great lout!" she cried, throwing herself at him with such force that he wheeled momentarily from the impact.

She had run the distance from her studio, through the back rooms and hallways, thinking, at first only faintly and then with greater assurance, that it was truly his voice she had heard, not some cruel twist of her imagination.

"Hey, gee, Ma, you're gonna squeeze me to death!"

Ralphie had always been affectedly fragile when faced with his mother's unrestrained enthusiasm. It had always been difficult for him to reconcile these moments with her usual reserve, and at such times he often appeared paralyzed with indecision. But she loved to hug him anyway, even if her tiny arms barely began to encircle his massive frame.

"Have we won the war, Ralphie?" she asked with delight, still clinging to him tenaciously.

"I dunno, Ma. I sure hope not. I got sent up here to recruit more men. What the hell are we gonna do with them if it's all over?"

"Ralphie, your language," she admonished him lightly.

"Golly, I'm sorry, Ma," said Ralphie. "You see, I've been living in male company for so long, I guess I've become uncouth. Again."

"It hasn't been that long, Ralphie," she replied. Actually she didn't care at all.

"I sent a telegraph from Tampa, saying I was coming home. Ah, jeez—I'll bet the messenger boys are all in the Army already, and I was hoping to recruit them."

Ralphie fumbled in his pocket with his free hand, still clutching his duffel bag with the other as Sophia let go of him at last. Blushing, he pulled out a piece of paper that he had thought for certain he'd given to someone in the telegraph office one week ago and stammered out an embarrassed few words. He was dressed in a new summer tan uniform, something she had not yet seen but had read about recently. It seemed to accentuate the darker shade of his face and hands after weeks in the semitropical sun. He was somewhat groggy and quite unshaved after his long train ride north, but to Sophia he seemed to glow. He lifted her into the air playfully, as he had so often in the past to her great annoyance. This time she did not mind. He was home and in one piece.

And then a second thought occurred to her.

"Were you wounded, Ralphie?" she asked apprehensively.

"No, no, I'm okay, Ma." He looked coy.

"Well then, why have they sent you home?"

"I told you. They want me to be a recruiter."

"Entirely possible," she agreed, "but you haven't, God forbid, contracted yellow fever?"

Ralphie quickly assured her that no such calamity had befallen him. He had simply got into some, well, little difficulties.

His sheepish demeanor and the blush that quickly blanketed his face caused her soon to suspect that the "difficulties" were of an embarrassing nature. She led him to a chair and sent a maid to the kitchen for coffee. Come to think of it, he did appear a trifle gaunt—for Ralphie, that is.

"I wish you wouldn't sit there with your mouth agape, Ralph. Your coffee is coming with all deliberate good speed. Now, tell me what happened to you in the military—please."

"Ah, gee, Ma. It's, well, kind of ticklish," he protested.

"And please don't call me 'ma', Ralph," she answered, her patience wearing thin.

"All right. Only. . .I have another name nowadays, and I like it a lot more than Ralph. The guys in the barracks used to call me, uh, Beef. *Beef* Blakeley."

Sophia sighed and acknowledged the maid, who had by now delivered the coffee.

"It has a certain ring to it. Alliterative, in any case."

American ways had not imposed themselves on Sophia without a struggle. When the maid departed, Ralphie began, uneasily, the history of his stay in the Army. Sophia quietly shushed him now and then, lest his words be overheard by one or another of the servants.

Some time ago Beef, as the sergeant had christened him, had been introduced to the military man's drink, beer. Throughout his life Ralphie had always avoided any form of spirits, preferring milk or mineral water or other liquids more conducive to the maintenance of his perfect form. Even coffee had been taken sparingly. She recalled his eager anticipation of the pitchers of natural fruit juices he'd expected to down in Florida and the combat zones, and he took great pains to remind her of that. The trouble was, he said, the water was scarce and the Army rationed it strictly. Even bathing was seen as a bit of self-indulgence; it could be done properly only if one had the good fortune to happen upon a friendly stream—that is, one relatively free of alligators and poisonous snakes. Sophia cringed and quickly reminded him that there were no such shortages now that he was home.

The only source of refreshment that Ralphie had found in abundance at the camp was beer. To his great surprise, he had enjoyed it. He had, in fact, enjoyed it very much. It was cold and invigorating, and someone had informed him of its unheralded nutritional properties. "Bully!" he exclaimed.

"How come Dad never told me about that?" he wondered aloud.

"I've no idea, Ral . . . er, Beef. Perhaps he doesn't know," she answered, humoring him.

During his years at the medical college Ian was said to be something of a legendary beer imbiber in his own right. Sooner or later she had always known Ralphie would inherit his father's taste for it. Ralphie's drinking seemed to her fittingly British in a way. Her ancestors had been drinking it for hundreds of years, at least since the fourteenth century, according to one family legend.

Ralphie wondered why she wore a look of mild amusement. She was thinking of the barrels that Ian had been hiding in a far corner of the wine cellar, thinking that she actually believed them to be casks of Madeira. Blakeley had always taken such pains to convince her that she'd refined his tastes to such a degree that he could never again tolerate beer or ale.

"Well, maybe I ought to tell him how good it is for you," Ralphie asserted.

"Of course. Now, go on with your story, dear."

Ralphie and his mates had got off duty late one afternoon and the sun was still burning the Gulf Coast as if it were noon. After a baseball game, in which Ralphie had hit a double, a triple, and three home runs, the company had repaired to one of those dingy wayside taverns one reads about in slice-of-life novels. They had been hot and thirsty, and Ralphie, having worked harder than the others, had been the hottest and thirstiest.

He grasped his neck with both hands and let his tongue droop grotesquely. She urged him to get to the point.

To make his long story short, as the sun fell below the palm tree horizon, he had consumed approximately one-quarter of a keg of beer. Before his friends could get him back to camp, the symptoms had already begun to manifest themselves. Sophia hastened to let him know that she understood the effects of beer on the digestive tract. The symptoms had remained for the next two days, during which period the military force had been sent on to Cuba while the Army surgeons scratched their heads over Ralphie's illness. Finally, reasonably certain that he was suffering from a problem of much less gravity than yellow fever, but still unconvinced of his stomach's ability to withstand a sea cruise, they had recommended that he be restricted to office duties for a time. Accordingly, he had been transferred to command headquarters in downtown Tampa, chastened, and somewhat lighter on his feet, and bored by his silly job.

For several days Ralphie had stood guard outside the office of an obscure functionary named Lieutenant General L. Bentley Starnes. On the third day General Starnes' wife had made an appearance. She was, as Ralphie haltingly described her, "sort of a painted lady but nice-looking anyway." She dressed in the height of fashion, smelled of heady cologne, undulated as she walked, and—to Sophia's shock—"talked kind of like you, Ma." Mrs. Starnes was also notorious, as Ralphie soon learned. One of his fellow guards had described her as a lifetime of worldly education in one evening and had reminded him that the look she'd thrown him was an all-too-familiar and unmistakable one. Several days later she had given him that same look—but this time the general had observed it. Thus, it had come as no surprise to any of Ralphie's confederates when the general had abruptly decided to transfer him to Philadelphia, where it was believed he could serve as a "paragon of military aesthetics," the general's aide had said.

"Recruitin's a pretty important job, you know," he reminded her.

"Well, I suppose you're hungry," she said after a time.

"I could eat my underwear."

"I fixem a dozen eggs, a pound o' bacom, an' a sack o' potatas, goddamn!"

Snopkowski had heard the voices in the downstairs room and had slipped into the dining room unnoticed. She stood before them in an ancient bathrobe, her toothless smile suddenly dominating the atmosphere. How many times, Sophia asked herself, had she asked Mrs. Snopkowski to remember to place her dentures in her mouth before leaving her room?

"*Cuba libre*, Snopkowski," said Ralphie.

"Ralphie, Ralphie—goddamn!"

Snopkowski pulled him from his chair and squeezed him as if he were the last item between her and the abyss. She led him into the kitchen with Sophia following uncertainly, and as they entered the room, Ralphie came to an abrupt halt.

Olga Wojdzekevicz had been standing in front of the new Acme Regal Steel Range, keeping a watch over the lentil soup. Before tending to the porcelain-lined reservoir, another of those extravagant properties that Snopkowski had talked Ian into purchasing, Olga Wojdzekevicz beamed momentarily at her visitors. It was a delightfully sunny smile, Sophia had to admit begrudgingly, and one could almost hear the bells ringing in Ralphie's head during that brief exchange. In her dirndl and long yellow braids she was the picture of pastoral simplicity. To complicate matters further, she turned again and flashed a blushing smile directly at Ralphie.

"She good cook, too, Ralphie."

Sophia glanced at Snopkowski, whose smile had become suddenly enigmatic.

"Bully, bully!" Ralphie exclaimed, taking a seat which afforded a good view of Olga Wojdzekevicz.

Somehow Sophia had the uncomfortable feeling that all this was not mere happenstance.

*   *   *

"Don't you think I look fetching, Max?"

Arthur's adopted falsetto was eerie, almost nauseating.

"I like you much better with the veil before your face, Arthur. That is the *only* saving factor in your ludicrous getups. My eyes need not be offended by that sieve you call a countenance."

Arthur Hartleigh had stumbled dopily into Toberman's study for inspection. He was clearly excited over his next assignment. These moments had become oddly stimulating to him, however much he might protest; with the elimination of Vincent, he felt he had gained a certain status. Max might despise him, but his usefulness was no longer in doubt.

"But, Max," he protested, "I shopped all over and found this dress just for you! You must admit, I still have the *figure* for it. What *are* a few blemishes, after all, but the chronicle of a life lived lustily?"

He pursed his lips as if to simulate a kiss. Arthur's transvestism, though convenient at times, always reminded Toberman of the depths to which he'd sunk in the struggle to finish his work.

"You know, Miss Meredith, the trouble with you is you never, *never* quit your damn probing. Why don't you take a night off like any normal guy?"

Allison bowed her head and seemed to be biting her lip.

Nathan McBride's melancholia had also seemed to fade, but those who knew him well enough were aware that it had merely gone deeper into his soul. There were little hints here and there, like prolonged daydreaming and unexpected touchiness.

One morning he had crawled out of bed and within minutes had realized that the lameness had disappeared from his knee. Ordinarily those first few steps had always been the most painful. The men at the precinct station had taken to riding him good-naturedly about his "newspaper knee." A few days after his knee had ceased to trouble him, Nathan had discarded the sling. The pain in his shoulder had diminished to the extent that it was now possible to exercise for short periods with light weights, but he was not yet ready for the punching bag.

Punching an inanimate object, stupid as it might appear, would have eased some of the psychological pressure. Beneath it all, Nathan still felt degraded, like some sort of a machine that could be turned off and forgotten. He had yielded, however, to Blakeley's prohibition, muttering only a few resentful words and nodding begrudging agreement.

Nathan settled into a satisfying morning routine. After a brisk workout and warm bath he would eat a breakfast of porridge, bacon, and eggs with tea and honey and would report to work by seven o'clock. It was by far the best part of the day.

The nights were, nevertheless, fraught with discomfort. Because he would tax himself to the bounds of exhaustion, hoping to put his disenchantment aside, the still-tender wound in his shoulder would start to throb just as he felt himself drifting uneasily into sleep. Then a sharp pain would awaken him abruptly, and soon the memories would take over.

Sometimes he would succeed in focusing his thoughts on the case, for it was supremely challenging. One would almost believe, Blakeley had grumbled recently, that Max Toberman was especially favored by the whimsical gods. They had expected, for good reason, to have put him away by now. But the best he could be called to this moment was a prime suspect. Max Toberman's motive, for one important thing, was no more than outlandish conjecture, and Blakeley was convinced that this was no random sadist. To barge into his office armed with nothing more than what had been gathered thus far would surely result in fuel to fire the pages of a hundred Stanley Butterfields. Repeatedly, during the past week, Nathan had assisted Owen Ward-Lattimore in the late hours as they sought the presence of secret passages and other telltale matters in Toberman's office. That alone was risking the greatest wrath of City Hall.

Just as they were convinced that he could at least be got on the obvious grounds of illegal entry into the country and fraudulent medical practice, Blakeley had been notified by the county medical association that Toberman did, in fact, exist. His records, unfortunately misplaced for a time, had been found and were impeccable. Now they ran the risk of being accused of harassing a noted surgeon and endocrinologist with degrees from Heidelberg, Bologna, and Edinburgh. On paper, not only did Toberman appear competent, but the impression was that of a dedicated medical practitioner of unselfish character and pristine work habits—a second Hippocrates working quietly on a modest middle-class street.

Miss Meredith had proved herself a marvel at the art of resurrecting pertinent odds and ends. This morning she had presented one piece of evidence, a fragment of an old diary, which had fascinated them. According to the anonymous writer, a slave from Virginia whose scrawled sentiments were both disjointed and touching, the house on Calvert had been part of the old Underground Railroad. The house in those days—it was forty years ago and the paper was brittle and yellowed by time—belonged to a German family named Lenhardt. Ernst Helmut Lenhardt, a minister from Dortmund, had been a leader in the abolitionist movement, a follower of John Brown, and a man who had campaigned among his countrymen for Thaddeus Stevens. Hence, the use of his house for the good of the antislavery cause was understandable. Much of the day had been devoted to attempting an interpretation of the document, but the private reminiscences of that unknown and probably unidentifiable young woman had also been in Toberman's favor. Key words were missing from eroded margins or blurred by water that had seeped through cracks in the ceiling of the museum room where Miss Meredith had been spending her spare hours lately. Occasionally Nathan, Hudson, and Ward-Lattimore had almost agreed on the location of one subterranean channel or another, only to fall into irritable bickering over the vagueness and cryptic language of the strange little work.

"That lady," Hudson had said finally, "if she could have imagined three grown men acting like this over her childhood fantasies!"

Ward-Lattimore had been, nevertheless, encouraged. Several evenings earlier, while feeling his way around Toberman's office, to which he had found access once again by way of a poorly latched rear entrance, he had all but determined that there was something, set into a hollow space, probably a safe, behind the instrument cabinet. More important, he had all but cracked the code to Toberman's safe. But the means had been perilous enough to cause Blakeley to order the curtailment of all such expeditions for the time being.

Ward-Lattimore had been tapping ever so gently on the wall when all of a sudden a door had swung open and a strange, bird-like creature had stumbled into the room. Ward-Lattimore had been able to ease silently into a corner in the darkness. The creature had seemed quite lost in its own cloudy world. Intent upon something within the safe, it had made its way through the office furniture, grunting odd little noises as it pulled the medicine cabinet aside and exposed the safe. Ward-Lattimore, gratified that he had been correct, stood frozen as his strange visitor fumbled with the combination. Since he allowed for occasional extra digits born of the creature's stupor, his trained ears had calculated the vital numbers with more precision— in his words—than most other human senses could have determined the shape and color of a melon.

This he had proudly averred later. But then Blakeley, under new pressure from City Hall, had got the full story and had issued his cease-and-desist order.

"Damned unimaginative of you, gov'ner," Ward-Lattimore said before going off to play billiards.

Hudson had been much less contentious than usual. There had been no more Hattie Rau cases. Besides his unexpected break in the Bowman case and the convenience of having Fatzinger quietly occupied in Zoltan Mroszek's cell, there had been further, incontrovertible evidence brought against the Reverend Richard Hopkins. To no one's real surprise, one of those who had stepped forward was Angela Whittingham's plain, older sister, Betsy. Although, for obvious reasons, her testimony was considered questionable, Betsy had attested to not one but several incidents in the young man's chambers. As she put it, the affair before her sister's death had not been traumatic, and she had dismissed it from her conscience. But last week, after Angela's tragedy had passed from the preacher's memory and he had proceeded to loosen her outer garments, Betsy Whittingham had found him and his holy crusade repulsive. "I want to be there when you hang him," she had sobbed. "I want to watch him kicking the air."

Hudson's "good holy pharisee" was now locked securely in a cell where the outraged Fatzinger could keep an eye on him. Fatzinger could not stand hypocrisy. Zoltan, improving physically but acting mad as a hatter, now tormented the furious Reverend Hopkins about his "teenage tattletales."

Life in Hudson's precinct would have been almost idyllic were it not for the activities of an exhibitionist operating in the area around Forty-sixth and Langley. The descriptions offered by the shaken observers had varied in size, color, and shape anywhere from a gray-haired, gaunt Caucasian to a Chinese dwarf carrying a long leathern club. Hudson's men had no doubt about his identity; his name was Daniel Irving Chamberlain, also known as Dirty Daniel, Irving the Bum, and the Lordly Lilywaver, once an almost successful playwright, now a hanger-on in the university district, who favored hashish and surprise encounters at sunrise. For the most part he had chosen to display his wares to the shopgirls and office workers who waited for trolleys at isolated stops, ducking out of wooded areas and disappearing just as suddenly after his performance. Hudson had run him in personally over the years, once for opening his trousers in the lobby of the Locust Street Theater during intermission of a production of *Romeo and Juliet* and again for displaying his backside through the window of the English Department at the university one morning as Professor Fitzwalter was preparing a lecture on dramatic form. The lieutenant's men were, however, unable to act on their suspicions since all of Chamberlain's victims had thus far either chosen to remain silent or gave their statements with such confusion that the department had been rendered helpless. Chamberlain, meanwhile, was obviously enjoying himself.

The early morning had been chilly, but with a heavy dew on the hedges under Nathan's window and the ladies draped in woolen shawls as they scurried past his door on the way to work. Watching them, he had thought of Hudson and the Lordly Lilywaver and laughed to himself. Most of the morning had been overcast, with the fog rising slowly, clouding the horizon until just before noon. It was a welcome departure after the oppressive heat of the early summer. By late afternoon a light rain had fallen, and in the evening a soft, steady mist hung in the air. In the parks, away from the crowds and street noise, the perfume of the foliage drifted in the breeze like the delicate, hypnotic call of a Lorelei.

One steaming mid-morning, while on his way from the precinct station to Dr. Blakeley's estate, he chanced upon Harry Hackett's place of business. Nathan thought it was somewhere on Sanders Road near Fifty-second, but he had never noticed it before. Hackett truly was a forgettable figure, and his funeral parlor was merely one of the precinct's many little establishments. It might have come to his attention earlier had burglars not had their superstitions, making it a custom to ignore such places. It had not occurred straightaway to Nathan that it was Hackett before him.

There stood a loud, officious man about thirty, a formal hat resting jauntily on the side of his head, frock coat slung over his arm, and perspiration staining the back of his shirt. He was mopping his brow and fussing with some attendants over the arrangement of the flowers in the rear of his hearse. He seemed particularly irked at one helper, an elderly man who, having seen many more serious storms in his time, found it easy to ignore him.

Presently the old gentleman waved Hackett aside with a trifling gesture, and Hackett walked away, flustered. Nathan looked on with disgust, thinking seriously of assault and battery, as Hackett cranked up his lustrous new Oldsmobile and putted away at the head of the funeral train. Vaguely Nathan could recall the portly little undertaker's interest in horseless vehicles that dark day in the hospital. He'd been dumped for that. It was degrading.

Hackett was the kind of creature, Nathan imagined, who probably had a perpetually runny nose as a kid and had no doubt had pimples in his adolescence. It was sickeningly obvious that a baby whale like that would need someone like Aidan beside him in his gaudy-new carriage. So much for impotent rage. . . .

"Why don't you have some lunch, Nate?" the bartender at Nellie's remonstrated in his unsubtle manner. "It's free."

"No poison tonight, Toes, whatever the price," Nathan answered pouring some ice water into his glass of rye.

He would sleep all night if it took a barrel of rye and the worst hangover in history to do it. It was the first night in a week that Blakeley had not given him a problem to solve, and he was beginning to feel his nerves departing. In that fashion Nathan spent the greater part of the evening.

It was chilly now. The evening drizzle had drenched the glen, and the fog had returned. It was not far from the river, and now and then the foghorns in the near distance sounded as if they were on the other side of the hanging willow trees.

The small clearing had been their favorite rendezvous, and he wondered as he shivered on the damp bench what had possessed him to come here. It was, of all places in the hemisphere, the most melancholy. So many times, in their stolen moments, he had met Aidan here in the glen amid the shrubs and ivy. They sat on this bench, sometimes in silence, sometimes speaking in hushed tones of their dreams and wishes for each other. Always close, always hand in hand, they had made it their place.

The chill cleared his head, leaving him with the taste of old whiskey and the familiar feelings of emptiness. He slipped a piece of candy into his mouth and sniffed the air. The scent of honeysuckle was all around.

Nathan rested his head against a post behind the bench. He had been there for a half hour, shivering occasionally, slumped like an inanimate object, lost in his depression. He closed his eyes to dream.

"Nathan." The voice was gentle, almost as if it were borne on the light rain. He turned slowly.

"Sometimes, Nathan, they say we learn to love our disappointments if we dwell on them long enough."

"Miss Meredith, what are you doing here? Does Blakeley want me?"

"No, Dr. Blakeley doesn't want you. I've come here on my own."

"I see."

He looked up and watched as she drifted out of the fog. Under the dull light from a gaslamp she was almost spectral in her black and gray autumn coat. He was not certain he wanted company, but he stumbled to his feet instinctively.

"I've seen you much more graceful, Nathan."

"I never told you I was Petipa."

"You never told me much of anything," she said softly.

His flippant comment made her turn abruptly silent. In a moment she regained her pride and began to walk away. But for some reason he could not bring himself at this moment to say something glib. He thought later that it was the sight of her damp, uncomfortable-looking shoes or the weary, almost vulnerable cast of her eye.

"Please don't go, Miss Meredith," he said impulsively. Her steps became hesitant as she drifted under the gaslamp.

He caught up with her there, and when she faced him, he detected tears in the corners of her eyes. He felt like someone who had just broken a delicate glass figurine.

"Miss Meredith, is there anything wrong?" he asked.

She shook her head.

"Look," he fumbled. "I'm terribly sorry. I guess—that is, I know—I'm a very inconsiderate man." He paused and gave her a moment to collect herself. "Is there anything I can do?" he asked awkwardly.

"You're going to make your rouge run that way, you know."

She remained motionless. He pulled a dry handkerchief from his lapel.

"I don't wear rouge, Nathan," she answered, accepting his handkerchief.

"Well, in that case, you'll wilt your eyelashes."

Both were silent for a few clumsy seconds. Nathan saw regrettable memories flash into and out of his brain. The setting was the same, but the figures were different: incongruous lines, incongruous motives. He wanted to caress her but did not dare, for he had no reason to believe that she would understand his hurt. He did not fully comprehend it. He only knew that right now he longed for something soft and warm in his arms.

"Why have you come here, Miss Meredith?" he ventured, his voice taut.

"You're very shortsighted, Nathan."

It dawned on him slowly that she had been calling him by his first name ever since she'd found him there. He grappled for a recollection of her own first name, not wishing to disturb the fragile peace that she had apparently been determined to make. The name came back to him. It was lovely.

"Let's just say I have a tendency to become absorbed in the commonplace, Allison."

He asked her if she wished to find a drier place in which to talk, and she replied that if he had no serious objections, she would prefer to go home. He steered the small carriage through the mist toward her apartment on the other side of the neighborhood. She had seated herself close to him, but told himself that was only for warmth. Steam rose as they talked, wreathing their faces. Smoke rose from chimneys in the neighborhood as fireplaces were suddenly pressed back into service by the shivering populace.

They talked at great length about nothing in particular, how or why she had tracked him down in the foggy glen tactfully avoided. The thin, fashionable striped blazer he had thrown on hours earlier clung to his body now like sodden burlap, and Dr. Blakeley had warned him about the danger of catching a chill before his strength had fully returned. It had sounded patronizing at the time. He braced himself and hoped that Allison would not detect his intermittent shuddering. As the drowsy clopping of the horse's hooves echoed through the quiet streets, he noticed her head tilting toward him as it had once before. This time he felt no pangs of conflict. It wasn't really bad the first time, whatever he may have told himself then. Something about Allison Meredith had been planted in his soul from the start.

"Why *did* you come looking for me?" he pressed finally. Nathan had the feeling that there were odds and ends to clear up before she drifted off to sleep.

"I allowed myself to dream," she murmured.

Arriving at her home after a half hour or so, he helped her from the carriage and walked her to the door, awkwardly struggling with his wants and needs on the one hand and his better judgment on the other.

"You look like a pneumonia candidate, Nathan," she said. "I have some brandy inside."

She was standing so near that he could pick up the scent of her cologne, despite the breeze wafting up the avenue. She was the only one who had ever worn it—several occasions now recurred to him— and he'd guessed it to be of French origin. A delicate gardenia, understated but intoxicating, it had always seemed appropriate for Allison Meredith.

"Are you, are you sure I'm not keeping you up?" It was past midnight.

"Don't you want to come in?"

"I'd . . . Well, I think I'd . . . "

"You're stammering, Nathan. Very unlike you. You've usually had something acute to offer." She smiled. "It's very good brandy. I've had it for some time, and I only pour it for special people."

She touched his hand lightly, and he stared back at her incredulously.

"Actually"—she shook her head in mock seriousness—"that's not true. In point of fact, Nathan, I've never opened it. When you come inside, you'll observe that the seal is as yet intact. You see, I've been waiting for the right company."

Nathan was having trouble convincing himself that he was not some sort of intruder. More than anything, he wanted to believe that this was all part of reality, but he had his own inexplicable misgivings.

"You have a funny way, forgive my saying, of selecting your company, Miss Meredith."

"How so, Detective McBride?"

Her tone was serious, but the look in her great blue eyes was playful as she peered up at him. Nathan was straining to keep his distance but losing ground by the minute.

"You haven't exactly led me to believe that I could tower over a gnat."

"You know, Detective McBride, the trouble with you is you never, *never* quit your damned probing. Why don't you take a night off like any normal guy?"

The words seemed out of place, coming from Miss Meredith, but the quote was well taken. They laughed at his earlier hostility.

"I've reached a point," she said, shivering now in a sudden breeze that had swept up the cobbled street, "when I have to make some sense of it. Peace of mind, I suppose, is what I'm talking about."

"You're going to catch cold, Allison. And then Dr. Blakeley will no doubt think I've kidnapped you and caused. . . ."

"Let me finish, Nathan," she whispered. "This is no easy thing for me, however it may seem to you."

There was a plea in her voice, and it silenced him. Somewhere in the distance a dog was barking in its backyard. Otherwise the section of town, with its fog and empty sidewalks, belonged to them. Allison's words, uttered haltingly, were clear.

"I've been waiting for you to come to me and say things like this, but I suppose the cards were stacked against me, what with your own concerns in recent weeks. And so I've come to you, sought you out, to make amends. We're both very headstrong, as I'm sure you've heard Dr. Blakeley mutter, and I don't really know how it all began, but, Nathan, ever since I've met you, whatever I may have said or done to drive you away from me, I've had you on my mind from waking to sleeping. Lord knows, I've tried to forget you. I've tried everything from pretending you didn't exist to cursing the sun over your head and the ground on which you've walked. Still, you remain. In the back of my mind or, worse yet, deep in my heart, you hang on. And so, you see, I felt I had to do something, *anything* to set matters straight between us."

Nathan had been standing still, listening intently even though the words were disquieting. As he started to answer, she stopped him.

"Anyone who heard me now would surely think me forward. I realize these are a man's prerogatives, chasing you down and saying such things, but, heavens, Nathan, I'd be an old woman before you'd ever get around to noticing me on your own!"

Her voice had suddenly risen above a whisper. Nathan, perhaps unconsciously, had taken her hand in his and was holding it tightly.

"I've wanted to clear the air, too, Allison."

He was about to take her in his arms when, somewhere in the mist, they heard a tapping. In a moment, while Nathan stepped back in awkward silence, a neat old gentleman in tweed cape and bowler made his way along the sidewalk with the aid of a cane, tipped his hat to Allison, and went on up the street.

They were still apart when the old gentleman had drifted back into the fog. Nathan's eyes followed him as his silhouette disappeared on the other side of a gaslight, then looked back to Allison, who seemed to be waiting anxiously despite the stolid look she tried to affect. He stepped forward and took her by the arms.

"Unless I'm dreaming this, Allison, you've come into my life at a time when it can only be good for me but may be very difficult for you. I don't suppose you've missed my darker moods lately. Your life could be a long series of that sort of thing—that is, if I follow your meaning correctly."

"If I were not a gambler, dear Nathan, would I have said as much as I have so far?"

He held her tightly and ignored the chill as she raised her lips to meet his.

"Do you like baseball?" he asked after a while, apparently out of caprice.

"I'll have you know," she answered steadily, "that I can run, throw, and hit better and with more consistency than do any of the men in my family, all of them superb athletes. And I go out to Baker Field at any opportunity. I can even tell you why Delahanty and Lajoie aren't meeting their averages. They have their minds only on home runs. They've forgotten how to get on base."

"Good Lord," Nathan whispered. "A rare gem. A truly perfect woman."

They entered her apartment. Nathan followed her somewhat uncertainly, taking a seat on the divan and studying the paintings that hung on the opposite wall. She had some excellent copies of Cezanne, Renoir, Seurat, and Van Gogh, all of them collected, he presumed, in her travels. The works in her bookcase were also European and up-to-date, and he felt just a bit alien to the tidy little room with the pastel shades and ubiquitous scent of musk. Off in a corner, facing the street, was a small office area with a desk, a typewriter, two or three note pads, and many heavily bound manuscripts.

The air was warm, and she had prevailed upon him to remove his coat in order to give it time to dry. She reappeared from the kitchen, bearing a glass of exquisite crystal. They shared the brandy. The candlelight flickered in the draft from the fireplace, casting shadows on the ceiling as they faced the soft flames, each forgetting the cold of the night outside.

How long Nathan had remained there, what conditions had obtained between him and Allison Meredith, never became matters of casual disclosure.

Following that evening, Blakeley often felt himself an outsider in their midst.

Twenty

"In truth, Mr. Mroszek, the Bowman case means nothing more to me than the outcome of a marbles match in Lithuania. I've been preoccupied with other affairs. There's a war on, for one thing. Or have you not heard? Silly question—of course, you haven't. It's much too mundane an affair for a man of your tastes."

"The Bowman case is no isolated matter, I'm certain. It has to be related to bigger and better things, such as the Butcher. Otherwise, I'd have been flung into the penitentiary instead of becoming your star patient. Is that not so?"

"Mr. Mroszek, if you do not stop waving your arms about, I shall have to put you into a straitjacket again. You could do damage to my instruments this way. Now, do be good and sit still while I administer this hypodermic."

"That means the tests are over. Will I then be permitted my morning glass of wine?"

"Certainly. I'm only injecting you with a vitamin and mineral complex. Nothing more exotic than that."

"Ah, good. . . . 'Rich the treasure, Sweet the pleasure—Sweet is pleasure after pain.' . . . Do you recognize that, *mon cher médecin?*"

"Most assuredly. It's from John Dryden's 'Alexander's Feast.' I've often quoted it to my children when they've sulked over having to eat their vegetables. This won't hurt, Mr. Mroszek. As you can see, the needle isn't very long. Just concentrate on those apothecary jars on the windowsill. Note how pretty the colors are."

"I'm not so completely worthless as all that, Dr. Blakeley. My life has simply taken some horrid turns, keeping me ever distant from the smallest of my dreams. When your Browning said, 'A man's reach should exceed his grasp,' he had no idea of the spaces *I* would someday encounter. *My* goals have long resembled the dark miles of the galaxy."

"Self-pity, Mr. Mroszek? You disappoint me."

"I may presume, then, You'll recognize these lines, also from Dryden, only from one of his tragedies, Dr. Blakeley. Quite à propos for my epitaph:

> When I consider life, 'tis all a cheat.
> Yet fool'd with hope, men favour the deceit;
> Trust on, and think tomorrow will repay.
> Tomorrow's falser than the former day;
> Lies worse, and while it says we shall be blest
> With some new joys, cuts off what we possest.
> Strange cozenage! None would live past years again,
> Yet all hope pleasure in what yet remain;
> And from the dregs of life think to receive
> What the first sprightly running could not give.

I believe I have you there, Dr. Blakeley. Surely, in all your efforts at the art of healing, or in the so-called honorable arena of the law, the good poet's words must have seemed an apt epistle to humankind."

"No. It's much too long for the ordinary gravestone, for one thing, unless you expect to be interred at Westminster Abbey. Why don't you consider these lines from the same poet, spoken shortly thereafter within the same act, same scene, if I may trust my memory.

> 'Tis not for nothing that we life pursue;
> It pays our hopes with something still that's new.

A better rhyme, I'd say; much less cumbersome, much less pompous, no?"

Blakeley carefully replaced the medicines and instruments in his heavy leather bag and suppressed a smile. He had grown to look forward to these little sessions. Zoltan was surprisingly acute, and his memory, astonishingly, had not suffered from all the abuse he had given his brain. Today it was Dryden, yesterday Donne, and Dostoevsky had been featured the day before that. Tomorrow it would have to be Emerson as Zoltan worked his way up the alphabet.

There had been times recently when he might have appeared jubilant over Zoltan's progress. It would not do to tip his hand just yet; Zoltan Mroszek would no doubt retreat deep within again if the challenge were taken away.

And then, too, there was the damned case. It made it so bloody difficult to smile over anything. Even Ralphie's abrupt return and the tale of his mysterious malady had offered only fleeting reassurance that the earth was indeed on its proper axis.

"Those paintings. They're mine."

"I say, you can't have it both ways."

"I can *prove* it. I shall describe the technique I used, and—supposing this expert of yours knows air from water—you shall see that Zoltan Mroszek is truly an unrecognized genius."

Blakeley envisioned Sophia's joy at being finally exonerated. If it were not a cruel jest, this, above all, would restore the peace at Blakeley manor.

"Tomorrow morning," he answered noncommittally.

Blakeley rapped on the bars of the cell. Zoltan reminded him that he had been promised a better quality of wine in that morning's ration. Blakeley nodded that it would be as stipulated, and after a bit of inconsequential growling on Zoltan's part, Fatzinger arrived to open the cell.

"Vell, vell," chirped Fatzinger with assumed heartiness, "und chust how iss our leedle patient procrastinatin' to treatment dis mornin'?"

"Dr. Blakeley—groaned Zoltan—"*must* I be exposed to this *rustic* for the entirety of my incarceration? It were far better to hang me."

"Eh? I thought you were close friends. If I may quote Izaak Walton: 'As the Italians say, Good company in a journey makes the way to seem the shorter.' I daresay you could not have been more appropriately mated had I selected Officer Fatzinger myself."

"Sir Izaak was no doubt speaking of *fish*. This odorous, worm-eaten offspring of a swineherd and a congenital imbecile. . . . One would think that I'd attempted to assassinate your President!"

"Huh?" Fatzinger looked about insipidly. "Vott iss. . . ."

"Yesterday, Dr. Blakeley, your constable sat in that chair by the window, cutting off what little light I have, staring at me with those beady eyes of his, ingesting the foulest-smelling sausages in the Western world. It's insidious!"

"Dott does it!" Fatzinger's face turned suddenly livid, and he threw his uniform helmet to the floor. Stumping about the cell he howled, "Dose vassn't sausages, by Christ! Dose vass chenuine *bull's balls* vott Strawberry Knockelknorr pickled herself chust for me. Dey vass gave to me outa true love an' emotion—an' she broke her big fat ass to do it! By Cheesuss, dott's no easy chob, yuh know."

"Officer Fatzinger, please," said Blakeley, stifling a smile.

"I'd like to see *him* chasin' down dott bull an' cuttin' off its personals. If yuh ask me, *he's* da sausage!"

"Officer Fatzinger, please," Blakeley repeated, "you shall overexcite our patient."

"I would call your attention, Dr. Blakeley," said Zoltan, "to the Eighth Amendment to the Constitution, which guarantees: 'Excessive bail shall not be required, nor excessive fines imposed, *nor cruel and unusual punishment inflicted.*' I ask you: Does my status as a suspect, witness, or whatever call for such treatment?"

Fatzinger's ire, still unabated, seemed to sublimate momentarily as he struggled to interpret Zoltan's question. His mouth fell open, and as he scratched his head, Blakeley was reminded of a rooster surveying a barnyard.

"Vell, if dott don't take da prize fer fibbin', den I'll be a sow's tiddy," Fatzinger said at length. "Fer two veeks in here I bin shtuck, vit him vorse den a billy goat shtinkin'. An' he says *I* offend *his* self-interests. It's enough to make a fella *lose* his appetite. To da commissioner I'm gonna complain about dis."

With that he took his seat under the window and, sulking, opened a lunch pail that was filled with pig's knuckles and Limburger and onion sandwiches. "Yah, dott's it," he reiterated with determination, "to da commissioner I'm gonna write—chust as soon as I finish off dese here eadts."

In his own way, Blakeley considered, Lieutenant Hudson had had the wisdom of Solomon when he had condemned these two to each other. It was a little like pairing Caliban with Launcelot Gobbo.

Ellen Sundgard arose at six, dressed hurriedly, and stole out of the house as quietly as possible. Moving carefully, so as not to soil her suffragette uniform, she cut across the bountiful fields of the old estate, hitched up the small surrey, and guided it out of the stable. It took more than a quarter hour to put the estate far behind her.

Ellen's grandfather had liked this location as soon as he had cast his judicious eyes upon it. That was shortly after he had left his native Norway in 1825, at a time when he had felt the new republic had finally achieved stability. Jens Olaf Sundgaard—the second *a* had been discarded by Ellen's father—had shed no tears of homesickness; he had already made as much money as his old country's economy would allow. And the young American government, with its unrestrictive policies regarding commerce and finance, seemed almost to beckon to men of his special acumen. He had chosen this site expressly because of its relative isolation. Adjoining the estate was the fifty-acre Brandywine Creek Battlefield, a national shrine to which few visitors ever came because the Colonial forces had been routed there by the British and Hessians in 1777.

The Sundgaard empire had grown vast by the year of 1898. Jens Olaf Sundgaard had wasted no time in investing where America most needed his dollars, the great, expanding West. And now the single-minded courage of young Ellen Sundgaard's grandfather had yielded a legacy of holdings in cattle, wheat, oil, and iron ore. With the outbreak of hostilities several months ago, those holdings had almost doubled in value.

Some tenacious gene had given Ellen Sundgaard a touch of her grandfather's grit. As Wandalee Hinch had said, and as she and Rosalie Blakeley had agreed, their cause was much more important than the liberation of a pack of filthy heathens on some faraway island. And they were not going to permit the men of Philadelphia to deter them with tales of the Butcher.

The march *must* go on. Wandalee had called this the supreme moment.

It was shortly after eight thirty when Blakeley left Mroszek's cell. He sat for a few minutes with Lieutenant Hudson and drank a cup of coffee. The one blessing that precinct stations had to offer was the constant flow of dark, rich coffee that seemed to be part of every office. The aroma was a pleasant change from the odors in the prison cell.

"You should have been here a few months ago, Doc," Hudson said. "It was really good then. I think the Army gets the best of it nowadays."

"Wait till we take Cuba," promised an officer at a nearby desk. "Then we'll have some real coffee. This stuff is half sawdust."

Hudson was worried about a lawsuit which was pending against the department because of something he had done last winter. Life, he complained, was governed not by justice but by the laws of irony.

The courts, he had good reason to believe, were never severe enough with those who had been cruel to children. The courts were never severe enough, period.

"They'd probably let John Wilkes Booth off with disturbing the peace if the lawyers and judges had had a chance at that one," he insisted.

"Two things really infuriate me, Dr. Blakeley, just two things: cruelty to animals and cruelty to children. The rest of it, as far as I'm concerned after all my years on the force, is just part of the goddamn game."

Respectable enough on the surface, Jack Ferris sold legitimate medicines for a living and attended church services regularly. Dressed in dark gray and always well groomed, he seemed to be the height of temperance and middle-class rectitude. Hudson had even attempted, on two occasions, to book Ferris, but both efforts had died in court, victims of legalistic red tape and cowardly rulings. Jack Ferris' little girl—five years old—had met with too many inexplicable accidents, and there had been so many head injuries that he had begun to fear the onset of brain damage. Being a neighbor of Ferris', Hudson had heard the cries in the night which had suggested something more than normal juvenile frustration. And finally, when one of the men, Officer Duffy, had brought Ferris in during the Christmas season, Hudson had heard quite enough. The little girl's cheeks were black and blue, and her eyes bore such a look of broken spirit that Hudson's heart sank when he noticed her. Ferris' wife, who had sworn she would press charges, stood by, nursing a swollen lip and an eye that was all but closed.

"Look at what you did to your wife and little girl. You'd have to be a pretty good boxer to do that, wouldn't you?"

No response.

"Answer me, you son of a bitch."

"What are you getting at?" Ferris had asked after another awkward pause.

Taking Ferris by the scruff of the neck, Hudson had dragged him into an isolated back room. Some three minutes later Jack Ferris had staggered semiconscious out of the room with one broken cheekbone, two broken ribs, a bloody nose, a three-inch cut over his eyebrow, and minus most of his front teeth. At the time the cowed, tubercular-looking Mrs. Ferris had sworn triumphantly that her husband had got only what he richly deserved, that she would still press charges, and that from that evening on she and the little girl would never again live under the same roof with Jack Ferris.

Hudson had personally telephoned for medical attention once it had been suspected that bone fractures were involved, and Jack Ferris had slept quietly through the night.

But that was all merely part of the fleeting spirit of the time. No charges had been pressed, Jack Ferris' wife had posted bond two days later, and the courts had reunited the Ferris family within the space of a week. Now there lay open on Hudson's desk a letter from the commissioner's office demanding an accounting from Hudson. Jack Ferris, with his wife and daughter as witnesses, was charging the police department with verbal abuse, assault with intent to maim, and assault with a deadly weapon—the latter, once again, because of Hudson's history as a prizefighter long ago. Another ambitious attorney had found in Hudson the perfect villain and the ideal catalyst for reams of cheap publicity.

"Why me?" Hudson asked wearily.

"Because you're too honest, Lieutenant," Blakeley replied thoughtfully. "You allow your sense of justice to get in the way. You'll never be devious enough to survive in the bureaucracy." Hudson sighed and sipped his coffee.

"And what of your exhibitionist, Lieutenant?" Blakeley inquired, thinking to introduce something of a lighter note. "Have you caught up with him yet?"

"Talk about a weasel," Hudson answered, shrugging. "We've had our plainclothsmen watching every cultural event in the vicinity; we've even had decoys posted here and there dressed as shopgirls. You know, around the trolley stops in the mornings—he pops up there mostly. So what does he do? Last night he stayed home evidently. Then this morning he showed himself to the nuns over at Saint Malachy's Convent. You should have heard the uproar *that* caused."

Stepping out of the station to look for a cab, Blakeley tipped his hat to some ladies. Their conversation went on uninterrupted as they acknowledged him and passed by. Perhaps, he thought wishfully, they'd forgotten his face by now. It had not appeared in the newspapers lately. A welcome change, that. He petted a passing mutt and watched a blacksmith at work in the shade near a livery stable. The rains of the previous night had bathed the air, leaving the morning sunny and cool with a steady breeze still gusting over the broader streets. For the first time in many weeks Blakeley had donned his plus fours and Norfolk jacket, a fashion he had favored after his last visit to London. Tweed was so civilized, but so impossible to wear in this damned climate. Of course, he could never be certain that Sophia approved of his looking so much like Bernard Shaw, whom she regarded as frightfully libertine. A windbag, yes, but no hedonist. In any case, Shaw dressed well. Not at all so conspicuously as some of those other artistic chaps. Like that strange Mr. Wilde used to dress, in his evening wear at noon or that Whistler fellow in his straw hats with the long, trailing bands—no doubt something Zoltan Mroszek would wish to wear, should he ever cease to equate personal squalor with self-denial and inner purity.

He hailed a cab and dodged the spray from its wheels as it pulled up beside him through a muddy section of the street. It was nine o'clock, and the neighborhood was fully awake by now. Through the narrow roadways vendors with pushcarts called attention to their goods while horse-drawn wagons rumbled over the inner lanes. In a short while his cab had made its way through the heavy traffic to the avenue and was able to move at a steadier pace.

Time was running out on the Lester Figge ultimatum. It was a matter of only a few more days.

Worse than that, Blakeley wondered just how much more time the Butcher himself would allow. According to the pattern, a disappearance was overdue.

"You there—Rosalie Blakeley. That will be quite enough out of you, young lady. Just hold that flag up where all can observe it and cease your banter." Wandalee Hinch, as the story went, had given up everything for her cause.

There were skeptics, even among her adoring suffragettes, who tended to place their belief in quite another story. For it was also said that Quentin Hinch, after years of oppression and dominance, had actually introduced his burdensome Wandalee to the suffrage movement in hopes of its carrying her off. Instead, after several meetings of the local chapter, Wandalee became more unpleasant. She had begun to stay up nights writing pamphlets, which tended to make her even more unreasonable the next day and prevented the hapless Quentin Hinch from escaping to the corner tavern after bedtime. And then, one morning, Wandalee had announced that she would never again cook a meal, wash a dish, change a diaper, or scrub a floor in obeisance to any man, "least of all you, you little nit."

Quentin Hinch had simply disappeared. It was said he'd gone off to South America. Others claimed he'd been seen in the company of a burlesque entertainer in Atlantic City. In any case, he had not reported to work at the insurance firm that day, and his presence in the world had not been verified since. Wandalee, momentarily stunned, had soon written off Quentin's disappearance as a typical case of male cowardice, and after putting her three children on a train to visit their grandmother in Altoona, had settled into the woman's suffrage campaign with a renewed vengeance.

There were those, though, who firmly believed her to be Elizabeth I reborn with echoes of Caesar and Christ.

"Why does she always jump on me," whispered Rosalie with a strong touch of resentment, "whenever you start acting up, Ellen?"

"Now, you know it works the other way around half of the time," said Ellen Sundgard with an impish smile.

Rosalie, who was carrying the blue and gold banner of the Commonwealth of Pennsylvania, raised it rather huffily into the breeze. Ellen carried the American flag, and a prim third girl who chose to walk somewhat apart from them, bore the purple banner of the movement. Waiting behind them stood some forty marchers bearing placards with angry messages. Wandalee had chosen the three of them for the advance guard because she felt their youth symbolic of a brighter future.

"I think she picks on me." Rosalie pouted.

"It's because you're both so lovely, my dears," said a strange falsettolike voice behind them. "We women are naturally jealous creatures."

They turned and noticed a tall, thin, older woman who was dressed fashionably in tailored plaid. They had seen her before at infrequent suffragette affairs. Leona Hartleigh was her name, Rosalie thought. Through her veil they could see the heavy layers of make-up with which she had tried unsuccessfully to conceal the many unsightly eruptions on her skin. Strength of numbers being of paramount importance to the cause, as they had heard Wandalee pontificate so many times, the members tolerated her habitual silence and sudden outbursts of gibberish.

"Tell me," she cackled, "which of you is the delightful Blakeley girl of whom I've heard so many wonderful things?"

Rosalie and Ellen glanced at each other and giggled; this brought on one more reprimand from the severe Wandalee Hinch. Another outburst of that sort, and they would have to yield their flags and go to the rear.

"Tell me the truth, my dears," pressed Leona Hartleigh sotto voce, holding in her palsied hand a paper bag filled with salt-water taffy. "Tell me which one of you is the daughter of the marvelous Dr. Blakeley, and I'll give you a sweetie. They come all the way from the seashore."

Sophia was at first inclined to regard her husband's tale of Zoltan Mroszek's paintings as something he had fabricated for the benefit of her shrinking self-esteem. When, after looking him straight in the eye for a moment, she found no hint of duplicity, she was so overjoyed that she wanted to kiss Ian. Instead, she forced herself to maintain a nonchalant pose, unaware that her blush was giving her away.

"I told you so," she said, and went on with her work. Having abandoned her portrait of Ralphie after his abrupt and rather embarrassing return, she was now attempting to paint from memory a scene of the pines of Rome.

A familiar din overhead told Ian that Ralphie was nearing the conclusion of his morning exercises. Beginning with a brisk round of calisthenics, Ralphie usually turned thereafter to the chinning bar and pulled himself up fifty or sixty times, raising his legs to a ninety-degree angle each time he did so. His record was one hundred and thirty-one, but he claimed that the Army had so disrupted his routine and that his, well, intestinal affliction had so sapped his strength that it would be weeks before that point could again be reached. After the chinning bar came the barbells. Beginning with light weights, he would work his way up to hundreds of pounds. Sophia had once remarked that standing rigid beneath them, he reminded her of one of those elaborate pillars which formed the bases of Hellenistic temples. Although Sophia found it all somewhat pagan in purpose, Blakeley himself had often sensed, admittedly atavistically, a kind of pride in his son's brute strength. It said something about the peasant origins of the Blakeleys back in the time of Becket and the Plantagenet kings, a stock said to be as sturdy as the best on the island. When at last Ralphie had pressed the ultimate poundage overhead, he was then ready for breakfast. The entire routine lasted anywhere from one hour to two and one-half hours, depending on Ralphie's humor at the time; it took place daily with religious dedication.

Gifted with an unusually powerful body, Blakeley had never been one to take such pains to honor it. There were better things to do in the mornings, especially with Snopkowski's breakfast skills.

The clanking on the floor meant that Ralphie was about to reach his finale. Out of idle curiosity, Blakeley climbed the stairs to Ralphie's room to watch. When he entered, his son, looking straight ahead, seemed nevertheless oblivious of his presence, concentrating on the task at hand.

In a second or two Ralphie squatted, took a very deep breath, and slung what must have been well over three hundred pounds into the air. Holding the weights overhead for a moment, he gritted his teeth until he was satisfied that his arms had locked properly and that he had surmounted the challenge. Then, as gently as if they were twin babies, he lowered the weights to the floor with a grunt.

"Damn," he muttered, "that one almost killed me."

"Good morning, Ralph."

"Oh, hi, Dad. I didn't see you there."

"I know. Tell me, how can you see right through someone of my girth when I'm standing directly before you?"

"Concentration, Dad. I have great powers of concentration."

"I see."

It was good to see Ralphie back to his normal self, tilting at windmills. The only thing that he and Sophia had found particularly annoying was Ralphie's newly adopted Southern accent. Ralphie said everyone sounded like that in the American Army, especially the sergeants.

"How are matters progressing between you and Miss Wojdzekevicz?"

"Hell's fire," grumbled Ralphie as he rubbed himself with a towel, "that ain't agoin' nowheres."

"Ralphie, please, for your mother's sake, do try to speak the language as you have been taught." As he watched Ralphie groping for the proper words, he wondered why he'd asked in the first place. Clearly, Ralphie had come to a difficult crossroads in his heretofore-uncomplicated life.

"It sure ain't easy, Dad."

"What isn't easy, son?"

"Sparking with a girl who doesn't speak a word of English. Gee whiz—she's just about the prettiest girl I ever saw, and I might as well be on the moon for all the closer I can get to her. "

Good heavens, thought Blakeley. He knew that there were at least three young ladies in London whom Sophia had intended Ralphie to meet eventually. That is, as soon as Sophia believed Ralphie to be suited for London society—and that was a process which could take another decade. Ralphie must simply be reacting to his long isolation from feminine companionship.

"Well," Blakeley replied, clearing his throat, "have you asked her aunt for assistance, perhaps by way of some interpretation? Snopkowski is her guardian, and she should be pleased by your interest in her niece."

"Oh, yeah, sure she is, I guess. Only I don't think she trusts me very far, Dad."

Not trust Ralphie? Preposterous. To any but the dullest observer, Snopkowski was ecstatic over Ralphie's interest in her niece. It must be some quirk of her mind.

"Has she said so, Ralphie?"

"She don't have to. If it isn't hard enough courting Olga in sign language, it makes a guy even more nervous knowing Snopkowski's sitting in the next room with a meat cleaver. And if she can't make it, she sends Olga's dumb brother Casimir. And he just sits there a few feet away from us. No kidding, Dad, he just bobs his head like this." Ralphie did what appeared to be an imitation of the village idiot, which brought a smile to Blakeley's serious eyes.

"And for that I get all spiffed up every evening, put on my uniform, pick some flowers, and go to visit her in the kitchen."

Blakeley decided to change the unsolvable subject.

"Does your Miss Wojdzekevicz prepare as ample a breakfast as her Aunt Snopkowski usually does? For a change I've come home to enjoy it and I have an appetite to rival yours this morning."

"Gosh, Dad, *does* she! That's how I know she likes me! Yesterday she must have given me twenty-five waffles. Jiminy!"

Ralphie put a robe over his exercise togs. The two repaired to the patio, where Olga Wojdzekevicz had placed liberal servings of Polish sausages, potato pancakes, and fried eggs before Ralphie's customary seat. When their eyes met, she and Ralphie exchanged coy smiles, which did not go unnoticed by the others.

"Bully, bully," Ralphie enthused, licking his lips and rubbing his hands briskly. From a window several stories overhead, Snopkowski beamed victoriously.

"Don't bully-bully me, young sir," snapped Sophia, who had already taken her place at the table. Ralphie, who had been grinning broadly at Olga, gradually turned and looked at Sophia curiously. "Wash your hands first," she explained. "You're no longer living in an Army camp."

"Ah, gee, my food will get cold." He withdrew his hands from the table.

Olga scowled at Sophia. In a moment her hands were on her hips, and her bounteous chest was puffed out like that of a defiant hen.

"Olga will keep it warm for you, I'm sure," said Sophia with a strong touch of annoyance. In England, she would remind Ian later, one never fraternized with the maidservants in quite so bold a fashion.

As if he had taken a cue from Olga, Ralphie frowned and started off toward his room, taking a potato pancake with him.

"And you might remind your sister that it's time for breakfast. In fact, it's one-half hour past the time for breakfast."

"She isn't here," said Ralph, his mouthful of potato pancake muffling his words.

"What? Where is she then?"

"I dunno. She left early this morning around seven thirty—in a big hurry."

Blakeley was suddenly suspicious. He interrupted.

"Did you notice what she was wearing?"

Ralphie was pensive for a moment.

"Oh, yeah," he said, laughing to himself, "those dumb suffragette duds. I was kidding her about them and she called me a dirty—"

"Oh good Lord," gasped Sophia, "the suffrage march! Ian—she's disobeyed us and put herself in danger."

"Get dressed, Ralph," Blakeley suggested calmly. "We must be prepared for any emergency."

"What emergency, Dad?"

"Get dressed, Ralph!" Blakeley repeated. Ralph dashed off to his room.

Olga, who had been observing with irate confusion, departed for the kitchen.

"Sophia, darling, there's nothing to cause us to be panic-stricken yet. Really there isn't. Do drink your tea while it's still warm. We can't very well have you falling ill on us. I've no time for any more patients, you know."

"But . . . you've repeatedly stressed the need for caution, and those warnings—"

"Have probably come from the great god Figge for all we know. He doesn't want me to forget he's watching."

During the past week and a half there had been messages left in odd places, messages which made it clear that someone had the ability to insinuate himself into the safest sectors of Blakeley's world. Indeed, Blakeley had all but made up his mind that it was time for Sophia to take Rosalie back to Kent to be introduced to her heritage. Yesterday, after finding one nailed to the wall of the gazebo, to which he had retreated from the irksome realities of his laboratory, he had contacted the Cunard Line about available berths. Whoever it was, he was certainly closing in.

"Ian. . . . "

"I say, those fried cakes do smell good. You don't suppose Miss Wojdzekevicz would resent my trying a few? And that Polska kielbasa looks exquisite. I've a hunger one could photograph, as they say."

As he started to transfer some of Ralphie's breakfast to his own plate, Olga returned from the kitchen, bearing a steaming bowl. She glared at him, and he placed Ralphie's potato pancakes back on Ralphie's plate. Then she placed the bowl in the center of the table and served them from the bowl, taking great pains to make it clear that she did it under protest.

"Boiled turnips!"

He looked up. Olga, arms crossed and face flushed, stared back at him.

"Is this some sort of correspondence?" asked Sophia angrily.

From above a skein of irate Polish erupted. Olga glanced up and answered in her own defense. This was the first time that either Blakeley or Sophia had realized Snopkowski's surveillance. It was clear that Olga had acted on her own. Once again Blakeley was thankful that Sophia understood none of Snopkowski's vocabulary; judging by the look on Olga's face, Snopkowski was mincing no words.

In a moment, after shaking her fist, Snopkowski slammed the shutters. Olga redistributed Ralphie's breakfast.

"Isn't it wonderful, my dear," said Blakeley, "to know you have such absolute power over all your subjects?"

"*She* is." Rosalie giggled, pointing to Ellen Sundgard as Leona Hartleigh crowed approval.

"Oh, you look just like your mother, Miss Blakeley," said Leona to Ellen. "So delicately beautiful."

Wandalee Hinch blew her tin whistle with grim determination.

The march proceeded down New Church Road, past a real estate office, a bank, and an arms factory, and turned into the brisk wind that blew up Lancaster Avenue. In front of Rosalie Blakeley and the others in the forefront, off-key cornets blared "Onward, Christian Soldiers" with unmistakable resolution. Crowds of curious children gathered, bustling with mischievous intentions. Rosalie steeled herself against the worst and plodded on, looking at Ellen Sundgard through the corner of her eye and listening to the shrill singing voice of Leona Hartleigh, close behind Ellen.

Lieutenant Hudson had just dispatched several more patrolmen to the parade route, just in case this suffragette march proved akin to many of its antecedents, when an attorney for the department entered his office, armed with a notebook and a set of questions. Hudson realized that the commissioner had decided to place the burden of the lawsuit squarely upon him.

"You can save yourself a lot of grief by cooperating with me, Lieutenant Hudson," the lawyer said after Hudson expressed his thorough contempt for all concerned. City Hall's timing was always so perfect.

"Now why the hell should I cooperate with you and that pack of rodents downtown?"

"Well, Lieutenant, then let's talk about rank or, better yet, pensions."

"Careful now. You'd like to go back to City Hall in the same condition in which you left, I'm sure."

"I am well aware of your penchant for fisticuffs, Lieutenant Hudson. Indeed, it's what has brought me here in the first place. Do calm yourself." The attorney backed up, Hudson having come around to the front of his desk.

The march continued to gather onlookers. Most were ominously silent, but a few shouted ugly epithets.

"Why are they so vicious?" Rosalie wondered aloud.

"As Wandalee puts it, 'Birth is never without its painful side.' We can't expect the New Dawn to come easily," answered Ellen. "Remember the Crucifixion."

The flags rippled in the wind and, at times, seemed almost to pull their bearers backward. Leona Hartleigh's eerie presence inspired Rosalie and Ellen to keep moving. Her high-pitched voice now seemed to overpower all the others. Leona had certainly got the spirit this morning. They trudged up Lancaster Avenue, private homes giving way eventually to the shops dominating the busy street.

Ellen began to joke about the gawkiness of some of the onlookers. Rosalie's uneasiness started to wane. The two were soon making light of other things: about Norma Williamson's crush on a biology teacher at their private school, the same young man's petrified look when Rosalie had asked him to explain animal, as opposed to floral, reproduction; about Jeannette Wheeler's secret desire to become a red-hot mama on the stage despite her flat chest and squeaky voice. Rosalie amended—more like a duck. They joked about Wandalee's mustache and Leona Hartleigh's horrendous singing voice.

"It's enough to take the vote away once we've got it," said Ellen. "Listen to her—it's like the end of the world."

"Maybe the law could exclude Leona," said Rosalie. "She'd never know who's running anyway."

"Leona would vote for both parties just to avoid confusion," said Ellen.

The marchers had begun to sing "The Battle Hymn of the Republic," Leona now louder and more annoying than ever. Tension was building both inside and outside the parade. The look of the crowd on the sidewalk had begun to change; familiar sights brought bitter memories of past incidents in this neighborhood. Why, they asked themselves in silence, had Wandalee insisted on *this* route?

When the local rowdies who had initiated trouble on earlier occasions appeared, Rosalie and Ellen prayed for a uniformed policeman. Both remembered having seen one on the last block, so it would probably be two or three more blocks before they would see another. The parade was too ambitious, and now Rosalie remembered her father's having said that the police were too overextended to pay proper attention to it. She wished she had stayed home.

"Don't worry, Rosie," said Ellen. "Leona's voice will scare them off."

Someone threw a firecracker, which went off several yards from Wandalee. Wandalee, for reasons understood only by her, screamed and grasped her breast as if she'd been shot.

In a moment the air was filled with missiles and with howls of confusion.

The high, well-trimmed hedges cut the chilly breeze but allowed the scent of Sophia's yellow roses to drift over the patio wall and across the breakfast table. When the Blakeleys had found the estate, Sophia had claimed that the soil texture was more similar to that of northern Italy, while he had maintained that it was identical to that of his beloved Kent and wished to keep the shrubs covering the grounds. To prove her point, Sophia had planted yellow roses, indigenous to the Venetian coast—and the flowers had thrived.

Detective McBride had arrived as the familiar talk of flowers was concluding. He was reminded by their conversation that he intended to send orchids to Miss Meredith to thank her for her kindness of the past evening. His sudden transformation went unnoticed. Frankly it was all Blakeley could do at the moment to keep himself from registering total panic. He wondered if the trembling of his hands was visible.

Ralphie, who had returned from his washbasin and had resumed the wolfing down of his breakfast, nodded mute acknowledgment of Nathan's presence, winked once again at Olga, and moved over to give Nathan room. Olga, meanwhile, had just noticed Nathan for the first time and was making a great effort to be visible to him. Her smile had broadened, her hips had taken on new powers of gyration, and her great chest seemed to be everywhere that his eyes might turn. Ralphie was now preoccupied with a large bowl of oatmeal. Snopkowski, however, stormed down in a wink from her vantage point. As Blakeley, Sophia, and Nathan looked on with reddening faces, the imperious Snopkowski dismissed Olga Wojdzekevicz with a few well-chosen words and a shake of her ominous forearm.

Olga deposited her pot of oatmeal on the table with an angry thud and huffed off to the kitchen.

"I send dot yonko back on next boat, goddamn. Nottink but trobble—her an' dumb brudder Casimir. Yesterday dey puttink cucumbers in bean soup. You know what dot do? Dot givem runs from now till Tanksgivink, goddamn!"

Suddenly realizing what had happened to Ralphie in Tampa, she looked at him and te-heed. He glanced back vacantly.

"I liked it," said Ralphie, his attention returning to the kielbasa and fried eggs.

"Drink your juice, Ralphie," said Sophia.

"Aww. . . . "

"Ralphie, you shan't ever be able to lift five hundred pounds if you neglect your vitamins," she reasoned soberly.

"Telephone call for you, sir," Victor intoned.

"That must be Rosalie."

"Oh," said Sophia with guarded enthusiasm, "I pray so."

"It's Leftenant Hudson, sir. Informed politely that this was my breakfast hour, he nonetheless *demanded* in words that I may not quote. . . . "

Blakeley hurried to the telephone. Victor arched a brow, muttered to himself, and strode away indignantly. Snopkowski, who had been glaring at him, waited until he was halfway back to the house before calling after him.

"I spit—ptui!"

"Would you care for more tea?" Sophia inquired of Nathan with a look of helplessness.

Over the telephone, Lieutenant Hudson's voice was subdued. "I don't want to alarm you, Dr. Blakeley, but there's someone here who needs your attention."

"Rosalie? Is she all right?"

"Just a bit shaken. She was marching with the suffrage ladies, and a ruckus developed over at Seventieth and Lancaster. She claims there's someone missing, and wants to see you right away."

Blakeley, with Nathan driving and Ralphie squeezed between them in the small buggy, took a shortcut through the woods that led to the river and ended at a bridge over the Schuylkill. They arrived at the precinct station in fewer than ten minutes.

Bandaged combatants sat about the room on wooden benches, arguing with one another and with various uniformed officers as they awaited either further treatment or fines and sentences. Wandalee Hinch, sporting a black eye, was howling lest she be overlooked. The outer office was bustling with legal and medical personnel, reporters, too, so Rosalie sat in Hudson's small, cramped private office.

"Daddy, Daddy!" The little girl still comprised most of her being. There were uneven cuts in her blouse and skirt, and her bonnet was missing. Muddy stains marred her crisp, well-tailored skirt. Blakeley knelt beside her chair and held her tenderly.

"What have they done to you, those barbarians?" he asked, thinking she might have been injured without realizing it. "Are you able to go home, where your mother and I can take care of you?"

"I'm all right, Daddy," she reassured him. "The crowd didn't do anything but jostle me. A strange woman in our own ranks did this. Daddy, you must find Ellen. I'm terribly worried about her."

"Ellen?" Blakeley asked, looking toward Lieutenant Hudson for an answer as Rosalie started to break down.

When the fight had broken out, Rosalie and Ellen had used their flag handles as weapons. Rosalie claimed to have broken hers over some brute's head. When Ellen was knocked to the ground, there had been a general disintegration of the ranks, and amid this confusion the two girls had become separated from their comrades. Rosalie had noticed the strange Leona Hartleigh assisting Ellen to her feet and escorting her out of the melee. She had followed them into an alleyway. At the time Rosalie had thought that Miss Hartleigh had discovered shelter from the rocks and bottles. In the alley, however, it had soon become apparent that Leona was not so concerned with rescuing Ellen as with carrying her off. As Ellen had screamed for help, Leona had pulled her toward a carriage some yards away; a small man had sat at the reins. Rosalie had gone to Ellen's aid. But Leona had shoved Rosalie back into the street, where she'd got caught up in the skirmish and had soon lost sight of her friend.

"Daddy, she had the strength of a *man*. She just threw me as if I were a rag doll," said Rosalie after Hudson had concluded his recount.

"The biggest factor, Dr. Blakeley," said Hudson, "is that your daughter believes that this Leona Hartleigh thought she was carrying *her* off rather than the Sundgard girl."

"Good Lord. . . "

Otherwise, one of the men would simply have taken Rosalie home, since there were no charges against her. The parade was legal if ill-advised, and above all, Hudson really wanted to nail that Hinch lady for something. Anyway, this Ellen Sundgard business was curious, and it might have serious repercussions. As Hudson spoke, he took Blakeley aside, and Ralphie moved to comfort his sister. Nathan, upon hearing portions of the story, went to the telephone and, on a hunch, summoned Owen Ward-Lattimore.

Lester Figge or the Butcher? One could almost toss a coin.

Nathan McBride's eyes had opened wide at the mention of a carriage.

"Where exactly was the alley, Lieutenant?"

"It's called Robinson's Way. You know where it is. It connects Lancaster to Rollins Avenue."

"Unpaved, right?"

"Oh, yeah. Decrepit and muddy."

"Good. I'll be back in five minutes with what you want to know, Dr. Blakeley."

"Rosie, next time you decide to go marching, you better take me along," said Ralphie.

Robinson's Way was little more than five minutes away on foot. It was now around eleven o'clock. Nathan made his way hastily through the streets and along the sidewalk of Lancaster Avenue. The chestnut trees and elderberry bushes that lined and shaded the avenue gave the world a deceptively peaceful appearance. Near the site of the minor riot he saw tradesmen nailing boards across the shattered windows of their small establishments. Others were sweeping glass into the gutter before their shops.

At Robinson's Way he stepped lightly over the muddiest areas, seeking the clues he had hoped to find on the ground. Few, if any, of the rioters had cared to enter the darkness of the alley. There. One set of wagon tracks. They led from Rollins Avenue into the alley, hugging the ground against the wall of the old Connery Building, leading in a tight circle back to Rollins. He squatted against the building and measured the width of the tracks, making allowance for their depth since the fat man was no longer driving. Then he measured the distance between the tracks and hurried back to the precinct station.

Running now, he hurdled and weaved his way over and through the natural obstacles of the midmorning, drawing curses and disapproving comments from shoppers and businessfolk. This time he could not afford to walk. He ran as fast as his legs could move.

"A constable will take you home," Blakeley was telling Rosalie, "where you may finish Ralphie's breakfast and read that shameless novel that your mother confiscated last week."

"It's not Lester Figge," Nathan announced, bursting into the office. "Let's take a calculated risk."

"Very good. There may still be time to rectify matters. Come along, Ralphie."

Owen Ward-Lattimore had been intercepted at his favorite billiard parlor just as he was about to win fifty dollars. He petulantly demanded of Nathan a concise interpretation of the phone call. Out of breath after his run from Robinson's Way, Nathan merely took him by the arm and led him to the buggy that waited outside.

"Now see here, McBride," he grumbled, "this is no way to treat a specialist."

Hudson offered to send along a paddy wagon with a contingent of men. Blakeley surveyed the havoc in the outer office and waved him aside politely.

"Catch up with us if you wish, thank you, Lieutenant."

Rumbling over the cobbled back roads as Nathan sought the briefest route to Calvert Street, the four of them crowded into the little buggy, the ride was enough to create the most hostile of feelings among his passengers. Ralphie, who found the adventure exciting, still complained of having to support Own Ward-Lattimore on his lap. Ward-Lattimore complained of Ralphie's tickling him, and Blakeley complained of both their elbows as they flailed about and jostled him. Repeatedly his monocle fell from its proper place.

To Nathan, whose mind was on only one thing, getting to Max Toberman's office before the Sundgard girl became another ugly statistic, their protests were petty.

"How I wish I could comfort you, Miss Blakeley. You are so very young and so very lovely. Not like the others."

Ellen Sundgard writhed in agony on the surgeon's table, unable to move a muscle under the heavy leather straps that bound her hands and feet and ran across her naked torso. For the time being there was no leather thong across her neck because he did not wish to risk her strangling prematurely. Instead, her head was fastened to the table by means of a clamp that gripped her hair. Nor could she speak through the gag that Toberman had placed securely over her mouth.

"Please," he urged her, "toss and turn and try to wrench your helpless body from the table, because in so doing you shall only tighten your bonds and so assist my efforts. You have no idea how great a service you are performing for mankind."

Toberman took a branding iron from the fireplace. Ellen's eyes jerked as the glaring red tip passed before them. Once before she had seen it, before Toberman had placed it on the arch of her foot. The pain had been so excruciating that she had almost passed out. Ever so cruelly, he had removed it in time to cause the greatest of torment.

"Let me do it," said Arthur Hartleigh. "You said I could." Toberman ignored the absurd figure in female clothing.

The new pain ran up her other leg and caused spasms in her back. She cried out, but again the gag muffled her screams, and she could feel the leather thongs cutting the skin on her wrists and ankles.

"I'm proud of you," said Toberman without a smile. He was rolling up his shirt sleeve and preparing a syringe. Against the dirt wall there rested an elaborate medicine cabinet dominated by apothecary jars filled with an almost colorless liquid. Ignoring Ellen for the moment, he inserted a needle into one of the jars and extracted some of the solution.

Toberman tensed his arm and shoved the needle into a prominent vein on the underside of his elbow. His eyes closed for a brief time, and upon opening, they seemed to have taken on an alien cast.

"You treat me as if I were a serf"—Arthur pouted—"and I am totally indispensable to you. I am all that stands between you and decrepitude."

"Hush up or I shall have to kill you."

The damp, underground room was silent but for Ellen's soft moans and the sound of water dripping from the walls to the dirt floor. Arthur looked up at Toberman's face in the torchlight and cringed.

"You don't have the courage to destroy someone who is not bound to a surgeon's table."

"Do you honestly think so, Arthur?"

Arthur's makeup was beginning to run with tears and nervous perspiration. He stumbled up the stone steps to the head of the first flight . . .

"Arthur!"

He stopped. "You bloody bastard!" he cried.

Toberman ascended the stairs calmly, flexing his hands as he stepped above the eerie shadows on the dark dirt wall. Arthur backed up and groped in the darkness for the door to the next level. When at last he had got hold of the door handle, Toberman grasped him by the shoulder and threw him to the floor.

"I'm served you well," babbled Arthur as he curled up in the corner, pulling his skirt up under his chin. "I've . . . loved you, Max."

"You're disgusting. Can you not make your final moment on earth a more manly one?"

"Go to hell!"

Toberman showed his teeth and reached down to lift Arthur by his throat just off the ground. In the torchlight he could see the hideous bulging of Arthur's eyes and the protrusion of his tongue as the grip became tighter. He held him above the ground, listening to the pathetic gurgling and smiling at Arthur's frantic efforts to kick at the air. Arthur tugged at Toberman's arms, trying desperately to pull the viselike hands away, but his efforts were useless. Toberman laughed low as the tugging grew weaker and Arthur's face turned gray under the heavy stage cosmetics.

In a moment Arthur's eyes rolled back into his head and his body fell limply to the floor. Toberman let Arthur drop like an empty sack. For a moment he looked down at the grotesquely protruding tongue.

"I'm terribly sorry, my child, that you've had to be exposed to that foul episode," he said, panting. "No doubt such creatures are quite foreign to you."

He returned to the medicine cabinet and adjusted another syringe. She could hear his heavy breathing as he worked. Closing her eyes, she prayed as she had never before.

God of mercy, God of hope. . . .

"Don't be alarmed. It's merely something to aid us both in our important work."

"I can't concentrate," Owen Ward-Lattimore admonished. He was tapping on the wall near the hole where the safe used to be in Toberman's vacant office. The echoes produced by the empty room made a world of difference to his sensitive ears. Properly chastised, Blakeley and Nathan held their breaths.

Ralphie had been left at the house next door, the erstwhile antique shop of Vincent Eliah Statler, in the event Toberman chose that avenue of retreat.

What if he had already gone? He asked Nathan with his eyes. Nathan, whom they called the Psychiatrist, Blakeley remembered, had argued before Ward-Lattimore had silenced them that there was little chance of that.

Toberman, Nathan had claimed, would wish to deposit the supposed Miss Blakeley in a location that was convenient to her father's discovering her. And that meant that this particular act would have to be committed here in Philadelphia, in Toberman's own grim laboratory. Not necessarily, Blakeley had argued.

The completely empty office had given him pause. Toberman could simply have wished to let Rosalie remain someone who had disappeared from the face of the earth, thereby inspiring an endless list of terrible imaginings in her father's mind.

"I've found the spot, I think," whispered Ward-Lattimore.

He was on his hands and knees, tapping lightly on a section of the wall just above the floor. There were no apparent seams in either the paneling or in the wainscoting, but he swore there was an empty area behind it.

"How are we to open that without alerting whoever is inside?" Blakeley asked.

"If I can find the perforations, I can get in there so quickly and quietly that a snake would have to admire me. The trouble is, Dr.

Blakeley—and if you ever breathe a word of this, I'll have you deported—my eyes aren't quite what they once were."

"Relax a moment," whispered Nathan, who slipped through the back window and ran off toward his buggy.

"Good heavens, Blakeley," whispered Ward-Lattimore, "listen to that."

Blakeley pressed his ear to the wall, and far away, as from deepest hell, he heard a long, agonized woman's scream. No doubt whatsoever anymore. He shuddered at the thought of what was taking place within.

"We've found our Butcher chap, sure."

"Despicable creature," whispered Blakeley. "We *must* find a way in."

Nathan returned, carrying a jar of black ink which he kept under the buggy seat in case he needed a witness' signature. Holding the jar halfway up the wall, he ran it across the paneling and let it run in a dark sheet to the floor. As they watched, there appeared a vivid outline of the neatly crafted entranceway. Nathan then produced a piece of chalk and quickly marked off the area in broad strokes.

Using a small knife of the finest Swedish steel, Ward-Lattimore pried deftly along the outline, and in a blink of the eye the entrance to the tunnel was open.

The cavity was barely wide enough to permit Blakeley to get through, but his companions squirmed through it with relative ease. For several yards they groped about in darkness. Indeed, the pitch black of the tunnel made all three think for a time that they were pursuing the least likely course, but soon they saw a dim flickering at the other end. The tunnel appeared to reach its terminus three or four feet above the floor of the dim corridor.

Nathan, the first to exit, scrambled through hurriedly, almost injuring himself at the other end when he misjudged the drop from the tunnel to the board-lined floor.

As he fell, he could hear the screams of the young girl more clearly. He got up quickly to pull Blakeley and Ward-Lattimore from the tunnel. Certainly now the time was measurable in minutes. When Blakeley was tugged free, the small tunnel collapsed, spilling dirt over the moist, warped lumber on the floor.

"Take off your shoes, gentlemen," Nathan whispered, bending down.

Another scream.

"What direction, Owen?" Nathan asked.

"This way, I believe," said Ward-Lattimore, removing his shoes after a brief pause. Blakeley and Nathan stood already in stockinged feet.

They turned left and followed the passageway for another fifty feet or so.

"It's like a damned coal mine in here," Ward-Lattimore grumbled. The few lit torches along the wall offered little illumination. "You'd think the bastard would at least invest in coal oil."

Halfway through the corridor there were puddles where the sodden ground had drained, and there were planks that teetered when one stepped on them unsuredly. At one point Blakeley even fell. In his fashion he salvaged most of his dignity, waving off the proffered assistance.

"There it is," he said on hands and knees, "a door up ahead."

"Go to work, Owen," said Detective McBride, holding a torch to the door. "Here, I'll place your hands on the knob."

Ward-Lattimore manipulated the lock for a few seconds, then took his knife to a small slit running beneath the steel plate. The door was moldering at the edges but essentially solid, placed there many years ago by the Reverend Lenhardt for the protection of his runaway slaves. The walls smelled of damp wood and rich earth. The air was close, but they had no trouble breathing.

Now, this one's a poser, thought Ward-Lattimore as he struggled to fathom the old lock.

He picked away with uncanny skill, making hardly a sound, so that each of them could hear the breathing of the others. One could become arthritic down here, Blakeley thought absentmindedly.

The door began to creak open. Owen stopped it after a few inches.

"You'd make a very good burglar, Owen," said Nathan, snuffing his torch on the damp floor. "Now, let's have a look."

Nathan crawled out onto the landing and came upon the body of Arthur Hartleigh. Uncertain in the darkness whether or not the body, still warm, was dead or alive or even whether it was male or female, he pulled it as quietly as possible back behind the door for Dr. Blakeley's inspection.

"My God, Nathan." In the matchlight he glanced at the terrible face. "He has all the characteristics of one who's been hanged. Someone of fantastic strength did this."

"This," said Ward-Lattimore, "must be the strange fellow who almost found me in the office that evening."

Nathan again crawled through the door and signaled the others to follow. Below them stood a thoroughly equipped laboratory and operating room laid out in strange fashion on a dirt floor.

As they looked on in horror, Toberman placed a branding iron to Ellen Sundgard's underarm. The sharpness of her scream drowned out the echo of their steps as they charged down the stairway. Toberman had scarcely a moment to look up.

"To him, Nathan!" shouted Blakeley. Nathan lunged at Toberman, who brushed him aside and tossed the branding iron at his head. Nathan crashed beneath the branding iron into the medicine cabinet, spilling bottles, instruments and accouterments about the room. Nathan immediately got up and dived again at the smaller Toberman, taking a backhand across his face. He fell to the floor, trying desperately to shake off his daze.

Blakeley came around the surgeon's table to attack Toberman from the other directon. Blakeley tried to pin him long enough to permit the others to join in. Toberman attempted to kick him in the face. He turned at the last moment, and the muddy foot glanced off his cheek.

Toberman ran for the stairs, running over Ward-Lattimore in the process, tipping over a small bookcase toward Blakeley and Nathan. Ward-Lattimore and Blakeley ran after him. Ward-Lattimore caught up to him on the stairs just as Blakeley reached their foot.

With a bestial growl, Toberman picked Ward-Lattimore up to toss him screaming through the air. He landed on Blakeley, and both tumbled down the stairs into a pile of rubble against the wall. Blakeley bent over Ward-Lattimore.

Dead. His neck had been snapped.

Toberman darted through the door at the head of the stairs. Nathan was still staggering around the far end of the room. He stumbled over to the pile of rubble, still shaking his head. Never before had he ever been brought down by a single punch—much less with a summary blow from a man as diminutive as Toberman.

"Are you all right?" he asked of Blakeley.

"I am, but I'm afraid Ward-Lattimore has seen his last day."

"Too bad," said Nathan groggily.

He pulled Ward-Lattimore's body off Blakeley. He started toward the stairs.

"Don't bother, Nathan. We've work to do here. He can't get through the tunnel and Ralphie's positioned himself in the other house."

"He's very strong, Dr. Blakeley."

"Stronger than Ralphie?"

As Blakeley gently closed Ward-Lattimore's eyelids and picked himself up from the pile of rubble, Nathan quickly draped his coat over Ellen Sundgard and loosened her bonds. She was breathing steadily, having fallen, mercifully, into unconsciousness.

Ralphie, hearing noises from below, got out of his chair and looked down at the trapdoor. The head which would soon emerge from the underground would actually be that of the West Philadelphia Butcher. Thinking of Rosalie, he pounded his fist and counted the steps, wondering what the Butcher would look like, and *oh, boy, was he ever going to be sorry he ever messed with Dad and me. . . . .*

Presently, the trapdoor began to rattle. Instinctively Ralphie stepped on it, thinking he had trapped the Butcher in a deep, dark pit, as if he were some kind of evil mole.

"Gotcha," said Ralphie gleefully.

Ralphie felt himself flying helplessly across the room, knocking over furniture and breaking the more delicate objects in his way. Going full tilt headfirst into the wall, he heard something crack.

"Holy cow!"

Toberman emerged from the lower depths and stared at him with fierce red eyes. Ralphie shook his head, staring back. The little man in shirt sleeves and leather apron seemed almost from another world, so intense and hypnotic were his eyes. Ralphie, had he not been so intent upon what he had to do, might have been frightened by them.

"Now you're really gonna—"

Ralphie charged across the room, braced himself, and threw a right cross with all his force, grunting with pleasure as he felt it landing squarely on Toberman's jaw.

Toberman's head gave way slightly. Stopped. Ralphie cried out in agony. His wrist and fingers seemed to snap. Toberman smiled weirdly, touches of saliva showing on his lips. He sprung at Ralphie and hit him solidly in the stomach.

Folding up, Ralphie felt a pain such as he had never felt before and, cursing his adversary, passed out.

"She'll be all right in a few weeks," said Blakeley, "but she won't walk for a time, and I fear there will be scars."

"Fortunately they're in places where few will ever see them."

Nathan wrapped Ellen Sundgard in a surgical robe and carried her in his arms up the stairs, hoping to find the passageway to the other house. Blakeley tarried briefly, studying the curious chemicals left behind by the fleeing Toberman. Some were utterly foreign; others only theoretically familiar. He sniffed one of the vessels and glanced over at the safe. It offered, he hoped, the answers to whatever the Butcher was really up to, and he wished fervently that Owen Ward-Lattimore had lived to open it. He would have enjoyed that.

"Thank you, English John," he said, and followed after Nathan.

The abolitionist Reverend Lenhardt had been a more cautious man than the world had thought. In any case, the channels led, mazelike, in various directions, some of them to dead ends. Cautiously, in the meager light of the infrequent torches, they traced a series of fresh muddy prints—those of a small man—leading, it appeared, toward the other house.

There Blakeley fully expected to find a smug, triumphant Ralphie. Blinking their eyes, they followed the prints up a wooden stairs to a ceiling and stepped out into a cluttered living room.

"Ralphie. Good heavens!"

"Jeez, Dad," groaned Ralphie, holding his stomach, "I hit him with my Sunday punch, and he never moved. I don't think he's *human*."

Ralphie was on his knees, gasping for breath and looking justifiably bewildered. The wall bulged in where the laths beneath had cracked.

Twenty-one

The vendors in the streets now advertised their corn, sweet potatoes, and acorn squash, and in the evenings the crickets seemed louder and more determined. Blakeley's hay fever made its annual appearance, and he was often heard to swear aloud in the middle of the night while shaking a fist at the rows of ragweed which thrived along the river. Though the heat of the summer had not diminished, it became more bearable as one grew used to it. In Blakeley's fields the dandelions thrived in the late-summer rains, and Snopkowski, coming out of retirement, had taken to brewing her favorite wine again. Her bouillabaisse and chicken Kiev were such a blessed relief from Olga's cabbage soup and knockwurst.

"Now you are knowink difference between forst-kloss chef an' dumb cheekum plocker, goddamn," she announced. Even Sophia had agreed wholeheartedly.

"Aw, Olga knows what she's doin'," Ralphie said loyally. "She just needs more practice, that's all. This is just a glorified fish stew, and you know it."

The cast on his hand made it difficult to handle the soup spoon, and his huge bib was heavily stained with bouillabaisse. The cramps in his stomach passed on in a few days, but the ignominy of his encounter with Max Toberman still weighed heavily. Informed that a lesser man would probably have died from the blow, he merely nodded his head and grunted. Making his life worse was the fact that the broken wrist curtailed his heavy exercise sessions, and he was reduced to running along the river and doing situps.

"Cripes, a healthy *girl* can do this much," he complained one day when Blakeley had walked in on him.

"Well, you've got one good hand. Can't you exercise with that?"

"Now wouldn't I look funny with one side bigger than the other?"

"Well, think of Detective McBride. Don't you think he feels equally embarrassed? After all, he's been a successful pugilist—one who has never lost a bout, and above all, he was never felled by a single punch before. *He* doesn't seem to be moping about as if his world had suddenly turned into an addled egg."

"First of all, Dad, he's just an ordinary guy. A nice guy but an ordinary guy. Second, he isn't in love with Olga Wojdzekevicz."

Olga, her own self-image having been reduced by her Aunt Snopkowski, had taken to showing her disdain for all things American by ignoring Ralphie. Three times within less than a week he had dressed up in his uniform and reported to the kitchen only to be met with a blank smile from her brother Casimir. "Olga no home," Casimir had said. It was the only English he had been taught, and he always recited it proudly.

"It might have been better if the newspapers would have talked up," Ralphie declared ruefully. "Then maybe she'd think I'm some kind of celebrity."

The almost miraculous rescue of Ellen Sundgard, the bizarre death of colorful Owen Ward-Lattimore, and the discovery of the Butcher's identity all received scant attention. To Ralphie's chagrin, the entire story was relegated to the inside pages of all the major dailies. It was as if the War Department had just become part of the conspiracy against Ralphie's romance.

Admiral Cervera's Spanish fleet had attempted to break the harbor blockade and was pursued by the American armored cruiser *Brooklyn*, and the battleships *Oregon*, *Iowa*, and *Texas*. The Spanish vessels *María Teresa*, *Almirante Oquendo*, and *Vizcaya*, driven ashore, had promptly surrendered; the *Cristóbal Colón* had been forced ashore and sunk; the torpedo destroyers, *Furor* and *Plutón*, had been wrecked near Santiago Harbor. Only one American seaman had been lost. General Toral's surrender to General Shafter on July 17 had given the American forces the city and province of Santiago de Cuba, while General Miles' campaign in Puerto Rico—where Ralphie would have served had he not drunk that cursed barrel of beer—had brought about complete possession of that island before the end of July. The Philippine Islands had been captured earlier in the month of August. The American troops, commanded by General Merritt and aided by Admiral Dewey's fleet, on August 13, had captured Manila and seven thousand Spanish prisoners.

Ralphie never complained outwardly about his disappointment over missing all the action, but it was obvious that the ridiculous turn of events in Tampa now seemed particularly humiliating. He went about his daily chores as a recruiter, speaking of the glory and excitement of military life, and Blakely often wondered whether Ralphie let his listeners think his hand had been injured in combat.

"Just for that," he had said, summarizing his disenchantment with Olga, "I *am* going off to school in North Dakota as soon as I get mustered out. That'll show her."

They had become closer, Blakeley and his son, ever since Sophia and Rosalie had gone off to England. After the scare during the suffragette demonstration he had made up his mind that both were better off out of his arena until the whole nasty affair was over and done with. He wished that Ralphie could converse on a few topics other than weight lifting and Olga.

It was encouraging, nevertheless, to have him about the estate. Lester Figge's operatives had let it be known that only a fraction of the strange contract had been fulfilled.

On the day after Ellen Sundgard's rescue, as Blakeley and Sophia sat in a quiet room in the twilight sun, listening to Gilbert and Sullivan music on the Victrola, a bullet had shattered the window and torn through a high-backed chair equidistant between them, lodging itself in the hardwood floor. A ballistics study had determined that the shot had come from a Winchester 73 pump-handle rifle, fired from behind one of the lilac bushes approximately one hundred and twenty-five yards away, atop the hillock, and further investigation had shown that the shadows falling upon the chair had given it a figure not unlike Blakeley himself. He had studied the chair silently for a moment, eyeing the hole in the cushioning where his heart had been supposed to be, then joked lamely about his not being at all so portly as the assassin had thought him. Sophia had merely bitten her lip and gone to bed.

Victor, thereafter, refused to go beyond the confines of the dining room. More often than not, he feigned a recurrence of his imaginary malaria whenever asked to perform a duty anywhere near a window. It was strongly suspected that he was seeking other employment.

"A wish devoutly to be consummated," Blakeley said, paraphrasing one of his favorite lines from Shakespeare.

"Not only that," Ralphie said, "but I think it's a good idea. He's starting to burn my wick. I think he sleeps under the bed."

One week later Figge had served his second notice. Blakeley had been at the Augustinian college, Villanova, delivering an address on the new legal implications of forensic psychology. Philosophers, especially the Thomists, with their impeccable sense of organization, had always been his most challenging questioners. He arranged a lecture at their school when he sought a reaffirmation of his theories.

It was after eleven when he had left the lecture hall and traversed the neatly kept campus following the cinder lane down to the highway. By arrangement with the cab company, a carriage and coachman had awaited him there. The ten-mile return trip was to have been uneventful.

The clear, fragrant air of the wooded drive had been a welcome departure from the closeness of the lecture hall. Had there been light in the cab he might have stayed awake reading the notes he had jotted during the questioning, but the carriage and the roadway had been dark. The driver had been singularly quiet as Blakeley stepped into the cab. The last of his wishes at the time was a chatty companion. Less than a mile from the college the monotonous rattle of the horses' hooves and the endless drone of the driver's humming had lulled him to sleep.

He would always recall the moment of his waking. In the midst of a cornfield, about five miles from the college, no one and nothing about—save the skunk that nested under the carriage.

The coachman had departed, evidently to join his confederates, and had stolen away in such thorough silence that Blakeley still had no recollection of his having left the highway. The driver had found a country lane, driven another half mile, and abandoned the carriage in the field. Even the horse was gone. Fortunately, the skunk—known ever since to the Blakeleys as Petunia—had chosen to take shelter from the night air under the cab in which Blakeley had been sleeping much too soundly. Its powerful scent had awakened him abruptly.

"Eh? What's that? Is Olga cooking something new?" he had murmured before realizing that he was alone in the cab.

As he had sniffed the air, the odor had grown stronger after a few minutes, and soon he had awakened with a sudden jolt. Amid the cacophony of the crickets and katydids, he had determined that the ticking was not simply in his mind, leaped from the carriage, and sprinted across the cornfield.

About fifty yards from the carriage Blakeley had been thrown to the ground by the explosion.

An occasional low-hanging cloud had drifted across the moon. After picking himself up with a grunt, muttering a few epithets, he had brushed the mud from his trousers. Standing there, he had realized with disgust that the skunk had gotten *very* close. He hoped poor Petunia had got out of harm's way, frightened by his abrupt exit from the cab.

By studying the stars and searching his mind for a rough memory of the remote area, he had been able to reckon his way back to the highway. Back at the estate, his clothing burned in the incinerator, it had been another two hours of soaking in tomato juice and bubble bath before the stench finally left him.

At breakfast on the following day Blakeley had announced to

Sophia and Rosalie that within a fortnight they were to board a ship for Liverpool. There they would proceed by coach to Kent, there to remain until Tobrensky, as he now thought of Toberman, and Lester Figge had been neutralized forever.

"*Daad-dee,*" Rosalie had balked. Her recent notoriety had made her something of a celebrity now among her social set. A romance was brewing with a sought-after quarterback from Swarthmore College.

"It's all arranged. I've spoken. Pack your trunk with warmer clothing should it be necessary to spend the autumn in England."

Rosalie had gone off to sulk. Sophia had smiled at him, fighting back a tear. She knew that he would miss her and that it pained him more than Rosalie could realize.

Tobrensky. The name evoked chills by now.

He stared at the solution, holding it to the light. At times he turned the small test tube around in his hand, thinking the color might change. He put it to the flame, wondering if a precipitate might collect at the base. He had run the tests for weeks now, and the look on his face was still freshly troubled. The customary use of chemicals had shown no impurities and refrigeration altered none of the components. Why, he asked himself, had he never seen it before?

It was wholly organic, a substance that could have been produced only by the human body. Yet search as he might and study as he had for wearisome hours, the substance defied description. It was a hormone; he knew that much, and it was probably a kind of adrenocortical secretion. And it contained an antigen that was useful in treating hemolysis. Such factors were not difficult to determine—he had got that far early in the investigation. No further. But what on earth Maxim Tobrensky had needed it for was perplexing. Tobrensky could not have been suffering from the debilitating effects of hemolysis, the destruction of red blood cells, and still possess such inordinate strength!

The only other material yielded by the underground laboratory had not been mysterious in the least.

"Bufotenine," he had told Lieutenant Hudson that afternoon as the bodies of Arthur Hartleigh and Owen Ward-Lattimore were being carted away.

"So old Regis was on to something after all," Hudson had remarked with a certain hint of satisfaction.

Bones Fatzinger, dreading another day in the cell with Zoltan Mroszek, killed some time before work devouring some of the spareribs left over from breakfast. Looking around for a quiet spot, he found a bench under a willow tree near the corner of Sixtieth and Jefferson. The air was still fresh and fragrant with wild flowers. The streets were still uncrowded, save for those whose working day began before most of Philadelphia.

Fatzinger, chewing on his spareribs, licking sweet and sour sauce from his chin, watching the trolleys rumbling along Jefferson Street, dreamed of Strawberry Knockelknorr. He wondered how long he could trust her around the eligible swains from Dinkler's Hollow. It had been days since he had last visited Ebenezersville.

As he was removing the wax paper from his molasses cake and cleaning the stickiness from his fingers with huge slurps, in improved spirits, he heard a chorus of feminine squeals from somewhere behind him. Fatzinger jumped to his feet, spilling the contents of his lunch pail across his lap.

"Who iss dott in da bush dere?" he shouted, but the screams had drowned him out. Reaching hesitantly for his revolver he shouted. "Come oudt or I'll shoot even!"

As Fatzinger gawked, a tall, thin fellow came out giggling. The culprit proceeded hastily to button up his trousers. When his eyes caught Fatzinger's, he stopped giggling and quickly closed his topcoat.

Holy horseshidt, Fatzinger told himself. *Diss here's da Lordy Lilywaver, by Cheesuss! Right back at me shtarin', too!*

"You're comin' wit me, Lordy Lilywaver," Fatzinger announced. "You chust been showin' yer filibuster at dose leedle ladies dere."

"I beg your pardon?"

"Und causin' an officer o' da law hiss vittles to shpill on hiss lap. Dott's salt n' battery, by Christ!"

The notorious exhibitionist regarded his arrester nonchalantly, seemingly more concerned with the task of breathing on his thick glasses and cleaning off the dust they had accumulated in the bushes.

That morning the Reverend Hopkins had been released on bond

posted by his bishop. Then came a telephone call directly from the office of the commissioner, reprimanding Hudson once again for the Jack Ferris mess.

A moment after hanging up he regretted calling the commissioner a melonhead and a pig's ass. When Fatzinger walked in with the Lordly Lilywaver in handcuffs, he greeted Bones with applause. That was enough to make the day worthwhile after all.

"Exposin' his privates I caught him, down by da trolley shtop."

"Put him in the cell next to Mroszek."

As Chamberlain was being escorted by a patrolman past a group of young file clerks, in a flash, he exposed himself to them as well. Squealing, the girls scattered in all directions.

"Bones, you're amazing." Hudson offered to make life on the force much better for the newly redeemed Fatzinger. Fatzinger had promptly requested his removal from the cell of Zoltan Mroszek.

"Whatever your little heart desires, Officer Fatzinger."

"Vell," he answered soberly, "dott's vott my leedle heart desires, Lootenant."

A grateful womankind began writing letters to the commissioner's office commending Officer Wilmer P. Fatzinger for his daring apprehension of the trolley stop terror. Shopgirls and secretaries, the wife of a prominent local architect, the Mother Superior of Saint Malachy's Convent, even the head of the Women's Christian Temperance Union, praised Fatzinger's part in the capture of the "depraved and desperate" Chamberlain.

The commissioner, who rarely read his mail, allowed the letters to pile up for the first three days before opening the first of them. Meanwhile, they had been brought to the attention of his niece—the one who had hired Fatzinger in the first place—and she saw to it that her uncle read the most influential of them. Soon the commissioner was convinced that Officer Fatzinger was no common man. Between his niece and the letters, he could not understand why that ninny Hudson had not argued for a promotion for this Fatzinger. "The man obviously deserves high praise, and he's being left to rot on Hudson's uniformed staff." His niece was lighting his cigar.

"I can't believe I'm doing this," Hudson grumbled. He signed the papers making Bones Fatzinger a member of his detective bureau. "The world must have slipped off its axis or something."

"No more o' dott randy-boo, Lootenant," Bones said soberly.

"City Hall says I'm a detectiff, an' dott's all dere iss to dott. Sign da papers. I gotta go up to Ebenezersville an' tell Strawberry Knockel-knorr da good news."

"Who says you've got the day off?"

"Da commissioner says. He likes me."

When Fatzinger returned, his first assignment was on a deserted road. His task was to count the number of horseless vehicles that crossed it weekly.

Life was only slightly better for Blakeley. The last time they had spoken, Hudson had been so angry that he could barely open his jaw to take another drink from his bottle of bourbon. The more he tried to explain his frustration, the angrier and more frustrated he had become.

Blakeley, on the other hand, when he was not looking out for Lester Figge's operatives, occupied his hours chiefly with the task of writing the last and most complicated chapter of his book on multi-cides; Maxim Nikolayevich Tobrensky, the West Philadelphia Butcher. By agreement with Miss Meredith, her work, already in progress, would treat the entire case in detail while his chapter would examine it only in scientific perspective.

The problem each faced was that neither had an ending. It had become a matter of waiting for the conclusion to manifest itself in all its macabre necessity. How long that would take was something known only to Tobrensky.

When Blakeley and Detective McBride had come upon the defeated Ralphie in the living room of the late Vincent Eliah Statler some weeks ago, they had had to face a sticky dilemma. Both Ralphie and Ellen Sundgard had needed medical attention. Nathan's reaction had been automatic; after placing Miss Sundgard on a couch with extreme gentleness, he had started out the door.

"Let him run, Nathan." Blakeley followed a well-educated guess. "He has to come back sooner or later, you know. We have everything he needs now."

The safe in the laboratory had yielded a wealth of disturbing data. The medicine cabinets had contained the greatest part of Tobrensky's research. In a hidden drawer of a desk a set of formulae had been discovered, but the mathematical interpretation of Tobrensky's theories was still lacking.

Losing faith in his own analytical ability, Blakeley had turned the material over to a police department chemist, who, cursing his own inadequacies had passed it on to the university. After a period of haggling among themselves, the university chemists had returned the formulae to Blakeley with a terse note accusing him of trying to be a practical joker; the theories were untenable, unprovable, and unimportant. With a chuckle of uncertain satisfaction, he read the note now and again.

Yet the formulas were not totally meaningless. Disgusted with his other efforts, he took a piece from one of the papers on which they had been written and tested it for age and manufacture.

The paper, as his tests had shown, had been manufactured in the year of 1785 in Saint Petersburg, Russia. Most unsettlingly the writing was Tobrensky's.

The search for Tobrensky actually began at that moment.

The few words that Blakeley could recall hearing as he'd grappled with the Butcher had been uttered in, of all things, Russian. Muscovite Russian. For hours, as he pored over Tobrensky's morbid case studies, Blakeley agonized over the connection suggested by these words.

The name of Maxim Nikolayevich Tobrensky had surfaced at one point during Miss Meredith's investigation months ago but had been dismissed as beyond consideration. But the case studies, written in French, brought another tantalizing aspect to mind. The Russian court, from Peter the Great on, had conducted all official business in that language. Similarly, scholars and scientists customarily worked in the French tongue, the only one that the court had ever regarded as civilized enough. Miss Meredith's research into the mysterious Dr. Toberman had uncovered no hint of French schooling. Italian, German, Austrian. No French. The language would have to be a matter of required formality, much as Latin had been in earlier centuries.

Marginal notes, scribbled on the impeccably scripted records and at first unnoticed, had, on second look, been written in Cyrillic script, some even in the French equivalent of Russian idioms. Clearly the earliest cases had been frustrating to the researchers. The marginal notes consisted mainly of expressions of disgust.

These clues had been so absurd that Blakeley at first wished to ignore them as possible temptations to chase wild geese. As the summer wore on, the coincidences continued to disturb his thoughts.

In the middle of one especially warm night he had been awakened by a dream inspired by his reading of the endless case histories: Over and over he had absorbed meticulous observations of tortures that would have taxed the imagination of the Spanish Inquisition. The cold, clinical, moment-by-moment recounts of levels of pain, methodologies, comparisons, durations of punishment, and amounts of bodily chemicals extracted led him unconsciously to see himself as the victim. As was obvious from the levels of testosterone included in the strange welter of organic materials, there had been a number of male subjects—young, untraceable peasants and prisoners of war, apparently, who had fallen into the hands of Tobrensky and his co-workers, to be strapped to the table, helpless to prevent the next torment. There were cases in which the methodology alone indicated a male. Reading such histories, Blakeley often felt a sharp pain rising from his pelvis to the pit of his stomach. The methods had been almost incredible in their imagination. He was unable to leave them behind. However vast his experience, the agony and torment on these pages were with him always, especially at bedtime.

The histories were undated. But the subjects had become exclusively female between the forty-eighth and sixtieth victims. There was, of course, the convenient possibility that there were sexual aberrations involved. Given the fact that the female threshold of pain was acknowledged to be greater than that of the male, the studies might have involved the physiology and psychology of pain and fear. Ugly thoughts, but as plausible as any.

He awakened around three o'clock in a cold sweat. Determined to rid himself of his doubts once and for all, he placed one of Tobrensky's papers under a very bright lamp to scrutinize it under a powerful microscope. The watermark on the paper, akin to that pinned to the body of Chantal de Rohan, was that of a Russian craftsman of the early eighteenth century. Blakeley had seen it before; unmistakable, featuring a Byzantine Saviour and the Dove of Peace on a background of clouds and seraphim. Very rare and elaborate, it was hard to discern on the old, heavily used paper.

He barely contained his impatience, summoning Miss Meredith immediately after a light breakfast.

"Yes, I know it sounds preposterous, Miss Meredith." She looked at him as if about to suggest he take a needed holiday. "But I must know. Humor me please." Hers was the task of reconstructing the history of Maxim Nikolayevich Tobrensky—a man who would have to be more than one hundred and fifty years old.

In Washington the Russian government, through its embassy, was most cooperative. With her captivating eyes and professional manner, Allison charmed her way through a battery of secretaries and into the office of the ambassador. She explained that she was doing an article on the life and times of Gregory Potemkin. The Russians were somewhat hesitant at first about revealing documents of a potentially serious nature, but at last they gave the enchanting Miss Meredith access to their archives. On the third day of her visit to the embassy library, she came across the name of Maxim Nikolayevich Tobrensky in a volume of an obscure registry.

"Does this say Tobrensky?" she asked the obsequious young man who had been assigned to assist her. She understood no Russian.

"Tobrensky, yes," he replied.

They never questioned her fascination with the scientific personalities.

"Oh? Do read it for me. You translate so well."

"Translate well? Really?"

"*Da*," she purred. It was the only word she could pronounce.

The aide smiled and proceeded with a guarded hint of excitement. Now and then she could sense his eyes moving from the printed page to her profile, but the pace of his voice remained steady lest it betray his infatuation.

"Maxim Nikolayevich Tobrensky: born, Moscow, September 19, 1742; educated at the court of Empress Elizabeth I; student of Sergei Alexandreyovich Tsutsov in the pure sciences, of Ivan Fyodorovich Orbzut in languages, and of Josef Ivanovich Boroditsky in metaphysics. From 1759 to 1762, a student at the Medical College of Saint Petersburg; licentiate in surgery at Bologna in 1765; in endo . . . endocrinologia at Heidelberg, 1767; resident surgeon at Edinburgh, 1768 to 1770, and at Vienna, 1771."

"A very impressive gentleman," Miss Meredith commented.

"Yes, of course," the young aide agreed. "What is . . . endocrinologia?"

"Endocrinology. A rare specialization among doctors, especially at that time. One who works with the benefits and disturbances of one's bodily chemicals."

"Oh." The description was to embarrass him. He blushed.

When she returned to Philadelphia, Miss Meredith's report proved many of Blakeley's suspicions. It did little to ease his qualms.

Had the research not been exhaustive, it might have seemed laughable.

Tobrensky, as the report read, had been a favorite at the court of Catherine the Great, commissioned an officer in the Imperial Army with the rank of major at age thirty. He had served at Azov against the Turks and in the Black Sea campaign of 1774. In the following year he had led a successful intelligence mission into the Crimea. In 1776, under special orders from the empress herself, he had taken part in an expedition on the east coast of Africa, probing the defenses of the overextended Portuguese there, meeting with moderate success before falling ill early in 1777. The precise nature of the ailment had never been determined; however, a fellow officer had described it as a curse which had befallen many in the expedition. Burning up with fever, Tobrensky had been transported back to Moscow, there to be released from duty because of poor health. Thereafter, he returned to his former practice of medicine and his absorbing pursuit of research. Eventually, in 1787, he had founded the Moscow Institute for the Study of Human Chemical Disorders.

"There is something conspicuously absent from your report, Miss Meredith," Blakeley said, removing his monocle.

"I do not deny that, Dr. Blakeley." She too questioned the nebulous conclusion of the biography.

"Well," the aide had told her with a weak smile, "if Dr. Tobrensky was born in 1742, I think it safe to presume the gentleman has passed on."

The Moscow Institute for the Study of Human Chemical Disorders was destroyed by Napoleon's shelling of the city. During her lifetime Catherine the Great, despite having lost interest in Tobrensky himself, had shown a great personal concern for his institute. According to one record, shortly before her death in 1769 the imperial endowment surpassed ten million rubles. This much Miss Meredith had learned from other documents, papers heretofore unacknowledged by the embassy librarian and clearly embarrassing to the smitten aide.

"Empress Catherine the Second was, as the French would put it, consumed by the joy of life."

"You mean," Allison Meredith had asked naively, "she was romantically involved with Dr. Tobrensky?"

"Well, that is only remotely possible, Miss Meredith," he had answered. "Perhaps in the most platonic of relationships. You see, Empress Catherine was quite up in years by that time, in her sixties at least. And that is quite old for a *true* romance! Pardon my levity. . . . "

"Of course. You're such a *dear* to explain these things."

The aide had smiled and collected himself.

"Yes . . . well, if anything, I would guess it was motivated by a desperate interest in science."

A *desperate* interest in science.

Nathan McBride, now Detective Sergeant McBride, had been returned to the department, and Lieutenant Hudson had assigned him to investigate the murder of a prominent insurance executive. The case was nothing much, and the evidence pointed to an early indictment. Hudson had been forced to act quickly. A downtown informant had told him that the commissioner, out to embarrass Hudson in any manner possible, had suddenly remembered that Detective McBride had been on a sabbatical of sorts.

Hence Blakeley rarely saw him anymore. He was never quite certain of the relationship between Nathan and Miss Meredith, although he had noticed that when Nathan had taken a week's vacation in Atlantic City, Allison announced that she would work on her book, turning up several days later with a sunburned nose. Allison had become an indispensable part of his world as of late, almost like another of his children.

One day, certainly unintentionally, Lester Figge did Blakeley a good turn.

The report from the Russian embassy, intriguing as it had been to read, left him with many unanswered questions, and each question only compounded his anxiety and burning desire to get to the bottom of it. Weary and red-eyed, he left his study one early evening to walk along the riverbank, where he noted with displeasure the growing clusters of ragweed and other pollen bearers which would annoy him until the first frost. Along the way he paused to listen to a band in the park across the water and watched a group of youngsters fishing on the shore.

As was his usual routine, he headed for the gazebo, where he would sit for a few minutes, watch the birds along the bank, and enjoy his pipe. It was always peaceful there, no matter how vicious the world outside.

While he watched the youngsters, a figure stole away from the gazebo.

Lieutenant Hudson had often warned, at times had begged him, to be more cautious. The Figge agents had shown that they could penetrate his property with ease. Quietly Hudson had posted men at the various entrances to the Blakeley estate and throughout the wooded sections. There was still access by way of the river. It was uncomfortable to know Blakeley was that vulnerable.

Sitting inside the gazebo and enjoying the warmth of the twilight sun, he lit up his pipe and began to write a letter to Sophia in Kent. Though he knew full well that she had not yet got there, he wrote, he hoped that she would find Maidstone agreeable and that Rosalie would not embarrass her by engaging in a sulking fit in front of the imperious Blakeleys. He was certain she would enjoy Uncle Reginald, whom she had never met because he'd been in the Orient during their courtship. Aunt Penelope, the main reason Uncle Reginald had gone off to the Orient, could be rather terrifying. Somewhere in the middle of his opening paragraph, Blakeley began to feel as if he were not alone. Without moving a muscle, he looked about the gazebo, focusing eventually on the ground.

Ever so slowly a copperhead snake crawled out from underneath his bench.

He remained still, holding his breath while the copperhead slid into the open. It was easy to observe that it was nervous, almost as nervous as he was, and it was all he could do to avoid agitating it.

The existence of snakes on the North American continent had been his principal reason for resisting emigration some years ago. He had often dreamed as a child, after reading adventurous tales of missionaries and explorers, that one of the scaly creatures had found its way into his pants leg. The sight of a snake, even of a harmless variety, usually caused him to break out in a rash.

A cudgel had been placed on the ledge of the gazebo by Snopkowski just after her terrible discovery earlier in the summer. Snopkowski had actually armed the entire estate during her period of recuperation, and Blakeley often chided her for it. Should soul and body united survive this moment, he would remodel the kitchen according to her specifications, regardless of cost or inconvenience.

The snake tarried briefly, motionless, confident, at ease in a warm spot where the sun came through the open wall. Then, as if bored, it crawled again in his direction, tongue flicking as it sought out the source of Blakeley's loudly thudding heartbeats.

When the snake raised its head, Blakeley swung the cudgel like a golfing iron. He picked the snake up and sent it against the wall with a quick series of slapping noises. As it curled up stunned on the floor, Blakeley broke the cudgel killing the snake.

"Are ye all right?" Officer Riordan asked, panting a bit after his long chase. With him was a sweaty figure whom he held in a hammerlock.

Blakeley, too, was out of breath, and he was still wondering whether all that just occurred had not been merely hallucinated. His shirt clung to his back, cooled by the draft from the river. Still, he maintained his composure.

"I believe we've met," he commented to the young man in Officer Riordan's custody. "You were driving a coach last time, weren't you?"

What an insidious method to employ, he thought later, sitting in a hot tub, trying to prevent a siege of ague and trying even harder to rid himself of the memory of the snake. The thought still caused shivers. He took comfort in the realization that although the operative would never dare betray his connection with Lester Figge, Figge would have to move more cautiously in the future.

When he had bathed, he congratulated himself privately for his calm, stealthy reaction to the crisis.

A snake. How perfectly filthy. . . .

"Tell him it's Ian Blakeley. Dr. Ian Blakeley."

"Does Mr. Figge know you, Dr. Blake?"

The woman's voice was cordial but icy. He was not supposed to have gotten this far.

"It's Blake*ley*, and I'm sure he does."

"I see. Well, do you think you can call back tomorrow, Dr. Blakeley? Mr. Figge is in conference at this moment."

It was shortly after nine o'clock on the following morning. Blakeley had once again dreamed all night of snakes. After the long bath and half of a bottle of Benedictine, he had decided that his mind could accomplish very little in what had remained of the evening.

That morning, over tea, he felt the game had gone on too long.

"Perhaps," he answered after reflecting, "simply informing Mr. Figge that you've spoken to me in person would convey my message adequately."

"I'm afraid you'll have to be more specific than that, sir."

Blakeley, angered as much by Figge's inaccessibility as by the attempts on his life, blurted out, "Tell him I'm alive, damn you! And tell him his efforts are as crude as his thinking is bourgeois!"

The secretary had begun to protest Blakeley's profanity when another voice interrupted.

"Blakeley, your methods are disgraceful. You must realize she's merely doing her job."

Figge's attitude seemed loathsomely confident. He lectured on until the secretary left the room. "I'd hoped to teach you to honor your commitments by now. I shall simply have to try harder."

"Begin with your lieutenants. They seem to have a penchant for selecting the most obtuse agents. Honestly, your actions seem to have been inspired by children's novels."

Blakeley's voice sank and became calm. Figge began to betray his ever more muddled state.

"That wasn't our only man, Blakeley. You know that. And you also know that you haven't seen the last of us."

"I just hope," said Blakeley, "that you're as diligent in attending to the other half of our agreement."

"It's all in trust, Blakeley, waiting for you and your teammates. They should do quite well, you know, since I doubt that you'll be around to have a share in it."

He returned to his laboratory, but the chilling thoughts of his recent encounters stayed with him, making him even angrier than he had been before the telephone call. It was warm, and he felt his collar chafing.

He stared once again at the test tube filled with Tobrensky's mysterious antigen. Shortly after he had hung up on Figge, Detective McBride had called to say that the case of the murdered insurance executive was all but settled—his wife had done it—and that, in light of the past evening's adventure, he was requesting reassignment to the Butcher case.

Thinking about it as best he could in more objective terms, he told himself that Figge's use of a venomous, crawling thing had been almost poetically appropriate. What better association of predators could one have imagined?

A snake. . . .

Good Lord, yes! How stupid not to have thought of it. . . .

He flipped through the pages of one of his reference books and read again the section on hemolysis. Miss Meredith's report had mentioned Tobrensky's African expedition.

Damn, how silly an oversight. It was snakebite! It *must* have been. Fever, dizziness, chronic weakness—why else would he have worked so ruthlessly to heal himself?

But then, once mended, what drove him on?

For the next few days Blakeley spent his hours searching through all available works on Tobrensky's period at the imperial court: his friends, of whom there were few; his enemies, not numerous either; his associates; his relationship with Catherine the Great. Miss Meredith was helpful as usual, but the identity and nature of the subject remained enigmatic.

One morning, as Blakeley stepped out of his laboratory to admire Miss Meredith's handling of Sophia's prize stallion, he tarried too long in the open. He had been warned repeatedly, but blast it, one can exist as an ant in a hill for only so long. The more he reflected upon the ignominious shadow of Lester Figge, the angrier and more rebellious he became. It was silly, he knew—he admitted so later— but in retrospect he had probably endangered himself deliberately.

Miss Meredith was a gem of a woman—unique in her professional dedication and very brave. For a time there Blakeley had worried about her safety more than he ever had worried about his own. Hudson had mentioned her lack of protection, not really wishing to add to Blakeley's cares. Living alone, leading a very unprotected existence, she was easy prey for potential kidnappers. Blakeley had prevailed on her to move into Rosalie's room. Whenever she had cause to leave the estate, Lieutenant Hudson saw to it that she was accompanied by an armed officer.

Detective McBride took a guest room on the next floor, much to Snopkowski's delight. She brushed Victor's objections aside with a terse comment. "You stay away from her keyhole, Veek-toor, or maybe I tellink him." Preparing her special potato soup for Nathan, she chortled impishly as Victor stalked off.

It took a lot of wheedling on her part before Lieutenant Hudson finally told Blakeley that he would again assign Detective Sergeant McBride to the case.

"Okay, Snopkowski, you win," Hudson had said over his third

plate of goulash, "but only for a few weeks. This leaves me only with Fatzinger."

"Fattinker? Vott's dott?"

"A kind of fungus that grows in police stations and eats everything in sight."

"Heehee—always you kiddink poor Snopkowski."

"Oh? I'll show it to you someday, then maybe you'll believe me. It looks like a scarecrow and sounds like a billy goat and eats anything that stands still long enough!"

"You tink maybe it eat bottlers? Heehee."

Victor, sulking in a corner because Snopkowski served the goulash to Hudson before he could get to it, muttered something about the peasant sense of humor.

Hudson, mired in his own troubles, did what he could, but without stronger evidence there could be no case of any credibility presented against Lester Figge. In his words, what they had so far "would be turned into scrambled eggs if Figge's lawyers went up against those assholes from City Hall." It was galling to think that Blakeley might have to submit to this harassment indefinitely.

As they looked on, Miss Meredith maneuvered the Arabian neatly over the riding rail and off onto the higher ground. With her atop, Sophia's horse no longer seemed so large. Thankfully Miss Meredith knew how to exercise it properly. Ever since Sophia had departed, the Arabian had become quite skittish. Blakeley also observed the proud smile on Nathan's face while, squinting into the sun, he watched Miss Meredith riding the beautiful animal over the hill.

"Excellent form," Blakeley mused.

"Yes."

Blakeley smiled. They made a very attractive couple.

Nathan went off to the kitchen for a cup of coffee and a continuation of his argument with Ralphie over the probable outcome of the baseball season. It was Saturday, and Ralphie did not have to rush off on a recruiting mission. The idle chatter around the breakfast table was a pleasant change from the usual talk of testing and speculating.

Blakeley lingered for a while to inspect the hedges. The symmetry of his garden was a minor obsession. He needed a little more time to ruminate about all that his tests suggested. With each experiment he had more difficulty believing his own notes.

The hedgerow wound across the front of the house, following the drive for a few yards before going its own way in the direction of the river. He would not go near the gazebo anymore. Instead, he stopped to admire the bed of begonias that Sophia had ordered him to see to daily. These, above all, had been the object of her almost fanatic attention since early June. Naturally he had promised to do all in his power to cultivate them while she was away.

"I dunno, Nate. Sometimes I think women are no good for anything except maybe wreckin' your good moods. Maybe you can tell me. Can a Protestant become a monk?"

Ralphie had begun to speak about Olga again. Nathan got up and rolled his eyes.

"I suppose so, Ralphie. Only you'll probably have to learn Latin."

"Really?"

Nathan was slightly uneasy, gazing out the window. He could not see Allison from his vantage point. There were some isolated areas in the woods beyond the hill. Lots of places in which to lie in wait. But then, as she had said, whoever wanted her would have to be able to outrun the horse.

"Then maybe," said Ralphie, "I can volunteer for duty out in the desert. Anywhere that you don't find a skirt will be good enough."

"Just don't take Snopkowski with you," Nathan answered absentmindedly.

He shifted his attention to the front of the house, coming to observe Dr. Blakeley near the begonia bed. As Nathan looked on, Blakeley turned his attention abruptly away from the flowers.

In a second he was scuffling with several men. They had got through the guards somehow, determined to finish what Figge's other agents had failed to do.

"It isn't Snopkowski that I'm interested in, Nathan," Ralphie was saying as Nathan darted out the door.

"Come on, Ralphie," Nathan said. "It's time to redeem ourselves."

Two of them had jumped at Blakeley from behind the hedgerow. Three came at him from the opposite direction. After felling the first with a quick punch, he had thrown the second over his shoulder into the hedges. But a third landed a blow to the side of his head. stunning him. As he struggled to clear his head, the fourth gripped him around the neck. Blakeley managed to bring his boot up into the last one's chest. He was wrestling with two of them as Nathan dived headlong into the melée and momentarily scattered the attackers.

Ralphie pried one of the thugs from his father's back with his good hand, landed an elbow on the attacker's forehead, lifted him off his feet, and sent him backward into the begonia bed.

Nathan set upon another of the attackers and landed four quick body blows and an uppercut before the startled thug had even realized his nose was bleeding profusely. Blakeley, amazing even himself with how much he remembered from his days in the queen's service, had all but devastated his weakening opponent. Ralphie distracted him then with some unexpected laughter, allowing the tough to butt Blakeley in the stomach and flee up the horse trail.

Ralphie was having a grand time. Two of the attackers, one extremely large, had come at him at once. He had been holding the squat one by the back of the collar, using him to absorb the larger man's blows. But when the short one had fallen unconscious to the ground, the bigger hooligan finally landed a wild punch near Ralphie's left eye.

"Damn! Now I'm not gonna fool around anymore!"

Seeing no sense in pushing his luck any further, the tough turned around and was intercepted in the begonia bed by Nathan.

"Hey! Don't you hit him, Nate. He's my goat!"

"Then hurry up, dammit!" said Nathan, dodging the huge man's punches, trying his best to accommodate Ralphie.

Ralphie tramped through the flowers and took over. Carefully using only his good hand he connected with a solid left hook as Nathan helped Blakeley to his feet.

"That's for hitting me in the face, jerk." The ruffian staggered in a fog.

"And that's for bothering Dad.

"And this is for lookin' like an ape."

A left cross landed with the sound of a stone hitting a wooden fence. After flying sideways into a rosebush, the hooligan had come to rest partially upright.

"Good move, Ralphie." Nathan applauded. He had been giving Ralphie lessons in boxing ever since he'd moved in a few days ago.

"Hey, Dad, look at that. Four out of five, and we're hardly even dusty."

"Speak for yourself," said Blakeley, sneezing. He had got a nose full of pollen in the flower bed.

"Five out of five," said Nathan as he saw Officer Riordan coming

up the lane with the last of the attackers. Behind them was Allison on the horse. She was grinning sheepishly.

"Riordan, you're pretty good when you finally get around to it."

"I can't be everywhere at once, Sergeant. There's only meself on the whole north end."

"Well, at least you got him," said Blakeley.

"I didn't get him, Dr. Blakeley. I was chasin' him, but it was the lady here that got him."

"Actually, he ran into the horse," Allison explained, leaning forward to pat it on the neck. "So it was Gladstone here who really got him."

As the five attackers were being herded into the paddy wagon, Ralphie, developing a black eye, nevertheless repeated that this was the most fun he'd had since coming home.

"What's the matter, Dr. Blakeley?" Nathan asked. "Those are five common street fighters. One of them is bound to talk, and we might have Figge where we want him."

"I know," Blakeley said despondently. "It's a good thing Sophia isn't here to see this." She would have extracted a reckoning painful to contemplate for each trampled plant.

On the way back to the house Ralphie marveled at Allison's unusual calm. There she was, cool as hell just after getting into an honest-to-gosh mix-it-up. And with all that moxie, she was still as pretty as a girl can be without being prettier than Olga.

"Wow, Nate, that's some *woman!*" he exulted, poking Nathan in the ribs. "Too bad she's so smart."

Blakeley ran some more tests and arrived at incontrovertible conclusions. There was nothing to do now but wait. He concentrated on concluding his book, realizing that its contents would bring accusations of charlatanry, however clearly he might word it.

Toward the end of the month Zoltan Mroszek was released from custody. Since the reason for his incarceration had been the damage he had inflicted on the church, Blakeley had come to an understanding with the little white-thatched pastor that Zoltan, gainfully employed, would repay the cost of repairs. As he watched Zoltan, now twenty-five pounds heavier and looking as sharp in his new clothes as his mind had been for weeks, stepping from the precinct station and out into the sunshine, Blakeley had a rare feeling of satisfaction.

Through Miss Meredith, a position had been secured as a teacher of literature and cultural history at a young ladies' academy in Wilmington. Zoltan had received the news with tears of joy.

Zoltan, using the few dollars that Blakeley had slipped into the vest pocket of his gray linen suit, rented a small apartment in Wilmington within a short walking distance of the school and established credit at bookstores. Blakeley had also included a note assuring Zoltan that his paintings would be sold—Sophia was never errant in her judgment of craftsmanship.

When he was settled, Zoltan returned to Philadelphia for one last look at his former habitat, the bohemian dens of the university district. It gave him the greatest relief to stand outside the old tenement and realize it would never again be his prison.

The evening was warm, and the overhead fans in the tavern seemed to move lazily. Most of the clientele complained of the heat, but Zoltan, sipping his light sherry and reminiscing with some old acquaintances, paid no attention to it. As he discussed Strindberg and Hauptmann with clarity, his auditors looked mildly amazed, listening attentively. And then in the second hour, someone, for reasons too perverse to define, had slipped a drug into his glass of sherry. Perhaps, as a sober friend tried to explain some time later, it simply bothered them to see their favorite clown turn serious.

Trying to find his way back to Wilmington, he became lost somewhere near the heart of the city, never getting beyond the circle in which he had wandered about for most of the evening. By eleven o'clock his new linen suit was soiled from first tripping into the gutter, then brushing up against a passing coal wagon.

Soon he found himself climbing the stairs of a tall building. For some reason he expected to see the wretched Bowman fellow and his mother haggling with the landlady as Mrs. Leibowitz looked on with that sickening smile. But they never appeared. He climbed past the turn on the stairwell where they should have been and continued to the top of the stairs. Knocking very angrily on the door of a hotel room he thought to be his old flat, he had been greeted by a belligerent man in underclothes.

"How would yiz like yer lights punched out, mister?"

"But that is not your prerogative. You see, *you* are trespassing on *my* property, and I fear I shall have to call the police."

"What's goin' on, Eddie?"

"Is this here yer old man, Charmain?"

The slattern, wrapped in a bed sheet like a native, denied it obscenely.

The man slammed the door in his face.

"Simians."

Atop the roof of the building Zoltan looked out over the city, studying its gaslights and silhouettes, and wondered if he could fly.

"Daedalus and Icarus, are you listening?" he shouted.

Daedalus and *Icarus* echoed faintly off the paving stones.

There were few mourners at Zoltan's grave: Blakeley, of course, and an awkward-looking Ralphie, plus eight or nine seedy persons from the cloudy past. Zoltan Mroszek's epitaph, on a stone purchased by Blakeley, was taken from Baudelaire: "Be always drunken, with wine, with poetry, with anything. . . ."

On the afternoon of Zoltan's burial, Blakeley was working on a paper that he would present at a criminology seminar at Harvard in the fall. Nathan was off at the precinct station catching up on his own paper work. At the moment he was approximately two months behind.

Ralphie, his broken hand no longer in a cast, was swimming in the river. And Allison Meredith, her book perplexing her for the time, had decided to take Gladstone for a ride.

"How is your work progressing, Miss Meredith?"

"It's good enough, I suppose," she answered pensively. "But I still think I'd be much better off had I gone to Cuba."

"Isn't it a bit warm for a ride?" Blakeley asked her. "It must be nearly ninety."

"I don't mind if Gladstone doesn't," she replied. "Besides, it's a lot more fun nowadays, without our strange visitors."

One of Figge's henchmen, the squat one, had spoken freely. Nick McNichol, according to Lieutenant Hudson—a gutless type. Though far from truly implicated, Figge ceased to make attempts on Blakeley's life. But the doctor knew the affair was far from over.

She rode off, a vision of grace in her yellow riding dress. Once, in a very sentimental mood, Nathan had called her a goddess on horseback, but Blakeley had thought that a bit much. A lovely young woman with magnificent style, excellent performance. But not even

Sophia was a goddess. This generation, Blakeley decided, had no sense of restraint.

After returning to his study, he removed his coat and went back to his research. The subject was a challenging one; he was attempting to refute the theories of six European scientists whose prestige was currently at its apex in this country. Nevertheless, he considered them fools. It was all he could do to temper his language. The mere thought that body types supposedly predisposed individuals to criminal behavior was to him so much twaddle.

After another hour he went to the kitchen and poured himself a glass of beer, as was his custom at three o'clock. Olga Wojdzekevicz was peeling potatoes, and Snopkowski was browbeating Casimir. Olga eyed him coldly, and he suddenly remembered Ralphie telling him she had decided to blame her demotion on him. It was easier than locking horns with Aunt Snopkowski.

"I say, Mrs. Snopkowski, what are you fixing for supper?" he asked cheerily.

She turned away from the hapless Casimir.

"Potatoes. What you tink?"

Abashed, he returned to his study and buried himself in the argument against body types.

Around three thirty Miss Meredith entered his study, out of breath. Her dark hair had fallen over her forehead, and her bonnet seemed atilt, as if she'd been in a struggle.

"Miss Meredith, have you met with an accident?" He got up from his chair.

"No. But I've come across someone who looks as if he has. Can you have a look at him?"

"Yes, of course. Let us take him to my laboratory."

"I think, sir, we'd better not move him that far. He's quite old. I found him on the trail."

Officer Riordan, who had assisted Miss Meredith in transporting the old gentleman back to the house, was lowering him from the horse to the ground as Blakeley reached them. They had propped him on Gladstone, and with Miss Meredith running ahead, Riordan had led the horse back to Blakeley. Ever so gently Riordan carried him toward the study. He was dressed in a well-worn black suit and appeared, by his sparse white hair and many wrinkles, to be well up in years.

"I think you'd better carry him into the laboratory anyway. Miss

Meredith, run ahead and get some cold water. He appears to be suffering from dehydration."

With Blakeley's aid, Officer Riordan carried the old man back to the laboratory. Actually Blakeley's help was not needed—the patient could not have weighed over ninety pounds. Riordan acted as if he appreciated it anyway. They placed him on a couch and moistened his lips. Then Blakeley felt his pulse.

"Seems to be suffering chiefly from exhaustion. Where did you find him exactly?"

"He was outside the fence," answered Miss Meredith.

"Do ye think he'll make it, Dr. Blakeley?" asked Officer Riordan.

"I don't know," said Blakeley, putting his hand to the old man's forehead. "I shall give him some medication and let him rest awhile. Then we shall see."

"Sunstroke, I'll bet," offered Riordan.

"Or simply old age."

Blakeley was silent for a moment, studying the old man's eyes, sunken above the bloodless gray cheeks. Then a suspicious smile came over his face. He rolled up the old man's pants leg. Miss Meredith and Officer Riordan looked on quizzically. Blakeley straightened out the one trouser, and turned his attention to the other leg. A look of satisfaction followed as he noted the crisscrossing scar tissue on the old man's calf.

"Hmm . . . Miss Meredith, do call Detective McBride and Lieutenant Hudson and apprise them of what has just transpired here."

"Yes, sir."

"And tell them I believe we've found Tobrensky. Or rather, Tobrensky's found us."

She ran off in search of the nearest telephone. Officer Riordan went out to round up the other policemen. Principally Blakeley was in need of witnesses. He knew how readily he could be called mad were he to recount this tale alone. The old man on the leather couch was without a doubt the mystery of the age.

He picked a needle from among the sterile instruments and measured out a very small dose of the antigen and injected it into the old man's body.

"Dr. Blakeley."

The stentorian voice startled him. He turned suddenly toward the couch, but the old man lay motionless.

"*Sir.*"

"What is it, Victor? I'm busy, as you can see."

"I *must* have a word with you about that young woman." Victor's face was flush with righteous anger.

Miss Meredith, finding him about to use the telephone, had, in her great agitation, taken it out of his hands. Since he had been about to call the Quimbys' maid, Clotilde, with whom he had been attempting for years to carry on a liaison, he was particularly put out by Miss Meredith's forwardness.

"And there I was, sir," he went on, "about to call my physician."

"Physician?"

"Yes. I hadn't wished to trouble you about my dizzy spells," he said nobly.

Victor, having said his piece, slowly cast his wet eyes upon the old man.

"As you were saying, Victor?"

"Is that. . . . Is that a . . . a. . . . "

"Yes. If you will observe the black suit, Victor, you will conclude correctly that he was a butler. I'm partial to butlers. I find they make excellent cadavers."

"Great Scot!" Victor gasped.

Victor dashed out of the laboratory.

With a fading look of amusement, Blakeley turned back to the old man on the couch and again felt his pulse. It had improved considerably. Likewise, the color had started to return to his cheeks. There was still no movement, however. Blakeley pondered whether to administer a greater amount of the antigen. He loosened Tobrensky's collar and draped him in a quilt, then left the laboratory for a few minutes.

"You must observe this closely, Miss Meredith," he said, finding her in the hallway. "What follows should be the highlight of your work. You must record it with meticulous care."

"I'm ready, Dr. Blakeley."

Through the professional veneer, the youthful excitement on her face was evident.

"You don't miss Cuba now, do you *Mr.* Meredith?" he asked heartily.

"No." She smiled nervously.

Instinctively he reached forward and hugged her for a brief moment. Then he told her where best to position herself in order to witness the climax of their little drama.

Within a quarter hour Nathan had arrived with Hudson and a

complement of patrolmen. The estate was soon completely encir-
cled by police. How absurd the entire business would appear,
thought Blakeley, should this turn out to be simply some poor old
man.

Detective Fatzinger, wearing a ridiculous set of plain clothes, had
also come along. Blakeley had to fight back a chuckle as he looked at
the combination of high-rise checkered trousers and green coat with
yellow-orange stripes.

"Come ahead back, youse," shouted the officious Fatzinger. Naturally confused, the patrolmen, who had been trying to station
themselves to proper advantage, stood uncertain.

Lieutenant Hudson waved Fatzinger aside and clarified the orders. When the men had been deployed, he looked about for some
means to occupy Detective Fatzinger. Blakeley, recalling similar occasions in London, understood immediately. The problem was to
deploy Fatzinger in the manner least potentially damaging to the
operation.

"Why don't you have Detective Fatzinger look for my butler,
Lieutenant?" said Blakeley in a tone conveying concern. "He's run
off to somewhere, and our cook, Mrs. Snopkowski, is terribly worried about him."

"Huh?" Fatzinger's frown, denoting great seriousness of purpose,
had not weakened since he had arrived. "You mean you think da
butler done it like in da shtories?"

"There is a very remote possibility, Detective Fatzinger," said
Blakeley.

"Vott's dott?"

"Find the butler, Fatzinger," ordered Hudson. "The cook may
thank you for it."

"Da cook?" Fatzinger's face registered opportunism, and he
strode off up the stairs with his characteristic high step, in search of
Victor.

"Dr. Blakeley!" called Miss Meredith, somewhat breathless after
running down the hallway from the laboratory. "Your patient is
moving about. He seems to have come to life all of a sudden."

They hurried down to the laboratory. Before entering, Blakeley
showed them where to place themselves in order to see and hear
what was about to occur without being noticed by the suspect. Nathan joined Miss Meredith at one vantage point, and Hudson positioned himself at the other. From their stations, set up by Blakeley

weeks ago, as soon as he had concluded his experiments and had begun to anticipate this moment, they could observe the action clearly. The wall panel had been removed from a space immediately behind a medicine cabinet, leaving Nathan and Miss Meredith a clear view through the glass. Another opening had been made in the wall behind a large still life, and Hudson was actually peering through a handful of grapes. Sophia had always considered the painting a monstrosity, and Blakeley knew she would be pleased to see it put to good use.

Blakeley opened the door and came face to face with his old enemy.

"Tobrensky!"

The old man had got up, and, as expected, sought the antigen, which he knew to be in Blakeley's laboratory. He turned around with an athletic agility seemingly incongruous with his ancient form.

"Blakeley," he said, showing his teeth in a manner unforgettable since their first encounter.

He was not at all so decrepit as the old man whom Blakeley had been nursing only minutes ago. The lines were still there, around the eyes and under the chin, but his cheeks were much more youthful. The antigen had worked with wondrous, if eerie, effectiveness.

"Are you looking for your formula, Tobrensky?"

"A formula suggests that it can be comprehended by ordinary minds."

"I shall admit, Tobrensky, that it has me stumped in certain of its features. I have difficulty in my endeavors to determine its actual components. But I have had some success, despite my antediluvian methods, in fathoming its purpose."

Tobrensky's face twisted into that of a patronizing adult addressing a child. "You have?"

"How else do you think I brought you out of your coma? I daresay you look better than you have in weeks."

"Brilliant." Tobrensky chortled. "I'm surprised that you don't expect me to fly about the room now."

"It must have made you quite popular for a time there, with the Empress Catherine, I mean, as she waged her own struggle with age."

Tobrensky moved about the room. "Blakeley, she would have given me half her empire had I not been retarded by my idiot associates. Blakeley, you are looking at *history*. I can tell you things about the world that no historian will ever be able to guess. I can also tell you about incompetence and all that it has done to the world of science."

"Incompetence or humanitarianism?"

"It depends on your point of view. High-grade morons the likes of you fumble their way into my life and my work, destroying mankind's greatest discoveries so many times. I only know that the wheel turns for all of us and that I, at least, have asked no quarter. The same cannot be expected of you."

Blakeley noticed Tobrensky's hand quivering ever so slightly, as if about to make a move. Just to be sure of his own safety, he felt for the derringer he had carried in his vest pocket since Lester Figge had begun his harassment.

"Strange," he said, "you are a prisoner on my estate. By my wits and scientific background, I've forced you into the web. Yet you persist in calling me ignorant. Do you come by your monstrous ego naturally? Rather than merely lengthening life. . . ."

". . . *Merely* lengthening life? There will come a time, Blakeley, when you shall not speak so blithely of my creation. Like the Empress Catherine, poor syphilitic that she was, you will grovel for the opportunity to prolong your worthless years. *Merely*. . . . "

Nathan and Allison at one corner, and Hudson at the other, listened mesmerized. With open eyes and sweaty palms they watched Tobrensky take a cigarette from a silver box near the sofa and with steady hands strike a match.

"Do you know, Blakeley," he went on, puffing smoke as he talked, seemingly at ease now, "I was actually relieved when you entered the case. Really. As I told my colleagues, your friend Captain Tolan, not far removed from a peat bog and a peasant's hovel, was the much greater threat. *His* was the mind, Blakeley. Sooner or later, in his uncommon sense, *he* would have found me out. As it is, you've been able to reap the benefits of chance: your enlistment of talented associates and my enlistment of pitiable subhumans. That is what has saved you from the scorn of your onlookers. You've been luckier than a crotchety Victorian deserves to be."

There was no graceful retort left to Blakeley. He only hoped they would realize that Tobrensky was trying to save face with himself.

"Indulge me for a moment, will you, Tobrensky?"

"Go on." Tobrensky snuffed out his cigarette.

"Well, if I were asked to describe you—and surely that is a logical request—I would no doubt say you are cold, shrewd, amoral. But I cannot judge you a mere sadist. Why then have you become so involved in such heinous cruelty?"

"I learned, Blakeley, during my own illness, that the human body is capable of manifesting remarkable powers when it is forced to the brink—powers of which science understands but a pitiful fragment. When one understands the nature of fear, fear capable of terrorizing whole cities, when one skillfully manipulates that fear, he can bring about incredible discoveries. I abhor cruelty. I am, as you've guessed, a very gentle man by nature, which is why I had to use the bufotenine. But, you see, I could only get the results I desired when my subjects were most desperate."

"And then?"

"You have seen the results. Their bodies have produced the most powerful drug known to science. Isn't it ironic, Blakeley? We carry it with us, unaware of our own worth."

To illustrate the power of his discovery, Tobrensky picked up a wrench that Blakeley had on one of the laboratory tables. As Hudson and the others looked on in disbelief, the little old man proceeded to bend the handle in his bare hands. Blakeley drew a deep breath.

"Apparently, your discovery was just a trifle late for the Empress Catherine."

"Alas, poor Catherine. Just one year short of my success. She remained a great believer to the end. She was desperate, of course. Only in her case it did no one any good."

In a flash Tobrensky had hooked the wrench against Blakeley's windpipe.

"Now, Tobrensky," he said cautiously, "you don't think I've encountered you without negotiating with the police. You've nowhere to go."

"Come, Blakeley."

He led Blakeley out of the laboratory and down a path. Hudson scurried out of his hiding place and signaled his men to drop their guns for fear of endangering Blakeley's life. One by one, they lowered their rifles and stepped aside. Before leaving the laboratory, Tobrensky had laughed at them.

"Tobrensky," Blakeley whispered as they made their way toward the stable, "you shouldn't have done that. I've only given you enough to enable you to stand up for a brief time."

"If I feel myself weakening, Blakeley, you will depart this world ahead of me."

They traversed the green and up the slight rise toward the stable, followed at a respectful distance by Blakeley's powerless allies. As they passed a patch of ragweed, he thought he might be forced to sneeze.

"How far do you expect to go, with or without me?" he asked.

"Far away, Blakeley. I've made it before, in Russia, Austria, France, even your own England, in circumstances much more difficult. I've done what I came here to do, you see, to destroy what you've stolen from me. I shall simply move on until another misguided creature interferes and I am forced again to move on again."

In the stable were a horse and buggy, ready to go.

Confound it, thought Blakeley; he had asked Ralphie over and over to unhitch his horse when he got home. The river had been too inviting.

Tobrensky shoved Blakeley toward the buggy and ordered him to climb into the driver's section. He obeyed, however reluctantly. He knew that he would never survive beyond the limits of the estate.

After Blakeley had climbed onto the buggy, Tobrensky grabbed the seat and started to pull himself aboard.

"Come down, you turkey's neck! Come down or I'll shoodt!"

Fatzinger stood peering into the darkness overhead, pointing his revolver at the rafters.

Tobrensky wheeled around and flung the wrench at Fatzinger.

The wrench hit the doorway, causing Fatzinger's gun to go off.

A body came down from above with a shrill cry, landing squarely upon Tobrensky. As Blakeley looked on, Tobrensky's jaw fell open. He let out a groan, and in a second his body fell limp.

Dead.

"Victor, Victor, are you all right?"

Blakeley was slapping Victor on the cheek. He was breathing shallowly, but there was no reason to believe he was anything but unconscious from fright. He bore no marks, save the few stains his clothing had collected when he had rolled into a puddle where the horse had been standing for too long.

Fatzinger peered over Blakeley's shoulder and inspected his catch with great pride.

"Vell, I chased dis here dog's pizzle all over da house an' up an' down da hillside, but I got him chust like da lootenant ordered," he announced uprightly. "But who da Cheesuss iss dott udder vun?"

They pulled Victor away from Tobrensky's body just as Ralphie was appearing in the doorway, his swimming suit dripping with river water.

"Hi, Dad. Did you yell for me just now?"

"No," answered Blakeley wearily, "You may return to the river, Ralphie."

"Oh, my God," said Hudson, who had hurried to the stable after hearing the sound of gunshots. "Fatzinger has caught the Butcher! Now just what the hell am I supposed to do?"

Epilogue

For a time they stood around, fascinated by the small, broken body of Maxim Tobrensky.

In the chilly breeze that wafted through the stable, ruffling the thin, white strands of hair, it was almost possible to see him through compassionate eyes. He looked so fragile and helpless, Miss Meredith was heard to remark absently. She appeared a bit shaken, grasping Nathan's arm and looking on uncertainly.

Blakeley concurred; it was difficult to fathom this creature in all his dimensions. To be sure, there was something of the museum curiosity about him, like a remnant of some dark, bygone era. And for some disturbing reason, Tobrensky now seemed at peace. Disturbing because, as he thought about it, he rather expected to see all the torments of hell in that small, wizened countenance.

Victor came to, blinked his eyes, then ran off still trying to summon up a scream. To no one's surprise, he was not seen for several days.

"Holy chumpin' alley cats! . . . " The gravity of the situation was beginning to dawn on Fatzinger. He backed up slowly and was turning pale. Eventually he sat meekly on a stool near the stable doorway, his trouser legs rising well above his boots and stockings.

Lieutenant Hudson continued to shake his head, alternately glancing at Tobrensky and Fatzinger. He pondered the vagaries of justice.

To Blakeley, however, the air felt abruptly cleaner. He breathed deeply, patted his waistline, and smiled at Hudson. "Capital!"

Inside the house a few minutes later, he poured himself two fingers of strong Irish whiskey, offered the same to Detective McBride and a rather diluted version to Miss Meredith. Then he took them aside to lead them into Sophia's studio. There they toasted their long, taxing adventure. It was fitting to do so in private.

At the sight of Sophia's paintings Blakeley was reminded that her exile in Kent might now be ended, and he could barely contain his happiness. His regard for Nathan McBride and Allison Meredith as associates and as people of estimable character was evident in his words. He saw in their eyes that they returned his admiration. All three were visibly relieved; the whiskey, it was understood, was intended as a tranquilizer.

They left him shortly thereafter, Nathan to assist the perplexed Lieutenant Hudson and Allison to begin work on the final chapter of her own book. She, too, had been awaiting this moment anxiously.

Blakeley poured himself a second helping of Irish and looked on fondly as the couple made their way past the hedgerow to the driveway. Nathan saw Allison to her carriage and kissed her tenderly on the cheek. In the other direction from his vantage point policemen were lifting Tobrensky's body and setting it down atop a buckboard. The shroud seemed hardly larger than one which might envelop a child. Blakeley drifted off to his laboratory. He had notes to complete.

"Damn!"

When Tobrensky tipped over the medicine cabinet, every last drop of the precious antigen had spilled. Blakeley cursed his own lack of common sense and wondered if perhaps Tobrensky had not been accurate in some of his contempt after all. The formula alone told but a fraction of what science would wish to know. His silly oversight—neglecting to keep even a small portion of it in a secure place—had wasted Tobrensky's thousands of hours of research. And much worse, what of the countless lives that had been spent in the process of its formulation and creation?

*   .   *

The autumn rains came, gently, at first, and warm. By the time the leaves had begun to change Sophia and Rosalie were on their way back to Philadelphia.

The Blakeley estate was not far from the main road. Set deeply enough amid the dogwood, birch, and linden, it seemed to be immersed in a sea of crimson, gold, and orange. There was a period of bright sun, and then, in late October, the rains returned. In the early-evening chill the smoke from burning leaves hung heavily all along the river. Blakeley rejoiced at length in his reunion with Sophia.

The season had in the end been kind. With his portion of the Figge reward, Nathan McBride had left the department to follow his dream as a Latin teacher. Miss Meredith, who was by now the celebrated chronicler of the Butcher case, had found him a niche in a private school, much as she had for Zoltan Mroszek. Only in this instance the school, select and parochial, was within walking distance of her apartment. Nathan—owner of a dark-blue Stanley Steamer, as well as several new pairs of shoes—was well over the fast. His times with Allison were especially precious: evenings before a fireplace, some cheese and fruit, chestnuts, warm wine, music from the Victrola. . . .

"Und dott'll be enough o' dott horseradish, Lootenant!"

The world had not been equally kind to Charlie Hudson. Jack Ferris, wallowing in gambling debts, had left town abruptly. The commissioner, reluctantly and with great loathing, had dropped the investigation of the aggravating lieutenant. Fatzinger, however, had become impossible. City Hall now regarded him as its golden lion; there was no way of hiding him. His actions had grown more outlandish and his presence more vocal by the day.

"I'm da guy vott da Butcher kilt und da Lordy Lilywaver reprehended, by Christ! Und don't you ferget dott!"

It was whispered that Hudson opened his bottle of bourbon shortly after noon, instead of waiting until it was customary after duty. Only whispered, of course.

Not that his life was totally devoid of fulfillment. In November, mostly as a result of Hudson's relentless efforts, the Reverend Richard T. Hopkins was convicted of indecent assault, indecent exposure, unnatural carnal knowledge, and statutory rape. The Commonwealth of Pennsylvania was now scrutinizing the Fundamentalist Church of Christ the Proselyte.

On December 10 a treaty of peace was signed in Paris. The once-proud Spanish Empire was forced to yield to the United States a large portion of its territories. It was wholly humiliating to the ancient kingdom, but the young American nation was jubilant and cast covetous, imperial glances elsewhere. The celebrations spilled over into the Christmas season; Blakeley, like so many of his adopted countrymen, toasted the victory as well as the coming New Year.

There seemed to be a greater meaning to the words uttered over wassail this time, one last opportunity to celebrate a moment of the century which had given them birth. Often that season the snows cut the estate off for days at a time. The solitude only added to Blakeley's happiness. He would then feel a rare moment far from the creeping progress of the outside world.

And then, one day after Christmas, he received two enigmatic visitors from Washington. Whatever the urgency of the matter, he left for the tropics shortly after New Year's Day.